SARATOGA

SARATOGA

DAVID GARLAND

St. Martin's Press ❧ New York

www.stmartins.com

Library of Congress Cataloging-in-Publication Data

Garland, David, 1940–
  Saratoga : a novel of the American Revolution / David Garland.—1st St. Martin's Press ed.
    p. cm.
  ISBN 0-312-32719-6
  EAN 978-0-312-32719-4
  1. United States—History—Revolution, 1775–1783—British forces—Fiction.
  2. United States—History—Revolution, 1775–1783—Fiction. 3. Saratoga Campaign, N.Y., 1777—Fiction. 4. British—United States—Fiction. 5. Soldiers—Fiction.
  I. Title.

PR6063.I3175S37 2005
823'.92—dc22   2005044235

First Edition: December 2005

10 9 8 7 6 5 4 3 2 1

To Benjamin and Sarah as a belated wedding present.
Wishing you health and happiness
on your journey through life together.

ACKNOWLEDGMENTS

Like any student of the American Revolution, I am heavily indebted to the generations of scholars who have written about the event. *Saratoga* tries to cut a fictional pathway through a veritable forest of histories, biographies, documents, articles, letters, and diaries. It should be stressed that this is a novel and certain liberties have therefore been taken with time and place. However, in striving to entertain and enlighten the reader, I hope that I have not offended the purists too much. Captain Jamie Skoyles, the hero of this saga, is essentially a figment of my imagination.

Countless sources have been consulted along the way. The most useful for my particular purposes were: *Saratoga*, Richard M. Ketchum (1999); *The Generals at Saratoga: John Burgoyne and Horatio Gates*, Max M. Mintz (1990); *The War in America (1775–1783)*, Piers Mackesy (1964); *John Burgoyne of Saratoga*, James Lunt (1976); and *Patriots: The Men Who Started the Revolution*, A. J. Langguth (1988).

The diaries of those who were there at the time—Captain Thomas Anbury, grenadier officer; Lieutenant William Digby of the Shropshire regiment; Lieutenant James Haddon, artillery officer; and the famous Sergeant Roger Lamb, surgeon's mate with the 9th Regiment—were invaluable. Lady Harriet Acland's journal was also fascinating.

For their help and enthusiasm, my gratitude must go to staff at Bennington Battlefield State Park, Fort Ticonderoga, and Saratoga National Historical Park. Those who took part in the reconstruction of the battles at Saratoga were unwitting coauthors.

Special thanks must be reserved for Benjamin Sevier, my editor, whose sharp eye and unflagging encouragement helped to improve the novel beyond all recognition; and for Judith, who kept me fed and watered throughout the time I spent on this book, and who offered a perceptive critique of each draft. Her support, love, and patience have been over and above the call of duty.

I have always thought Hudson's River the most proper part of the whole continent for opening vigorous operations. Because the course of the river, so beneficial for conveying all the bulky necessities of an army, is precisely the route that an army ought to take for the great purpose of cutting the communications between Southern and Northern provinces, giving confidence to the Indians, and securing a junction with the Canadian forces. These purposes effected, and a fleet upon the coast, it is to me morally certain that the forces of New England must be reduced so early in the campaign to give you battle upon your own terms, or perish before the end of it for want of supplies.

—GENERAL JOHN BURGOYNE, 1775

SARATOGA

CHAPTER ONE

Crown Point, October 1776

The musket ball hit him right in the middle of the forehead and burrowed into his brain. With a stifled cry, Private Samuel Farrar dropped straight to the ground, his body motionless, his hands still gripping his weapon, his grotesque third eye weeping blood. Nicholas Ottley was horrified.

"They've shot him," he gulped.

"Get down!"

"Sam is dead. They've killed him."

"Come on, lad!"

Captain Jamie Skoyles dived instinctively for cover and tried to pull the young soldier behind him, but he was too late. A second shot was fired from the other side of the clearing and Ottley felt as if a hot poker had just been thrust into his stomach. Knocked back on his heels, he lost all control of his body and collapsed in a heap, tossing his Brown Bess musket into the bushes as he did so. Ottley clutched his wound and stared at Skoyles with utter disbelief.

"I've been hit, Captain," he said, his face contorted with pain.

"Sharpshooters. Hidden in the trees."

"Am I going to die?"

"Not if I can help it," said Skoyles, retrieving the fallen musket and checking that it was loaded. "Lie still until this is all over."

"I thought I'd be safe with you, sir."

There was a note of accusation in Private Ottley's voice and disenchantment in his eyes. He was blaming the officer for failing to protect him in the way that he had always done in the past. Ottley was a spindly, fresh-faced youth of seventeen summers who reminded Skoyles of himself at that age. For that reason, he had gone out of his way to help him adapt to the rigors of army life, teaching him to make the most of his lot and saving him from some of the ritual bullying that new recruits invariably suffered. All that now remained of Skoyles's patient instruction was a frightened boy, robbed of his dreams of military glory and doubled up in agony beside him.

One soldier dead, another disabled. Skoyles was on his own. The first thing he had to do was to assess the strength of the enemy. Two shots had been fired, but he sensed that the ambush might involve more men. To find out, he pretended to crawl out of his hiding place to collect the discarded musket from beside Private Farrar, who was lying several yards away. A third shot bit the ground less than a foot in front of him and sent a flurry of dust up into his face. Skoyles rolled quickly back out of sight, certain now that there were at least three of them because neither of the first two would have had time to reload his weapon and fire again.

Jamie Skoyles and his men were part of a patrol that had been combing the woods for enemy soldiers who had fled from the fort at Crown Point as the British army pushed south. Separated from the other members of the 24th Foot, the three redcoats had gone deeper and deeper into the woodland, unaware that they were about to walk into a trap. British uniforms were colorful targets. Two soldiers had already been hit. Distant gunfire confirmed that Skoyles and his companions were not the only ones who had met resistance. It was bad news. It meant that nobody from the main group would be able to come to their aid.

Lying flat on his stomach, Skoyles poked the musket through the bush and tried to ignore a twinge of guilt. Sam Farrar had been a veteran soldier, older than his captain, a man who had cheated death in combat a dozen times. His luck had finally run out. Farrar would be missed but not mourned. Nick Ottley was different. He was young, innocent, burning with the fire of youth, eager to do well, but untried in action. He had worshipped Captain Jamie Skoyles, willingly entrusting his life to him. Yet he had now been cut down by a solitary musket ball, a brave soldier turned into a whimpering animal. Skoyles felt responsible.

Survival was his priority. If he could pull through, there was an outside chance that Skoyles could help the wounded Ottley back to camp before he bled to death. But the odds were stacked against him. Armed with a musket, a pistol, and a sword, Skoyles was up against at least three men, each of whom had now had time to reload his weapon and decide on his next move.

2

While they knew exactly where he was, Skoyles had no idea where they were concealed. They could come at him from any direction. One of them might even work his way around the clearing so that he could stalk Skoyles from behind.

"It *hurts*, Captain," Ottley gasped. "It hurts like hell."

"Be quiet, lad."

"I can't stop the blood."

"Hold still," snapped Skoyles. "I need to *listen*."

Scanning the trees on the other side of the clearing, Skoyles pricked up his ears when he heard the snap of a twig off to the right. Someone was on the move. He waited, watched, and eventually caught a glimpse of a body, creeping stealthily through the undergrowth. It was enough. In a flash, Skoyles raised the musket, took aim, and fired. A loud grunt and the sound of a body falling into the bushes told him that he had hit his target.

The momentary feeling of triumph gave way instantly to a sense of alarm as two figures suddenly emerged from the other side of the clearing and ran toward him with their weapons at the ready. They knew that Skoyles would have no time to reload his musket or to grab the one that lay beside Farrar. The decoy had been sent ahead to draw his fire. With the two men only twenty yards away, Skoyles pulled his pistol from his holster and leveled it but he had no chance to pull the trigger. One of the oncoming rebels discharged his musket and the ball went into Skoyles's right shoulder, forcing him to drop the pistol and stumble backward. A searing pain made his eyes mist over. There was another loud report as the second man fired, but the lead ball sailed past Skoyles's head and buried itself in the trunk of a tree.

Wielding their muskets by the barrels, the men surged even closer, intent on beating his brains out with brute force. Skoyles tried to draw his sword with his right hand but he set off an inferno in his shoulder. Only his left hand could save him. Using it to extract the weapon, he dodged the first man, then lifted his sword to parry a blow from the other's flailing musket. Skoyles ducked, feinted, then thrust home. The point of his blade sank deep into the man's chest before being pulled out with a practiced flick.

As one rebel collapsed to the ground, the other swung his musket hard and caught Skoyles across the back, making him lurch drunkenly forward and sending fresh tremors of agony through his shoulder. He spun round to face his attacker and was momentarily shocked. Looking at him properly for the first time, Skoyles saw that his adversary was even younger than Private Ottley, a scrawny lad, no more than fourteen or fifteen, with ragged clothes and bare feet. The boy's cheeks were pinched with hunger, but his eyes were alight at the thought of his prize. To kill a redcoat officer would earn him status and respect. Charging in again, he swung his musket with murderous power.

Skoyles ducked beneath it and jabbed with his sword, drawing a trickle of blood from the other's thigh. If he was old enough to kill, he decided, the boy was old enough to die. For his part, he would certainly not spare Skoyles. Coming at him with renewed energy, he tried to batter the wounded man into submission. All that Skoyles could do was to parry the blows with his sword as he retreated. Skoyles could feel his strength waning, his options closing down. The pain in his shoulder intensified. Blood was dribbling down his right arm. His vision was impaired. He could not hold out much longer.

When the musket was swung at him once more, he used his sword to deflect it and kicked out hard with his foot, catching the boy in the groin and making him howl with anger. With a slash of his blade, Skoyles sliced open his wrist and forced him to drop his weapon. Though writhing in agony, the boy was not finished yet. As Skoyles stood over him, panting for breath, the rebel soldier pulled a knife from his belt with his left hand and lunged at the redcoat in front of him. Skoyles stepped smartly out of reach so that his attacker was thrown off balance, then he put all of his remaining energy into one final thrust, impaling the boy on his sword point and watching the life drain out of him like water being poured from a jug. His victim made a futile attempt to spit his defiance before sinking to the ground.

Bruised and bleeding, Skoyles needed a few minutes to recover. A cry of desperation from Ottley reminded him that someone was wounded more seriously than he was. He staggered across to inspect the injured private. Ottley was in a bad state. Weak from loss of blood, he could do little more than groan pitifully. He had never realized how much torment a musket ball could inflict. Using only his left hand, Skoyles removed Ottley's canvas knapsack and undid the strap. Inside the knapsack, he found a shirt, three pairs of white yarn stockings, and two pairs of linen socks. Bundling them together, he used them to stanch the bleeding from the other's stomach.

"Press them against the wound," he advised.

He left Ottley and went across to Private Farrar. Inside the other soldier's knapsack were items that could used as emergency bandages for Skoyles's own wound. Unbuttoning his coat, he thrust a handful of stockings and socks up to his injured shoulder. He did not wish to leave any weapons for foraging rebels to find so he gathered up all the muskets and hid them quickly in the bushes, intending to recover them when he returned with a burial detail. Armed with his sword and pistol, he came back to Ottley. To leave him there would be to expose him to the risk of being caught by the enemy or, worse still, of being attacked by some of the predatory animals that inhabited the woods. Yet Skoyles had no strength to carry Private Ottley to safety. When he tried to lift him, the pounding in his right shoulder was unbearable.

"Sorry, lad," he said. "We'll have to do this the hard way."

Grabbing him by the collar, Skoyles began to drag him slowly across the grass with his left hand. Ottley did not protest. He pressed the bundle of clothing against his stomach, gritted his teeth and prayed. They had gone almost a mile before Skoyles passed out.

"Take a swig of this, Jamie," Tom Caffrey suggested, offering him a bottle of rum. "It's going to hurt."

"Where am I?"

"Not far from the camp. One of the Indians found you."

Skoyles had opened his eyes to look up at the reassuring face of his closest friend, Sergeant Tom Caffrey, an assistant surgeon with the regiment. The wounded officer lay on the ground where he had fallen. Caffrey had stripped him to the waist so that he could get at the wound to extract the musket ball, exposing a slim, muscular body that bore the scars of earlier battles. Brain still swimming, Skoyles recalled how he had come to be in that part of the wood.

"Where's Ottley?" he asked.

"Forget about him."

"See to him first, Tom. I can wait."

"The boy is way past my help," said Caffrey sadly. "There was so much damage to his innards that no surgeon in the world could have recovered him. Besides, I got here too late. He was already dead, Jamie."

"Damnation!"

"They've taken him back to camp for burial."

"I let the poor lad down."

Burning with remorse, Skoyles was also furious with himself for having unwittingly led Farrar and Ottley into an ambush. Both of the soldiers had paid for the mistake with their lives. Killing three rebels did not atone for the deaths of his men. Skoyles was chastened. His attempt to get Ottley to a place where he could receive medical attention had been doomed from the start. During the latter part of the exhausting journey, Skoyles had probably been dragging a corpse.

"Tell me what happened, Jamie," said Caffrey. "It will give you something to think about while I'm hunting for that piece of lead you've got lodged inside you." He held a bottle to Skoyles's lips. "Only drink this first. You'll need it."

Skoyles took a long sip of rum and let it course through him. It helped to steel him against what lay ahead. With his eyes closed, he told his friend what had befallen them in the wood. Caffrey, meanwhile, cleaned away the dried blood so that he could ease open the wound and search for the musket ball with his probe. Skoyles felt as if he had been shot all over again, and he winced, but he made no complaint. He simply raised his voice to tell his tale with more deliberation.

Caffrey worked quickly but carefully. He was a solid man in his forties with broad shoulders, a barrel chest, and thick arms. His face had a ruddy complexion, a broken nose, and the kind of pleasant ugliness that women somehow found disarming. The son of a Devon butcher, he had unaccountably ended up as an army surgeon. The irony of the situation never ceased to amuse him.

"We lost our way, Jamie," he said, probing gently until he made contact with the ball. "Both of us. We betrayed our birthright. Your father was a doctor, saving lives, whereas you get paid to take them. I come from a family of butchers, yet I spend all my time treating the effects of butchery—for what else are British soldiers except sides of beef, ready for the slab?" He twisted the instrument then pulled it gently toward him. "Got the little bugger!" he declared, holding the blood-covered musket ball on the palm of his hand. "You were very lucky. It missed the bone."

"I don't *feel* lucky, Tom."

"No, it must have hurt like hell." He cleaned the wound again so that he could stitch it up. "What you need now is a long rest."

"No," said Skoyles, trying to sit up, "I've got to lead a burial detail back to the place where it happened."

"Lie still," said Caffrey, pushing him gently down again with a hand on his chest. "I need to do some embroidery on you. And don't worry about Sam Farrar. The Indian scouts will find him easily enough. All they have to do is to follow the trail of blood that Nick Ottley left behind."

"I have to show them where I hid those muskets."

"All in good time, Jamie."

Skoyles recoiled slightly as the needle penetrated his skin, but he made no sound. Now that the musket ball was out, he was ready to bear any pain. What he was not prepared for was the shock that awaited him.

"You'll have plenty of time for this shoulder to heal," said the other with his soft West Country burr. "The fighting is over for this year."

"What do you mean?"

"General Carleton has decided to turn back."

"The devil he has!" exclaimed Skoyles, stung by the news. "Have we come all this way to let the rebels off the hook? It's lunacy, Tom!"

"It's orders."

"Then they're bloody stupid orders. Why, in the bowels of Christ, must we retreat when we're only fifteen miles from Fort Ticonderoga? Take that and we destroy their northern army."

"Only after a long siege and that would take us into winter."

"Not if we strike hard enough."

"There are twelve thousand men in Ticonderoga, Jamie. They could hold out for months. By that time, we'll all have frozen to death."

"There are *reports* of a large garrison," argued Skoyles. "But I don't believe a word of them. They're devised to frighten us off. And even if there were that number at the fort, what state would they be in?"

"A better one than you at this moment."

"No, Tom. They'll be like those three ragamuffins I killed this afternoon—human scarecrows without a decent uniform or a pair of good boots among them. They looked as if they hadn't eaten for a month." With an effort of will, Skoyles sat up, glad that his friend had finished his sutures. "For heaven's sake, we have them on the run. Doesn't our commander appreciate that?"

"General Carleton is a cautious man."

"This is not caution—it's fucking madness!"

"Calm down, Jamie," said Caffrey.

But Skoyles was seething. "We chase the rebels out of Canada," he said with passion. "We build a fleet so that we can pursue them down Lake Cham-

7

plain. We demolish their makeshift navy, and when we reach Crown Point, we discover that they've burned the fort and taken to their heels." He pointed with his left hand. "You saw those corpses that we found littering the ground. They were riddled with smallpox. The garrison was so anxious to escape that they didn't even bother to bury their dead. The rebels are there for the taking, Tom. What else does General Carleton *need?*"

"Warmer weather."

"Strike now or we lose a golden opportunity."

"I agree with you, Jamie," said the other, wiping the blood off his probe and needle before putting them away with his other instruments, "but, for some strange reason, I wasn't consulted on the matter."

"General Burgoyne would have been consulted, and so would General Phillips. Neither of them would want to give up when victory was within our grasp."

"They were overruled, Jamie. We head north tomorrow."

Skoyles was rocked. "*All* of us?"

"Every man jack."

"We give Crown Point back to the rebels?"

"So it seems."

"Then why bother to take it from them in the first place?" Anger had dulled the pain in his shoulder and roused his spirit. "Whoever controls Crown Point has mastery of the lake. At the very least, we should leave a garrison here."

"It would take too many men to rebuild the fort."

"The rebels will rebuild it. As soon as we move out, they'll occupy it again and strengthen its defenses. Christ Almighty!" said Skoyles in exasperation. "We're supposed to be at war with the bastards. We should hold on to every inch of land that we take from them."

"Not with the winter coming, Jamie. It can be very harsh." Caffrey stood up and gave a shrug. "General Carleton has made the decision. We pull out tomorrow and withdraw to St. John's."

"Shit!" cried Skoyles.

The word summed up his day perfectly.

CHAPTER TWO

When he set sail for America for the third time, Lieutenant General Sir John Burgoyne did so with mixed feelings. He was still grieving over the death of his wife, Charlotte, dogged by guilt and haunted by the fact that he was three thousand miles away when the tragedy occurred. The prospect of another voyage across the treacherous waters of the North Atlantic was not an enticing one and was bound to induce a certain amount of dread even in someone as supremely confident as Burgoyne. But his sadness and his apprehension were tempered by a quiet elation because he was returning to the colonies with an exciting new status. After some skillful lobbying in London, Burgoyne had gotten himself appointed to command the army that was to launch another invasion from Canada. It was the ideal cure for seasickness.

Burgoyne's ambition had been fulfilled. His plan of campaign had been approved, and he had been given command in place of his erstwhile superior, Sir Guy Carleton, governor of Canada. There remained the small problem of handing over the letter communicating the news to Carleton—a proud Irishman who would take it as an insult—but Burgoyne believed that he could soften the impact with some honey-tongued diplomacy. In doing so, he would take special care to conceal the fact that he had deliberately undermined Carleton's position during meetings with the secretary of state for the colonies. Burgoyne had no qualms about doing that. He was convinced that he was the better man for the job, and the more deserving of the glory that it would surely bring.

His ship was the *Apollo,* a square-rigged, three-masted frigate that traveled in convoy with various transports. Burgoyne's reinforcements consisted largely of hired soldiers from Germany. The holds of the vessels were packed with muskets, bayonets, ammunition, private tents, bell tents, drum cases, powder bags, hatchets, kettles, canteens, knapsacks, axes, forage ropes, picket ropes, blankets, water buckets, and all the other paraphernalia of military life. While Burgoyne ensured that the *Apollo* carried a substantial store of champagne, brandy, and claret, the Germans had less control over their baggage. Instead of the consignment of boots that had been ordered, they were sailing with a vast quantity of dancing pumps and ladies' slippers, clear evidence that the contractor was either monstrously inefficient or possessed of a wicked sense of humor.

A single day in oceanic waters could be a trial by ordeal. To spend, as they did, almost five weeks at sea was a test of nerve and endurance that many were destined to fail. Crammed together belowdecks, the men who were due to fight for paltry wages were fed on the meanest rations and subjected to the stink of vomit, the stench of unwashed bodies, and the most primitive sanitary arrangements. Water was green with algae, hardtack was alive with weevils, beef was like salted teak. Scurvy and other diseases soon began to claim some of the passengers.

But it was the sea itself that was the greatest danger. Whipped by the wind and rain, it frothed with fury and tossed the vessels, making it almost impossible for them to remain in convoy. On good days, there was the ceaseless swell and the stiff breeze; on bad ones, there was a violent tempest that turned the sea into colossal liquid mountains that threatened to drown every last one of them. Sudden waves could scour a deck and sweep even the most sure-footed sailors overboard. The noise was deafening, the discomfort extreme. As the convoy zigzagged its way across the Atlantic, the death toll slowly rose.

Burgoyne took advantage of periods of calmer weather to enjoy the voyage as best he could. He dined with the captain and with his officers, drank copious quantities of claret, played cards, and listened to a trio of musicians. Parading his men on deck, he tried to keep up their spirits with words of encouragement, telling them, with a confiding smile, that the horrors they were now suffering were worse than anything they would meet in the line of fire. Burgoyne could see the misery etched in their faces, and he knew that not all of them would survive to step ashore on Canadian soil.

It was not something that troubled him overmuch. Casualties were unavoidable. Burgoyne was about to write an important new chapter in his life, and he tried to direct all his attention to that end. Brooding on the fate of some of his fellow passengers would only hamper him. His prime objective was to wage a successful campaign against the American rebels. Having left England with some misgivings, he was certain that he would return as a national hero.

Everyone was heartened when land finally came into sight. There was even greater relief when the flotilla entered the huge St. Lawrence estuary. Winter had been relatively mild, and the ice had started to melt earlier than usual. As they sailed upriver, they had to contend with a continual uproar as the surging runoff buffeted the massive chunks of ice that came floating down from the Great Lakes. There were compensations. In place of the turbulent sea that stretched for miles in every direction, the passengers could now look out on spectacular panoramas.

Thick forest adorned both banks, broken from time to time by a sudden clearing, a sparkling river, or a glistening lake and dominated by majestic mountain ranges that seemed to stretch to infinity. In the distance, a first waterfall was glimpsed, bursting over some rocks with foaming power before disappearing from sight among the pine and maple trees. Colors were dazzling in the bright sunlight. The enormous scale of it all was breathtaking.

Burgoyne was content. Thanks to the timely thaw, they would be arriving in Quebec a fortnight earlier than he had anticipated. It was a good omen. His ship finally sailed into the harbor on May 6, 1777, and he celebrated his arrival in characteristic fashion. Making light of the onerous voyage, he donned his dress uniform and took up his stance on the quarterdeck, adopting the military pose he had used when having his portrait painted by Sir Joshua Reynolds.

They were waiting for him. Regiments stationed in the city were lined up to greet him and to welcome the reinforcements he had brought from England. When the gangplank of the *Apollo* was eventually lowered, the first person to walk down it was the tall, handsome, debonair Lieutenant General John Burgoyne in his scarlet coat with gold piping and epaulets, white waistcoat and breeches, and gleaming black boots. Now in his midfifties, he was a warrior in his prime, looking less like a weary passenger than a triumphant leader about to claim a coveted prize. Showing the white lace at his cuffs, he waved a friendly greeting to the assembled ranks of redcoats. A resounding cheer went up from the soldiers at the quayside.

Gentleman Johnny was back.

"Is there nothing you could do?" asked Tom Caffrey with concern. "The punishment may kill him."

"I'll raise the matter with Major Featherstone."

"Go over his head."

"No, Tom," said Skoyles, "that's not the answer. The only way to do this is by persuasion. I'll talk to Harry Featherstone."

Caffrey was bitter. "Well, it's no use appealing to his finer feelings," he said, curling a lip, "because he doesn't have any. Major Featherstone is a cruel, bloodthirsty, black-hearted devil."

"I disagree. He's a good officer."

"Good at inflicting unnecessary pain on his men."

"Let me speak to him."

"Is there any point, Jamie?"

"I think so," said Skoyles.

They were in the island city of Montreal, a community whose population of some four thousand souls had been swelled by the British soldiers billeted there throughout the winter. Captain Jamie Skoyles and his regiment had joined the newly arrived General Burgoyne in the city. Though it could boast many appealing features, Montreal had neither the size nor situation of Quebec, and its architecture was less imposing. Beginning as a trading post, it still had vestiges of a frontier town about it. Indians, trappers, and voyageurs could be seen in its streets alongside the moneyed and sophisticated Canadians. Throughout the city, a quintessentially French air prevailed.

Like the rest of the soldiers, Skoyles was eager to leave Canada and cross the border into New York. After a long, enforced rest, he wanted to close with the enemy again, especially as his wounded shoulder had now healed. Meanwhile, however, he and Tom Caffrey were on the heights behind Faubourg des Recollets, where a grand review was to be staged for General Burgoyne. Troops, artillery pieces, and bands were already starting to move into position. As the two friends chatted, the very man they had been discussing was marching toward them in his dress uniform. Shooting him a look of disgust, Caffrey slipped quickly away.

Major Harry Featherstone was a striking figure, of medium height, well built, straight-backed, and so impeccably dressed that he made Skoyles feel shabby in his faded uniform with its fraying cuffs. Dark-haired and dark-eyed, Featherstone had high cheekbones and a neat black mustache. His face was arresting rather than handsome, finely chiseled, but too long and too tapered at the chin. Exuding a sense of importance, he moved with an arrogant strut. When he reached Skoyles, he clicked his tongue in disapproval.

"Fraternizing with the lower ranks again, Captain?" he said. "That's a bad habit for an officer."

"Sergeant Caffrey is a friend of mine."

"Sergeant Caffrey is a sergeant and should be kept in his place. How can you expect the men to respect you if you sink to their level? Yes," he went on, raising a hand to stifle the protest on Skoyles's lips, "I know that you came from the ranks yourself, but you must shake off old allegiances. You simply must learn to distinguish between them and us, Jamie. We are, in every sense, a race apart."

"General Burgoyne might disagree with that," noted Skoyles. "I've heard him stress the need to treat soldiers as thinking beings. There are times, he believes, when officers may slacken the reins in order to talk to the men. When he formed his own regiment, the 16th Light Dragoons, he advocated as much in his code of instructions."

"Fear and discipline are the only things that keep an army in order. General Burgoyne understands that."

"There are shades of fear and degrees of discipline."

"Not in my opinion."

"Excessively harsh treatment only breeds hatred and resentment."

"Arrant nonsense!"

"I beg to differ, Major."

"Go easy on the men and they see it as a sign of weakness. You know that as well as anyone, Jamie." Featherstone slapped him amiably on the shoulder. "Severe punishment teaches them obedience."

"That depends on the circumstances," said Skoyles, trying to reason with him. "Look at the case of Private Higgs, for instance."

"Ah," said Featherstone, raising an eyebrow, "so *that* is what this is all about. You and Sergeant Caffrey are in conspiracy, are you?"

"Not at all, Major."

"The pair of you have the impudence to question my authority."

"We simply ask you to reconsider."

"There's nothing to reconsider," declared Featherstone with a peremptory snap of his fingers. "I found Higgs drunk on duty and he used foul language when I reprimanded him. I had no choice but to have the wretch flogged. What would you have done in my position—award him some kind of medal?"

"No, Major," said Skoyles, "I would have looked more closely into the case. Do you know *why* Private Higgs was in that state?"

"Too much rum on an empty stomach."

"But why did he take to drink in the first place? By the standards of the others, he's usually quite abstemious. Higgs also has an unblemished record as a soldier and how many can say that? So what made him act out of character?"

"Who cares?"

"I do, Major—and so does Sergeant Caffrey."

"Higgs must take his medicine."

"Some punishment is in order," Skoyles conceded. "We both accept that. But I feel that you should know that Higgs had some distressing news. Word came from England that his wife and child have died of smallpox. It was a crippling blow for the poor man. *That* was why he reached for the bottle."

"The punishment stands. Sixty lashes."

"Reduce the number and you still make your point."

"No," said the other with a hollow laugh. "If I were stupid enough to do that, I'd lose face entirely. Lessen the severity of the flogging? Absolute madness! The men would think that I'd gone as soft as you."

"I can be strict when strictness is called for, Major."

Though they were hardly natural allies, there was a comfortable friendship between the two of them, based on a mutual respect for each other's abilities. Harry Featherstone, a wealthy man in his thirties from an aristocratic family, had bought his commission in the way that most officers did. Skoyles, by contrast, the son of a country doctor in Cumberland, had worked his way up through the ranks and been promoted lieutenant as a result of conspicuous gallantry. From the start, he lacked the airs and graces of his fellow officers, and his rough North Country vowels made him stick out even more. The same age as the major, Skoyles was taller and more athletic, with rugged features and close-cropped fair hair.

Featherstone smiled at him "Do you know what your trouble is, Jamie?" he said, helpfully. "You're neither fish nor fowl. In trying to keep a foot in both camps, you're neither officer nor soldier. Your fellow officers distrust you because you're simply not one of us while the lower ranks despise you because you try to befriend them. You are in limbo."

"I care nothing for that. My concern is for Private Higgs."

"Sixty lashes. My only regret is that I can't administer them myself. I'd appreciate the exercise."

"Flaying a man until there's no skin left?" said Skoyles with distaste. "Is that what you call exercise?"

"Yes, Captain—and pleasant exercise at that. Man or woman, I'd lay it on hard and leave my signature across their backs so they'd never forget me." He gave a thin smile. "As it happens, I had a woman flogged once—a corporal's wife. The provost marshal gave her thirty lashes for stealing some potatoes. A shapely wench, she was, too. It was good to have an excuse to see her stripped to the waist. Mind you," he went on, smirking broadly, "I'd have preferred to see those lashes applied to her bare buttocks. Nothing quite as exciting as watching a naked woman squirming in pain, is there?"

Skoyles accepted that his embassy on behalf of Private Higgs had failed. A hapless soldier, whose only crime had been to seek solace from his grief, would be flogged into insensibility on the orders of the major. Higgs was one Thomas Lobster who would live up to his nickname, for his back would be turned into a large, raw, lobster-red wound. What irked Skoyles most was the fact that Featherstone himself drank to excess on a regular basis and used the most obscene language when he was in his cups. Yet he was above reproach.

Featherstone emphasized the point. "You missed a splendid dinner yesterday," he announced, proudly. "Thirty of us in all. I'm told that we got through seventy-two bottles of claret, eighteen of Madeira, and twelve of port—that's not counting a little porter and punch, of course. It reminded me why I love the army so much."

"You love being able to inflict punishment on your men."

"That, too, can be very agreeable."

"Not to all of us, Major," said Skoyles.

Featherstone laughed. "I'll not let you put me out of countenance," he said, punching him playfully in the chest. "Not today of all days. Come, let's go and put on a show for Gentleman Johnny. He's deservedly in command now."

"We can at least agree on that."

"You'll notice the difference now that the general is back to set the tone. We'll be able to get down to some serious tippling again."

"Private Higgs might find that rather ironic," said Skoyles.

"Forget him," advised the other with a companionable chuckle. "You're one of us now, Jamie. Enjoy the privileges of officer life. Damn it all! Isn't that why you joined the army? It was certainly what tempted me into uniform—that, and the pleasure of reminding inferior nations why Britain is supreme on the field of battle."

The army was hamstrung by unnecessary delays. Even though he knew that an invasion would inevitably take place, Sir Guy Carleton had made little preparation for it. Burgoyne did not hurry him. After his arrival in Montreal, he waited two whole weeks before he wrote to Carleton about his transport requirements. There was no sense of urgency. A humane, experienced, conscientious soldier-politician, the governor was deeply wounded when he first learned that he had been superseded. Nevertheless, he behaved toward Burgoyne with perfect decorum, concealing his outrage and offering whatever assistance was needed, making it clear, however, that as long as the army was in Canada, he still outranked the General.

While the troops remained in Montreal, the governor held a ball in honor of the new commander, one last glittering social occasion before the important business of war was resumed. The venue was Chateau Ramezay, the magnificent residence built at the start of the century by former governor, Claude Ramezay, who wanted to be reminded of the castles of his native Normandy. It was a high stone structure with a series of dormers set into its copper roof. All of its rooms were exquisite and well proportioned with elaborate carved paneling by a French architect as the distinguishing feature of the Nantes Salon. Standing on the Rue Notre-Dame, the chateau had formal gardens to the side and to the rear.

Captain Jamie Skoyles was among the first to arrive. He knew the building well, having been part of the army that had expelled the rebels from the city in the previous spring. Punch was being served, but Skoyles took care not to have too much of it. He needed to keep his wits about him for the main business of the evening, which was to revel in female company. Skoyles had always had an eye for the ladies, and his elevation to officer rank had certainly aided his pursuit of pleasure. Canada had been an education for him. During a dalliance with some of its pretty *demoiselles,* he had greatly improved his command of French.

As the room slowly began to fill, the orchestra played a medley of English and French melodies. Skoyles watched from a quiet corner. A few of the officers were traveling with their wives, but it was members of the civil administration, and notably the Canadian families, who provided most of the feminine interest. Skoyles was soon reminded how large the average Canadian family could be. One middle-aged couple swept into the room with no fewer than five attractive young daughters in tow as well as four sons. Skoyles admired the French fashions of the Canadian women though he was less enamored of their powdered and ornamented coiffures. They looked too artificial to him.

He was still surveying the room when he heard a nervous voice.

"I find them so intimidating," Charles Westbourne confessed.

"Who?" asked Skoyles, turning to him.

"The fairer sex."

"You'll soon learn to conquer that fear, Lieutenant."

"I doubt it."

"Women were put on this earth for our delight."

"Then why do they always unnerve me so?"

Lieutenant Charles Westbourne was a plump, fresh-faced young man in his twenties, relatively new to the regiment and still—an incongruity in a British army—obviously in possession of his virginity. There was no hope of his losing it at the ball. Skoyles could see the glass of punch trembling in his hand and the first beads of perspiration on his brow. Unlike some of his fellow officers, however, he did not mock Westbourne. He tried to protect him from the scorn of the others, and an unlikely friendship had grown up between them as a result.

"What are we supposed to do, Captain?"

"Dance with them, of course."

A note of panic sounded. "Dance? I don't know how!"

"What better time to learn?" observed Skoyles. "Make the most of it while you can. Before too long, we'll be dodging enemy fire."

"I think I'd prefer that to dancing with a woman."

"Coward!"

"They all look so unapproachable to me."

"An optical illusion."

"How does one get to *meet* them?"

Skoyles grinned. "Watch me," he said. "I'll show you."

Putting his glass on a table, he adjusted his uniform and pulled himself up to his full height before striding purposefully across the floor. General Burgoyne had just entered the room with a group that included a young lady who caught Skoyles's attention at once. Pale and slender, she had a radiance that set her immediately apart from all the other women. Her auburn hair was brushed up on her head into an oval shape with a series of curls trailing artfully down. She was wearing a beautiful blue silk dress with a hooped skirt and a wide décolletage, partially covered by a chiffon bow but still advertising the full breasts. Even at first glance, Skoyles noted a strange mixture of vulnerability and self-possession about her.

Seeing him approach, General Burgoyne gave him a warm smile.

"There you are, Skoyles," he said. "Have you heard the news?"

"What news, sir?"

"I thought I'd arrived in Canada with a secret plan of action, yet I find a paper circulating in Montreal that contains infernally accurate details of my strategy. How on earth could that happen?"

"There are spies everywhere, General."

"They'll hang from the tallest tree when I catch up with them!" He turned to his companions. "You all know Captain Skoyles, don't you?"

"Yes," said Brigadier General Simon Fraser. "One of my best men."

"Thank you, sir," said Skoyles.

Anxious to be introduced to the only woman in the group, Skoyles had first to exchange greetings with Simon Fraser, Major General William Phillips, the renowned artilleryman, Adjutant General Major Robert Kingston, Major John Dyke Acland, and Major Alexander Lindsay, the Earl of Balcarres. Including the general, there were three members of Parliament in the group. Clearly, the young lady moved in exalted company, all of them wearing powdered wigs and sporting their epaulets.

"Let me introduce our charming young guest," said Burgoyne, beaming at her. "Miss Elizabeth Rainham." She gave a polite smile. "Miss Rainham, this is Captain Skoyles of the 24th Foot."

"Delighted to make your acquaintance," said Skoyles, inclining his head in a token bow.

"Thank you, Captain," she said.

"Are you a resident of Montreal?"

"Oh, no. I only arrived in the city this morning."

"Why don't you find Miss Rainham a glass of punch, Skoyles?" suggested Burgoyne. "Then she can tell you what she's doing here—apart from lighting up the room with her beauty, that is."

She laughed softly. "You flatter me, General."

"A feat well beyond my competence."

"And mine," added Skoyles with an admiring smile.

"Be careful, Miss Rainham," Burgoyne warned her genially. "Whatever you do, don't let Skoyles lure you to the card table. I speak from bitter experience. He has the luck of the devil."

"I can vouch for that," said Balcarres. "I'm another of his victims."

"Is that true, Captain?" she asked.

"Not entirely." Skoyles intercepted a passing waiter to take two glasses of punch from his tray. He handed one to Elizabeth before raising the other in tribute to her. "Your good health, Miss Rainham!"

"Thank you."

Sipping their drinks, they moved aside from the others and took a moment to weigh each other up. She looked at Skoyles through large, intelligent, curious blue eyes.

"The general did not mention your Christian name," she noted.

"It's Jamie."

"Short for James?"

"No, Miss Rainham," he explained. "Jamie, as in Jamie. My mother was Scots. I was named after her grandfather."

"Yet you don't have a Scots accent."

"My father was English. I was born and brought up in Cumberland." He took another sip of punch. "But you sound more like a southerner to me. Surrey, perhaps? Sussex?"

"Kent, actually. We have a home near Canterbury."

"What brought you to this part of the world?"

"A ship," she said, grimacing. "A small and extremely smelly frigate. I can't say that I took any pleasure from the voyage, Captain. It was a nightmare. But," she went on, bravely, "that's all behind me. I can start to enjoy myself now."

"Enjoy yourself?"

"I'll be traveling with the army."

Skoyles was taken aback. "I can't guarantee much enjoyment for you in that, Miss Rainham. It promises to be a testing campaign."

"Not according to General Burgoyne," she said brightly. "He's a family friend of ours and he assures me that there'll be no real danger. Why should there be?" she asked, hunching her shoulders. "He'll be leading an army of professional soldiers against a disorganized rabble of amateurs. There can only be one result."

"I hope that you're right," said Skoyles, worried by her optimism, "but it would be foolish to underestimate our enemy. When we fought against them last year at Valcour Island, they gave a good account of themselves. We lost several men."

"I'm not frightened by the sight of blood, Captain Skoyles."

"Just as well. You'll see lots of it."

"Are you trying to scare me off?"

"Not at all," he said. "It's just that I don't think that life in the shadow of Canterbury cathedral will have prepared you for the ugliness of what might lie ahead."

"I'm treating it all as an adventure."

"Adventures can have unseen hazards."

"That's what makes it all so thrilling."

"There's nothing thrilling in the sight of dead bodies," he said. "Or in seeing your men sustain horrific injuries. This is not a cricket match on the village green, Miss Rainham."

"Please!" she said, her cheeks coloring slightly. "Stop treating me like a child. It may interest you to know that my father fought alongside General Burgoyne in Portugal. I also have a brother in the Horse Guards. So you see, I do have some insight into army life."

He was blunt. "I doubt that."

"Why do you take such pleasure in vexing me?"

"I don't, Miss Rainham. I just feel that you should be warned."

Skoyles was torn between desire and anxiety. If she accompanied the army on its journey south, he might have the chance to improve his acquaintance with her. Nothing would please him more. On the other hand, he knew that she would be come face to face with the more hideous aspects of warfare and he wanted to save her from that. There was another consideration. Skoyles had experienced the climate in the Hudson Valley at that time of the year. He would hate to see that delicate complexion of hers ruined by the hot sun.

Elizabeth was brusque. "Unlike you, I have total confidence in General Burgoyne."

"We all do, Miss Rainham."

"No, Captain," she said, crisply. "I sense a flicker of doubt. You are not as certain of victory as you should be. Fortunately, that's not an attitude shared by my future husband."

Skoyles was checked. "You're betrothed?"

"What else would bring me all this way in the such discomfort? It was not to have my upbringing derided by you, I can assure you. Only the compulsion to be with my beloved could have got me to Canada. In fact, I reached Montreal somewhat earlier than expected so I'll be able to surprise him." She looked around. "I can't wait to see his face when he realizes that I'm already here."

"What regiment does he serve in?"

"Your own—the 24th Foot."

"Then I must know him," he said.

"I'm sure that you do, Captain."

"May I ask his name?"

"Of course. It's—" She broke off abruptly as a newcomer sauntered into the room. "There he is!" she said, joyously.

Picking her way through the crowd, Elizabeth Rainham went off to greet her betrothed and to receive a kiss on both gloved hands. Skoyles was filled with a sudden envy. During their brief conversation, Elizabeth has aroused more than his interest. Skoyles had felt the first stirrings of lust, only to discover that she was hopelessly beyond his reach. The man she had sailed an enormous distance to be with was none other than Major Harry Featherstone.

"Lucky bastard!" said Skoyles.

CHAPTER THREE

June, 1777

The flogging was carried out in full view of the regiment, formed up in hollow square. Drunkenness was a problem that bedeviled the British army, and punishments for offenders were stern. Every man in the ranks felt sorry for Private Roger Higgs, the latest scapegoat to be paraded in front of them to serve as a dire warning. They knew his story and understood his lapse only too well. When he appeared, there was a collective murmur of sympathy for him. Higgs was marched to the wooden triangle that had been set up and he stood there, shivering with fear, while his sentence was read out by the adjutant. Ordered to strip, he removed his shirt. As he was tied to the triangle, Higgs looked thin, pale, and defenseless.

Captain Jamie Skoyles was forced to watch along with everyone else but—though he did not condone drunken behavior—he had never found flogging an edifying spectacle. At its best, it broke a man's spirit and rendered him unfit for duty for a length of time; at its worst, it flayed its victim to death. Skoyles hoped that Higgs would survive but it was open to doubt. The soldier was not robust. Even the hardiest of men had perished when their backs were cut to ribbons.

The signal was given and a brawny drummer stepped forward to select a cat-o'-nine-tails from its green baize bag. Higgs did not dare to glance over his shoulder at the short whip. He simply tensed his body against the first stroke. When it came, it ripped open his skin and made him convulse wildly. Before the first yell had left his throat, the strands of twisted rope bit into his back again and set the blood running down it. Higgs struggled to get free but there was no escape. His ordeal had merely begun. Almost five dozen lashes were still to come, each one more agonizing than the last as it pierced his skin to the bone and found a fresh place to inflict torture.

What made it worse for Higgs was that he suffered such pain and humiliation in front of his fellows. Others had got through their ordeal without yelling for mercy, but Higgs let out a cry of despair with each succeeding stroke. He was a blood-soaked skeleton, twisting and turning like a rag doll in a high wind. Standing beside the triangle, Tom Caffrey waited to help him, wondering how much life would be left in the man's body when the flogging ceased. The drummer had built up a rhythm now, striking the bare flesh at a steady and unvarying pace, making sure that no portion of his target was spared the sting of the cat-o'-nine-tails.

When the flogger finally tired, a second man stood by to take over, choosing another whip and attacking Higgs's back with gusto. Some of the soldiers looked away, others kept hoping that someone would intercede on the victim's behalf, most of them vowed that they would never let themselves be flogged into delirium in front of the entire regiment. Skoyles looked across at Major Harry Featherstone, clearly relishing the occasion, his smile broadening as the sergeant major called out the strokes. When it was all over, when Higgs was left hanging there with his back dripping blood, and when Tom Caffrey moved in to help him, Featherstone was obviously disappointed. There would be no more pleasure for the major to take from another man's pain. Skoyles was appalled by the streak of cruelty that had been revealed.

Harry Featherstone went down sharply in his estimation.

After a series of reviews and festivities at St. Johns on the Richelieu River, the army finally set sail on June 13. The Royal Standard was unfurled aboard the *Thunderer,* an ungainly vessel, and the makeshift armada made its way toward Lake Champlain with high hopes of a successful expedition. Their ultimate destination was Albany, the northern base of the American rebels, where they expected to be joined by an army dispatched up the Hudson River from New York City by Sir William Howe, commander in chief of British forces in America.

When the two armies met, Burgoyne predicted, they would have split their enemy in two, creating a barrier between New England, the stronghold of the rebellion, and the rest of the colonies. It would, he felt, be the decisive blow needed to bring the conflict to an end. The capture of Albany depended on taking a series of intervening forts from rebel hands, and Burgoyne had no worries on that score. In Major General Phillips, he had a master of artillery, a man who had distinguished himself in the Seven Years War by achieving the almost impossible feat of bringing up his guns at a gallop.

While the main army would travel with Burgoyne, a smaller force had been assembled in Montreal under Brigadier General Barry St. Leger. Its aim was to sail three hundred miles up the St. Lawrence River and across Lake Ontario before making its way toward Fort Stanwix by means of Lake Oneida and Wood Creek. The fort had been built on the bank of the Mohawk River in order to guard the portage from Wood Creek. Though renamed Fort Schuyler after General Philip Schuyler, the commander of the Northern Department of the Continental Army, it was still referred to by the British as Stanwix. They recognized no honor bestowed on a renegade general.

St. Leger's orders were to head for Albany along the Mohawk Valley, a route of immense strategic importance since it was the gateway to the west. It was also Indian country, the home of the powerful Confederacy of the Six Nations that included the Mohawks, Iroquois, and Senecas, tribes that had fought with the British against the French in the past. Since almost half of his two-thousand-strong force consisted of Iroquois, St. Leger believed that he would have excellent guides and, in the event of resistance, a brutally effective fighting unit. Having closed off the rebels' western supply line, he intended to rendezvous with Burgoyne at Albany.

The general, meanwhile, was already in transit. Most of his fleet had been constructed during the previous summer and winter. Well-armed frigates such as the *Inflexible* and the *Royal George* had been built with a shallow draft, enabling them to sail close to the shore. Some two hundred bateaux had also been hastily completed and soldiers were trained how to row them. Instead of the 12,000 men he had hoped to have at his disposal, however, Burgoyne—when his reinforcements finally caught up with him—would have only about three-quarters that number. His army comprised almost 4,000 British regulars and just over 3,000 Brunswick and Hesse-Hanau troops.

In addition, he had a small detachment of loyalists and Canadians at his command, and would be joined in time by some hired Indians. The fleet was encumbered by the massive artillery train, and by the best part of a thousand noncombatants—transport and commissariat men, cooks, wives, children, and camp followers. Though horses, wagons, and food rations were in far shorter supply than Burgoyne had requested, he was not daunted. Indeed, from the moment they set off from St. Johns and left Governor Carleton behind them, he was positively elated, able to take full control of his army at last. It was something to be savored.

As a personal favor, he invited Elizabeth Rainham to sail with him on the *Maria* on the first stage of the journey. Grateful that she was not traveling with the baggage train, Elizabeth stood on deck beside the general and took the opportunity to probe for detail.

"I trust that we shall be in no danger," she said.

"None whatsoever, my dear," Burgoyne assured her. "You'll be kept well behind the lines with the others. You'll hear the artillery, of course—especially the twenty-four-pounders—but it's a sound to which you'll soon become accustomed."

"Captain Skoyles thought it foolhardy of me to come."

Burgoyne chuckled. "If you were engaged to *him,* Skoyles might think differently. I'm certain that Major Featherstone does."

"Oh, yes," she said. "Harry has no fears at all for my safety. He's delighted that I made the effort to be with him. Harry has this curious inclination to be married on American soil."

"British colonial soil," he corrected her firmly. "But I can't imagine your parents agreeing to anything as bizarre as that. If I know Richard Rainham, he'll insist on Canterbury Cathedral for his daughter's wedding. Yes, and I daresay that he'll settle for nothing less than the archbishop himself."

"We shall see. No final decision has been made."

"You just wished to be with the man you love, is that it?"

"Yes, General," she admitted with a coy smile. "Absence may make the heart grow fonder, but it has many drawbacks. That's why I had to come. If I'm going to be an army wife, I want to have a better understanding of what that means, and the only way to do that is to go on a campaign with Harry. Mark you," she added with a twinkle in her eye, "that's not what I told him."

"Oh?"

"I teased Harry that I only made the journey in order to visit Uncle David in New England. Somehow, I don't think that he believed me."

"I wonder why," said Burgoyne with another chuckle.

A sudden gust of wind made the brim of her straw hat flap and she put up a hand to steady it. Elizabeth found river transport much more agreeable than battling across the North Atlantic and she gazed at the pristine beauty of forest and mountain as they scudded along. She was also intrigued by the variety of colorful birds that flew overhead, hundreds of them daring to land on the ship's rigging as feathered stowaways. After a few minutes, she raised a topic that had been on her mind for days.

"Harry tells me that Captain Skoyles won his commission by bravery in the field," she remarked. "Is that true?"

"True and fairly unusual," he replied. "Most British officers follow tradition and purchase their commissions. I did so myself, Elizabeth, when I was barely older than you, so there's no disgrace in it. Somehow I scraped together two thousand pounds to buy a captaincy in the Royals. Heaven knows how I managed it!"

"We're all eternally grateful that you did, General. Father says that you were heroic when you fought against the Spaniards in Portugal. He knew then that you were marked out for great things."

"*This* will be the greatest," said Burgoyne with passion.

"Coming back to Captain Skoyles," she said, trying to sound casual, "what exactly did he do to earn his commission?"

"Best person to ask is Brigadier Fraser. There when it happened, so he was a witness. It was on his recommendation that Skoyles got his lieutenancy."

"I see. And when a captaincy became vacant, he bought it."

"No, my dear," Burgoyne explained, "it was exempt from payment because it had been obtained by the incumbent through seniority. Real scramble for the position, I can tell you."

"I'm sure."

"Dozens of fellows in the race. Skoyles beat them all, strictly on merit. Buy a commission!" he exclaimed with a short laugh. "I can see that you don't know Jamie Skoyles."

"I know that he can be blunt."

"Speaks his mind. Good quality."

"Not if he criticizes you. I found him rather rude."

"A trifle untutored, that's all. Skoyles would never be deliberately rude to a woman. Underneath that roughness, he's a real gentleman."

Elizabeth was about to reply when she noticed that someone had come out on deck, a buxom woman in her early thirties with a mass of brown curls exploding from beneath her hat. Assuming that she herself was the only female aboard, Elizabeth was very surprised to see her.

"Who's that lady?" she asked.

"That?" replied Burgoyne, collecting a smile from the woman as he looked in her direction. "Oh, that's Mrs. Mallard," he went on, smoothly. "Her husband is one of our commissary officers."

Captain Jamie Skoyles was part of the advance corps under Brigadier Fraser that was dispatched ahead of the main army to reconnoiter. When they reached Cumberland Head, north of Valcour Island in Lake Champlain, they made camp and awaited the arrival of the others. Unlike his friend, Lieutenant Charles Westbourne was making the journey for the first time.

"I had no idea there'd be so many mosquitoes," he complained.

"It's always worse when we get hot weather after a few days of heavy rain," said Skoyles. "Ideal breeding conditions for them. At least, you get a moment's warning from the mosquitoes. It's the other insects that I hate—the ones you don't see until they've bitten you."

"The men are very unhappy. Every time we step ashore, they have to go through the same boring routine of clearing brush, digging latrines, collecting wood, and lighting fires."

"The smoke is the only way to keep the mosquitoes at bay."

"Even then, we've had to sleep with our hands and faces covered."

Skoyles was sympathetic. He could see the bites on Westbourne's cheeks and knew how much they must itch. "Take heart, Lieutenant," he said. "Think of all the wonderful things you've seen for the first time. Where is it you hail from—Nottingham, isn't it?"

"Yes, Captain."

"I'll wager that you've never found fish of this size in the River Trent. The pike and salmon are huge, so is the bass. And don't forget all those delicious passenger pigeons we've been eating every day. Some of them were so tired after flying across the lake that they fell out of the trees. All we had to do was to catch them."

"I know," said Westbourne, rallying, "and I enjoyed every mouthful. But it was the animals that fascinated me. I've never set eyes on moose and beaver before, nor on bears. I saw my first turtle yesterday. It was enormous."

"One day, you'll be able to boast about it to your children."

Westbourne was uneasy. "Oh, I'm not sure about that, Captain."

"Why not?"

"I don't think I'm the marrying type."

"You don't need to be married to have children," said Tom Caffrey, jovially, as he joined the two men. "Two minutes of naked lust is all that it takes, Lieutenant. You'll succumb to it one day, sir."

"I'll take your word for it, Sergeant," said Westbourne, backing away in embarrassment. "Do excuse me, gentleman. I have things to do."

Caffrey watched him go. "I didn't mean to frighten him away."

"He's suffering badly, Tom. That fair skin of his tempts every insect within range. The worst of it is that we've camped here on swampy ground. Venture into the woods and you find swarms of the little devils."

"Yes, I know," said the other ruefully. "As soon as I lowered my breeches over a latrine, my ass came under attack."

Caffrey had accompanied the advance corps in case anyone was injured along the way, but all that he had done was to fend off the dozens of soldiers who begged him for something to soothe their insect bites. His supply of salve had been exhausted on the first day. Caffrey had been waiting for a moment alone with Skoyles.

"Have you managed to see her again, Jamie?" he asked.

"Who?"

"A certain young lady you took a fancy to."

"There are plenty of those to choose from," said Skoyles happily.

"I was thinking of Miss Elizabeth Rainham."

"Ah—now she was rather special."

"Such a pity that she'll end up in Major Featherstone's bed."

"He wooed her and won her."

"Given the chance, you could do the same."

"Too late. She's spoken for, Tom."

"You've changed your tune, haven't you?" teased Caffrey. "Since when has Jamie Skoyles been frightened off by competition? That woman you knew in Quebec was married, yet you charmed her away from her husband for more than one night. And she wasn't the only conquest of yours who was well and truly spoken for, was she? Last year, there was that lady who—"

"Miss Rainham is different," said Skoyles, cutting him off.

"You mean, you'd have to lay siege for much longer?"

"No, Tom. I mean that she's betrothed to a fellow officer."

"What better way to get back at Major Featherstone?"

"Why should I want to do that?"

"Because you were as sickened by that flogging as I was."

"Yes," conceded Skoyles, "but that's no reason strike at him through Miss Rainham. While I might have lost some respect for the major that day, I still admire him as soldier. I've seen him in action."

"Wouldn't you like to see *her* in action?"

"Tom!"

"I'm only going on what you said yourself," argued Caffrey. "When you got back from that ball, you couldn't stop talking about Elizabeth Rainham— even though you went on to spend the night in the arms of another lady altogether. What was she called—Mary?"

"Maria."

"There you are. You sleep with one woman but think of another. It was the major's intended who really set your blood racing, wasn't it?"

"She struck me as an attractive woman, that's all."

"Especially with her clothes off."

"I'll never know."

"But you'd *like* to, wouldn't you?"

"Any man in his right mind would like to, Tom."

"Then go and get her!"

Skoyles laughed. When they had met in Montreal, he had been quite intrigued by Elizabeth Rainham, and he still felt a pang of regret whenever he recalled the way that she had hurried to greet Major Harry Featherstone so joyfully at the ball. It had been more than a case of simple jealousy. He could see at a glance exactly the kind of married life that awaited her with a man who was much older and seasoned in the kinds of pleasures that would inevitably exclude his wife. Skoyles was very sorry for her. It was apparent that Elizabeth did not really know the man to whom she was betrothed, nor could she guess at the disillusion that lay ahead for her.

"Well?" Caffrey goaded him. "What's stopping you?"

"Common sense, Tom."

"You don't give two hoots for common sense."

"Miss Rainham wouldn't look at me twice."

"How do you know?"

"Because she's made her choice. Leave her to it."

"If it were anyone but Major Featherstone, I would. We can't sacrifice her to that supercilious turd. She deserves better, Jamie. I think you should do the lady a favor."

"I will," said Skoyles, "by keeping well clear of her."

"Coward!"

"Tom, I hardly know her."

"That's not the impression I got."

"I talked to her for a few minutes at the ball and sat opposite her at dinner but that was that. Since then, I haven't spared Elizabeth Rainham a moment's thought."

"Liar!"

"Stop calling me names."

"Then stop provoking me," said Caffrey with a good-humored grin. "At the very least, you might admit that the lady interested you."

"I confess it freely."

"Then I'll satisfy your curiosity."

"What do you mean?"

"I'll ask Polly to see what she can discover," said Caffrey, smacking away a mosquito that tried to land on his chin. "She has a gift for picking up gossip. I know that Polly won't be able to meet this lady on equal terms, but Miss Rainham will be traveling with a maid. *She's* the person that Polly might get to know."

Though he made some token protest against it, Skoyles found the offer appealing. Polly Bragg had been with Caffrey for over a year now, and she had proved herself to be loyal and discreet. If nothing else, she could find out more detail about Elizabeth Rainham, and Skoyles was interested in any scrap of information about her. He would certainly not get such information from Featherstone or from any other source.

"There's no need for Polly to do this," said Skoyles, pretending to be indifferent to the notion. "Leave well alone, Tom."

"I'm always ready to help a friend."

"Supposing that he doesn't want to be helped?"

"Then I'll tell him that he can't fool me," said Caffrey genially. "I know you too well, Jamie. I've seen that light in your eye before, and the only thing that can put it there is a beautiful woman."

———

30

On the first night when his army assembled at Cumberland Point, General Burgoyne elected to sleep aboard his ship. Most people believed that he wanted to stay clear of the mosquito-infested swampland, but there were a few whispers that he might have another reason for wishing to remain afloat. The sound of female laughter was heard from within his cabin. When he came ashore next day to inspect his troops, there was a jaunty optimism about Burgoyne. It gave the soldiers heart.

At four o'clock on the morning of June 24, the order for general march was beaten on the drums and the men clambered into their bateaux. Two cannon boomed aboard the *Maria* to signal departure. As the sun was coming up, they rowed away from Cumberland Bay. Wearing brilliant war paint and bright feathers, the Indians led the way in birchbark canoes that held thirty or more, paddling rhythmically and skimming over the placid water with apparent ease. Then came a succession of bateaux, four abreast, containing regulars in scarlet coats with white breeches and waistcoats, as well as light infantry in black leather caps and red waistcoats, grenadiers in their heavy bearskin hats, and Canadians in Indian attire. It was a striking show of military power.

Behind the massed ranks of troops came the gunboats with their blue-clad artillerymen, their guns glinting proudly on deck. The *Royal George* and the *Inflexible* came next, their progress slowed by the massive booms they had in tow. Two dark-hulled frigates, the *Maria* and the *Carleton*, took their turn in the procession and, astern of them, was the first British brigade in scarlet coats, faced with yellow, red, or white. Three pinnaces followed, each bearing a general. John Burgoyne was in the central craft, flanked by William Phillips and Lieutenant General Friedrich von Riedesel, Baron Eisenbach, commander of the German contingent, a short and rather portly man in his late thirties.

Riedesel's troops rowed in serried ranks behind him—infantrymen in dark blue coats, white breeches, and waistcoats, and jägers in green with red cuffs and facings. Officers sported plumed caps, while the grenadiers, in contrast to their British counterparts, wore tall miter caps with shiny metal plates on the front of them that acted as so many mirrors in the sunlight. Even when propelling their bateaux, the Germans somehow looked supremely controlled, a well-drilled professional force that was watched with interest and wonder by the sutlers and camp followers bringing up the rear.

It was an awesome sight, an army on the move with disciplined grandeur, its size doubled by its reflection in the shimmering waters of the lake, its potency somehow increased by its splendor. To the east were the looming peaks of the Green Mountains, to the west were the dark and craggy Adirondacks. Gliding between them across the widest part of the lake was a dazzling flotilla of death.

Gentleman Johnny had a true sense of theater.

Major Harry Featherstone was not a man who could easily conceal his anger. After making his feelings known to the brigadier, he sought out Jamie Skoyles in his tent.

"*I* should have been sent on this mission," Featherstone insisted.

"Brigadier Fraser made the decision."

"It was the wrong one."

"That may be so, Major," said Skoyles, trying to calm him, "but there's no point in berating me about it. I've no power to change the situation. Take the matter up with Brigadier Fraser."

"I've already done so—to no avail."

"I'm sorry to hear that."

"When all is said and done, I'm the senior officer."

"Of course."

"But that counted for nothing," said the other irritably. "Listen, Jamie, I know that you have a lot of experience as a scout and I don't want us to fall out over this, but you can appreciate why I'm furious."

"Yes, Major."

"This assignment should have been given to me."

"All I can do is to obey orders, sir."

Skoyles was delighted that he had been selected for such an important scouting mission, but he could understand why Featherstone was so upset. Hoping to be given the task himself, he had probably boasted of the position to Elizabeth Rainham. Instead of being able to go on a daring expedition, he would now have to cool his heels in the advance camp while someone else had the opportunity to gain kudos. It was galling for the major.

Ready to depart, Skoyles had shed his uniform and changed into a hunting shirt that would be far less conspicuous than his redcoat. He picked up his Brown Bess musket and checked that it was loaded. Featherstone watched him with muted resentment. When Skoyles tried to walk past him, he blocked his way.

"You could always ask for me to assist you," he said.

"No, I couldn't."

"Why not?"

"Because it would be the other way round," Skoyles pointed out. "You'd be in command and I'd be at your elbow. If that's what the brigadier had wanted, he'd have said so."

"Simon has too much on his plate at the moment."

"Perhaps that's why he chose the wrong person."

"That's the only excuse I can think of," said Featherstone with ill grace. "Next time, I'll expect him to turn to me."

"I'm sure that he will, sir."

There was a tension between the two men that had not been there before, and it puzzled Skoyles. In being preferred over the major, he had clearly ruffled his feathers. Featherstone was still obstructing his exit.

"I'll have to be on my way," said Skoyles.

"Of course. I'm sorry." Reverting to his normal bonhomie, Featherstone moved back so that the other man could leave. "Good luck, Jamie! I know that you won't let us down."

Once outside the tent, Skoyles forgot all about his exchange with the major. The task ahead demanded all his concentration. Accompanied by three Indians, he was being sent on a scouting mission to find out the strength of the American forces that lay ahead and to determine the quality of their fortifications. It gave him an opportunity to make amends for the mishap that had occurred nearby the previous year.

Progress had so far been uninterrupted. Under the leadership of Brigadier Simon Fraser, the advance corps had approached Crown Point. Bracing themselves for combat, they instead found the fort completely abandoned and decided to camp there until the main army could catch them up. Meanwhile, the scouting party was being sent on toward Fort Ticonderoga, a much more formidable bastion. Jamie Skoyles had learned his trade as a skirmisher, able to move fast, shoot straight, and survive in enemy territory. They were skills that would now be called into play. Watch boats had fled before them at every point in their journey down the lake. The rebels knew that they were coming.

The Iroquois braves chosen to go with Skoyles were lithe, muscular young men who, apart from a breechcloth and a set of beads apiece, were virtually naked. They each carried a hunting knife and a tomahawk, a fearsome weapon that they could use as a club or throw with force and unfailing accuracy. Of the three Indians, only one understood English well. Unable to pronounce their names, Skoyles opted largely for sign language.

He had grave reservations about the inclusion of four hundred Indians in the army. While they were fine scouts, they could be unreliable in combat, ever likely to act on impulse, scalp, mutilate, rape, or plunder with indiscriminate savagery. Their loyalty was also questionable. When the army had earlier assembled at Bouquet River, General Burgoyne had issued two proclamations. The first was addressed to American colonists, warning them that those who sided with the rebels would be severely punished and threatening that he would unleash his Indians against them. Since it was directed at a farming population—some of whom could not even read—its flowery language and grandiose claims were somewhat wasted.

The second proclamation had been delivered to the Indians, and Skoyles could recall some of the exact words used by Burgoyne, *"I positively forbid bloodshed when you are not opposed in arms. Aged men, women, children, and prisoners must be held sacred from the knife even in time of actual conflict."*

The Indians had cheered the general to the echo even though most of them did not realize what he was saying. Skoyles had fought with Indians beside him before, and he knew that it would take more than a humane and well-intended edict to prevent them from resorting to their traditional methods of warfare. After the proclamation, drink had unwisely been served to the Indians, and they performed an impromptu war dance, so wild and uninhibited that even some of the hardened soldiers were shocked.

Suppressing his doubts about them, Skoyles set off with his three companions. As they passed through the picket line, he was interested to see that Roger Higgs, the private who had been flogged a fortnight earlier, was back on duty. Morose but watchful, Higgs gave him a nod, aware that Skoyles had at least tried to speak up for him. It was clear from the way he kept shifting position that the sentry was still in pain from his beating, but he was nevertheless doing his duty.

When they plunged into the woods, Skoyles let one of the Indians take the lead. Clouds of blackflies rose up to envelop them, but the Indians seemed unaware of them. Carrying his musket in one hand, Skoyles used the other to swat the insects away, grateful for the wide-brimmed hat that gave him a measure of protection. He stayed close behind the leading man and marveled at the sureness with which he picked his way past swamps and through dense undergrowth.

They had gone over five miles when the incident occurred. It was Skoyles who first sensed danger. Hearing and seeing nothing, he nevertheless had a warning of peril. Tapping the man ahead of him to bring him to a halt, he waved to the two men behind him. They fanned out and crouched behind cover, listening intently. One of the Indians then decided that it was a false alarm and he stood up. It was a fatal error.

Somewhere ahead of them, a weapon was fired and the ball hit the Indian in the eye before making an untidy exit through the rear of his skull. He collapsed in a heap, his feathers sodden with blood. Enraged by his death, the other Indians waited to see if there would be more firing. Instead, they heard the sound of hasty departure and set off quickly in pursuit. Skoyles went with them, hoping to catch the attacker before they did so that he could take the prisoner alive. The rifle shot had been deadly, but the weapon was slow to reload, so its owner had taken to his heels, hoping to outrun the pursuit.

Skoyles was moving fast, but he soon lost sight of the Indians among the trees. All that he could do was to guess the direction in which they went and keep up a steady pace. He had covered some distance before he saw a flash of color ahead of him. Slowing to a trot, he went forward with more care, his musket at the ready. Skoyles had not been deceived. What he had glimpsed was the figure of a man, clad in a green jacket and breeches, loading something into the saddlebags of a horse. He appeared to be unarmed.

It was only when Skoyles got near the clearing that he saw the rifle on the ground. Before the man could stoop to pick it up, Skoyles rushed forward and pointed his musket.

"Leave it there," he ordered. "You are my prisoner."

The man stared belligerently. "And who, in God's name, are you?"

"Captain Skoyles of the 24th Foot. You shot one of my men."

"I did nothing of the kind," said the other indignantly. "I've been out hunting, as you may see." He indicated the game protruding from his saddlebags and strung across the rump of his horse. "When was your man killed?"

"Minutes ago."

"I haven't fired my rifle today. I prefer to snare my quarry. It's more effective. Fire a shot and you frighten the animals away. If you don't believe me," he went on, "look at my rifle. It's still loaded."

Skoyles knew that he was telling the truth. Apart from anything else, the man was not out of breath, whereas Skoyles was still panting from the chase. Motioning the man back with his musket, he checked the rifle and found it loaded. The man would never have had time to do that. He took a closer look at the prisoner, a thin, wiry man of middle years with wispy gray hair curling out from under his hat and a grizzled beard. He had spoken with a light Scots accent.

"Who is your commanding officer, laddie?" asked the man.

"Brigadier General Fraser."

"Would that be *Simon* Fraser?"

"The same."

"Then you can stop pointing that musket at me," said the man with a hearty laugh. "I served under Brigadier Fraser when he was in command of the 78th Regiment of Foot. A gallant soldier, if ever there was one. Where is he? I'd like to meet him again."

"I insist on it," said Skoyles without lowering his weapon. He retrieved the rifle from the ground. "You must come with me."

"Willingly," agreed the other. "My name is James McIntosh, by the way. I live near Fort Ticonderoga."

"That remains to be seen."

Skoyles was wary. He had met too many plausible American spies to take them at face value. If his prisoner really had served in the British army, that claim could soon be verified. He was about to question him in more detail when he heard loud whoops from the distance. The Indians had got their man.

With prisoner and horse ahead of him, Skoyles set off toward the sounds of celebration, fearing what he might find. The Indians had seen their companion's head split open by an enemy rifle shot. No mercy would be shown. It was some minutes before Skoyles got there. When he eventually found the Indians, he saw that they had taken their revenge. Their victim had been beaten to a pulp with tomahawks before being scalped, stripped naked, and hanged by his feet from a tree. His genitals had been cut off and stuffed into his mouth. A swarm of insects buzzed greedily around the corpse.

Skoyles felt sick.

CHAPTER FOUR

rigadier General Simon Fraser had spent most of his adult life as a soldier, and it had left its mark on him. He was only a youth when he was wounded in combat in the Low Countries. Then he had sailed to America to serve in the 78th Highlanders under Amherst and Wolfe. Service in Prussia had followed. Still short of fifty, the dashing Fraser had had an illustrious career in the British army and was known for his bravery, his tactical acumen, and his inspiring leadership. It had been his idea to select and train the elite corps of marksmen of which Jamie Skoyles was such a valued member.

Arriving back at camp, Skoyles had gone to his commander's tent to hand over his prisoner and give his report. Fraser recognized the man at once and confirmed that it was James McIntosh, shaking his hand warmly. The two Scotsmen exchanged a few brief reminiscences before Skoyles gave his account of events. When he heard what had occurred on the scouting expedition, Fraser's handsome face darkened.

"You've Captain Skoyles to thank for bringing some decency to bear on the situation," said McIntosh. "He insisted that the Indians cut the man down and bury him. They didn't like that idea at all."

"I can imagine," said Fraser.

"The pair of them ranted and raved, but Captain Skoyles wouldn't be moved. He stood over them until they'd dug a shallow grave and buried their victim. Only then did he let them see to their own man."

"Well done, Jamie."

"Thank you, sir," said Skoyles. "There were no papers on the man, but he wore the uniform of a local militia. I brought back his rifle and ammunition."

Impressed with his handling of the situation, Fraser let him stay while he interrogated McIntosh. Skoyles was fascinated to listen to the interview, the sound of two Scots accents reminding him so closely of his mother's voice that fond memories were rekindled. Professing neutrality, McIntosh was nevertheless ready to help the British army all he could. Since he lived in the shadow of Fort Ticonderoga, the retired soldier was able to give them precise details of its outworks, its fortifications, its garrison, and the number of ships at its disposal.

It took hours to hear all the information that poured out of the garrulous old Highlander but Fraser was tireless in his pursuit of the facts. Invited to ask questions on his own behalf, Skoyles looked deep into McIntosh's eyes as he spoke.

"Somebody is lying," he said.

"We'll it's not me, laddie," retorted McIntosh, bridling.

"Two prisoners were captured yesterday. They told us that there were twelve thousand troops at Fort Ticonderoga, yet you claim there are only a third of that number."

"There are, Captain Skoyles."

"Who do we believe—you or them?"

"Me, of course," urged McIntosh. "I've got no reason to mislead you. Those other men have. They gave you false estimates of the garrison to try to frighten you off. I'm telling the truth."

"I know that you are," said Fraser supportively.

"If we invest Ticonderoga," Skoyles resumed, "it could be a protracted siege. How long do you think their provisions will hold out?"

McIntosh shrugged. "Six weeks. Two months at most, I'd say."

"Could fresh supplies be brought up from Lake George?"

"Not if you put your artillery in the right position," said McIntosh, scratching his beard. "You could isolate the fort completely. As I told you, it's understrength in every way. Last December, there were less than two thousand troops there, and many of them didn't even have shoes on their feet. I felt sorry for them. Winters are grim around here. Ticonderoga is especially bleak. The only reason they put Colonel Anthony Wayne in charge of the fort was that he was felt strong and fit enough to survive the climate." He gave a wry grin. "Do you know what Mad Anthony is supposed to have said when he was eventually replaced?"

"What?"

"That Ticonderoga was the last place on earth that God made, and that there were grounds for believing He finished it in the dark." He gave a harsh laugh. "The colonel could never get over the number of human skulls that were lying around. For want of any other vessel, some of his men drank out of them. Yes," he continued, "and they even used the bones of dead soldiers as tent pegs. It's like living in a graveyard."

"It was always called the Gibraltar of the North," said Skoyles.

"Well, it doesn't deserve that name now, Captain. From what I've seen, the fort is far from impregnable."

Delighted with all that he had learned, Fraser was anxious to pass on the intelligence to Burgoyne as soon as the general arrived. He thanked McIntosh and asked him to remain in camp until the main army joined them. McIntosh was only too pleased to be among British soldiers again. Skoyles wanted a private conversation with the man. The two of them stepped outside the tent.

"Thank you for what you said about me in there," said Skoyles.

"It was the truth, Captain. If you hadn't stopped those savages when you did, they'd have carved up that man's body for sport. You forced them to behave in a more civilized way."

"We couldn't leave that man just hanging there."

"*They* would have," said McIntosh.

"Be that as it may. What I really wanted to ask you about was a friend of mine. If you've lived in the area so long," said Skoyles, "you might just have come across him."

"I might. Who is he?"

"Ezekiel Proudfoot."

"Proudfoot . . . Proudfoot," McIntosh repeated, thinking hard. "Now why does that name mean something to me?"

"His father is Mordecai Proudfoot," Skoyles explained. "He owns several hundreds of acres on the eastern bank of Lake George. I was billeted at the house with other troops many years ago. I was only fourteen at the time, around the same age as Ezekiel. That's why we became such good friends. We've tried to keep in touch ever since."

"So this Ezekiel Proudfoot works on the family farm?"

"No, that's what made him so unusual. Ezekiel was the youngest of three brothers. The other two were happy to become farmers but Ezekiel had other leanings. He defied his father's wishes."

"What did he do?"

"He got himself apprenticed to a silversmith in Albany."

"*That's* how I've heard the name," McIntosh declared, slapping his thigh. "Of course. Ezekiel Proudfoot is an engraver."

"Yes," said Skoyles, "he turned out to have a real talent for it. I've seen some of his work. But I lost track of him a couple of years ago and wondered if he's still in Albany."

"I doubt it, Captain."

"What do you mean?"

"Your friend is a true patriot," said McIntosh. "He makes and sells prints that celebrate the American cause. It seems that Ezekiel Proudfoot has a knack of being in the right place when action breaks out. He was at Trenton and at Princeton last winter, and his prints of both American victories were on sale within three weeks. They were very popular. I saw mention of them in the newspapers."

"He's obviously making a name for himself," said Skoyles.

"So are you, from what I can gather."

"Me?"

"I could see the trust that Brigadier Fraser places in you. He wouldn't do that unless he had a high opinion of you." He sucked his teeth and shook his head sadly. "Great pity, really."

"What is?"

"This clash of loyalties, tearing the colonies apart."

"I agree. It's tragic."

"People who once wore British uniforms now try to shoot holes in them. Old comrades are intent on killing each other. Take your own case, for instance," said McIntosh. "You and this fellow Proudfoot have obviously been friends for years, then this happens."

"Yes," said Skoyles reflectively, "we've probably only met a dozen times or so, yet we feel very close to each other. Or, at least, we did," he added with a frown. "You're right, Mr. McIntosh. War ruins everything. Ezekiel and I are now on opposite sides."

Fort Ticonderoga was a forbidding sight, enclosed by the old French lines and heavily guarded by fortifications on top of the lofty Mount Independence to the east and, a mile to the west, by those on the summit of Mount Hope. Ticonderoga, "the place where the lake shuts itself off," was an ideal location for a bastion that could command the narrows, a mere quarter of a mile wide. By way of protection, a log-and-chain boom was stretched across Lake Champlain. A floating bridge gave easy access between the fort and the earthworks and batteries on the eastern bank.

Major General Arthur St. Clair, a well-featured, upright man of forty with chestnut hair, had taken over the stronghold from Colonel Wayne and, with the help of his engineers, done his best to reinforce it. Glaring weaknesses remained. The fort had been built by the French to repel a British advance from the south. If an attack were launched from Canada, Ticonderoga was facing the wrong way. St. Clair had a more worrying problem. To defend the fort properly, he needed twelve thousand men, and his garrison fell woefully short of that number. With limited supplies and low morale among the soldiers, he was far from sanguine.

"Congress gave me false hope," he grumbled, pacing up and down his office. "When I was in Philadelphia, they swore to me that the British would sail from Canada to New York by sea. Yet here they are—only fifteen miles away at Crown Point."

"You know my opinion," said Wilkinson. "I think that we should fall back to Fort George. It will be much easier to defend."

St. Clair was appalled. "Abandon this place without a fight?"

"We could never hope to win, General."

"That's not the point, Colonel. If we ran away from battles we never expect to win, then our cause would have been lost at the start. Besides, we can't be absolutely certain that Burgoyne's army *will* attack."

"Why else have they come?"

"To deceive us by making a feint."

"That's highly unlikely."

"General Burgoyne is a man who usually has a trick up his sleeve."

"With an army of that size, he doesn't need to rely on tricks."

James Wilkinson, the fort's adjutant, was an alert, intelligent, zealous officer of twenty-one. Inclined to be opinionated and overeager, he had not endeared himself to all of his colleagues, but St. Clair valued his comments. In suggesting evacuation of Ticonderoga, the bumptious adjutant was advocating a course of action that his superior would once have believed unthinkable. Even now, it had little appeal to St. Clair. He turned to the other person in the room, a tall, rangy, round-shouldered man in his thirties with a lean, pock-

marked face and long, straggly brown hair. Seated in a corner, Ezekiel Proudfoot had a board across his knee and a piece of charcoal in his hand.

"What do you think, Ezekiel?" asked St. Clair.

"We must always bear in mind the fort's prestige," replied the artist. "It's a
potent symbol. To surrender it would be quite shameful."

"Not if the decision were made on practical grounds," Wilkinson argued.
"We have some idea of the size of the British forces and we can be sure that
their artillery will be formidable. How can we defend the indefensible? Our
ammunition is limited. Our men are ill disciplined and poorly armed. Think
how they'll behave under heavy fire."

"They'll fight like Americans," said St. Clair bravely, "or I'll know the reason why. We've been outnumbered before, Colonel."

"Yes," Proudfoot added. "Our victory at Trenton was against a larger
force than our own. The general and I were there."

"That may be," said Wilkinson, "but, on that occasion, you had the advantage of surprise. That doesn't obtain here. We can't cut and run this time.
The fort is a trap. It's only a question of time before they pound us into submission or starve us out."

"Not necessarily."

"There's no hope of relief. General Schuyler made that clear."

"He also made it clear that Ticonderoga must not fall."

"That was before he knew details of Burgoyne's advance."

"It's our duty to fight, Colonel," said Proudfoot.

"Even if it results in the loss of the fort and the entire garrison?" asked
Wilkinson. "Congress wouldn't thank us for that."

"I've a feeling that they'd admire us nevertheless."

"No, Ezekiel. With respect, you don't think like a soldier."

"I do," attested St. Clair.

"Sacrifice everything here and we leave the country defenseless."

"I prefer to take a more optimistic view," asserted St. Clair, putting his tri-
corn hat on at a rakish angle. "Hold out against the British and we strike a major blow for freedom. That's what we must do." He opened the door. "I'm
going to visit the hospital to see if any of the patients are able to hold a
weapon. We need every man we can muster."

"A complete waste of time," said Wilkinson under his breath.

"Keep that drawing board handy, Ezekiel," St. Clair advised. "You may have some real action to record very soon."

"Thank you for the warning, General," said the artist, with a lazy smile. "That's exactly what I was hoping to hear, sir."

"Have you ever sketched a disaster before?" asked Wilkinson.

"No, sir. I was too busy running away from it."

"Then have the sense to do the same thing now."

"Not when we have a chance of a famous victory," said Proudfoot with sudden passion. "I side with the general here. Ticonderoga is the gateway to New England. We must defend it tooth and nail to keep the British at bay. While you fight with muskets, my only weapon is a stick of charcoal but— long after the echo of gunfire has died—my sketches of what happened here will have the power to bring more and more soldiers to the American flag. Give me some heroism to immortalize," he pleaded. "Repel the British and strike a major blow for freedom."

There were four of them in the general's tent. Having arrived at Crown Point that morning, Burgoyne was anxious to hear the latest intelligence. Brigadier Fraser introduced him to James McIntosh and gave him an abbreviated account of the information supplied by the Scot. It served to bring a real glint to Burgoyne's eye. Next to speak was Jamie Skoyles, back in uniform, on hand to explain what had happened on the scouting expedition. He felt obliged to offer his counsel.

"We mustn't rely too much on the Indians, sir," he warned.

"But they're the eyes and ears of the army," Burgoyne insisted. "All that we have to do is to keep them in check."

"That will be impossible in the heat of battle. They just follow their own murderous instincts. We saw an example of that yesterday."

"They had provocation, Captain. Their companion was shot dead."

"They were under orders to take prisoners, General, not to kill and mutilate an enemy like that."

"It was a grisly sight," said McIntosh, wincing. "Scalping is one thing, but they would've hacked him to pieces if Captain Skoyles hadn't intervened. Indians are a law unto themselves."

"Not when they're under my command," affirmed Burgoyne, thrusting out his chin. "I won't stand for disobedience. They know that." When he turned to Skoyles, there was amusement in his voice. "It seems as if you've altered your stance, Captain. If memory serves me aright, you once stood up for the Indians. Is that correct, Simon?"

"Yes," replied Fraser, "but it was a very long time ago."

"These things stick in the mind. I heard it from Jeffrey Amherst's own lips. He regaled us with the story at Brooks's one evening. At the time, he didn't know whether to laugh or explode with anger."

Skoyles was astonished to learn that his moment of youthful boldness had actually been discussed in one of the leading London clubs. All that he could recall of the event was that he had been given a stern reprimand and sent on his way.

McIntosh was curious. "What exactly happened, General?"

"Skoyles can tell you."

"Must I, sir?" asked Skoyles. "I was very young at the time."

"Yet with sufficient daring to confront your own commander."

"Not everyone agreed with General Amherst's actions," said Fraser, trying to spare Skoyles the embarrassment of telling the story himself, "but few people would have done what Jamie did. When he heard that the general had given smallpox-infected blankets to the Seneca, he was so upset that he complained to him in person."

"I'm a doctor's son," said Skoyles. "I thought that inflicting such a dreadful disease on anyone was wrong. I told General Amherst that it was an immoral way to wage war."

McIntosh was amazed. "You told him *that?*"

"Words to that effect, anyway."

"Then you're a braver man than I am, Captain."

"I stand by what I said."

"Even though the men were vicious savages?"

"I've seen people die of smallpox," said Skoyles. "Lots of them. I'd not wish that kind of death on anyone. It's hideous."

"War is war," Burgoyne announced seriously. "When faced with atrocities, we sometimes have to resort to extreme measures. It may be regrettable, but our hand is forced." He smiled at Skoyles. "I'm pleased that, after his brush with General Amherst, one audacious young soldier learned the importance of abiding by the decisions of his superiors."

"I did, sir," Skoyles admitted.

"Jamie's point is still valid," Fraser reminded them. "We have to keep the Indians on a tight rein. They're far too unpredictable. That's why he's volunteered to go to Ticonderoga on his own."

"Is that wise?" asked Burgoyne. "You'd be taking a big risk."

"I don't think so, General," said Skoyles. "Now that the horses have arrived, I can move much faster. Mr. McIntosh has kindly offered to act as my guide. I can carry out the reconnaissance that I'd hoped to complete yesterday."

"You'll find that everything I told you is accurate," said McIntosh.

"There are some things that you didn't tell us."

Burgoyne hesitated. "Are you happy about this, Simon?"

"Yes, sir," Fraser replied, confidently. "Jamie is very experienced in this kind of work. I have complete faith in him."

"For what it's worth," said McIntosh, "so do I."

"In that case," Burgoyne decided, "the pair of you can get on your way. Oh, one moment," he added before the two men could move. "You might find this useful, Skoyles." He searched in a bag and extracted a small telescope. "Be sure to bring it back to me, mind. It has great sentimental value. It was a present from General Amherst." He held it out. "And it's not infected with any disease, I promise you."

"Thank you, sir," said Skoyles.

Taking the telescope, he led the way out and headed for his tent. McIntosh went off to get the horses so that Skoyles could change out of his uniform. Before he reached his tent, however, Skoyles was waylaid by Major Harry Featherstone.

"I hear that your scouting trip was a failure," he remarked.

"We were ambushed in the woods," said Skoyles.

"One man against four of you? Pretty good odds, I'd say."

"Not when the man is concealed in the undergrowth with a Kentucky rifle. It's much more accurate than our muskets. Besides, he paid with his life."

"With his life, his balls, and his American prick," said Featherstone, laughing harshly. "Serves him right in my view. The mistake you made was to cut the bastard down. He was an enemy soldier. I'd have left him dangling there as a warning to others."

"Enemy or not," asserted Skoyles, "I believe that a dead man should be treated with some respect—not mutilated for sport. Instead of warning others, a dangling corpse would only have incited more rebels to fight against us."

"All the more of them for us to kill!"

"There'll be no shortage of targets for us to aim at, Major. When I get back from Ticonderoga, I'll bring details of the garrison. General Burgoyne is sending me there on my own this time."

Featherstone was incensed. "I've been passed over *again?*"

"Don't take it personally, Major."

"But it's an insult to me."

"Only if you choose to take it as such."

"How else am I to take it, man?" the other demanded. "I'm ideally suited for this work, and the opportunity has been denied me because you managed to curry favor with Gentleman Johnny."

"I resent that, sir," said Skoyles, squaring his shoulders. "The one thing that I'll not be accused of is using flattery to achieve my ends. I must ask you to take that back."

Harry Featherstone glared at him for a second, then regained his composure. Emitting a brittle laugh, he patted Skoyles on the arm.

"I take it back at once, Jamie," he said smoothly. "Banish the words from your memory. You wouldn't know what flattery was. The reason you were selected is that you are considered the better man and I must live with that judgment."

"Thank you, sir."

"Good fortune go with you!"

Featherstone's smile did not reach his eyes.

Taking part in a military campaign was not at all as Elizabeth Rainham had envisaged it. Though there had been no action yet, she was finding the experience tedious and uncomfortable. Outbursts of torrential rain had hindered their progress, followed by days of muggy heat that made her itch and perspire. Dinner was the only pleasant occasion of the day, taken, more often than not, with General Burgoyne and his senior officers, and involving some heavy drinking on the part of the men. There was a mood of gaiety that struck Elizabeth as strangely out of step with a major military undertaking.

Only two other women usually joined her at table. One of them was Friederika von Riedesel, wife of the German commander, a short, slim woman with an elfin beauty that was quite luminous. Elizabeth admired her bravery in traveling with her three young daughters into what would soon be hostile territory. Neither Friederika nor her husband spoke any English, but Elizabeth knew enough French to communicate with both of them. She was surprised to learn that their marriage had been arranged, when it was patent that it was a true love match.

The presence of the other woman at the table was more puzzling to Elizabeth at first. She could not understand why Lucinda Mallard, the wife of a lowly commissary officer, was given the privilege of dining with the general. It took time for the truth to emerge, for she had always known John Burgoyne as a respectable and trusted family friend. When she realized that he had taken another man's wife as his mistress, she was deeply shocked, all the more so because the general behaved as if there were nothing untoward in such an arrangement. Elizabeth was confused. General Riedesel and his wife were a perfect example of a happy marriage. Burgoyne and Lucinda Mallard represented a very different side of army life.

She was still disturbed by it all as she wandered through the camp in search of her maid. Nan was talking to another woman when Elizabeth approached, and she immediately broke off the conversation to come across to her mistress.

"Who was that?" asked Elizabeth.

"Oh, that was Polly Bragg," Nan replied, cheerfully. "She's such a pleasant woman. I could talk to her for hours."

"Could you?"

"Yes, she's been with the 24th Foot for a year now. Polly knows everybody, ma'am. She was telling me about Captain Skoyles."

"Indeed?"

Elizabeth's interest was immediately aroused. Even though she had not seen him since they met in Montreal, she was still curious about him. Nan Wyatt knew her well enough to sense that curiosity. Plump, amiable, and rosy-cheeked, Nan was a bustling woman in her forties, with an effervescence of someone half her age and a readiness to meet any challenge without a whisper of protest. During the worst days of their horrendous Atlantic crossing, Nan had been a great support to Elizabeth and was more like a second mother than a maid.

"Why is Polly Bragg traveling with us?" Elizabeth wondered.

"For the same reason as you—she wishes to be with her man."

"Is her husband in Major Featherstone's regiment?"

"He's in the regiment," said Nan, "but he's not her husband. Not yet, anyway, but Polly hopes that he will be one day." She saw the slight blush in Elizabeth's cheeks and gave a tolerant smile. "It's not the sort of thing that would be allowed in Canterbury, ma'am, but it obviously works. Polly is able to help him."

"Who?"

"Her man—Sergeant Tom Caffrey. He's an assistant surgeon. Polly acts as a nurse. She's seen the most gruesome sights in battle. Some of her tales made my stomach turn, yet she takes it all in her stride. It was Polly who tended Private Higgs."

"Private Higgs?"

"The man who was flogged for being drunk on duty," said Nan. "I'm surprised that Major Featherstone didn't tell you about it, ma'am."

"Why should he?"

"Because he was the person who caught the man and ordered his punishment. Sixty lashes, apparently." Elizabeth blanched. "Polly says that there was hardly any skin left on his back when they finished. She and Sergeant Caffrey nursed him through it."

"Very commendable of her," said Elizabeth, keen to get off the subject of the flogging. "But you mentioned Captain Skoyles."

"Did you know that he went on a dangerous scouting expedition?"

"No, I didn't."

"It was yesterday, ma'am. It turns out that Sergeant Caffrey is a particular friend of Captain Skoyles. That's how Polly got to hear of it."

"What happened, Nan?"

The maid needed no more encouragement. Taking a deep breath, she launched into her narrative, recalling as much as she could of what Polly Bragg had told her and introducing a few dramatic flourishes of her own. Elizabeth listened with growing concern, fearing for Skoyles's safety until she was assured that he had returned to Crown Point. One thing perplexed her.

48

"Major Featherstone told me that *he* was likely to lead a scouting expedition to Fort Ticonderoga," she recalled.

"Captain Skoyles was chosen before him, ma'am."

"Oh, I see."

"He has a reputation for this kind of work."

"He obviously brought some decency to bear on a disgusting situation. I know that they're supposed to be on our side, but what those Indians did to their prisoner was barbaric. It was almost inhuman."

"That's why he didn't want them with him today," said Nan.

"Who?"

"Captain Skoyles, of course. He told Sergeant Caffrey that he was hoping to go to Ticonderoga on his own."

"On his own?" Elizabeth was alarmed.

"Don't fret about it, ma'am," said Nan, squeezing her arm. "Polly told me that the captain is very resourceful. He's well able to look after himself."

The journey to Ticonderoga was slow. Jamie Skoyles's real problem was to stop his loquacious companion from talking too much and thereby distracting him. He wanted to remain alert to any potential dangers. On the other hand, he was very grateful for McIntosh's help in finding a way on horseback through the thick woodland. Skoyles was wearing his hunting shirt and a pair of buckskin breeches again, enabling him to blend into his surroundings. Tucked away in his saddlebag was the telescope entrusted to him by General Burgoyne.

"I doubt that there'll be many pickets out," McIntosh decided. "If I were General St. Clair, I'd have every last man behind the walls of the fort or in one of the redoubts. He must know that the army is coming."

"What manner of man is he?"

"A veteran soldier. He fought at Louisburg and Quebec—just like you and me, Captain. St. Clair was in the 60th Foot."

"The Royal American Regiment," noted Skoyles.

"Times have changed. He'll have no truck with King George now."

"What about you, Mr. McIntosh?"

"Oh, I've no quarrel with His Majesty," said the other, easily, "but, then again, I don't condemn the patriots. They have good reason to fight. This is one war that I'd prefer to keep out of, that's all."

"You're bound to lean toward one side."

"Then that side is the British, which I why I was ready to help you. At the same time, I consider myself an American now. It's a beautiful country, Captain. I intend to spend the rest of my life here."

"I may well do the same," Skoyles confessed. "The war won't last forever. I've been saving up money to buy myself some land. Who knows? When the fighting eventually stops, I might meet up with Ezekiel again."

"You're assuming that the British army will win."

"We must win, Mr. McIntosh. If we don't crush this rebellion now, it will grow and grow. We simply won't let that happen. We fought hard to build an empire, and we won't let any part of it crumble away."

A distant shot brought the dialogue to an end. Skoyles had his musket at the ready in a split second, but it was not needed. When a second shot was heard minutes later, it was much farther away.

"Someone's out hunting," said McIntosh. "Plenty of wolves, foxes, and wildcats about. Raccoons, too. I prefer hares and wild turkey," he went on, patting his saddlebags. "Easier to catch and nicer to eat. The reason you found me hunting so far from home yesterday is that I like to have plenty of space. The woods near my house are usually crawling with men from the fort in search of a decent meal for once."

Skoyles soon came up against another denizen of the forest. As he guided his horse past a clump of trees, it suddenly shied as a rattlesnake raised its head and shook its seven rattles until they produced an eerie sound. McIntosh had difficulty controlling his own mount, but Skoyles was out of the saddle at once, tethering his horse to a branch before unslinging his musket. He took aim, fired, and sent the snake's head bursting in all directions, its lifeless body collapsing in the brush, its menacing rattles silenced forever. Both men took time to calm their horses down.

McIntosh was impressed. "You certainly know how to shoot."

"The brigadier insists on regular practice," said Skoyles, reloading his weapon with meticulous care. "Shooting practice and bayonet practice."

"Damn rattlers are everywhere—and blacksnakes. I killed one last week that was all of seven feet long."

"I just hope that the shot didn't give us away."

"We're still a long way from the fort."

Nevertheless, they waited and listened carefully for some time before they were certain that nobody was in the vicinity. Skoyles remounted his horse and they pressed on. When they were a couple of miles short of Ticonderoga, they parted company. Living nearby, McIntosh was known in the garrison, and Skoyles did not want to imperil him in any way. If he were caught with a British spy, no amount of protestation would save the Scotsman's life.

Skoyles was also motivated by self-preservation. Though he had no reason to expect betrayal, he acted as if it were at least a possibility. McIntosh had only to warn the pickets and they would come searching for Skoyles. The latter therefore set off in one direction before doubling back as soon as his companion was out of sight. Staying close to the river, Skoyles moved furtively in the direction of the fort. It was over twenty years since he had seen Ticonderoga and, on that occasion, he had been coming from the opposite direction, but he remembered it well and had a sketch map drawn by McIntosh to guide him.

When he found a quiet spot to leave his horse, he tied the reins to the branch of a tree and left the animal in a shaded grotto. Musket in one hand and telescope in his pocket, he set off along the western bank of the river before using the cover of the woodland to move in a wide arc to his right so that he could get to the rear of Mount Hope. An outwork had been built to protect the sawmills and the La Chute River that twisted along from Lake George. Since the battery and blockhouse were on the southeastern corner of the summit, Skoyles began to ascend from the northwestern side, using the butt of his musket as a walking stick and checking every so often that he had not been spotted.

At length, he reached the top and made his way across it with circumspection, getting as close as he dared to the blockhouse in order to have a vantage point. Lying flat on his stomach, he was now able to view the fort with the aid of the telescope. At first sight, its defenses were intimidating. Inside the fortifications built by the French were the tents of the summer camp, protected to the east by two newly constructed redoubts. Fort Ticonderoga had a daunting solidity, and Skoyles did not need reminding how many soldiers had perished while trying to take it. The skulls of which McIntosh had spoken were relics of General James Abercromby's disastrous attempt at capturing the fort in 1758. Some of the tents that Skoyles had seen were pegged to the ground by the shin and thigh bones of dead British soldiers.

Set on a tongue of land that poked into Lake Champlain, the fort showed signs of activity, though it was difficult for Skoyles to estimate the number of men in the garrison. Judging by the size of the camp, it was not large. Across the water, on the Vermont shore, were a series of earthworks and batteries that extended the perimeter defenses around the base of Mount Independence, where the hospital, the dock, and workshops were located. Through the lens of his telescope, Skoyles could see the gun emplacements on top of the mountain, an array of firepower that could bombard any vessels that foolishly tried to sail between the promontory and the fort opposite.

Directly below him to the south was the sawmill on the La Chute River outlet from Lake George. There was a blockhouse beside it but no sign of life in either building. Skoyles surmised that men had been withdrawn to the fort to prepare for its defense. Even with their reduced garrison, the Americans would be able to offer stiff resistance. To take the fort, the British army would have to be prepared to sustain heavy casualties, but that would not deter Burgoyne. Having set out his plan of campaign, he would follow it to the letter.

Some distance to the south of the fort, on the western bank, was another mountain, a steep hill, shaped like a sugarloaf and rising to over eight hundred feet. McIntosh had insisted that it was undefended, but Skoyles wanted to see if it was possible to drag heavy artillery up the face of the incline. Guns mounted on the summit would have the fort at their mercy. Skoyles was not given any time to study the problem. There was an angry shout from the direction of the blockhouse, and a shot was fired.

Someone had seen him.

CHAPTER FIVE

The bullet missed him by a matter of inches, whistling past his ear and spending its fury in the ground behind him. Skoyles reacted quickly. Without even looking to see who had fired at him, he jumped up and scurried away as fast as he could, keeping low and zigzagging to present a more difficult target. When he reached the edge of the summit, he opted for the swiftest means of descent. With the telescope in his pocket, he clutched his musket tight to his chest like a lover and hurled himself down the slope. It was a perilous descent, rolling over uneven ground that was full of awkward bumps, sharp stones, and unexpected hollows, but he gathered momentum with every yard.

Skoyles hoped that time was on his side. Having fired one shot, the man who had aimed at him would take half a minute to reload his musket. That was the fugitive's margin of safety. It soon disappeared. Roused by the alarm, two other soldiers ran after Skoyles and tried to pick him off as he rolled crazily down the side of the mountain, but their shots went harmlessly past their target and bounced off some rocks. Cursing themselves, they reloaded as fast as they could, but they were much too slow. Skoyles hurtled on downward, losing his hat, collecting cuts and bruises as he went, ignoring the pain in the interests of survival, and praying that no better marksmen aimed at him.

When he reached the bottom, he hauled himself up, risked a look at the summit, then sprinted toward the nearest trees. They were some distance away as the garrison had denuded the woodland in its immediate environs for firewood during the winter. Skoyles reached the cover of a tree stump and crouched behind it only an instant before another venomous bullet came hissing after him. It buried itself in the wood. Three soldiers were now scrambling down the side of Mount Hope in pursuit of him, choosing a far safer but much slower route. Two more had appeared at the top of Mount Hope. Delay would be fatal.

Skoyles sprang up and darted off into a stand of trees, snaking his way through the trunks as fast as he could. When the woodland thickened, he began to feel that he was clear of immediate danger, but he was determined to complete his survey before he returned to camp. With that in mind, he headed south toward the river outlet that connected the two lakes, staying hidden all the way. To cross the river by means of the bridge near the sawmill would bring Skoyles out into the open again, and there would be several rifles trained on him this time. He had to get out of their range and find another place to cross the water.

His search took him well over a mile along the outlet. All that he had to do was to find a spot where it was possible to wade across, enabling him to keep his musket and powder dry. They were his essential lifeline. Eventually, he came to a bend in the river where the water was so shallow that he could see the pebbles at the bottom of it. Making sure that he was neither watched nor pursued, Skoyles stepped in and waded across with the cold, refreshing water up to his waist.

As soon as he found cover on the other side, he paused to take stock of the injuries he had picked up. There was blood on his hands and face, and his head was pounding from the blows it had taken during the reckless descent, but it was his hip that throbbed with the most insistent pain. The reason was self-evident. Stuffed in his pocket, the telescope that had been so invaluable had dug into him time and again as it revolved its way down Mount Hope. Skoyles lifted his shirt to see an ugly black bruise already starting to form around his right hip. There were a few dents in the telescope itself. He hoped that General Burgoyne would not notice them.

With his sodden breeches clinging to his legs, the bottom of his shirt dripping, and his feet squelching in his shoes, he continued on his way until he came to the foot of the steepest mountain. Once called Sugar Hill, it had been given a more appropriate name less than a year earlier. Mount Defiance had defied all attempts to hoist cannon up its sheer sides. Knowing that General Phillips would not be so easily frustrated by the problem, Skoyles decided to reach the top, spurning the easier northern face because it would make him visible to sentries on Mount Hope, Mount Independence, and at the fort. He was not the only person with a telescope.

Forced to take the precipitous southeastern route, he could see why the engineers at the fort had abandoned the notion of hauling any artillery up there. It was a long, hazardous climb, and Skoyles had to make frequent changes of direction, using his musket to steady himself yet again and making light of the dull ache in his whole body. When he felt yet another trickle of blood down his face, he wiped it away with the back of a hand that was itself badly lacerated. By the time he reached the top, he was so fatigued that he needed a long rest before going on.

As he had guessed, Mount Defiance not only commanded the fort, fifteen hundred yards away, it overlooked the battery on the summit of Mount Independence. Both targets would be within range of British guns. There was an additional benefit. Guns on Mount Defiance would cut off escape routes up Lake Champlain and up the river that led to Lake George. The only other route that needed to be blocked off was the wagon track that ran from the rear of Mount Independence. Fort Ticonderoga would then be completely surrounded.

Lying flat as before, Skoyles used the telescope to good effect, taking a careful inventory of the defenses and troop numbers. Since the climb had been so difficult, he had no fears that anyone would try to follow him. When he had a strange feeling that someone was watching him, he took no notice at first, assuming it was a trick of his imagination rather than a warning of imminent danger. Only when he heard a noise directly behind him did he realize that he was not alone.

Fear made him tense his muscles. He grabbed his musket and rolled quickly on to his back to aim at what he expected to be a rebel soldier. Instead, to his utter astonishment, he found himself looking into the large, brown, inquiring eyes of a goat.

Skoyles laughed with relief.

Presiding over dinner that afternoon, General Burgoyne had fewer guests than usual. General Riedesel and his wife were there, and so were General Phillips and Brigadier Fraser. The party was completed by Major Harry Featherstone and Elizabeth Rainham, all of them sitting around a table that was laden with rich food and drink. Elizabeth was relieved that there was no sign of Lucinda Mallard, though she was a trifle worried at the amount of claret that Featherstone was consuming.

Burgoyne held forth with his usual geniality, favoring them with some an- ecdotes of his success as a playwright and boasting of his friendship with the actor David Garrick. In order that his German guests would not feel left out, he translated into French as he went along, a language in which he was quite fluent after living in France for so long. Talk soon turned to the campaign it- self, and William Phillips, a big, beefy man in his forties with a forthright manner, complained about the shortfall in manpower.

"Ideally," he said, "I'd need six hundred trained men for the movement and operation of the guns but I've less than half that number. General Riedesel has been kind enough to supply me with a hundred gunners but the rest are raw recruits from the infantry."

"They'll not let you down," Burgoyne assured him.

"I'd prefer regular artillerymen, General."

"I'd prefer more troops, more horses, more provisions, and three times as many wagons, William, but I have to make do with what Sir Guy Carleton managed to scrape together for me. No matter," he went on, slapping the table for emphasis. "We've an army that will sweep aside everything that gets in our way."

"Hear, hear!" said Featherstone.

"It may not be quite as easy as that," suggested Fraser.

"Come now, Simon," teased Burgoyne. "I'll have no defeatism."

"I'm not being defeatist, General. I'm as certain of success as you are, but there'll be bruising battles ahead. We must accept that."

"We accept it and relish it," said Phillips, reaching for his claret.

"And we push forward regardless," Burgoyne insisted, "whatever our setbacks. Remember what I said in my general order—this army must not retreat."

"Out of the question," Featherstone agreed. "We never retreat."

Riedesel had not been able to follow everything that was said, so Bur- goyne acted as interpreter once more. Phillips and Fraser fell into conversa- tion about tactics, leaving Elizabeth free at last to have a quiet word with Harry Featherstone. Having emptied his glass, he was signaling to the steward to refill it for him.

"Don't you think that you've had enough?" she asked.

"No, Elizabeth," he replied with a laugh, "not nearly enough. I can drink all afternoon and still walk back to my tent in a straight line."

"I'd rather not put that claim to the test, Harry."

"Would you deny me the pleasure of carousing with friends?"

"Of course not," she said.

"I'm glad to hear it. We can't have a daughter of Colonel Richard Rainham objecting to alcohol. Your father would never forgive you. He can hold his wine and spirits with the best of them."

"That's certainly true."

Elizabeth chided herself for making any comment. Several glasses of claret had had no visible effect on him. Throughout the meal, Harry Featherstone had been loving and attentive toward her, clearly pleased to be part of a couple and thus able to show Elizabeth off to the others. By the same token, she was reveling in his company, thrilled that she was sitting beside the youngest and, in her view, most handsome man there. In his immaculate uniform, he cut quite a figure. One day, she hoped, they would achieve the deep marital contentment displayed by Riedesel and his wife. Elizabeth felt an upsurge of love.

Then she recalled what Nan Wyatt had told her earlier.

"Is it true that you had a man flogged?" she said.

"I've had a number of men flogged," he answered breezily. "Necessary part of army life. You have to punish them hard, Elizabeth, or you forfeit their respect. A good flogging will keep the rest of the men on their best behavior for weeks."

"But sixty lashes—isn't that a bit extreme?"

"I'd order a hundred, if it was needed—even more. You don't realize what we're up against. All you've done is to see the troops on parade. If you knew them better, you'd see what scum they really are."

Elizabeth was dismayed. "That's a harsh judgment."

"It's a compliment to some of them," he told her, "believe me. Our army consists largely of the lowest of the low—thieves, drunkards, wild Irishmen, ignorant farm boys, ruffians, riffraff, and downright villains. But for officers like me who know how to impose discipline, that rabble would run scared when they heard the first shot."

"General Burgoyne speaks so well of his men."

"Only because we've licked the unlettered wretches into shape."

"You talk of them with such contempt, Harry," she said.

"It's all they deserve."

Elizabeth was shocked by the undisguised hatred in his voice. He obviously despised the men he commanded. Burgoyne rose from his seat to signal the end of the meal. After exchanging pleasantries, his guests dispersed. Featherstone escorted Elizabeth back to her tent on his arm. She took the opportunity to touch on a more sensitive topic.

"There's something I've been meaning to ask you," she began.

"Then ask it," he invited.

"It's rather embarrassing, I'm afraid."

"There should be no embarrassment between us, Elizabeth."

"It's the general," she ventured tentatively. "Have you, by any chance, noticed his interest in a particular lady?"

Featherstone grinned. "It's an open secret," he said. "Mrs. Mallard warms his bed at night, and has since we left St. Johns."

"But she has a husband."

"A complaisant one, it seems."

"Weren't you shocked by that, Harry?"

"Not at all," he replied. "General Howe is doing exactly the same down in New York City, except that he's a little more brazen about it. He has Mrs. Loring with him wherever he goes—another married woman whose husband is happy to look the other way. I'm told there are even some saucy rhymes about Mrs. Loring," he continued. "I daresay that there'll be the same sort of mockery for Lucinda Mallard."

"I find the whole thing extraordinary."

"That's because you don't understand army life."

"Are you telling me that this is *normal?*"

"Calm yourself," he soothed, seeing the anxiety in her eyes. "There's no need to be so narrow-minded about it. General Burgoyne no doubt sees it as one of the perquisites of his rank. It's a pleasant way of relieving the boredom of a campaign."

Elizabeth was scandalized. "Do you mean that you condone it?"

"Not exactly—but, then, I don't gainsay it either."

"You think that the general is *entitled* to take a mistress?"

"He's certainly not the first to do so, Elizabeth."

"That doesn't make it right."

"Moral standards are not the same in a situation like this."

"Well, they should be," she insisted. "General Riedesel's wife feels that. I know that she disapproves as much as I do—and as much as I hoped *you* would."

"It's not a question of approval or disapproval. It just happens."

"And what about you, Harry?" she demanded, stopping to face him. "Will you see it as a privilege of rank when your earn promotion? Is that what I'm to expect as wife—a husband who intends to relieve the boredom of a campaign by betraying his marriage vows?"

"General Burgoyne is a single man now. He has no wife to betray."

"I'm talking about Harry Featherstone."

"Then you can still your fears, Elizabeth," he said, conjuring up a persuasive smile. "I could never betray you, my darling. Were I to become lieutenant general in my own right, there's only one lady I'd wish to travel with me on a campaign—and that's you."

Taking her by the shoulders, he tried to plant a kiss on her cheek, but she raised a hand to stop him. His answer had been far too glib to satisfy her, and she began to look at the man she was engaged to marry in a rather different light. Featherstone offered his arm again. There was a long pause before she took it. They walked on together.

It was late evening when Skoyles finally returned to camp. Darkness was starting to fall and that made it even more difficult for Jamie to find his way back. When he reached the picket line, the man who stepped forward to challenge him was Private Roger Higgs, a tall, stringy individual with cadaverous features. Covering the rider with his musket, he demanded to know who he was. Skoyles dismounted and moved forward so that the sentry could see more clearly.

"It's me, Private Higgs," he declared.

"Captain Skoyles," said the other. "I never reckernized you, sir."

"You did what you were supposed to do. Well done, Higgs."

In the gloom, Higgs could not see the marks on his face. Skoyles had washed off most of the blood but he could do nothing about the livid bruises on his cheekbones and temple. The sentry shifted his feet.

"Sergeant Caffrey says I got you to thank, sir. You tried to get my sentence reduced."

"I tried," said Skoyles. "I did my best to talk him round, but Major Featherstone wouldn't budge."

Higgs spat on the ground. "That's what I think of the major."

"Let's have no disrespect, Private Higgs."

"I 'ates the bastard, sir, and I'll not pretend I don't, not even for you. Sergeant Caffrey should've let me die. I'd no will to live, I can tell you that. What's there to live for when my wife and child are gone?"

"I heard about your bereavement," said Skoyles with obvious sincerity. "I'm very sorry. You have my sympathy."

"Thank you, sir."

"It's all the more difficult to bear with you being so far away."

Higgs was bitter. "Made no difference to Major Featherstone, did it? Get more sympathy out of a bleedin' cannonball."

"Try to put it all behind you," Skoyles advised him gently. "I know that's hard but it's the only way. We've a battle to fight soon, and we'll need every man's mind to be directed solely at that. You're a soldier, Private Higgs. You know what's expected of you."

"I'll kill the major," vowed Higgs in a low voice. "If I gets the chance—God 'elp me—I'll do for 'im. I swears it, Captain Skoyles."

Skoyles grabbed him by the arm. "You'll do nothing of the kind, do you hear?" he said, sharply. "You'll behave as you've always managed to do in the past and be a credit to the army. This is not what your wife or child would have wanted of you, is it? They were proud of you and they had good cause. Yes, I know," he continued before Higgs could speak, "there's injustice here, there's pain and torment, there are grounds for rancor, but you have to bear it all like a man. Do you understand?" Higgs was shamefaced. "Do you understand?" repeated Skoyles, tightening his hold. Higgs nodded and Skoyles let go of him. "This conversation never took place."

"No, sir."

"You know quite well what would happen to you if it had."

"Yes, sir," muttered Higgs. "Thank you."

Skoyles gave him a friendly pat on the shoulder and went past, leading his horse by the rein. He was soon swallowed up by the shadows.

Lifting the cup, Sergeant Tom Caffrey took a first sip of his tea, gave a nod of approval then patted her affectionately on the rump.

"Delicious!" he said, licking his lips. "Nobody makes tea like you, Polly. I knew that there was a reason why I wanted to bring you."

Polly Bragg put her hands on her hips. "Is *that* all I'm fit for, Tom Caffrey?" she asked with mock scorn. "I'm your tea maker, am I? That's why you keep me on. Not because I take care of the laundry or make you bandages or nurse your patients or share a tent with you. It's simply because I keep you supplied with tea."

"Of the best quality."

"*Everything* I do is of the best quality."

"I won't argue with that, Poll," he said, slipping an arm around her. "But for you, I'd have frozen to death in the Canadian winter. You're the best thing that's happened to me since I crossed the Atlantic."

"As long as you remember that."

"Will you ever give me the chance to forget?"

"No, Tom."

He kissed her on the lips and she responded. It was the end of the day and they were in his tent, having a last cup of tea by candlelight that threw flickering shapes on the canvas. Caffrey could not recall what life had been like before he met Polly Bragg. It was certainly less pleasurable. Since he had met her, she had settled in with him so well that she seemed always to have been there. Polly was the widow of a corporal in the British army who had been killed while repulsing the doomed American raid on Quebec. She was an attractive, shapely woman in her thirties with a healthy look of a countrywoman about her. Like Caffrey, she hailed from Devon.

He was still embracing her warmly when the flap of the tent opened and Jamie Skoyles popped his head in. The newcomer withdrew immediately.

"Pardon me," he called to them.

"No need to be sorry," said Polly, opening the tent flap to pull him inside. "Come on in, Jamie." She saw his face in the candlelight. "Dear God!" she exclaimed. "What's happened to you?"

"Let me take a look at you," said Caffrey, holding up one of the candles so that he could examine the facial wounds. "What've you been up to, Jamie? You look as if you've been trampled by a herd of buffalo."

"That's what it felt like at the time," Skoyles admitted, "and they had very sharp hooves."

While Skoyles told them how he had come by his injuries, Caffrey sat him on a stool and tended his wounds, cleaning away the remnants of dried blood before putting ointment on his lacerated face and hands. Polly was more disturbed by the sight of the bruises, but Skoyles assured her that they had been earned in a noble cause. His reconnaissance visit to Ticonderoga had been a success, adding vital new detail to what James McIntosh had been able to tell them. When he delivered his report to General Burgoyne and to General Phillips on his return to the camp, Skoyles had won both praise and gratitude.

"You should've come to me first," Caffrey scolded, "so that I could make you look human before you spoke to them. What did they say when they saw the state you were in?"

"General Burgoyne said that he'd seen me looking better, Tom."

"I've seen corpses looking better," said Polly, peering at his wounds. "I just hope that Miss Rainham doesn't catch sight of you in this condition, I really do."

"You've spoken to her?" said Skoyles.

"I've spoken to her maid, and that's almost as good. Nan Wyatt, that's her name. Motherly soul, she is. She's looked after Miss Rainham for years and won't have a word said against her."

"She'll hear none from me, that's for sure."

"According to Nan, her mistress has the sweetest disposition. She's talented, too. Elizabeth Rainham sings, she plays the harp, she does all kinds of interesting things—things that I never had the chance to do when I was her age."

"Tell Jamie about Major Featherstone," Caffrey urged.

"Oh, yes," she said. "Nan has her doubts about him."

"What sort of doubts?" asked Skoyles.

"Well, it turns out that he's a family friend. He knew her father very well. When he first came to the house, he used to pay his addresses to Cora Rainham, the elder sister. But she died tragically of the fever some years ago, so he slowly turned his attentions to Elizabeth."

"She's a lot younger than Featherstone."

"She'd always admired him," said Polly with a worldly air. "Well—let's be honest—what woman wouldn't admire an officer like him? All that brass and scarlet is very fetching."

Caffrey was indignant. "What about my sergeant's uniform?"

"You look very smart in it, Tom, but it's not the same as being a major. I can see why Miss Rainham was dazzled. Nan reckons that, because the sister had died, it was almost as if her mistress felt obliged to marry Major Featherstone in her stead. Not that she doesn't love him," she added, quickly. "Nan went out of her way to tell me how much she dotes on him. But it's not as if Elizabeth Rainham was his first choice."

Polly retailed all the other snippets of information she had gleaned from the maid, and Skoyles listened attentively. Every new detail about Elizabeth Rainham made her more appealing, but he accepted that she was hopelessly beyond his grasp. Betrothed to a fellow officer, she could never be more than an object of curiosity to him. In any case, Skoyles was not in search of any female companionship. Unknown to his two friends, he already had that within easy reach. The woman whom he had met in Montreal—Maria Quinn—was traveling with them and awaiting his call. He had no need of a prim young virgin from Canterbury.

"Thank you, Polly," he said. "I'm deeply grateful."

"So is Miss Rainham," she said.

"What do you mean?"

"Well, Nan Wyatt was as nosy as me. She wanted to hear all the scandal, so I told her what I knew. Nan also asked about people whose names she's heard on Miss Rainham's list."

"Such as?"

"People she's met since she's been with us—General Phillips, Brigadier Fraser, and so on. But there was one person," said Polly with a giggle, "that she knew her mistress would really like to know about."

"Oh? And who was that?"

"Captain Jamie Skoyles."

At the very start of hostilities, Major General Arthur St. Clair was given stark proof of the shortcomings of his defenses at Fort Ticonderoga. When a skirmish party of Indians and British light infantry approached the stronghold, St. Clair saw how exposed his men on Mount Hope were, and he ordered them to withdraw, protecting the movement with a sortie. Driven back by the Indians, he sustained only small losses, but, during the exchange of fire, one bold and inebriated Irishman crept up until he was a mere forty paces from the

American lines. Hiding behind a tree stump, the man fired a shot and set off such a concerted volley from the rebels that the noise scattered the Indians.

The Irishman was captured and imprisoned in the fort, but he was stubborn and insolent under questioning, refusing to tell them anything about the strength of the British army. St. Clair discussed the case with Ezekiel Proudfoot, and the other man had a suggestion.

"He may not talk to *us,* sir," he said thoughtfully, "but I'll wager that he'll confide in Captain O'Driscoll."

"Why on earth should the prisoner do that, Ezekiel?"

"For two good reasons, sir. First, O'Driscoll is an Irishman, and you know what happens when two sons of Hibernia get together. Second, if we put our man in the same cell, we'll let him have a bottle of rum concealed about him."

"I begin to follow you," said St. Clair, smiling. "We pretend that O'Driscoll is a damn Tory and lock him up. All he has to do is to play the part well enough to win the prisoner's confidence."

"The bottle of rum will do that."

The plan was put into effect immediately and soon bore fruit. The obstinate prisoner, a member of the 47th Light Infantry, was much more outgoing in the presence of a fellow Irishman and, warmed by a few long swigs of rum, gave him the name and number of every corps under Burgoyne's command. He was even able to list the guns available. When the information was passed on to St. Clair, it confirmed his worst fears. He adjourned to his office with Ezekiel Proudfoot and Colonel Wilkinson.

"It's the strength of that artillery that troubles me," he confessed. "They have six-pounders, twelve-pounders, and twenty-four-pounders as well as howitzers and mortars. Worst of all, they have William Phillips in control of the weapons, a man who showed what he could do at the Battle of Minden. He's a genius."

"Even a genius needs a target," said Wilkinson.

"He has one right here."

"Only if we stay, General."

"You still want us to run away with our tails between our legs?"

"I'd rather call it a tactical withdrawal."

"It would be a cowardly retreat," said Proudfoot angrily. "Or, at least, that's how it would be seen. What will that do to our reputations?"

"We have to take the long view, Ezekiel. If we make a swift and orderly withdrawal, we can at least preserve our men to fight another day. And not just our troops," said Wilkinson, looking at St. Clair. "Your eleven-year-old son is with us, sir. Is this the kind of military experience you want the boy to have? It would be terrifying for him."

"Leave my son out of this."

"Why put his life in danger? Keep him here and he'll suffer the same fate as the rest of us. He'll either be killed or taken prisoner."

"I dispute that," said Proudfoot as he saw a shadow of doubt fall across St. Clair's face. "We may well hold out here. The French had a very small garrison when General Abercromby tried to take the fort, and they still scattered the British army. We'll do the same."

"Supposing we fail?" asked Wilkinson.

"Then we earn recognition for our courage."

"There's nothing courageous in being overrun by superior forces," reasoned the other. "That's arrant folly. General Burgoyne has only to lay siege to Ticonderoga and we're at his mercy."

"That's not true, Colonel. He'll suffer his share of casualties. My feeling is that he'll launch an assault as a matter of honor. When we withstand it, he'll simply march around us and continue south."

"I'm inclined to agree," said St. Clair.

"Why should he do that?" Wilkinson argued. "Gentleman Johnny has more men, more firepower, and every advantage. British and German soldiers have been honed to perfection. They're not a ragbag army like ours. And think of those Indians," he added, running a hand across his skull. "I don't know about you, General, but I'm very fond of my hair. I'd prefer it to stay attached to my head. I don't want my scalp dangling from an Indian's belt."

"Indians are fair-weather warriors," said Proudfoot with contempt. "They only fight on if victory is in sight. Look at the way they vanished when that volley was fired earlier on. They ran away in complete panic."

"What I remember was the way that our men fired willy-nilly before they'd been given the command," said Wilkinson. "They lost all discipline. That would be a catastrophe in a battle."

"Their nerves need to be steadied, that's all."

"And how do we do that, Ezekiel? When they see the size of the British army, they're going to be shaking in their boots—those lucky enough to *have* any boots, that is."

St. Clair turned away, conscious of the immense problems that a defense of the fort would entail but reluctant to yield it to the enemy without offering stern resistance. Colonel Wilkinson was not the only senior officer who would advise an evacuation of the fort, but there would be others to whom such a course would be anathema. Their task was to halt the British advance in its tracks for as long as possible, not to assist it by deserting their posts. He reached his decision.

"Ezekiel is right," he said. "We must stay."

"That's suicide!" cried Wilkinson.

"He's here to record our actions for posterity."

"So?"

"Whatever we do will one day appear in a popular print for all to see. Do you want to be portrayed as a brave officer, fighting for your cause to the last bullet? Or would you rather let Ezekiel show the world the coattails of your uniform as you run away in fear?"

"That kind of print would inspire nobody," Proudfoot observed tartly. "Unless you think your backside is a good advertisement for our cause, Colonel."

"I resent that comment," said Wilkinson hotly. "It's not fear that makes me want to leave—it's common sense. I have my faults, I concede that, but nobody has ever questioned my bravery."

"Nor do I, James," St. Clair said, holding up a conciliatory hand. "You've shown your true colors often enough. I'm vain enough to believe that I've done the same. No coward would dare to take up arms against the British, as we've done. Ticonderoga is full of brave men."

"Then save their lives by withdrawing them from the fort."

"There'd be no hint of bravery in my sketches, if you do that," Proudfoot warned. "I'll draw what I see—an undignified retreat. Leaving the fort without even firing a token shot. I'd call it blatant cowardice."

"I see it as a sensible tactic."

"One that would delight Burgoyne."

"General Washington has employed that strategy on a number of occasions. He'd rather quit the field than fight a pitched battle to the finish against a much bigger army. As a result," said Wilkinson, "he's reduced the number of losses in combat."

"You're forgetting what Ticonderoga *means* to us," said Proudfoot, standing up to reinforce his point. "It's our talisman. It has a powerful hold on the American mind. As long as this fortress survives, it will give hope and encouragement to our army. Let it fall or, even worse, hand it over to the enemy as a gift, and we inflict the most terrible wound on ourselves. That would be unforgivable."

"We stay," St. Clair announced. "We defend the fort and trust in our own men to hold it. I expect you to abide by that decision, James."

"Of course, sir."

"Then let's have no more discussion of the matter."

"If you wish," said Wilkinson, clearly disappointed. "All I ask you to bear in mind is one thing. Retreating from a position that you cannot expect to hold is not the action of a weak commander. It may sometimes be an indication of his strength."

"I accept that."

"Then remember the name of George Washington."

"I always do," said St. Clair loyally, "but, in the circumstances, I must also keep another name in mind—that of Ezekiel Proudfoot. He'll tell the truth about what happens here."

"Oh, I will," Proudfoot vowed. "You can be certain of that."

Since he had carried out the reconnaissance of Mount Defiance, it was left to Jamie Skoyles to escort General Phillips, Brigadier Simon Fraser, and a detachment of light infantry to the spot. Skirting the fort so that they would not be seen by any of the sentries, the party arrived at the foot of the mountain. They studied the rocky incline of the southeastern face. William Phillips needed less than a minute to reach his decision.

"We can do it," he said confidently.

"Are you sure, sir?" asked Skoyles.

"Didn't you say that you saw a goat up there, Captain?"

"He was as close to me as you are."

"Then I have no qualms at all about the enterprise," said Phillips. "Where a goat can go, a man can go, and where a man can go, he can drag a gun."

"It will take a lot more than one man, General."

"It will take hundreds, but we'll get a couple of twelve-pounders up there somehow." He stared up at the summit. "The ascent is almost perpendicular here. However did you manage to climb it, Skoyles?

"Very slowly, sir."

Fraser chuckled. "Don't blame you, Jamie."

"You'll find it slightly easier on the northern face," advised Skoyles, "but that would put us within sight of the enemy."

"It's a risk we'll have to take," said Phillips, turning to Fraser. "We need to build a road to the summit, Brigadier. We must use every possible expedition to get cannon to the top."

"We will," Fraser promised. "I'll have an abatis constructed on the top. That's work for axmen."

"They'll be kept busy clearing the side of the mountain," noted Skoyles, "and the approach from the camp. If you want oxen to drag guns up there, the road will have to be wide enough."

"Sixteen feet at least," Phillips confirmed.

"I don't foresee a problem," said Fraser.

Skoyles did. "They'll have to work under fire, sir."

"They're soldiers. It's what they expect to do."

"Yes," Phillips added. "Better that we lose a few men now than a large number in a long and bloody siege."

"Provided that the enemy don't see us hauling artillery up there," warned Skoyles. "That would give the game away."

"Surprise is everything," Fraser agreed.

Phillips rubbed his hands together. "And won't they be surprised when we start firing!" he said chirpily. "We'll be able to pick them off at will from up there. This is all due to you, Captain."

"And to that goat," said Skoyles.

Work on the road began immediately. Experienced woodsmen with sharpened axes began to clear a way through the undergrowth, working long hours in sweltering heat and supported by British troops pressed into service. Skoyles estimated that, in all, the road would need to be some three leagues long, and he admired the speed with which the men labored. There were early casualties. As soon as they began to build a track up the northern side of Mount Defiance, they came under fire from the fort and from Mount Independence. Three artillerymen had their heads blown clean off, and another man had his leg fractured, but the work continued regardless. It took a detail of some four hundred men to complete the road and to construct a battery on the summit.

The two heavy artillery pieces were dragged up Mount Defiance under cover of a morning mist and concealed among the trees. They were joined by a detachment of troops under the command of Jamie Skoyles. Alongside him was the excited Lieutenant Charles Westbourne.

"That was a splendid gesture of General Burgoyne's," he observed.

"But well deserved," Skoyles commented.

"No question about that, Captain. Those men worked like Trojans to build the road and get those twelve-pound cannon up here. I can see why the General would have rewarded *them* with a refreshment of rum, but he ordered it for the entire army."

"Everybody gained that way, Lieutenant. The axmen and the laborers not only got what they'd earned, they also got the respect and thanks of everyone else. It was a wise move by General Burgoyne."

"He makes nothing but wise moves," said Westbourne.

Skoyles did not reply. Privately, he had questioned more than one of their commander's decisions—not least Burgoyne's readiness to linger in Canada after his arrival—but he knew that Westbourne would never agree with him. To the impressionable lieutenant, there was an air of infallibility about Gentleman Johnny, and he could never bring himself to offer any criticism of him. Skoyles was pleased to have Westbourne with him. Naïve in other respects, the lieutenant was nevertheless a good officer, tireless, committed, and cool in an emergency.

In addition to their men, they had a number of Indians with them, all of them given strict instructions to remain out of the sight on the summit of Mount Defiance until the moment for attack came. It was Charles Westbourne who first noticed that the order had been disobeyed, and he took immediate steps to remedy the situation.

"Look!" he cried, pointing toward the Indian camp. "The idiots have lit a fire! What, in God's name, do they think they're playing at?"

Followed by Skoyles, he ran off in the direction of the smoke. When he reached the Indian tents, Westbourne kicked the blazing embers apart, then stamped on them in an attempt to extinguish the flames. Skoyles did the same, chastising the Indians as he did so. Both men used the sides of their boots to push earth over the flames but smoke continued to rise up into the blue sky. Westbourne was alarmed.

"Do you think they saw anything at the fort?" he asked.

"Probably," said Skoyles, glaring at the Indians with annoyance. "So much for the element of surprise! We were supposed to wait until General Riedesel was in position at the rear of Mount Independence."

"We might still be lucky, Captain."

"I doubt it."

"You never know."

"They were told to stay in the trees and keep their heads down."

"The Indians can be a menace at times."

"That's what I said to General Burgoyne."

"We'd be far better off without them," said Westbourne.

At that moment, from somewhere behind them, there was a deafening explosion as one of the twelve-pound cannon fired its first shot and made the ground tremble. Seconds later came the sound of a huge splash as the shot hit the water. The suddenness and the sheer volume of the noise startled them all. Skoyles was absolutely livid.

"Hell and damnation!" he yelled, swinging angrily round. "Whatever made those imbeciles do *that?*"

General Arthur St. Clair was standing near the rampart with Ezekiel Proudfoot when he heard the commotion. The two men looked up at Mount Defiance. Smoke from the fire was still curling up into the sky, but it was the reverberations of the gunfire that claimed their attention. Horrified that the British had somehow got cannon on top of the mountain, the general could see why one of the guns had been used. A small boat was sailing through the narrows toward the fort. An eager British gunner had tried to blow an enemy vessel out of the water.

"God defend us!" cried St. Clair.

"We agreed that I'd be sketching a battle here tomorrow, General," said Proudfoot, trying to restore the other man's confidence, "because we believe in our hearts that we can hold out against the enemy attack. That may be still the case, sir."

"Not if they have cannon on top of Mount Defiance."

"Ticonderoga has thick walls."

"Yes, but Major Phillips can shoot over them, Ezekiel."

"Send men up there to disable his artillery."

"They'd be mown down before they'd gone ten yards," said St. Clair, chewing his lip with anxiety. "We've been outflanked. The British have done what we found impossible. They've turned Mount Defiance into a virtually impregnable redoubt. Nothing we can do will shift them from there."

"That doesn't mean we should cut and run, General."

"What's the alternative?"

"Fight to the last man and show them our true character."

"Fine rhetoric, Ezekiel, but poor leadership. If we stay here, we're all doomed. The British have the upper hand. Taking the fort will be like shooting fish in a barrel."

"As one of those fish," said Proudfoot, alarmed by the vacillation of his commander, "I'm still ready to put up some resistance—and so are the men. That's why they're here. We'll be judged by our deeds, General."

"Yes," said St. Clair, "I know. But I'm not sure that I want to be remembered as a man who allowed a whole garrison to be wiped out. Loath as I am to admit it, I'm coming to see the wisdom of Colonel Wilkinson's argument."

"What's happened to your resolve?"

"It's tempered by discretion, Ezekiel."

"Discretion!"

"It's the better part of valor."

"I don't see anything remotely discreet or valiant about abject surrender, because that's what it would amount to, General. Abandon the fort and you'd be betraying our cause."

"That's a dreadful accusation!"

"I speak as I find."

"Then it's my fault for listening to you," said St. Clair crisply. "You're entitled to your opinion, Ezekiel, but I have to remind you that you have no military authority here. You are merely an artist, nothing more. Since I agreed to defend the fort, the situation has altered radically. That calls for a change of plan."

Proudfoot was bitter. "The only thing that's changed is you, General," he said. "Yesterday, you were full of courage and determination to withstand whatever the enemy could throw at us. Today—because of one shot fired from a cannon—you've lost your nerve."

"Don't you dare accuse me of that!"

"Why else are you even considering a retreat?"

"Because I have a duty of care for my soldiers," retorted St. Clair, bolt up-right and quivering with rage, "and I do not choose to have them blown to pieces by artillery that can pick us off at will. Now let's have no more carping from you, Ezekiel, or I'll have you put under restraint."

"For being honest?"

"For being insubordinate."

"I'm only saying what you said yourself earlier."

"That's enough!" the other barked. "You've exceeded your latitude. I give the orders here—you simply obey them."

"Yes, General."

"I've been far too indulgent with you."

"If you say so, sir."

St. Clair heard the faint note of insolence in his voice. He was fond of the artist and respected his work immensely. Not wishing to lose his friendship, he adopted a more conciliatory tone.

"One day, Ezekiel," he said, "you'll thank me for saving your life."

"All that I'll remember," Proudfoot returned, still smoldering visibly, "is how you lost your reputation as a soldier at Ticonderoga. You also threw away a golden opportunity to show just how bravely American patriots will fight for their independence. You let this country down, sir. Don't expect any gratitude from me on that account."

CHAPTER SIX

When night came, a full moon lent Fort Ticonderoga a ghostly quality. It floated like an apparition on the brilliant waters of Lake Champlain, surrounded by the phantom peaks of Mount Independence, Mount Defiance, and Mount Hope, three giant silhouettes that seemed at once to protect and threaten the beleaguered fortress. Under cover of darkness, the evacuation began in earnest, the speed and secrecy with which it was conducted leading to all manner of confusion. It was less of a controlled departure than a headlong flight.

Hustled without warning onto a series of bateaux, the sick and wounded were rowed away from the dock, escorted by armed ships and galleys that carried the female members of the garrison, as well as six hundred soldiers under the command of Colonel Pierce Long. They sailed due south at a leisurely pace toward Skenesborough. The vast majority of the soldiers, however, crossed the bridge from the fort and assembled on top of Mount Independence so that they could make their escape overland. With a collection of sketches in his satchel, a reluctant Ezekiel Proudfoot went with them.

Two serious blunders were made by the departing troops. They failed to destroy the bridge behind them and—thanks to the French commander on Mount Independence—they let the cat out of the bag. General Roche de Fermoy, a colorful but erratic adventurer, was a seasoned tippler. While the rest of the army was on the move, the slothful Frenchman was still sleeping off his latest drinking bout. Awakened by the noise of departure, he stumbled about so clumsily that he contrived to knock over a candle and set fire to his tent. The ensuing blaze was a clear signal to the British and German troops that something dramatic was happening.

On the eastern bank, General Riedesel saw the fire and promptly urged his men on. Their attempts to reach the wagon track behind Mount Independence had been delayed by marshes but, with a final push, they arrived in time to harry the rear guard with a few parting shots. Brigadier Simon Fraser, meanwhile, had verbal confirmation of what was afoot. Three deserters from the American ranks arrived to tell him that General St. Clair had ordered an abrupt withdrawal from Ticonderoga. The presence of artillery on the top of Mount Defiance meant that it was impossible to make a successful defense of the fort or of the battery on the summit of Mount Independence.

Fraser's response was characteristically prompt. Without waiting for a direct command from Burgoyne, he advanced with his men, sending word of his movements to his commander, who still lay asleep in the capacious arms of Lucinda Mallard. With a party of Indians in tow, Fraser's men were braced for fierce resistance that never materialized. The four American gunners, who had been posted on the eastern bank with a loaded cannon, could not resist plundering the discarded supplies and drinking themselves into a stupor. Unable to fire at anyone who attempted to cross the bridge, they were sprawled on the ground, dead drunk beside their cannon, allowing the British troops to take instant control.

It was an Indian who then caused unnecessary danger to his own men. When he saw a lighted match beside the snoring rebels, he picked it up out of curiosity and dropped a spark upon the pinning of the cannon. The result was ear-splitting. Loaded with all kinds of deadly shot, the cannon went off and sent its contents flying over the heads of the British troops and into the lake. It was only by a miracle that there were no casualties from this random act of madness.

Minutes later, the British flag was hoisted over Fort Ticonderoga.

Captain Jamie Skoyles was among the first to join his commander. Having seen the fire on top of Mount Independence and realized that the garrison was making a run for it, he brought his men down Mount Defiance to approach the fort from the south. By the time he got there, British troops were ransacking the stores and carrying some of the provisions away. Brigadier Fraser was staring at a sheet of paper.

"Good morning, sir," said Skoyles.

Fraser looked up. "Good morning, Jamie."

"The birds have flown, I see."

"But not as silently as they would've liked," said Fraser. "With luck, General Riedesel may have peppered their arses as they took the road out of here. The main thing is that we've seized the fort without any loss of life. General Burgoyne will be delighted."

"What are his orders, sir?"

"I await them. The general was still in his cabin on the *Royal George* when I set out. My guess is that he'll order us to pursue the rebels west to Hubbardton while he sails on down the lake to Skenesborough."

"We watched the boats leave," said Skoyles. "They were not rowing with any urgency. They obviously think we'll be held up here for a long time by the boom across the lake, and by the men left to guard the bridge."

"Then they're in for a nasty shock, Jamie. The bridge has been secured and I reckon that our gunboats will smash a way through the boom in well under an hour. Take a look at this," he said, handing him the sheet of paper. "I found it scrunched up in the courtyard. Someone obviously thought they were going to mount a courageous defense of Ticonderoga."

Skoyles looked down at the sketch. Even in the dawn light, he could make out a dramatic scene, drawn by a talented hand, showing a group of Continental soldiers inside the ramparts of the fort. They were firing their muskets bravely at the enemy and, in some cases, engaging in hand-to-hand combat with the British as they attempted to storm the fortress. It was a patriotic celebration of American heroism. Jamie Skoyles had seen the work of this particular artist before, and his emotions were deeply stirred.

"What do you make of it?" asked Fraser.

"Ezekiel Proudfoot."

"Who?"

"It was drawn by a friend of mine, sir," said Skoyles. "An engraver named Ezekiel Proudfoot. He was here."

"Are you certain of that?"

"No doubt about it."

"Then he's not a friend any longer, Jamie. He's an enemy."

Ezekiel Proudfoot was hurt and profoundly dismayed by the order to flee from Ticonderoga, refusing to accept the arguments in favor of immediate withdrawal. Some of the scenes he had witnessed verged on the chaotic. Discipline was lost, bickering broke out, officers gave contradictory commands, soldiers bumped into each other in the dark, knapsacks and even weapons were left behind in the headlong retreat, and the whole hurried exercise was symbolized by the folly of the inebriated French general who had accidentally lit a beacon on Mount Independence to alert the enemy.

What irked Proudfoot most was that he had been deprived of an opportunity to commemorate American resolution during a prolonged siege. The sight of an entire garrison scurrying away like rats from a sinking ship was hardly a fit subject for one of his prints, and would certainly not arouse the patriotic instincts of his countrymen. A once unassailable stronghold had been yielded to the British without even a semblance of resistance. Ezekiel Proudfoot felt so ashamed that he voiced his disgust to General St. Clair.

"I never thought to see such a thing," he complained. "The mighty Fort Ticonderoga, abandoned in haste by a whole army."

"That army was more apparent than real," said St. Clair briskly. "We had barely two thousand men fit for duty, a corps of artillery and fewer than a thousand militiamen. If the enemy launched a simultaneous attack from both directions, there was no way that we could hold them off."

"How do you know if you wouldn't even try?"

"My hand was forced, Ezekiel."

"Even though we might have—"

"And I'll brook no criticism," said the other, interrupting him with a peremptory glance in his direction. "Not even from a friend."

"My apologies, General," said Proudfoot through clenched teeth.

"Better to lose a fort than sacrifice a whole garrison."

"That's your opinion, sir."

"I'm not interested in yours."

"That won't stop me from having one."

"Make sure that I don't have to hear it," said St. Clair.

After a forced march of several miles that had lasted for most of an oppressively hot day, they had reached the tiny settlement of Hubbardton in Vermont. Knowing that there would be pursuit, St. Clair elected to take the main body of men on to Castleton, some six miles or so away. Colonel Seth

Warner was left in Hubbardton with 150 men and told to wait there until the rear guard caught up with him. Instead of continuing to retreat with the others, Ezekiel Proudfoot remained behind, eager to be where action might take place. It was quite late when the rear guard, comprising the 11th Massachusetts and the 2nd New Hampshire regiments, finally arrived in the town. Ignoring an express order to keep moving, Warner chose instead to spend the night in Hubbardton.

Proudfoot sensed a battle ahead. Excited by the prospect, he was glad that he had spurned the opportunity to go on to Castleton with the others. St. Clair might have let him down, but Seth Warner was made of sterner stuff. American heroism would be displayed, after all.

"Confounded Germans!" sneered Major Featherstone. "We've lost them."

"They don't march as quickly as we do, Major," said Skoyles.

"No—damn them! Riedesel is far more interested in keeping his troops in formation than pushing them on."

"They'll catch up with us in time, Major."

"Brigadier Fraser is furious with them."

"I think that he accepts that they move at a slower pace," Skoyles said tolerantly. "Especially in the kind of hot weather we've had today. Their uniforms are too thick and their boots too heavy. But I dispute that the brigadier's shown any real anger toward our German allies. When all is said and done, General Riedesel is nominally in charge of this operation. He does outrank the brigadier."

"He'll never outrank Simon Fraser in the things that matter," said Featherstone, curling his lip. "That's why he defers to the brigadier, who has twice the military brain of that lumbering foreigner and ten times the experience of fighting in America. General Burgoyne understands that. The brigadier, quite rightly, is always taken into his confidence while the German commander is often excluded from any meetings."

"That may not be a sensible policy, sir."

"It is to me. The power of decision must be ours."

"Nevertheless, we rely very heavily on the Brunswickers."

"Then where the bloody hell *are* they, Captain?"

Jamie Skoyles and Harry Featherstone were with the force that had been dispatched after the fleeing Americans. Checked from time to time by sporadic gunfire from the rear guard, they had pressed on hard to get within striking distance of Hubbardton. Tents had been pitched at night at Lacey's Camp, a place vacated by the Americans only an hour earlier. Since they traveled without provisions, the hungry British troops had slaughtered a cow in the woods to eat for supper. Somewhere behind them, under the command of Riedesel, were regiments of Brunswick grenadiers and riflemen, unable to catch up and pausing to rest for the night. The chasing army was split in two.

While they waited for reports from Indian scouts, Skoyles found himself talking to Featherstone. Aware of the man's defects, Skoyles had always conceded that the major had his finer points. He was fearless in battle and led his men from the front. Other officers would prefer to wait until the German reinforcements arrived, but Featherstone was ready to join battle without them. He loved action as much as Skoyles himself, and always showed gallantry in the field. He was also a keen student of military strategy.

"Gentleman Johnny wants to finish them off," he said with obvious approval. "While we drive the rebels toward Skenesborough, he'll sail down the lake and meet us there. St. Clair and his army will be caught between the two of us and annihilated. It's a brilliant plan."

"Only if the Americans oblige us by sticking to it," said Skoyles.

"What do you mean?"

"They may not want to be pushed in that direction, Major. This is the kind of territory in which they fight best—thick woodland where sharpshooters can stay hidden and pick off our men before we get within a couple of hundred yards of them. Besides," he went on, "General St. Clair is an intelligent man. I don't think it will take him long to work out what Burgoyne's strategy will be. For that reason, he'll keep well away from Skenesborough."

"Not if we hound him all the way."

"We'll need more men to do that."

"As long as they're not those lazy, putrid, pox-ridden Germans!"

"We'll never win without them, sir."

Featherstone bit back an expletive. Extracting a silver snuffbox from his pocket, he opened the lid, took a pinch between forefinger and thumb, then inhaled it noisily. Skoyles watched him as he put the snuffbox away. The captain was in a quandary. One of the men who had marched with them in the 24th Foot was Private Roger Higgs, still nursing the wounds inflicted on his back and still brooding on revenge. Though he had ordered the man to forget such murderous thoughts, Skoyles was not at all certain that Higgs would obey. That left him with two options. Skoyles could either warn Harry Featherstone of the possible danger or keep him in ignorance of it.

Problems attended both courses of action. If Skoyles were to tell the major of the threat made against him, then Higgs would immediately be put under arrest and the captain would be asked why it had taken him so long to issue a warning to his fellow officer. If, on the other hand, nothing was said and Higgs actually carried out his threat, Skoyles would be left feeling guilty. His silence would not only have cost the major his life, he would have separated Elizabeth Rainham from the man whom she loved. Even though he barely knew the lady, Skoyles did not wish to do anything that would make her unhappy. For her sake, he appointed himself as the major's protector.

"What's the trouble?" asked Featherstone, eyeing him shrewdly.

"There is no trouble, sir," replied Skoyles.

"I feel as if you're on the point of saying something."

"Not really."

"Come on, Jamie. Share your thoughts with me, man."

Skoyles hesitated. Before he could utter another word, however, he saw Brigadier Fraser approaching out of the gloom. Despite the lateness of the hour, the newcomer was in a sprightly mood.

"Good news!" he announced. "Scouts have just returned to tell me that there's an encampment at a place called Sucker Brook. They've only posted a few sentries so the Indians were able to get close enough to estimate their numbers."

"What are they, sir?" asked Skoyles.

"Well short of our own, Jamie."

"That sounds promising."

"It sounds irresistible," said Featherstone, beaming at the thought of action. "When do we attack, Brigadier?"

"Before dawn."

"Alone?"

"I've sent word to General Riedesel to make all speed to join us," explained Fraser, "but we can't delay our assault until they do. We must strike when the enemy least expect it."

"They've no idea that we're here," said Skoyles. "If they have so few sentries, then they clearly underestimate the speed at which we marched. We should take them unawares. Who is being deployed?"

"Two companies of the 24th Foot along with half the light infantry and the grenadier battalions. Colonel John Peters won't be left out. He'll bring up his loyalist corps and, of course, we'll have the Indians as well."

"That could be a mixed blessing, sir."

"They've done well so far, Jamie," said Fraser. "They haven't lit a fire or set off a cannon this time. They'll guide us to the exact spot."

"I can't wait!" said Featherstone, bunching a fist. "This is what soldiering is all about—blood and glory!"

"Some of that blood will be ours," Skoyles cautioned.

"No matter for that. Men are expendable. They'll give their lives in a noble cause—the maintenance of the British Empire." He turned to Fraser. "What are our orders, Brigadier?"

Fraser was crisp. "Have your men ready to march in an hour."

The assault was well timed and swiftly executed. Achieving complete surprise, the British launched the attack on Sucker Brook at five o'clock that morning, waking the New Hampshire regiment from their slumbers and throwing them into disarray. Casualties were relatively light in the ranks of the 24th Foot—though a senior officer was killed—but the Continental Army lost several men. Over 350 soldiers had bivouacked near the little stream that drained the valley to the east, with a large group of stragglers in attendance. Realizing that they were outnumbered and outmaneuvered, those who had not been killed or wounded simply fell slowly back. The battle of Hubbardton had commenced.

Jamie Skoyles was in the thick of it, fighting on foot and leading a detachment of men with spirit and purpose. When the bullets began to fly, he ordered his troops to respond, knowing that their smoothbore Brown Bess muskets might not have the accuracy of the hunting rifles that they faced but confident that his men could fire and reload three times in a minute. In close combat, that gave his army a distinct advantage over weapons that took much longer to reload. The advantage was increased by the fact that the British—unlike the Continentals—had bayonets fixed on their weapons and the sight of so much flashing steel helped to put fear in the hearts of the New Hampshiremen.

Mounted on his horse, Harry Featherstone was as intrepid as ever, bellowing orders, leading by example, throwing discretion to the winds. When Skoyles looked across at him, the major's horse was suddenly shot from under him, keeling over and neighing in agony. Featherstone leapt from the saddle, dodged the flailing hooves of the stricken animal, then ran forward a dozen yards before taking aim with a pistol to shoot dead the man who had brought the horse down. He let out a roar of satisfaction and beckoned his men to follow him.

It was an unequal contest. The Continentals soon deserted the field, abandoning the camp and leaving the wounded to the mercy of the enemy. Brigadier Fraser's men had secured an early success. Most of the Continentals whom they had frightened out of Sucker Brook would take no further part in hostilities. Their departure left Fraser able to turn his attention to the remaining Americans—the men of Vermont under Colonel Seth Warner and the Massachusetts regiment under Colonel Ebenezer Francis. Surging across the stream, the British swarmed up the slope with alacrity toward the American forces. They had tasted victory, and they wanted more.

Ezekiel Proudfoot heard it all from a vantage point by a cabin up on the ridge. Roused from their slumbers by the sound of gunfire, the rest of the Continentals watched in dismay as part of their army was routed, but their officers were at least given warning. They were able to rally and draw up a line of battle that was anchored on the extreme left by Zion Hill, a steep, wooded incline that rose to twelve hundred feet. While most of the American soldiers were armed with long rifles, Proudfoot had only paper and a charcoal pencil in his hands.

As the redcoats marched relentlessly toward them, he began his first sketch. Staying within earshot of Colonel Francis, the engraver was distracted by the sound of a galloping horse that came from the direction of Castleton. Proudfoot surmised that the messenger had arrived with such desperate speed that he must have brought important news, and he made sure that he overheard it.

Pulling his horse to a halt, the breathless rider jumped from the saddle, ran to Francis, and thrust a letter into his hand.

"Dispatch from General St. Clair, sir," he announced.

"Thank you."

"He wanted you to have it as soon as possible, Colonel."

Francis tore open the letter and read the contents. Proudfoot could see the look of alarm in his eyes. He soon understood what had put it there. Francis turned to the officers at his side.

"God help us!" he wailed.

"What's happened, sir?" asked a young lieutenant.

"The British broke through the boom at Ticonderoga within an hour. They sailed on to Skenesborough and caught up with our vessels. All of our baggage, powder, and cannon have been captured."

The lieutenant was aghast. "They've taken Skenesborough?"

"Yes," said Francis. "Our escape route to the south has been cut off. General St. Clair is being forced to make a wide detour in order to reach the Hudson. We are ordered to join him at once."

"How?"

"A good question, Lieutenant."

"The British are coming to block our retreat."

"Then let's give them a warm welcome, shall we?" said Francis, steeling himself. He scanned the approaching line of redcoats, marching boldly along a half-mile front to the beat of drums. "Let's show them what the Continental Army can do, shall we?" he went on, warming to the prospect of battle. "We've more men, higher ground, we can move faster and shoot straighter. We stand and fight, gentlemen."

There was general agreement among the officers, though Proudfoot could see how shaken they had been by the news from St. Clair. Ebenezer Francis tried to instill some confidence in his officers.

"Forget what happened at Skenesborough," he urged. "This is Hubbardton—the place where we strike back and show the British how gallantly we can fight for our freedom. If they want a battle, let's give them one. Take up your positions. We must move with great expedition or the enemy will be upon us."

The officers ran off, and Ezekiel Proudfoot moved to the cover of some trees. Far below him, the British advance continued inexorably across a patch of open ground. When he lifted his pen to sketch the scene, Proudfoot's hand did not tremble for an instant. He felt no fear and had no regrets. This was what he had come to see—a pitched battle that would bring out American fortitude and prove to the redcoats they had a worthy adversary in the men scattered along the ridge. Here was no discreditable retreat. It was a stand for freedom, and Proudfoot felt privileged to be there to witness it.

Buoyed up by their victory at Sucker Brook, the British troops marched in formation toward what they believed would be another triumph in the field. Captain Jamie Skoyles shared their conviction that the Continental Army, recently formed and made up of a curious assortment of men, was no match for a force of highly trained professional soldiers. Even against the greater numbers of the rear guard, he did not doubt their ultimate success in the battle. Brigadier Simon Fraser showed no hesitation in ordering a second attack. Riding up and down the line on his horse, he exhorted his men on with words and gestures, telling them what an important blow they could strike against the rebels and warning them not to fire until the command was given. The drums continued to beat out their stirring prelude.

When the long red line came within range, the Continentals fired their first volley with lethal results. Several of the oncoming troops were wounded and fell to the ground. Three of the officers were killed outright. Discipline, however, did not falter. The British infantrymen simply stepped over the bodies of their fallen comrades and marched on, needing to get much closer to the enemy before their muskets could be used with any effect. A second volley from the Americans claimed some more victims and, once again, officers were among the selected targets.

The brigadier was undeterred. He ordered the light infantry and the 24th Foot to ascend the steep, wooded slopes ahead, telling them to fan out and roll up the enemy's right, thus forcing them away from the escape route to Castleton. Major Acland and his grenadiers were given the more difficult task of scaling the unoccupied Mount Zion to the right, the summit of which commanded the road beyond. Jamie Skoyles was part of the force that began to scramble up the slopes with their muskets slung across their backs. Ahead of them was the light infantry and it was they who reeled back from the first shower of ball and buckshot that came down from the ridge above. It was going to be a perilous climb.

Skoyles was less concerned about the enemy than about one of his own men. Instead of following the others, Private Roger Higgs, he saw, was moving determinedly sideways until he got within a dozen yards of Major Featherstone. He lifted his musket and took aim. Unable to make himself heard above the crackle of gunfire, Skoyles did the only thing that he could. Racing toward Featherstone, he tackled him hard around the waist and knocked him to the ground, saving him from being hit by the musket ball discharged a split second later by Higgs.

Featherstone protested wildly, but the danger was not over. Failing to shoot the man he hated, Higgs charged at him with his bayonet at the ready, intending to stab him to death. Skoyles was on his feet in a flash, using his sword to parry Higgs's vicious thrust. Before the private knew what was happening, he was struck hard in the stomach by the hilt of Skoyles's weapon and expertly deprived of his musket. Higgs was in despair. Cheated of his revenge, he yelled abuse at Featherstone, then ran frenziedly up the slope without any care for his fate. Within seconds, he was brought down by enemy fire.

Skoyles offered a hand to the major, who was still lying on the ground. It was spurned. Hauling himself to his feet, Featherstone could not even bring himself to offer a word of thanks to the man who had just saved his life. Instead, he pushed roughly past him. Enraged by the attack on him, he hurried up the slope until he came to the dead body of Private Roger Higgs, twisted into an unnatural shape on the grass. With cruel deliberation, Featherstone used the butt of his pistol to smash open the man's skull, hitting it time and again in his fury. Skoyles had to rush forward to grab him.

"He's dead, sir," he shouted. "Leave him be."

"He tried to kill me!" Featherstone howled, shaking himself free.

Skoyles pointed a finger. "The enemy is up there."

As if to confirm the fact, a volley came down from the ridge above and felled some more of the redcoats. One of them—hit simultaneously by several bullets—came tumbling helplessly down the slope to end up at Featherstone's feet. Setting his jaw, the major abandoned his assault on Higgs and went on up the slope. Jamie Skoyles was close behind him, sickened by the man's needless brutality and sending up a silent prayer for the soul of Private Roger Higgs. A hail of bullets made him flatten himself on the ground for an instant. Then he took cover behind a tree and returned fire. Victory no longer seemed so certain.

While the left flank of the British force was taking on the Massachusetts regiment with its seasoned riflemen, the right flank was trying to climb the precipitous Mount Zion. Slinging their muskets, they had to pick their way slowly upward, clinging to tree roots, balancing on outcrops of rock, and using any means at hand to stop themselves from falling off the sheer face. Major Acland did not shirk his task. Leading the way, he brought his grenadiers inch by laborious inch up the incline, taking risks, scornful of danger, determined to reach the summit. In doing so, he knew, they would be able to harass the enemy from the rear and relieve the embattled light infantry and 24th Foot.

When he and his men finally dragged themselves to the top of the mountain, Acland was able to get a clear view of the action on the left flank. Brigadier Fraser's brave advance up the wooded slope had been halted by enemy fire. The redcoats were gathering their strength for a second assault. Urgent help was needed. Drawing his men together, Acland set off across the summit, having achieved their first objective of barring the way to Castleton. They came out into open ground to be met by a welcome sight. Approaching them across the grass were some fifty or more American soldiers, members of the Continental Army in ragged blue uniforms, their heads bent forward in defeat.

Seeing that their arms were clubbed in a gesture of surrender, Acland assumed that he was about to take prisoners of war. He ordered his men to refrain from firing or from showing any hostility. It was an expensive mistake. When the Americans got within ten yards, they lifted their rifles and fired, sending dozens of British soldiers to the ground. Struck in the thigh by a musket ball, Acland was horrified at this flagrant breach of military rules. It was unimaginable that British soldiers would adopt such a shameful ruse. As the guileful rebels took to their heels, the major barked an order.

"After them!" he shouted. "And show them no quarter!"

Under a darkening sky, the fighting continued on the British left flank with increased ferocity. Two assaults had now failed. At the instigation of Brigadier Fraser, a third assault was launched, and the infantry pressed up the wooded slope once more. The resistance was even fiercer. As the red uniforms surged up the hill through the trees, they were highly visible. Crouched behind fallen logs and a stone fence on the crest of the ridge, the men of the 11th Massachusetts unleashed volley after volley. Another batch of infantrymen crashed to the ground.

From his high eminence on the ridge, Colonel Ebenezer Francis was able to watch how the battle was unfolding. When he saw a detachment of British troops trying to lap around his right flank, he gave the order for a sudden counterattack and threw his men down the slope. At point-blank range, the Americans were able to inflict great damage among an infantry that was bunched too closely together, and they drove them back for the third time. The British had to leave even more dead and wounded behind them as they recoiled from the unexpected assault.

Fraser was quick to realize the intense danger of their situation, and he blamed himself for being overconfident. In sending the grenadiers off toward Zion Hill, he had weakened his line considerably, and enemy fire had taken an additional toll. Advantage had definitely swung to the Americans. They had not only shifted their defenses on the hill to nullify the flanking movement by the grenadiers, they had proved that frontal attack against the light infantry and the 24th Foot was highly effective. If they could collapse the damaged British line, they could sweep it from the field. It was the sort of victory that would give an immense fillip to the American cause.

Captain Jamie Skoyles caught a signal from the brigadier and dodged an enemy fusillade to scuttle across to him. Harry Featherstone soon joined them, his spotless uniform now sullied and torn, but his will to fight on as strong as ever.

"We can't hold them much longer," Fraser decided.

"We must, sir," said Featherstone, wiping the sweat from his brow. "Let me take another detachment to outflank them on their right."

"That would only weaken the line still more, Major. If they were to break through, we'd be done for." He turned to Skoyles. "Captain?"

"We may have bitten off more than we can chew," said Skoyles resignedly. "Perhaps we should spit some of it out."

Featherstone wrinkled his nose with distaste. "You're surely not suggesting that we retreat?" he said. "That would be unforgivable."

"My advice would be to dig in and maintain our position. Another attack would be far too costly. We've been repulsed three times now. Let the enemy come to us."

"I'd prefer to hit them from the rear with a flanking movement."

"No," said Fraser with authority, "it would only fail again. Captain Skoyles is right. We must form a solid defensive line and make sure that it's not breached at any point. It's our only hope."

Skoyles gave a weary smile. "That's not true, Brigadier."

"Isn't it?"

"Listen, sir."

"All I can hear is gunfire," Featherstone grumbled.

"*Listen!*" Skoyles urged them.

The other men pricked up their ears. Above the incessant noise of the guns and the groans of dying men, Skoyles had picked up another sound. From across the valley, carried on the light wind, came the distant clamor of hunting horns, the squeal of hautboy, the roll of drums, and the sound of voices raised in song. Misunderstanding what he heard, Harry Featherstone was worried for the first time.

"Jesus!" he cried. "There are *more* of the devils!"

"No, Major," said Skoyles. "What you hear is a battle hymn being sung by the Brunswickers. General Riedesel is coming at last."

"Thank heaven!" exclaimed Fraser with a gasp of relief.

"Not before time," Featherstone grunted.

"I knew that they wouldn't let us down."

"So did I, sir," said Skoyles, before flicking his eyes towards Featherstone. "What about you, Major?" he asked with light sarcasm. "Does it offend your English sensibilities, being rescued by lazy, putrid, pox-ridden Germans?"

The complexion of the battle changed dramatically. Ezekiel Proudfoot's hand paused over his latest sketch. The triumphant charge down the hill that he had begun to draw might not now take place. Once the Germans came into sight, marching to music and singing lustily, the spirit gradually began to drain out of the Continental Army. The prospect of victory slowly melted before their eyes. Heartened by the approach of their reinforcements, the British fought back with renewed vigor, and it was dead rebels who now rolled down the hillside.

Proudfoot saw it all. The German commander deployed his men with skill. Appraising the situation through a telescope, he sent a detachment of riflemen to support the British left flank while some eight hundred grenadiers were ordered to encircle the hill, gain the crest on the right of the American defenses, then turn southward to envelop them. The troops from Massachussetts fell back in disorder, and when he saw the British scrambling up the hill again, Proudfoot went with them. Clutching his satchel, he dived behind a log fence where Colonel Francis was trying to rally his men, ordering them to reload.

Having gained the crest of the hill at last, the British troops joined the Brunswick riflemen and dressed their ranks for a charge. With great bravery, Francis jumped over the breastwork and called upon his men for one more volley. But the words died in his throat. A German bullet pierced his heart and killed him outright. Ezekiel Proudfoot heard the collective sigh of despair from the men around him. Saddened by what had happened to their leader, fearing a bayonet charge from one side and a concentrated volley from the German grenadiers on the other side, they started to panic and dashed off into the woods.

Proudfoot was unarmed and unwilling to risk flight when there were so many stray musket balls flying about. All that he could do was to stay behind the fence, curled up on the ground. There was no prospect of relief. Farther along the ridge, Colonel Seth Warner saw that they had lost and ordered his Vermonters to scatter at once and to meet him in Manchester. The rear guard had been put to flight, and over three dozen of its men had perished during the sharp encounter. In less than an hour, the battle of Hubbardton was over. It remained only for the British to see to the wounded, bury the dead, and round up any prisoners.

The first man to be taken was Ezekiel Proudfoot. When a redcoat peered over the fence, he saw a figure lying on the ground against the timber. He gave him a tentative prod with his bayonet and produced a yell of protest. Sitting up immediately, Proudfoot raised his hands in surrender.

"I'm not a soldier," he said. "As you see, I've no weapon."

"Who are you?" the infantryman demanded.

"My name is Ezekiel Proudfoot. I took no part in the battle."

"Nevertheless, you're a prisoner of war, Mr. Proudfoot." The man turned to call over his shoulder. "I've found another one, Captain."

Proudfoot stood up and saw the officer walking toward them. He stared intently at the bruised features of the newcomer.

"Jamie Skoyles!" he cried in surprise. "Is that *you?*"

Lieutenant General John Burgoyne preened in front of a mirror. He was in his cabin aboard the *Royal George* and had just received a verbal report from Brigadier Fraser of the events at Hubbardton.

"Excellent, excellent!" he said.

"It was a Pyrrhic victory, General."

"A victory is a victory."

"There were heavy casualties," said Fraser sadly. "We lost nearly fifty men— including Major Grant—and one hundred and forty-five were wounded."

"Yes, but you killed plenty of *them,* Simon. More to the point, you took over three hundred prisoners, a rebel colonel among them. They won't be able to fire in anger at a redcoat again." He swung round to face his guest. "By George!" he went on. "This is beyond all my expectations. In the space of a mere ten days, we've crossed the border, captured Ticonderoga, seized two hundred vessels, a hundred cannon, and a prodigious quantity of stores, powder, and shot. When the rebels had the gall to turn and fight, you gave them a good hiding."

"Only because of General Riedesel's timely arrival, sir."

"He shouldn't have lagged behind you in the first place." His face shone once more. "But I apportion no blame to anyone. It's an occasion for celebration. We've not only dealt the enemy a crushing blow, we are now, unbelievably, within seventy-five miles of our target—Albany."

"Have you received word of General Howe's movements?"

"Not yet."

"Will he have already dispatched an army up the Hudson?"

"Who knows? William Howe is not the most efficient of men."

Fraser was concerned. "But we will be joined by reinforcements from New York City?" he asked. "We can be certain of that?"

"Of course," Burgoyne replied airily. "It was all part of the plan that I explained to King George and to Lord Germain. They were made well aware of my requirements. When we reach Albany, we'll meet up with Howe's men and also with St. Leger. What tales we'll have to tell them!" He chuckled happily. "I mean to win that wager, Simon."

"Wager?"

"It's recorded in the betting book at Brooks's. Fifty guineas are at stake. I swore to Fox that I'd return victorious from America within a year. Ha!" he said, clenching his fist. "Within a year? At this rate, the job will be done in a couple of months."

"There's still some way to go yet, sir," Fraser cautioned him.

"But every step of it will be paved with success. I feel it in my bones, Simon." Burgoyne struck a pose. "I've written to the king to inform him of our success in taking Fort Ticonderoga. He'll understand the true significance of that. King George will also be able to read between the lines of my dispatch. Nothing can stop us now!"

CHAPTER SEVEN

It was days before Jamie Skoyles was able to have a proper conversation with his friend. Ezekiel Proudfoot was one of the many prisoners of war who were rounded up after the battle at Hubbardton, searched, deprived of any weapons or papers, and kept under armed guard. They and their captors spent a long, wet, sleepless, uncomfortable night on the ridge, uncertain whether the Continental Army would launch a nocturnal attack or had quit the field for good. In the event, St. Clair did not return with his main force. The only danger that the British and German soldiers faced was from fugitive sharpshooters, hiding in the woods.

On the following day, the troops were marched to Skenesborough while the wounded of both sides were evacuated with the prisoners to Ticonderoga, where a small British garrison had been left. It was only by the direct intercession of Jamie Skoyles that Proudfoot was not sent back to the fort with the others. The engraver was curious as to why he had been singled out.

"How did you persuade them to let me come with you, Jamie?"

"It was not easy," said Skoyles.

"I can imagine."

"Major Featherstone was adamant that you should stay with the others. When I argued that you bore no arms and took no direct part in the fighting, he pointed out that one of your prints could do just as much damage to the British army as a hail of grapeshot."

"I'm vain enough to believe that that's true," said Proudfoot with a half smile. "A print can be a powerful weapon. You only have to look at the famous engraving of the Boston Massacre. That was so effective."

"But a gross distortion, Ezekiel."

"It was an artistic interpretation of the event."

"There was certainly more art than accuracy in it," said Skoyles with asperity. "I was in Boston at the time and spoke to some of the soldiers involved in the so-called massacre. Yes, and I talked to some of the civilian bystanders as well. None of them thought that Paul Revere's engraving was a truthful portrayal of what actually happened."

"Truth is not an absolute, Jamie."

"It is to me."

"I think that Paul Revere did the American people a great service."

"Only by telling them a lie."

"Shots were fired. Five people died. Those were the facts."

"No, Ezekiel," Skoyles returned. "One of those killed was a mulatto by the name of Crispus Attucks. What sympathy would the death of a black man arouse? Very little, I suspect. Paul Revere clearly thought the same because, in his print, he changed Crispus Attucks into a white American. What do you call that—artistic license?"

"An insignificant detail."

Skoyles let out a sigh. "You've changed, Ezekiel."

"We both have," said Proudfoot sadly. "We used to be so close."

"I hoped that we still were."

"Not as long as you wear a red coat."

Skoyles had been astonished and pleased to see Proudfoot again, albeit on the opposing side in a battle. Since the other man had been at Fort Ticonderoga for some while, Skoyles convinced Fraser that the prisoner would be able to give them valuable intelligence about the garrison there, and that he—as a former friend of Proudfoot's—would be the best person to extract such information from him. Accordingly, he was interrogating Proudfoot in the privacy of his tent with an armed guard outside to prevent any attempt by the prisoner at escape.

"Why did General St. Clair abandon the fort?" asked Skoyles.

"He was frightened away by the artillery on Mount Defiance."

"What was to stop the Continental Army having its own guns up there? We'd never have been able to sail down Lake Champlain with the threat of heavy artillery trained on us from the summit."

"The engineers thought that Mount Defiance was too steep."

"A fatal miscalculation—one of many."

"The British army has made its share of mistakes," said Proudfoot sharply.

"I daresay that it will make many more before we're done. Let's be frank, Jamie. If your reinforcements hadn't arrived when they did at Hubbardton, your commander's folly would have been exposed for what it was. He attacked the ridge with too small a force. You were saved by your hired killers from Germany."

"You have hired killers in your ranks as well, Ezekiel."

Proudfoot nodded slowly. "I agree," he said. "Unfortunately, it's the only way we could raise an army. It would be nice to think that everyone in the uniform of the Continentals was spurred on by patriotism, but that's simply not the case."

"I know."

"Many of them couldn't give a damn about England's persecution of us. Our infantry consists of murderers, robbers, wife-beaters, hunters, mountain men, Negro slaves who've run away from their masters, and European adventurers who can't resist a fight—especially when they get money for it." He studied Skoyles. "How much do you get paid, Jamie?"

"Why?"

"A captain in the Continental army earns forty dollars a month and can expect at least two hundred acres of land as a reward for his service."

Skoyles grinned. "Get thee behind me, Satan."

"Can't you be tempted?"

"Not by you, Ezekiel."

"Are you so dog loyal to that tyrant back in England?"

"No," Skoyles admitted. "It's not simply love of king and country that made me wear this red coat—though I'll defend to the death every inch of our empire. It was the lure of army life. It can be an ugly life at times—a brutal, heartless, painful kind of existence that makes you do things in which you can take no pride whatsoever. But," he added with a resigned shrug, "it's what I chose, and it's where I feel at home."

"Crawling over the dead and dying on a wooded hillside?"

"Battles are never pretty."

"How many years have you been a soldier now?"

"Over twenty," replied Skoyles. "I'm beyond redemption."

"No thought of marriage and settling down?"

"In the fullness of time."

"You may not have too much of it left, Jamie."

There was a note of sorrow in his voice that revealed a lingering affection for Skoyles. The physical changes in Ezekiel Proudfoot were obvious. He looked older, sparer, and more world-worn. He had retained his philosophical air and his delight in argument, but there was a harder edge to the man than Skoyles remembered. Proudfoot had been tempered by war into a flintiness that made him seem almost truculent.

"What about you, Ezekiel?" asked Skoyles. "No wife and children?"

"Not any more."

"You lost them?"

"No, Jamie," said Proudfoot, recoiling from the stab of a memory. "They were taken from me by the army that you so blindly serve. If I told you how, I daresay that you'd accuse me of gross distortion, so I'll spare you the details."

"They were killed?"

"Massacred—along with everyone else in the village."

"And this was by British soldiers?"

"By Hessian mercenaries in your pay. That comes to the same thing. One day, I had a family; the next day, it was gone."

"I'm very sorry to hear that, Ezekiel. I really am."

"We commit atrocities just as bad," Proudfoot conceded. "What can you expect when you put weapons in the hands of violent men? But that's no consolation to me. Perhaps you'll understand now why I chose to put my humble talents at the disposal of your enemy."

"Most men in your position would have joined the Continentals."

"I fight more effectively with a pencil in my hand."

"What about your father? Is Mordecai still alive?"

"He died a year ago."

"And your brothers—Reuben and Silas?"

"Silas took over the farm. He's the eldest of us. He has a lovely wife and six fine children. Reuben was always the most hot-blooded member of the family," he said. "He joined one of the Massachusetts regiments, so you might meet up with him on a battlefield in due course. My brother is a true patriot, inspired by a vision of a free America. It gives him an excuse to kill British soldiers. Reuben enjoys that."

"It's a dangerous habit. We'll have to cure him of it."

"There'll be plenty more to take his place."

Personal tragedy had robbed Proudfoot of his gentle manner and his ready sense of humor. He was a driven man, willing to court jeopardy in order to do his work, determined to help the American cause with his skills as an artist and engraver. In the middle of a raging battle at Hubbardton, he had had no weapon with which to defend himself. Proudfoot had been there to observe, record, and disseminate. Only a mixture of obstinacy and foolhardiness had kept him on the battlefield. Even when he had a chance to flee, Proudfoot had stood his ground.

"Tell me what happened at Ticonderoga," Skoyles said.

"You already know that."

"I know only that the fort was evacuated. Who made the decision and who advised against it? How many men did St. Clair lead away from Mount Independence? What were his plans? Did he intend to join up with General Schuyler? I want information, Ezekiel."

"Look at my drawings," counseled the other. "That's where you'll find your information. During my stay, I must have drawn almost every man at the fort—the Negroes as well as the whites."

"I'm glad that you can tell the difference between the two."

"There *is* no difference, Jamie. They're all Americans."

"Slave owners would disagree."

"They'll learn," said Proudfoot. "They'll learn." He raised a hopeful eyebrow. "I suppose that it's no use asking for my satchel back?"

"None at all."

"I feel naked without pencil and paper."

"Then you'll have to get used to it," Skoyles warned. "General Burgoyne has been looking through the contents of your satchel with interest. He says that you have a rare talent. But neither he nor I will let you have your things back again. You'd only spend your time making notes of the strength and disposition of our army. We can't let that sort of intelligence fall into the wrong hands."

"All that I wish to do is to make some sketches. What harm is there in that? Listen," said Proudfoot, touching his arm, "I'll strike a bargain with you. Give me my satchel and I'll tell you everything you want to hear. Is that fair?"

"Yes," answered Skoyles, "it's extremely fair. But fairness is not on offer here, I'm afraid. Your choice is a stark one. Tell me what I need to know or I'll have you sent back to Fort Ticonderoga to be put on short rations with the rest of the prisoners." His smile was cold. "Which is it going to be, Ezekiel?"

After all this time, Tom Caffrey had not become accustomed to the smell of death. It still offended his nostrils and haunted him for days afterward. While the rest of the British army had fought tooth and nail at Hubbardton, he came up behind them, making instant decisions about which of the injured would recover if given medical attention and which were beyond help. When the burial detail was later formed, he had recognized a number of corpses being lowered into graves as belonging to men who had begged for his attention while they lay in agony on the battlefield. Caffrey felt the usual pangs of guilt. With such limited resources, he had been compelled to ignore many more wounded soldiers than he was able to tend.

Polly Bragg knew better than to pester him with questions after a battle. She let him brood in silence, waiting patiently until he was ready to confide in her. About one thing, however, Caffrey had been eager to talk on his return, and it came up again when Nan Wyatt walked past their tent. The two women immediately fell into animated conversation. Cleaning his instruments in a bucket of water, Caffrey only half-listened to their gossip.

"What did Miss Rainham have to say about it?" asked Polly.

"About what?" replied Nan.

"Major Featherstone, of course. His narrow escape."

"Escape?"

"Yes," said Polly. "Tom told me all about it. He was close enough to see the whole thing. The major is lucky to be alive, isn't he, Tom?"

"What's that?" asked Caffrey, looking up.

"We were just talking about the rescue at Hubbardton."

"It's the first I've heard of it," said Nan, anxious to know more. "Major Featherstone was rescued, you say? When? How?"

"Tom should be the person to tell you."

"What happened, Sergeant Caffrey?"

Caffrey began to dry his instruments with a piece of cloth. He had been introduced to Nan Wyatt while they were camped at Crown Point and found her pleasant company. For the sake of Jamie Skoyles, he had encouraged the friendship between Nan and Polly Bragg, and he now saw an opportunity to show Skoyles in a good light. Caffrey was not surprised to learn that no mention of the incident had been made to Elizabeth Rainham. Had he raised the topic, the major would have had to praise another officer, and he was unwilling to do that. Caffrey repaired the deficiency.

"One of his own men tried to kill Major Featherstone," he began.

Nan was shaken. "One of his own men?"

"Private Roger Higgs."

"He was that young soldier I told you about, Nan," said Polly, nudging her with her elbow. "You remember, the one who was flogged on the major's orders."

"Higgs could never forgive him," Caffrey went on, rubbing the last speck of moisture from his saw. "He wanted revenge and bided his time."

His account was concise but lucid. Inured to the abominations of the battlefield, Polly Bragg had pressed for more detail, but Caffrey did not wish to upset Nan Wyatt with a full recital of the facts. He merely stressed how much Major Featherstone owed to the alertness of Jamie Skoyles. Nan was amazed that the major had not volunteered the information himself, and she could not wait to pass it on to her mistress.

"Thank you, Sergeant Caffrey," she said. "I'm very grateful."

"It's the major who should be showing a little gratitude."

"I can't believe that a British soldier tried to shoot him."

"He's by no means the only man to do that to an officer," said Caffrey. "During a battle, you've no idea where the danger comes from. In my time, I've extracted musket balls from the back of more than one unpopular officer."

"That's dreadful!"

"Passions run high in combat. Anything can happen."

After thanking him again, Nan Wyatt scuttled off to report to her mistress. Caffrey exchanged a glance with Polly Bragg.

"We both know why Major Featherstone held his tongue," he said harshly. "He's too proud to admit that someone saved his rotten carcass from a British musket ball."

"I thought he was Jamie's friend."

"Of a sort. They got on well enough at first. Jamie started to look at him differently after that flogging. The major enjoyed it so much. Then there was that scouting mission to Ticonderoga. It rankled with Major Featherstone. He never forgave Jamie for that. The major believed that he should have been sent instead. He couldn't accept that Jamie was chosen ahead of him on merit."

"Was that because Jamie is a better scout than him?"

"He's a better *everything* than Harry Featherstone. He's certainly a better card player," he added with a cackle. "Jamie has emptied the major's pockets time and again."

"But if someone saves your life, you'd become his friend."

"Not in this case, Polly."

"Why not?"

"Because a rift has opened up between the two of them. I suppose that the truth of it is that the major has never really looked on him as an equal. How could he? Jamie rose from the ranks," he explained, "where he rubbed shoulders with the likes of me."

"There's nothing wrong with that, Tom."

"There is to Major Featherstone. No matter what Jamie does, he'll never be fully acknowledged by some officers. The major just happens to be the worst of them. Jamie Skoyles will always be an outsider to him. Put it this way," he went on. "If Higgs had aimed his musket at Jamie's back, I'm not at all sure that Harry Featherstone would've lifted a finger to save him."

One of the things Jamie Skoyles liked about an army was the extraordinary variety of human beings it contained. Uniforms might achieve a common appearance and constant drilling might impose a rigid discipline, but a man's essential character was unchanged by it all. Sinners did not become saints when they took the King's shilling. Skoyles was reminded of that once more when, on his way to report to General Burgoyne, he encountered two men from his regiment in the middle of a heated argument.

Private Daniel Lukins and Private Marcus Wolverton could not have presented a sharper contrast. Lukins was a diminutive Cockney with a face like a squashed tomato and a voice like the croak of a frog. Convicted of forgery, Lukins had been released from prison to join an army that was in desperate need of recruits, whatever their criminal tendencies. Wolverton, on the other hand, was an educated man who had once had a promising career as an actor in front of him. Stage fright of such intensity had seized him one night during a performance at Drury Lane that it was impossible for him to continue in his role. After fleeing from the theater, he drank steadily for a whole week to calm his nerves, only to find—when he finally sobered up—that he had somehow volunteered to serve in the British army.

Tall, slim, and stately, the actor towered over the forger, but it was the latter who was clearly getting the better of the exchanges. When they saw Skoyles approaching, they stepped apart and gave him a salute.

"Why are you two always at each other's throats?" asked Skoyles.

"Us?" replied Lukins, an expression of complete innocence on his face. "Wolvie an' me is the best of friends. Ain't we, Wolvie?"

"No, Dan," the other said loftily. "I'd not dignify our relationship to that extent but I would accept that we are well acquainted."

Lukins laughed. "That's 'is way of sayin' 'e loves me, Captain."

"What was the dispute about this time?" said Skoyles.

"Old Red 'Azel."

"Dan is referring to General Riedesel," Wolverton explained with careful enunciation. "I happen to admire our German ally."

"Then buy the bugger a watch," Lukins suggested sourly, "so 'e can arrive at the battlefield on time. Red 'Azel left it until the very last moment at 'Ubbardton an', when 'e did come, 'e brings that bleedin' band with 'im, like they was goin' to a concert."

"We owe the Brunswickers a debt of gratitude," noted Skoyles.

"That's exactly what I told him, Captain," said Wolverton, "but all that Dan can do is to hurl abuse at them."

Lukins thrust out his chest aggressively. "Old Red 'Azel can't 'old a candle to Gen'lman Johnny."

"General Burgoyne," corrected Skoyles.

"I'd foller 'im through the gates of 'ell, so I would."

"I have the same respect for General Riedesel," said Wolverton.

"Did you 'ear that, sir?" demanded Lukins, red with indignation. "Wolvie thinks them turd-faced Germans is better than us redcoats. That's treason, that is, an' no mistake."

"Wolverton is entitled to express an opinion," said Skoyles.

"It deserves a floggin' at least."

"I've already had one from that vicious cat-o'-nine-tails you call a tongue," Wolverton told him, "but my view remains the same. General Riedesel is the equal of General Burgoyne. He has more experience, for a start. He always thinks deeply before he acts. General Riedesel takes his time."

"Yes—we found that out at 'Ubbardton, didn't we?" Lukins challenged him. "While 'e was takin' 'is bleedin' time, we was all but blown to bits on that 'illside. That's what thinkin' deeply does for you."

"How would you know when you're incapable of such a thing?"

Lukins squared up to him. "You callin' me iggerant?"

"No," said Skoyles, grabbing both men by the scruff of their necks. "Now let's have an end to this nonsensical bickering. You're comrades in arms, not sworn enemies. Keep out of each other's way until you can behave in a civilized fashion—or I'll bang your silly heads together." He pushed them apart. "Understood?"

"Yes, Captain," said Wolverton apologetically.

"Lukins?"

"As long as Wolvie don't call me—"

"*Lukins!*" snapped Skoyles, cutting him off. "Did you hear me?"

"Yes, sir," Lukins said reluctantly.

"Then settle your differences before I do it for you."

Skoyles waited until the men had gone off in opposite directions before he continued on his way. While he had great respect for Burgoyne, he was inclined to agree with Wolverton's estimate of Riedesel. Once the favorite staff officer of the duke of Brunswick, the German was a more versatile soldier than General John Burgoyne. He could be mocked for his emphasis on drilling his troops but he was not prone to some of the overhasty judgments that the British commander occasionally made. Skoyles was reassured by the presence of the German troops. Unlike the Indians, they could always be relied on in a battle.

As he strolled toward the house where Burgoyne had set up his headquarters, the first person whom he saw was the man who owned the place. Colonel Philip Skene, one of the loyalist commanders, was staring at a fresh grave that had been dug in his garden. He was a big, burly Scotsman in his early fifties with a wealth of military experience behind him, but he looked a sorry figure now. The sound of footsteps made him glance up and he contrived a weak smile.

"Captain Skoyles," he said. "Welcome to my home—what's left of it, that is. The rebels were untidy guests. They made rather a mess of the house." He gazed down at the grave. "And they even had the gall to move my dear wife from her last resting place."

"Your wife, Colonel?"

"She was buried in the cellar in a lead coffin. That was far too big a temptation for soldiers who were short of ammunition, so they dug up my wife, brought her out here, and melted the lead down to make musket balls." He turned to Skoyles and grimaced. "I don't relish the idea of being shot by a piece of my wife's coffin."

"I can understand that, sir."

"Still," said Skene, brightening a little, "at least I can occupy my own home again. This is a wonderful spot, Captain—rich soil, an endless supply of good timber, and a lake nearby that's a busy highway for trade and travel. I spent years developing this site. I own well over fifty thousand acres and created my own community here."

"Largely made up from Scots, I'm told," Skoyles observed.

"We have the pioneer spirit."

"I know. My mother was Scots. I inherited that spirit from her."

"There was already a barracks and a blockhouse when I came here," said Skene with a proprietary wave of his arm. "I added a sawmill, an iron forge, a coal house, a stone barn and stables, and, of course," he went on, indicating the two-and-a half-story limestone building behind him, "my home, Skenesborough House."

"It's an impressive achievement, Colonel."

"I like this country. Wouldn't dream of living anywhere else."

"I've a feeling that I'll see out my days in America as well."

"Let's put these rebels in their place first, shall we?"

"Yes, Colonel."

Skoyles took his leave and went into the house. When he was admitted to General Burgoyne, he was amazed to find him in a room that had a wooden coffin on a table. Seated in a corner, Burgoyne beckoned the visitor across to him. He gestured toward the coffin.

"Allow me to introduce Mrs. Skene to you, Captain."

Skoyles was bewildered. "The colonel's wife?"

"The colonel's *mother*," said Burgoyne cheerfully. "It appears that, by the terms of a will, the old lady will continue to receive an annuity as long as she is above ground. Philip Skene is a true Scotsman. He'll not part with a single penny if he can find a way to hold on to it. So—there she lies—dead as a doornail but still able to earn her keep."

Skoyles was amused. "Colonel Skene is a strange man, sir."

"Strange but resourceful," said Burgoyne. "Who else would travel through this wilderness, attended by black servants in splendid livery and powdered wigs? Eccentric he may be, but he's also invaluable to us. He knows the area like the back of his grasping hand. That's why I made him my political adviser."

"A wise choice, General."

"I think so. This house of his is certainly more comfortable than a tent or a cabin aboard ship—even if we do have to share it with the late Mrs. Skene." He chuckled quietly. "By the way, I hope that you'll join us for a game of cards this evening."

"Thank you, sir. I will."

"Excellent. You always provide a challenge." He glanced down at the sheaf of drawings in his hand. "Been taking another look at your friend's handiwork. Man has a sharp eye."

"Not much eludes Ezekiel Proudfoot," said Skoyles. "He did much more than draw some sketches at Ticonderoga. He took careful note of everything that went on at the fort."

"Was he willing to part with the information?"

"When he'd been sufficiently persuaded, sir."

"What have you learned?"

Taking a deep breath, Skoyles retailed the intelligence that he had gathered from Proudfoot, giving details of troop numbers, decisions made by General St. Clair, and the likely movement of the garrison now that it had been forced to make a detour around Skenesborough. Burgoyne was struck by his ability to remember so much without needing any notes. When Skoyles had finished, the general congratulated him.

"Well done, Captain," he said. "You've discovered exactly what I'd expected and wanted to have confirmed. There is, however, one point that puzzles me."

"What's that, General?"

"According to this fellow, Ezekiel Proudfoot, we'd be deluding ourselves if we expected any loyalist support in the surrounding countryside. Colonel Skene is of the opposite opinion," said Burgoyne. "He's convinced that, once people know they have the protection of the British army, they'll flock to join us."

"Ezekiel poured scorn on that notion, General."

"Perhaps he was deliberately misleading us."

"I think not, sir."

"We need additional men. They must come from somewhere."

"The most we could expect to recruit is a mere handful."

"Then why does Skene argue to the contrary?"

"You'll have to take that up with the colonel."

"What's your feeling?"

"That it would be foolish to count on many coming forward, sir."

"Even though they can clearly see that we have the upper hand?" said Burgoyne. "In the past, I know, some Tories have been tarred and feathered. Others have been shot."

"Or hanged."

"While they fear such reprisals, as now, any loyalists will obviously keep their heads down. Released from that fear, they'll rush to throw in their lot with us."

"I hope that proves to be true, General."

"You sound unconvinced."

"In all honesty, I am, sir."

"Then let me put a question to you," said Burgoyne, sitting back. "Whose judgment do we trust? That of a man who's deliberately stirring up resistance against us with his artistic skills?" He dropped the sketches onto the chair beside him. "Or that of someone who joined the British army as a boy of eleven and served it loyally for three decades? Ezekiel Proudfoot or Philip Skene?" He nodded toward the coffin. "My vote goes to the man who has the wit to keep the body of his mother above ground in order to benefit from her annuity. Colonel Skene has a nose for business. Don't you agree?"

"Yes, General. But he has been away from the area for some time."

"Proudfoot or Skene? Who do you put your money on?"

Skoyles needed a few moments to consider his decision.

"Ezekiel Proudfoot," he said. "I think he's telling the truth."

Elizabeth Rainham was thrown into confusion. When she heard about the attempt made on Major Featherstone's life by one of his own men, she was deeply shocked. The thought that the man she was hoping to marry might have been shot in the back by a British soldier did not merely alarm her. It showed her that Harry Featherstone was not as universally respected as she had assumed. Elizabeth was even more disturbed to learn that he had not even expressed his thanks to the person who saved his life. So ruffled was she by what she heard from Nan Wyatt that she went in search of Featherstone with the other woman trotting beside her.

Unable to find him in his tent, the two of them decided to look elsewhere for the major. It was then that they chanced upon Jamie Skoyles, returning from his meeting with General Burgoyne. Pleased to see her again, he gave an involuntary smile. Elizabeth was disturbed to see the bruising that still marked his face.

"Good day, Captain," she said.

"Miss Rainham."

"I wonder if I might speak with you for a moment?"

"Of course," he replied, mystified by her sudden interest in him. "Would you care to step into my tent? It will afford us a little privacy."

Elizabeth hesitated. "Very well," she decided after a pause. She followed him across to his tent. "You can stay outside, Nan."

"Yes, ma'am," said Nan dutifully.

Skoyles opened the flap and held it back so that she could step inside. When he joined her in the tent, he felt an immediate frisson. Alone with her for the first time, sharing a confined space, gave him a new awareness of her charms. Elizabeth displayed a blend of curiosity and embarrassment, looking around the tent with interest while knowing she should not really be there alone with him. She fell back on a stilted formality.

"Is it true that you were involved in an incident at Hubbardton?"

"A battle is rather more than an incident, Miss Rainham," he said.

"I was referring to Major Featherstone."

"Ah, I see."

"My understanding is that you saved his life."

"I prevented one of our men from killing a fellow officer, that's all."

"That is not all, Captain," she said, gazing intently at him. "You rescued Major Featherstone by your prompt action and you spared me the most unspeakable suffering. I'll never be able to thank you enough."

"Kind of you to say so, Miss Rainham."

"And I must also thank you on behalf of Major Featherstone," she resumed, hands twitching nervously by her sides. "I'm led to believe that he has been unduly remiss in that respect."

"I need no thanks from the major," said Skoyles.

"You're entitled to far more than that."

"Take that up with him, Miss Rainham. Though I should perhaps warn you that you may not find him very forthcoming. As far as I'm concerned, the whole business is best forgotten."

"Forgotten?" she echoed in wonderment. "You save a man's life on the battlefield and you want to forget it? Did it have no more significance than that, Captain?" Her eyes were glistening with subdued passion. "Tell me what happened."

"The major can do that, Miss Rainham."

"If he'd wanted to, he would already have done so. Besides, I want to hear it from your own lips. All that I have is a second-hand account that was picked up by Nan, my maid. She heard very few details."

"I suspect she heard enough."

"What do you mean?"

"That some of the facts are too distressing to recall," said Skoyles, not wishing to add to her discomfort. "I prefer to leave the incident where it belongs—firmly in the past."

Skoyles was in a dilemma. Wanting her to stay so that he could relish her company, he was loath to talk about the one thing that would keep her there. There was a silent battle of wills. Elizabeth tried hard to persuade him but he refused to comply. When she looked at the injuries to his face again, she assumed that he had picked them up at Hubbardton.

"This is not the first time, is it?" she said with admiration. "You've distinguished yourself on the battlefield before."

"I'm a soldier. I do what I have to do."

"Not everyone would have acted as bravely as you did in a skirmish some years ago." She smiled at his look of surprise. "Brigadier General Fraser told me about it. You not only took on four enemy soldiers single-handed, you rescued a wounded officer and carried him to safety under fire. That was how you earned your lieutenancy—or is that something else you prefer to keep firmly in the past?"

"No, Miss Rainham," he confessed readily. "As it happens, I cherish that particular memory. It was an important event in my career."

"And so is this. You should receive some recognition."

"The circumstances are very different."

"But the outcome was the same. You saved a man's life."

Skoyles was touched that she had taken the trouble to ask his commander about him and flattered by her praise, but he still refused to provide her with the details she wanted. He could imagine how she would react if he told her that the person to whom she was betrothed had pounded the skull of a dead British soldier in a fit of uncontrollable rage.

"Thank you for coming, Miss Rainham," he said.

"It was not really my place to do so."

"You'll always be a more welcome sight than Major Featherstone."

"That's an improper remark, Captain," she scolded. "You know my reason for being in this country and you should respect it."

"I do, believe me."

"Then let us leave the matter there."

"If you say so, Miss Rainham."

It was her turn to be perplexed. Knowing that she should leave, she could somehow not bring herself to do so. Her mind was telling her one thing but her body was countermanding the order. All she could do was to stand there in a state of indecision, wondering what it was about the rough-edged captain that made him so oddly appealing. There was no battle of wills between them now, just an exploration of each other's eyes, a soundless declaration of something beyond casual interest.

The mood was broken by the arrival of Major Harry Featherstone.

"Elizabeth!" he exclaimed, stepping abruptly into the tent. "What, in the devil's name, are you doing here?"

"Miss Rainham asked to speak with me, sir," said Skoyles.

"I'm not talking to you," snarled the newcomer before changing to a gruff politeness. "Well, Elizabeth?"

"It's exactly as Captain Skoyles told you," she replied. "I wanted to have a word with him."

"*Alone?* In here?"

"He was kind enough to invite me in."

"Then you should have refused," said Featherstone, barely able to conceal his annoyance. "Or, at the very least, your maid should have been in here with you."

Elizabeth bridled. "I need no instructions on decorum."

"It seems that you do."

"Harry!"

"This is not what I expect of you."

"The fault was mine, Major," said Skoyles, coming to her aid. "I should have spoken to Miss Rainham outside."

"You should not have spoken to her at all!"

"Surely, that's a decision that only Miss Rainham should make."

"I agree," she said spiritedly, "but it's not one that I would even have had to consider if you'd been more honest with me, Harry. Why didn't you tell me that Captain Skoyles had come to your rescue in the nick of time at Hubbardton?"

"The opportunity never presented itself," he said dismissively.

"But we've spoken on a number of occasions."

"I didn't wish to upset you with unsavory details."

"It's far more upsetting to be kept deliberately in the dark," she argued. "How do you think I felt when Nan told me what happened? I was distressed, Harry. You might have been killed."

"We'll discuss this later, Elizabeth."

"Captain Skoyles saved your life."

"I'd like you to go now," he said with studied civility. "I need to speak to the captain alone." When she hovered, he became more forceful. "Goodbye, Elizabeth."

"Goodbye, Miss Rainham," said Skoyles.

She was plainly discomfited by the turn of events but she accepted that it was no place to start an argument with Featherstone. After giving Skoyles a smile of farewell, she went swiftly out of the tent.

The major immediately rounded on Skoyles. "Don't you *dare* do that again!"

"Do what, Major?"

"Speak to Miss Rainham in private."

"She raised no objection herself," said Skoyles.

"Well, I do," asserted Featherstone. "A very strong objection."

"I could hardly turn the lady away when she asked to talk to me. That would have been ungentlemanly. And I didn't go in search of Miss Rainham, sir. It was she who came here."

"What did you tell her?"

107

"That's between us," Skoyles said bluntly.

"What did you tell her—damn you!" Featherstone roared. "Her maid said that the pair of you had been in here for several minutes. Were you portraying me as a helpless victim at Hubbardton? Did you boast about how you just happened to see Private Higgs before I did?"

"No, Major. I declined to go into any detail."

"Is that what Miss Rainham wanted?"

"Yes, sir. As far as I'm concerned, the incident is best consigned to history. I said as much to her."

"You gave no account of what occurred on the battlefield?"

"None at all," said Skoyles. "Miss Rainham is still unaware of the savagery with which you attacked Private Higgs."

"The man tried to kill me!"

"That was no reason to assault him. He'd already been shot dead."

"I don't have to answer to you, Skoyles," said Featherstone with vehemence. "Higgs got what he deserved, and there's an end to it. There was no need for Elizabeth—for Miss Rainham—to hear anything at all about the incident."

"It did not come from me, Major."

"Then where *did* it come from?"

"In truth, I've no idea. There were several witnesses."

"I'll find out which one of them spread this story. However," he added, straightening his shoulders, "that's not what brought me here. I came to ask if your interrogation of the prisoner was worthwhile."

"Extremely worthwhile, sir."

"Have you reported to General Burgoyne?"

"He was very pleased to hear what I'd gleaned from the man."

"He'll be less pleased when I talk to him."

"About what?"

"That friend of yours—Ezekiel Proudfoot. I knew that it was a mistake to bring him here. He should have been sent to Fort Ticonderoga under armed guard with the other prisoners."

"But he's no soldier," said Skoyles. "Ezekiel is a harmless artist."

"Harmless?"

"He poses no threat to us, Major."

"A peaceful man, is he?" mocked Featherstone.

"Ezekiel Proudfoot will give us no trouble."

"Not anymore, he won't—because he's no longer with us. The man you describe as harmless overpowered his guard and stole his musket."

Skoyles was astounded. "Ezekiel has *escaped?*"

"Yes, Captain," said Featherstone angrily, "and he's had time to take stock of our army. Thanks to you, he came here as a prisoner and escaped as a spy. Now get after the bastard at once and bring him back here—alive or dead!"

CHAPTER EIGHT

The search began immediately. With a dozen redcoats and a couple of Indian scouts, Captain Jamie Skoyles went off in pursuit of Ezekiel Proudfoot. Two major difficulties confronted them. The fugitive had over an hour's start on the posse, and they had no idea in which direction he had gone. Skoyles had to wrestle with an additional problem. He found himself almost wanting his former friend to get away. Though Proudfoot was committed to the rebel cause, he was no enemy soldier with a blood lust. He was a man with a genuine love of his country and an urge to shake it free from the grip of an army that had slaughtered his wife and child. Prompted by revenge and the desire for liberty, he was doing exactly what Skoyles would have done in his place. He was hitting back in the way he knew best.

The circumstances of his escape defined the man. Overpowering the guard, he had made no attempt to kill him. Proudfoot simply knocked the man unconscious long enough to take his uniform, bind, then gag him. His disguise helped him to slip through the British lines and vanish into the forest. Skoyles was sure that he had not stolen the musket in order to kill anyone who went after him. It was taken solely as a defense against the wild animals. If caught, Skoyles believed, he would surrender the weapon without a fight. Ezekiel Proudfoot was no soldier.

The search party made what speed it could. Ahead of the redcoats, the Indians moved along at a steady lope as they tried to pick up a trail. Skoyles followed on horseback with his soldiers behind him, fanned out in a wide arc that nevertheless left each man within sight of his fellows. Believing that Proudfoot would make for Castleton, they had set off in an easterly direction. After a couple of miles, however, they had found no scent of their quarry. Skoyles ordered a sweep to the south, guessing that Proudfoot must instead be heading for Fort Anne. As the redcoats combed the forest, they heard the howling of wolves in the distance.

The farther they went, the more certain Skoyles became that they would never catch up with Proudfoot. He would not only be miles ahead of them, he was traveling through woodland he had known since childhood. Skoyles was soon obliged to dismount in order to lead his horse. They had found the route taken by the American rebels who had departed in haste from Skenesborough and felled trees in their wake to delay any pursuit. The search party was slowed to a painful crawl. Where tree trunks did not block their way, they had to wade through steamy swamps, black with clouds of angry insects.

Skoyles could hear the protests of his men getting louder all the time. Soaked by the water, stung by mosquitoes, pestered by gnats, and frustrated by obstacles in their path, they were getting farther away from the safety of Skenesborough. The Indians finally called a halt. They had seen something up ahead that alerted them to danger, and they came back to report to Skoyles. Tethering his horse to a branch, he followed the scouts until they reached a small clearing. Through the trees on the other side, he could make out what looked like the figure of a man, hanging from a bough. With his sword in hand, Skoyles inched his way around the clearing with the Indians at his back.

When he got closer, he realized what he had seen. It was the stolen British uniform, stuffed with brushwood and dangling from a tree. Having served its purpose, it had been abandoned by Ezekiel Proudfoot, but not before it had been shredded with a knife and covered with excrement. Skoyles was positive that the desecration was not the work of Proudfoot. Evidently, he had met up with some of the rebels who lurked in the forest to pick off any British targets that presented themselves. The fact that the red coat had no holes in it showed that the fugitive had not been mistakenly shot. Realizing that Proudfoot had got away, Skoyles felt a curious mixture of disappointment and pleasure.

"That's enough," he decided. "I'm calling off the search."

Major Harry Featherstone took a long time to compose himself before he called on Elizabeth Rainham. She was in her tent with Nan Wyatt, sitting in front of a mirror propped up on a rickety table while the maid brushed her hair. As soon as the visitor announced himself from outside, Nan put the brush down and left, collecting a censorious glance from him as she did so. Elizabeth got to her feet.

"Come in, Harry," she called.

He entered the tent, smiled fondly, then took her hand to kiss it.

"This is no place for you, Elizabeth," he said, looking around. "Why didn't you take a room at the house when it was offered to you? It would've have been much more comfortable."

"I had no wish to be under the same roof as that woman."

"You've nothing to fear from Mrs. Mallard."

"It's not fear that stopped me," she said. "It was disapproval. If I'd moved into the house, I'd be countenancing the arrangement that General Burgoyne has reached with another man's wife, and I'm simply not able to do that."

"You'll come to accept it in time."

"No, Harry. I can assure you of that."

"Very well," he said, careful not to argue with her. "What I really came to do is to offer you my apology. I was unnecessarily brusque earlier on and didn't mean to speak to you like that."

"It was rather upsetting."

"Skoyles was to blame. He caught me on the raw."

"You were extremely rude to him."

"He deserved it, Elizabeth."

"What—after saving your life?" she asked incredulously. "That's a strange way to repay the captain for what he did. And you still haven't explained to my satisfaction why you made no mention of the incident."

"I told you. I didn't wish you to hear about it."

"Why not?"

"Because of the danger I was in, Elizabeth. I thought you'd be terrified to hear that one of my own men became so crazed that he attempted to kill me. Combat has peculiar effects on some people. Private Higgs was one of them."

"Every time you see action, there's danger," she said reasonably. "I know that and I accept it as part of military life. What I never envisaged was that an officer like you ran the risk of being shot by a British soldier, a man who's trained and paid to fight at your command. It's frightening, Harry. Yet, from what I hear, this is not an isolated case."

"What do you mean?"

"Nan said that other British officers have sometimes been killed or wounded in battle by someone who's actually on their side."

"Who told her that?"

"Sergeant Caffrey."

"Ah," he said, teeth clenched. "So that's who it was—Tom Caffrey."

"Nan has become friendly with a woman called Polly Bragg. It was she who first mentioned the incident to Nan. She was amazed that I hadn't heard anything about it. So—for that matter—am I."

"The whole thing was over in a flash," he insisted. "Why make so much of it?"

"Because I want you to stay alive, Harry."

He smiled. "Oh, I intend to be around for a long while yet. I have such enticing prospects ahead of me, don't I?" he said, taking her hand to squeeze it between both palms. "Am I forgiven?"

"For what?"

"Trying to protect you from something I felt you shouldn't know."

"As long as it never happens again," she said, enjoying the feel of his warm hands. "I'm not a child anymore. I'll not have a fit of the vapors if you tell me what happens on the battlefield. I want to know *anything* that concerns Major Harry Featherstone. It's my right, isn't it?"

"Of course." He kissed her hand again. "Am I forgiven now?"

"Yes."

"Good." His facial muscles tightened. "With regard to your maid, I suggest that you forbid her to go anywhere near Polly Bragg."

"Why? She likes the woman."

"Do you know who Mrs. Bragg is?" he asked. "She was the wife of a corporal—though I doubt very much that their marriage had the Church's blessing. In any case, he was her second 'husband.' When the corporal died, she took up with our assistant surgeon, Tom Caffrey. Do you understand what I'm saying, Elizabeth?"

"What?"

"The woman is practically a whore."

"Harry!" she protested.

"Well, what other word can I use? She's a camp follower, an unpaid harlot, someone with a compulsion to have a soldier in her bed. Polly Bragg is like dozens of others who follow the British army. Ten women per company is the specified number for us, and they're certainly not all on the Married Roll."

"Mrs. Mallard is."

"That's irrelevant."

"Not in my view."

"We're talking about Polly Bragg," he said, reining in his temper. "I'm sorry to disenchant you, but her friendship with Nan was not accidental. It was very deliberate. Mrs. Bragg was obviously suborned by Sergeant Caffrey."

"Why?"

"Because the sergeant is a close friend of Captain Skoyles," he said, spitting out the name. "Skoyles is behind all this. He's taken an unhealthy interest in you, Elizabeth. Since he can't get close to you himself, he finds out everything he can by using Polly Bragg as his spy."

"No," she said, refusing to believe it. "Captain Skoyles strikes me as an honorable man. He'd never do such a thing."

"Oh, yes, he would. But he won't get the opportunity again."

"Why not?"

"Because you'll cut off his supply of information at the source. Your maid is never to speak to Mrs. Bragg again, do you hear?" he ordered. "It's not the innocent friendship that it appears."

"Nan clearly thinks so."

"Then she's been duped. As for Captain Skoyles," he added darkly, "leave him to me. Since he's too pigheaded to listen to a verbal warning, it will have to be delivered more forcefully."

When he returned to Skenesborough with his men, Jamie Skoyles first reported to Brigadier Fraser that they had been unable to recapture the prisoner and that he had thought it unwise to pursue him deeper into the forest. Tired, perspiring freely, and itching from insect bites, Skoyles then repaired to his tent to wash, shave, and change into a clean uniform. He was troubled by the sense of relief he felt that Ezekiel Proudfoot had eluded them, and he struggled to explain it to himself. Was he simply sorry for the man, or did he have a grudging admiration for the way he had nailed his colors to the American cause? Had he caught any other rebel prisoner trying to escape, Skoyles would have shot him without compunction. First and foremost, the captain was a British soldier with a heightened sense of duty.

Why did Proudfoot make him react so differently? It was much more than the pull of an old affection. The engraver served the enemy, producing prints that would glorify the actions of the patriots while denigrating those of the British. Spread far and wide through the newspapers, Proudfoot's work was an effective recruiting tool. In taking him out of commission, Skoyles would be removing an important weapon of the American cause, yet he could still not bring himself to regret the man's escape. It puzzled him.

Having made himself presentable again, he set off toward Colonel Skene's house for an evening at the card table. Sergeant Tom Caffrey came striding around the angle of a tent to intercept him.

"Hold on, Jamie," he said. "I need to speak to you."

"I'm late already. General Burgoyne has asked me to play with them again and that's an invitation I can't refuse. There's money to win."

"Or to lose."

"I'm prepared for that as well," said Skoyles easily.

"Not that it happens very often, mind you. When it comes to cards, you've got the luck of Lucifer. What are you going to do with all your winnings?" asked Caffrey. "You surely don't still have that dream of buying a little land in America?"

"No, Tom," replied Skoyles with a grin. "I want to buy a *lot* of land."

"Only if we crush the rebellion out of these hotheads."

"Whatever happens, this is the country for me."

"Then I'll do my best to keep you alive to enjoy it." Caffrey's face clouded. "There's something you need to know, Jamie."

"Can't it wait until tomorrow?"

"That may be too late. You have to be ready for them."

"Them?"

"I've just had Dan Lukins in my tent," said Caffrey. "He claims that he tripped over and hit something hard as he fell, but the little devil had obviously been in a fight again."

"I think I can guess who his opponent was—Private Wolverton."

"Exactly. I bullied the story out of Lukins as I patched him up. It was over a watch, apparently. Wolverton took it from a dead rebel officer at Hubbardton and was delighted with his booty. It was a fine watch."

"Then Lukins stole it."

"Inevitably."

"There's always some bone of contention between those two," said Skoyles, wanting to get off. "Excuse me, Tom. I don't have time to listen to this now."

"You must," asserted the other, putting out a hand to detain him. "The fight took place behind some baggage wagons, it seems, where there was nobody about. Wolverton was furious at the theft of the watch, even though he'd stolen it himself, of course."

"Did he batter Lukins?"

"Yes, Jamie. He made that ugly little face look even uglier. It was covered in blood. Wolverton eventually knocked him down, then got his watch back. All that Lukins could do was to lie there on the ground, dazed and bleeding."

"So?"

"It meant that he wasn't seen by the two men who slipped behind the wagons for a private conversation—about Captain Jamie Skoyles."

Skoyles was suddenly interested. "*Me?*"

"Lukins recognized Harry Featherstone, but he'd never seen the other fellow before. One of the Canadian axmen, he thought."

"Go on."

"The major asked the man if he'd like to earn some money by setting upon a certain officer and giving him a sound beating." He gave a mirthless laugh. "He did confess that it was a job for two of them as you wouldn't be an altogether defenseless victim."

"Coming from Featherstone, I take that as a compliment."

"Lukins swears that it's due to happen tonight," said Caffrey. "On your way back from the card game at the house, when you've had plenty of Gentleman Johnny's claret and are completely off guard."

"Thanks, Tom. I appreciate the warning."

"Count on me to be there as well."

"I'll make sure I don't drink too much of that claret."

"See if you can smuggle out a bottle for me."

"You deserve a dozen bottles for this," said Skoyles.

"Don't forget Dan Lukins. He's the man who overheard them."

"But only because Wolverton had that fight with him. I'm grateful to both of them. Lukins may have lost a little blood, but he's prevented mine from being spilled too freely tonight. Forewarned is forearmed." He straightened his shoulders. "At least, I know what to expect now."

"Two of us against two of them," said Caffrey gleefully.

"I wonder how much the major is paying them."

"They only get their money when their work is done."

"Not a bloody chance!" said Skoyles with a smile. "I do believe that I'm beginning to feel sorry for them."

General John Burgoyne was in his element. Seated in the dining room at the house, he looked around the table at the senior officers who were gathered there and raised his glass in yet another toast.

"To King and Country!" he declared.

"King and Country!" they echoed in unison.

Glasses were emptied, then replenished with more wine. Everyone was in good humor. The atmosphere was relaxed and convivial. Burgoyne and his guests might have been carousing in a London club rather than pausing in the middle of a campaign. As the owner of the house, Colonel Skene was, technically, the host, but he was happy to cede that role to his commanding officer. Alongside the two of them at the table were Brigadier Simon Fraser, General William Phillips, and Major Harry Featherstone. They wanted to enjoy the break in hostilities before moving on to what they were convinced would be further victories.

Featherstone leaned over slightly in the direction of Burgoyne.

"Have you had chance to consider my request, General?" he asked.

"Forgotten what it was, Harry," Burgoyne joked. "How much did you want to borrow from me this time?" The others laughed. "You sought my permission, didn't you?"

"Yes, General."

"Colonel Skene might be the best person to consult. He knows the temper and the geography of this wilderness far better than we do. What do you think, Colonel?" said Burgoyne. "Harry wishes to escort Miss Rainham to visit her uncle, who has land somewhere to the northeast of us. His name is Lansdale—David Lansdale."

"I know the fellow," said Skene heartily. "A trueborn Englishman. It would be wrong to claim him as a friend exactly, but, then, most of my neighbors find me a trifle outlandish, if not downright bizarre." There was general amusement at the remark. "Lansdale owns couple of thousand acres near Bitter Creek, best part of a day's march away."

"Should I sanction a visit there?"

"It would not be undertaken simply to enable Elizabeth to meet her uncle," said Featherstone quickly. "Our principal aim would be to find recruits. As well as three sons, Mr. Lansdale has many workmen, tenants, and slaves on his estate. And there's a village nearby, I believe."

"We can certainly count on his loyalty," Burgoyne affirmed. "Met him once at a family gathering, many years ago. Elizabeth was no more than five or six at the time. For some reason, Lansdale was about to sail to the colonies, start a new life here. Never understood why."

Philip Skene beamed. "I do, General," he said, tapping his chest, "because I share David Lansdale's instincts. By all accounts, he's done very well for himself, and I'd be surprised if he didn't furnish us with some men and some horses."

"Is it safe to travel to Bitter Creek?"

"Oh, yes—as safe as it is for me to look for recruits in Castleton tomorrow. The rebels have fled to the south or gone much farther east. Some have even deserted to join us—the most encouraging sign of all."

"More to the point," said Burgoyne complacently, "loyalists are starting to trickle in at last. We still need plenty more, of course, so I'm inclined to let Harry go and find them for us."

"Thank you, General," said Featherstone.

"Be sure to ask David Lansdale if he remembers me."

"Nobody would ever forget you, sir."

"You stick in the mind in perpetuity," Fraser added, raising a glass to his commander, "like a first beautiful love affair."

"I've had several of those in my time," Burgoyne confessed.

Jamie Skoyles walked in on the laughter. After apologizing for his lateness, he took the empty seat at the table and was immediately given a glass of claret. Everyone except Featherstone offered a cordial welcome. Though he was the junior officer there, Skoyles did not feel in any way overawed. Among fellow gamblers, rank did not apply.

Burgoyne reached for his glass. "I spy another toast, gentlemen," he announced. "To Captain Skoyles—the hero of Hubbardton."

"I'll drink to that," said Fraser, willingly.

"Captain Skoyles!" they chorused.

Featherstone joined in the toast without enthusiasm. Noting his reluctance, Burgoyne clicked his tongue reproachfully.

"Come, come, Harry," he admonished. "Skoyles saved your life. *You* should be the one who proposed the toast and not me."

"I'm very grateful to him," said Featherstone, forcing the words out.

"So are we all. Hate to lose a splendid officer like you. Well, my friends," he went on, picking up a pack of cards from the table, "are we ready to do battle? I suggest some games of faro and macao until two of you retire hurt, then the last four of us standing can turn to whist."

"You seem to assume that you'll be one of the four," noted Skene.

"I can play cards all night," boasted the other.

"Even when someone is waiting for you in bed?"

Burgoyne chuckled. "The lady will not be neglected."

A privileged outsider, Skoyles always enjoyed his evenings at the card table. He was not only accepted by the others—apart from Harry Featherstone—he was able to join in the table talk, ranging, as it did, from inconsequential gossip to serious discussion of military strategy with occasional lapses into drunken obscenity. When it came to appetite and capacity for wine, port, and brandy, Skoyles could match anyone there, but he was careful to restrict himself that evening. Featherstone, by contrast, was in no mood to hold back, drinking hard and shooting him sly glances from time to time. They were studiously ignored.

Unlike the others, Skoyles was not a man of personal wealth with money to throw carelessly away on the turn of a card. What allowed him to compete with them was the fact that he had built up some substantial winnings over the years, much of it coming from some of the very people at his elbow now. In his experience, nothing revealed the true character of a man as comprehensively as a game of cards. It stripped away the outer covering and revealed the essence of a person.

General John Burgoyne was a born gambler—bold, impetuous, unwilling to accept defeat. Whenever he lost, he tried to double the stakes. There was a sophisticated recklessness about him. Nobody would have guessed that his father, ruined by gambling, had died in prison after being been hounded there by his creditors. Simon Fraser was more cautious, the dashing soldier of the

119

battlefield turned into a watchful and calculating player. William Phillips was the most ebullient man there, laughing uproariously when he won and using the ripest language when he did not. Having made a career out of amassing wealth, Philip Skene was not ready to part with any of it lightly, playing with a high seriousness and taking little part in the conversation so that he could devote all his attention to the cards.

Skoyles had played with Harry Featherstone enough times to know that gambling brought out the worst in him. Drinking far too much at too fast a rate, the major was an erratic player whose attention frequently wandered for a fatal second or two. His language could be as coarse as that of William Phillips. During games of whist, Skoyles had learned to read his face and guess what cards Featherstone was holding.

The six of them had been playing for half an hour before talk turned once more to the campaign. Burgoyne emptied another glass of claret and sat back with contentment.

"This is how a war should be conducted," he said. "A short, sharp victory followed by a decent interval during which we can celebrate our success in the appropriate way."

"I still believe that we should have barked at their heels when we had them on the run," Phillips opined. "The rebels will have time to lick their wounds and call upon their militias to reinforce them."

"I agree with General Burgoyne," said Featherstone. "We have the finest army in the world and they know it. That's why they scampered off like frightened rabbits. We can destroy them, as and when we choose."

"I have more respect for them than that, Major," said Skoyles.

"So do I," Fraser added. "They gave us a fright at Hubbardton."

"We won the battle," Burgoyne contended. "That's what matters."

"Had we chased them harder," said Phillips, emitting a snort of disgust when he turned over a card, "we might have finished them off properly and brought this damnable war to an end."

"We need time for all of our supplies to be brought up, William. In any case, too rapid a pursuit would be unwise. Colonel John Hill discovered that when he headed for Fort Anne with too few men. They were lucky not to be routed. The rebels will not get away," said Burgoyne calmly. "We'll hunt every last one of them down when we've built a road through the forest. That, alas, may take some time."

"I can vouch for that, General," said Skoyles, recalling the search for Ezekiel Proudfoot. "There are obstacles almost every step of the way, and we'll have to construct dozens of bridges. I'm not convinced that the overland route is the one to take."

"Nobody sought your opinion, Captain," said Featherstone.

Burgoyne was tolerant. "We're all friends here, Harry," he pointed out. "Everyone is entitled to speak. Never let it be said that I was deaf to sensible advice."

"What Skoyles is about to advocate is not sensible."

"How do you know until we've heard it?" He smiled invitingly at Skoyles. "Well, Captain?"

Skoyles was well informed. "Our baggage train is too large," he said, "and we have a desperate shortage of horses and oxen to pull it. We have one hundred and eighty carts, each carrying eight hundred pounds of stores. Then there are a dozen heavy guns to drag with tons of shot and powder. If we travel overland, we move at a snail's pace and stretch our supply line to the limit. Water is our best ally," he urged. "We should sail down Lake George, as the bulk of our artillery will do. I know that we'd have to transport the boats across the portage at Ticonderoga and overland from Fort George to the Hudson River, but I still believe it would be the better route."

"An absurd suggestion," snapped Featherstone.

"Not at all," Fraser countered. "It has much to commend it. Jamie is only saying what many others think."

"Well, it's not what *I* think," Skene ventured, keeping his beady eyes on the next card that was turned over. "We should hack our way through the forest to Fort Edward and gather new recruits and fresh horses as we do so. I've no qualms about provisions. We'll gather all we need from the hundreds of loyalists hereabouts."

"It could take us weeks to reach the fort," said Skoyles, "and we'd lay ourselves open to attack from sharpshooters hidden in the trees. Those swamps are very unhealthy—we'd lose several men to disease. Water is a much safer way to travel."

Fraser nodded. "It's an argument that's worth considering."

"Only to be discarded, sir," said Featherstone. "To reach Lake George, we'd have to return to Ticonderoga and that would be seen by the army as a retrograde step."

"Quite so, Harry," said Burgoyne, bringing the discussion to an end on a peremptory note. "An army marches on confidence and we'd only weaken it by withdrawing from Skenesborough now. We press on, gentlemen," he decreed, raising a magisterial finger. "You all heard my proclamation: We never retreat. And a return to Ticonderoga would be perceived by our friends and enemies alike as a retreat." He turned over a card and laughed. "Ah, I appear to have won yet again!"

Philip Skene was the first to quit the table. Having held his own for most of the evening, he began to lose money and elected to cut his losses. Simon Fraser was the next to leave, pleading fatigue and wishing to be up early on the morrow. The four still at the table played whist for an hour or so until Burgoyne remembered that Mrs. Lucinda Mallard was awaiting him. Since it had been a profitable evening for the general, it seemed like an excellent time to bring the proceedings to a close. Skoyles was ready to do so even though he had won only a small amount.

The real losers had been William Phillips and Harry Featherstone. While the two of them remained behind to exchange profanities and console themselves with brandy, Skoyles slipped away into the night. Featherstone could not resist a smirk at his departure. Skoyles walked back through the camp, ready for an ambush and looking forward to some physical exercise. He got within yards of his tent before the attack came. Two burly figures suddenly charged up behind him out of the gloom and tried to grab him. Skoyles was ready for them. He swung round to face his attackers, catching the first man by his coat and hurling him to the ground.

Sergeant Tom Caffrey appeared out of nowhere to take on the fallen man, delivering a blow to his ear that sent him rolling over onto his back, then diving on top of him to pummel away with both fists. Skoyles, meanwhile, was grappling with the second assailant, a giant of a man who was intent on earning his reward by overpowering his victim with his superior strength. Pulling Skoyles toward him, he got in a couple of telling blows to his ribs. Skoyles winced and replied with a flurry of punches to the face that the huge Canadian took without flinching. When Skoyles dislodged a tooth, the man simply laughed and spat it out. The giant lunged forward to clasp his opponent in a bear hug, tightening his grip slowly to squeeze all the energy out of him.

Skoyles tried in vain to break his hold. Having knocked his own adversary unconscious, Caffrey jumped to his feet and came to the aid of his friend, but his help was not needed. Unable to break free, Skoyles put his head back then brought his forehead down sharply against the bridge of the man's nose, splitting it open and making him stagger backward. With a grunt of pain, the man steadied himself, wiped away the blood that was cascading down from his nostrils, then swung a massive leg in an attempt to kick Skoyles in the groin.

Had he made contact, the fight would have been over, but Skoyles had been in too many brawls to be caught unawares. Moving swiftly aside, he grabbed the man's foot and pulled it with all his might so that the Canadian fell to the ground with a dull thud, landing on some sharp stones that opened up a deep gash in his skull. Skoyles did not spare him. Twisting the man's ankle until he produced a yell of agony, he bent down to haul him up into a sitting position so that he could catch him on the chin with a thunderous uppercut. This time, the man did flinch. He flopped to the ground and stayed there.

Tom Caffrey had a serious complaint to make.

"You should have left that big bugger for me," he said.

Although he had lost a sizable amount of money at the card table, Harry Featherstone left the house in high spirits. His request to escort Elizabeth Rainham to see her uncle had been granted, he had drunk some excellent wine and brandy in the company of his commanding officer, and—most pleasing of all—a person against whom he had a grudge would by now have been beaten to a pulp by hired Canadian axmen. He had cause for satisfaction. As he rolled unsteadily along, he was grinning broadly.

Once inside his tent, however, his bonhomie vanished in a flash. By the light of the candle, he saw two men sprawled on the ground, each stained with blood and groaning in pain. Featherstone was incensed. Instead of handing out a severe beating to someone else, they had been the victims of assault themselves. Skoyles had obviously escaped his punishment. In leaving the wounded men in the major's tent, he was signaling that he knew exactly who their paymaster was.

"You idiots!" cried Featherstone, kicking one of them.

"You never told us there'd be *two* of them, Major," the man bleated. "Just give us our money and we'll get out of here."

"Yes," said the giant axman, holding his broken nose. "We deserve something for what we suffered out there tonight. We want our reward."

"Oh, you do, do you?" asked Featherstone. "Then you'll get it!"

Seizing a riding crop, he began to whip them unmercifully, driving them out of his tent like a pair of miscreant dogs. Featherstone's wrath knew no bounds. Jamie Skoyles had turned the tables on him, and the major took out his anger on the Canadians.

The next day brought in many more recruits, loyalists who had been sufficiently heartened by the success of the British army to declare their allegiance and who were brave enough to risk any reprisals against their families or their properties by the rebels. As he watched them stream in, Skoyles was not persuaded that all were genuine Tories. Some would be informers, sent by the enemy to get exact details of the strength of the army and liable to disappear when their work was done. Skoyles took particular note of those he felt were worth watching.

Some of the newcomers had unwelcome tales to tell of atrocities committed by the Indians. Ignoring the orders they had specifically been given by General Burgoyne, many of them had run riot. One report told of two white women being raped and of the Negro who had tried to protect them being scalped and left for dead. Another report claimed that Indian scouts had stolen drink and money from a house and killed a guard dog. A third story concerned the murder of a boy who had been herding his pigs in the forest. His scalp, too, hung from someone's belt.

Lieutenant Charles Westbourne was outraged by what he heard.

"They're nothing but unprincipled savages," he protested. "General Burgoyne should take them to task."

"He's done that repeatedly," said Skoyles, "but threats have no effect. The mistake lay in bringing them with us in the first place."

"I was appalled by their conduct at Ticonderoga, Captain. While we moved on, they stayed behind to plunder and drink—and you know the terrible effect that alcohol has on them. They behave like wild animals."

"General Burgoyne visited their camp this morning to remonstrate with them. I accompanied him, Lieutenant. What shocked us was the number of scalps hanging up to dry in the sun. Many of them probably came from innocent people who've taken no part in the hostilities."

The two men were standing between a row of tents in the middle of the camp. They moved aside to let a column of soldiers march past under the eye of their drill sergeant. Westbourne was unsettled.

"The Indians are supposed to scare the enemy," he said, "but they put the fear of death in me. What will they do next? Discipline is a concept that's entirely foreign to them. As for their appearance," he went on with a hint of a blush, "it beggars description. One of their chiefs is completely naked, except for a dead bird that covers his manhood. It's disgraceful, Captain. Imagine how distressing it would be if any of the ladies were to catch sight of him."

Skoyles laughed. "With respect, Lieutenant," he said, "I suspect that most of the women traveling with us are well accustomed by now to the sight of a naked man. They're more likely to be amused than upset. Nobody who trails after an army can retain her innocence indefinitely."

"That's certainly true of the camp followers," Westbourne agreed, "but I was thinking of people like Baroness Riedesel, Lady Harriet Acland, and Miss Elizabeth Rainham. They shouldn't be subjected to such a disagreeable spectacle. To be honest, I was rather troubled when I saw Major Featherstone set off at dawn."

"Why?"

"Because he had two Indian scouts with him, as indecently clad as most of their tribe. Do you see what I mean, Captain?" he asked. "Miss Rainham is forced to ride behind primitive men whose bare buttocks are clearly visible. She'll have to avert her eyes throughout the entire journey."

Jamie Skoyles also had reservations about the expedition that Elizabeth Rainham was undertaking, but his misgivings were not related to the Indians. His concern was that she was leaving the safety of the camp to make her way through country that might still harbor pockets of American rebels. Notwithstanding the presence of Harry Featherstone and a small detachment of redcoats, Skoyles feared for her safety. He was also envious of the major's opportunity to spend so much time with Elizabeth away from the stink and bustle of the camp at Skenesborough. Whatever else he told her on the way, Skoyles mused, Featherstone would certainly not mention the two Canadians whom he had hired to exact revenge on his behalf.

"It's her birthday in a month or so," said Westbourne.

"Who?"

"Miss Rainham."

"How do you know that?"

"The major told me. The lady will be twenty-one, apparently. When we reach Albany, there's even a possibility that they'll ask the chaplain to marry them."

Skoyles was alarmed. "Are you sure?"

"Major Featherstone sees no point in waiting," the other explained. "Miss Rainham's family talked of a wedding in Canterbury Cathedral but that would be a year or more away. I must say that she looks far too young to become a wife but, then, I hear that Baroness Riedesel was married when she was only *sixteen*. I find that extraordinary."

"Yet you can see how happy their marriage is, Lieutenant."

"Yes, I have noticed that," said Westbourne, "and, as you know, I rarely take account of such things. I'm not minded to take a wife myself, but I wish the major and Miss Rainham well. I'm sure they'll be extremely happy together."

"What on earth makes you think that?"

"Major Featherstone told me so himself. He's just dying to wed."

Elizabeth Rainham had not been deterred by the prospect of many hours in the saddle. Eager to see her uncle again after such a long time, she had brought letters for him from various members of her family. She was also relieved to get away from the camp at last to see something of the countryside at close quarters. Elizabeth was treating the visit to Bitter Creek both as an adventure and as a welcome chance to spend some time with the man she loved. Enjoying the sensation of freedom, she could not understand why Harry Featherstone was so distracted.

"Don't you feel well?" she asked.

"Yes, yes," he replied. "I'm fine."

"You've not spoken for the last few miles."

"I'm sorry, Elizabeth."

"Did you have too much to drink last night?" she teased. "Is that why you're so quiet today? How late did you play cards?"

"Not late at all," he said, managing a smile. "And I don't mean to neglect you. This is the best day I've had so far in the campaign. We're together at last, away from the hurly-burly of the camp."

"Yes, Harry."

"It seems like an age since we last went riding together."

"It was almost exactly two years ago to the day."

"How can you remember that?"

"Because I had good reason," she said with a nostalgic smile. "We rode across Chartham Downs on a Saturday afternoon. When we got back to the house, you proposed to me."

"Bless me!" he exclaimed. "Did I?"

"Don't tell me you've forgotten."

He laughed. "No, Elizabeth. You had the kindness to accept my hand." He looked around. "When you did that, however, I don't think you expected that our next ride would be through the Green Mountains."

Guided by two Indians and followed by twenty redcoats on foot, Featherstone and Elizabeth were mounted on two of the finest horses available. Though she rode sidesaddle, she had complete control over the animal and even kicked him into a brisk trot across open land. For the early part of their journey, they had accompanied Colonel Skene, who was going to Castleton with some German soldiers in search of recruits, but they were now on their own. With the redcoats to protect her, Elizabeth felt completely safe. The only thing that worried her was the howling of wolves up in the mountains.

"They sound as if they're getting closer," she said.

"Wolves are a menace. We shot dozens of them after the battle at Hubbardton. They came down in large packs to feed off the dead."

Elizabeth was shaken. "Feed off them? Surely, all those who died were given a decent burial?"

"Our own men were, of course," said Featherstone, "and we buried Colonel Francis out of respect for the fight he put up against us. But we didn't bother to dig graves for all the rebel casualties."

"You just left them on the battlefield? How revolting!"

"It was necessary. In any case, burying them would have been a wasted gesture. When we rode away, the wolves were starting to dig up bodies from the ground." She grimaced. "You can see now why I choose to keep certain things from you."

"Yes," she agreed. "The very thought of it induces nausea."

They rode on in silence for a couple of miles before cresting a hill that commanded a view of the valley below. Elizabeth's heart lifted. Beside the creek that snaked its way along for over a mile was a large, two-storied timber house with a series of outbuildings forming a courtyard in front of it. A mill had been erected at the water's edge, and its wheel was turning steadily. Cattle grazed nearby. Horses were penned in a field adjoining the house. In the evening sunshine, it looked like an idyllic spot and Elizabeth believed that she recognized the place.

"This must be it," she exclaimed with excitement. "Isn't it beautiful, Harry? Exactly as Uncle David described in his letters. I can see now why he came here."

"Why is it called Bitter Creek?" asked Featherstone.

"I don't know but it ought to be given a much nicer name. Can we go down there?" she pleaded. "Uncle David is going to be so thrilled to see us."

Featherstone smiled indulgently and nudged his horse forward. She kept pace with him on her own mount. Relieved that they had at last reached their destination, the soldiers trudged behind them. Eyes on the house below, they followed a winding track down the hillside. There was no whisper of danger. When the column got within fifty yards of the house, however, shots rang out, and one of the Indian guides dropped dead on the ground. Two of the soldiers were badly wounded. The noise of gunfire was so loud and unexpected that it made Elizabeth scream in horror. Her horse bucked wildly, tossing her onto the grass.

Leaping from his saddle, Featherstone crouched beside her to shield her from any attack. On both sides of them, he could see long-barreled rifles protruding from the bushes.

"Scatter!" he yelled to his men. "It's an ambush!"

CHAPTER NINE

Jamie Skoyles had always believed that the only way to get a woman out of his mind was to take another woman into his bed. Accordingly, he invited Maria Quinn to join him that evening and share a bottle of wine that he had been keeping for just such an occasion. Maria was more than compliant. A vivacious young woman with red hair that hung in curls and a pretty face that was lit by a bewitching smile, she had joined the ranks of the camp followers in the hope that Skoyles would seek her out again. The night they had spent together after the ball in Montreal had been the culmination of a dalliance that had gone on for days. It had been such a riot of love and lust that it prompted Maria to abandon the safety of Canada for the uncertainties of an American campaign.

She was delighted that Skoyles had finally remembered her, and as they lay entwined in his tent, he wondered why he had not done so before. An hour of raw passion with Maria Quinn had obliterated all trace of Elizabeth Rainham from his mind. After caressing her naked back and buttocks, he ran an index finger down her nose and onto her lips. She gave the finger a playful bite.

"Are you happy?" he asked.

"Very happy," she purred. "I thought you'd forgotten me."

"After what happened in Montreal? Impossible, Maria."

"Good."

"It's just that I've been rather busy since."

"I can see that from the state of your face and these bruises all over your body." She nestled into his shoulder. "You've been in the wars, Jamie. It's just as well you've got me to kiss your wounds better."

"You do it so beautifully."

"Does that mean I'll be seeing you again soon?"

"I can't promise anything," said Skoyles, drawing slightly away. "I told you before, Maria, that a soldier's life is not his own. This is the first chance I've had since we left Canada to spend time with you."

"I'm a patient woman."

He laughed. "You were impatient enough earlier on."

"Didn't you like that, Jamie?"

"I loved it."

He kissed her full on the lips and she responded willingly. Skoyles was about to roll on top of her again when he heard a noise outside his tent. He held Maria away from him so that he could strain his ears. A second later, the voice of Polly Bragg called out to him.

"Captain Skoyles!" she said. "Are you awake in there?"

"Wait a moment!" he replied, anxious to conceal the presence of his visitor from her. He blew out the candle beside the bed. Snatching up his breeches, he clambered into them before crossing hurriedly to put his head outside the tent. "What is it, Polly?"

"I'm sorry to rouse you at this time of night," she said, holding her candle close to him, "but Tom sent me. There's bad news, I fear."

"Bad news?"

"You're to come at once."

"What sort of bad news?"

"It concerns Miss Rainham," she said anxiously.

"What's happened to her?"

"There's been an ambush."

"I'll come immediately."

Having no details to impart, Polly went off into the dark and left him to scramble into the rest of his clothing and pull on his boots. When he had lit the candle again, he turned to Maria with a gesture of apology.

"Do you want me to wait?" she asked hopefully.

"No, I may have to ride out of camp."

"You know where to find me, Jamie."

"Yes, I do."

"Then don't leave it too long next time."

After giving Maria a farewell kiss, Skoyles ran all the way to Tom Caffrey's tent. When he lifted the flap to burst in, he saw his friend dressing the wounds of a soldier who lay on the camp bed. Polly Bragg was helping him. By the light of the candles, Skoyles could see that Private Marcus Wolverton was in poor condition. His jacket had been removed so that a musket ball could be removed from his upper arm, there was heavy bandaging around his thigh, and his hands were covered with abrasions. Pain was chiseled deeply into his face. When he recognized the newcomer, Wolverton gave him a pale smile of deference and spoke with a voice slurred by fatigue.

"No, Captain," he said with a weak smile. "I haven't had a fight with Dan Lukins this time. It's more serious, sir."

"You were part of the escort to Bitter Creek," noted Skoyles, crouching down beside him.

"They took us by surprise."

"Was anyone killed?"

"Five dead, at least."

"What about Miss Rainham? Was she hurt?"

"I've no means of telling, sir. Major Featherstone told us to scatter, so that's what we did. Before I could fire a shot, I was hit in the arm. Another ball grazed my leg. I dropped my musket and limped away. Since I couldn't hold a weapon to fight," he went on, "I thought the best thing I could do was to come for help."

"Yes, yes, Wolverton. You did the right thing."

"He's exhausted, Jamie," said Caffrey. "I had to give him a tot of rum to get any sense out of him."

"I want to hear about Miss Rainham."

"There's nothing I can tell you, sir," said Wolverton. "I wish I could. They seemed to be all round us, hidden in the bushes. We didn't stay long enough to see how many of them there were."

"*We?*" repeated Skoyles.

"He came back with one of the Indians," Caffrey explained. "The other one was killed. They were lucky. Miss Rainham's horse threw her and bolted up the hill. They managed to catch the animal."

Skoyles was disturbed. "She was thrown from her horse?"

"Yes, Captain," Wolverton replied. "The last I saw of her, the lady was being helped toward cover by Major Featherstone."

"But she was still alive?"

"Yes, sir."

"It was Redsnake who caught the runaway horse," said Caffrey, who had prized some of the story out of the wounded man. "He's one of the Mohawks helping to guide them to Bitter Creek. I know that we've heard some blood-curdling tales about the Indians but this man is a real hero. Instead of riding off himself, he helped Wolverton into the saddle."

"It's true," Wolverton agreed. "I'd never have found my way back here, especially in the dark. But Redsnake seemed to know exactly where to go. He was my savior. If he'd not bound my arm for me, I might have bled to death."

"Where is he now?" asked Skoyles.

"Back in the Indian camp," said Caffrey, "reporting to his chief."

"Was he injured?"

"Apparently not."

"Good," said Skoyles. "I'll need him to lead us back to Bitter Creek. And I'll give him thanks on your behalf, Wolverton."

"He deserves my apologies, Captain," said the other.

"Why?"

"Because the only way that I could stop myself from falling asleep was to quote from some of the plays I've acted in. Redsnake had hour after hour of William Shakespeare inflicted on him."

"I doubt if he understood a word of it."

"I'm not sure that *I* did, sir."

Skoyles stood up. "Who else knows about this?"

"You were the first person I sent for, Jamie," said Caffrey.

"Thanks, Tom. Brigadier Fraser needs to be told immediately so that a detachment can be formed. I'll make sure that I lead it."

"I'll ride with you. It sounds as if I'll be needed there."

"Take me as well, Captain," said Wolverton, trying to sit up.

"No," said Skoyles.

"You must, sir."

Polly Bragg eased him back down. "You're in no state to move," she said, solicitously. "Just try to rest."

"But I *have* to get back."

"Why?" asked Skoyles.

"Because I left poor Dan Lukins there," said Wolverton with evident affection, "and I feel guilty for having deserted him. I've simply got to find out what happened to him."

There were eight of them still alive. The other two in the group had died from their wounds in the night. Locked in a shed that had no window, the soldiers were bound hand and foot. Every so often, the guard who was posted outside the door opened it and shone a lantern in to make sure that they were still securely tied up. All of the prisoners had suffered cuts and bruises during the ambush. One of them had a musket ball embedded in his calf, another man had broken three fingers. The shed was dark, filthy, and uncomfortable, reeking with a compound of foul smells. Rats darted to and fro. All that the men could do was to lie there in a trough of self-pity.

Propped up against a wall, Harry Featherstone brooded on the calamitous turn of events. He was angry with himself for leading his men into an ambush and for being unable to fight his way out of it. He was also furious with his captors for incarcerating a man of his rank with common soldiers, forcing him to listen to their inane babble. It was a deliberate affront to his dignity. But his overriding concern was for Elizabeth Rainham, unhurt by her fall from the horse but now in the hands of a cruel and vindictive enemy. Featherstone chided himself for agreeing so readily to take her to Bitter Creek.

While the soldiers had been herded into the rat-infested shed, Elizabeth had been taken into the house to face unknown horrors. The major feared for her virtue. The American rebels who had captured them were part of the rear guard of the Continental Army that had been routed at Hubbardton. They had already killed David Lansdale and looted his house. It was unlikely that they would show any mercy to his niece. Patriots had little sympathy for anyone suspected of being a Tory. The lucky ones were only severely beaten. Hanging was a more likely fate, followed by the rape of their womenfolk and the destruction of their property. David Lansdale had been one more victim.

Featherstone was fuming with impotent rage. Elizabeth was in the house with a group of violent men and there was nothing that he could do about it. He took no consolation from the fact that he had heard no screams from her during the night.

Daniel Lukins had heard something else in the dark hours.

"I wonder what 'appened to Wolvie," he said sorrowfully. "I'd 'ate to think they left 'im out there with the others to feed them wolves. They never stopped 'owling, did they? Wolvie, eaten by wolves—it's not right."

"Be quiet, man," Featherstone ordered.

"But 'e was my friend, sir."

"Then mourn him in silence."

"What's goin' to 'appen to us, Major?" asked Lukins.

"I wish I knew."

"It's alright for you, sir. I mean, you're an officer. You're important. They'll exchange you for one of our prisoners." He peered at the others in the gloom. "What about the rest of us?"

"Yes," said another voice. "What about us, sir?"

"We'll just have to hope for the best," replied Featherstone.

"As long as it's not left to that sergeant with the scar across his face," said Lukins with a shiver. "An 'eartless devil, 'e was. I 'eard 'im say 'e'd like to put us in 'ere and set fire to the place. If I ever gets out alive," he vowed, "then that sergeant's goin' to 'ave a lot more scars across 'is ugly face—or Dan Lukins is a liar."

"Hold your tongue," Featherstone demanded. "It's bad enough to be locked up in here without having to listen to your stupid remarks."

Lukins was cowed into silence and nobody else dared to speak. The tension in the shed was almost tangible. The soldiers remembered only too well what had happened to Private Roger Higgs, flogged on the orders of Major Featherstone. Even in captivity, they were afraid to disobey the officer. After another hour, however, the pangs of hunger were too much for the little Cockney to bear and he had to speak out.

"Aren't they goin' to feed us, Major?" he wailed. "I can stand anythin' but bein' starved to death—that'd be against every article of war. I'll write to that turd, George Washington, to complain, so I will."

His absurd boast provoked some half-hearted laughter, but Harry Featherstone did not join in. All that he could think about was the fate of Elizabeth Rainham.

Back at Skenesborough, swift action was taken. Brigadier Fraser not only agreed that Skoyles should lead a detachment to Bitter Creek, he insisted on

134

getting General Burgoyne out of bed to hear details of what had happened. As a result, Skoyles was given the loan of his commander's telescope once again. The news that Elizabeth Rainham was caught in the ambush upset Burgoyne. As a friend of the family, he felt that he was—to some extent—*in loco parentis*. The thought that Elizabeth might be dead, badly wounded, or, at the very least, taken prisoner by the rebels made him curse his decision to allow her to travel to Bitter Creek.

Redsnake needed no persuasion to act as their scout. It emerged that the Indian who had been killed in the ambush was his brother, and he was eager to wreak revenge on his behalf. Four other Mohawks joined the detachment of fifty men, all of them mounted to ensure speed. As they left the camp, they were waved off by General Burgoyne himself, wishing them well and still praying for the safe return of Elizabeth Rainham. With the Indians leading the way on their ponies, the detachment followed a track that seemed to meander aimlessly through the forest. Jamie Skoyles rode beside Lieutenant Charles Westbourne.

"We were wrong to condemn all the Indians," said Skoyles. "Because of Redsnake's prompt action, one of our men was saved and the alarm was raised."

"I know, Captain," returned the other, watching the Indians ride bareback in front of him. "I just do wish they'd wear something more than a string of beads and a few feathers."

"This is no time for maiden modesty, Lieutenant."

"You'd think they'd want to protect their bodies."

"They prefer freedom of movement."

"So I see."

Sergeant Tom Caffrey brought his horse alongside them. Knowing that there would be wounded men when they reached their destination, he had his instruments and bandages in his knapsack.

"How long will it take us, Jamie?" he asked.

"Hours yet."

"Do you think that they'll still be at the farm?"

"There's only one way to find out, Tom," said Skoyles. "I can't believe they'd kill the entire detachment and move on. My guess is that they'll take prisoners and steal their guns and ammunition. The sight of captured redcoats is a powerful symbol for them."

"What about Miss Rainham?"

Westbourne gulped. "I shudder to think what might befall her."

"Let's just hope that the lady is still alive," said Skoyles.

"And unmolested."

"What puzzles me," said Caffrey, "is how they walked into the ambush in the first place. They were experienced soldiers with two scouts to help them, yet they were taken completely by surprise."

"They simply weren't expecting rebels in that part of the country," Westbourne explained. "Colonel Skene assured them that they'd be safe."

"I think I've worked out what must have happened," Skoyles decided, turning it over in his mind. "From what Wolverton told us—and from what I could get out of Redsnake through an interpreter—there's a hill that overlooks the approach to Bitter Creek. The rebels must have had pickets up there. When they spotted Major Featherstone and his men coming, they had ample time to set up the ambush."

"What if the pickets are still there?" said Caffrey.

"Then they've chosen the wrong day to be on duty."

They pressed on hard, breaking into a canter whenever possible and only stopping to water the horses once during the journey. Urged on by Skoyles, they were soon back in the saddle, exposed to the beat of the hot sun that glinted off their bayonets and sent trickles of sweat down their faces. When they got their first distant glimpse of the hill near Bitter Creek, Skoyles called them to a halt and ordered them to conceal themselves among the trees. He and the Indians went forward on foot, remaining under cover all the way.

Half a mile from the hill, he used the telescope to scan the summit. As he had expected, two sentries had been posted there to keep the approach road under surveillance. Skoyles was gratified. It meant that the rebels had not yet left Bitter Creek. He gave the telescope to Redsnake and showed him how to use it. The Indian was amazed at what he thought were its magical powers. Fascinated by the instrument, each of the Mohawks had to take his turn with it, sharing their excitement as they did so. Skoyles reclaimed the telescope and sent them off. They knew what to do.

It was a long wait. At first, Skoyles thought that they might have lost their way or been caught in a trap somewhere. Though he scanned the undergrowth on the slope ahead, he could see absolutely no sight of the Indians. They had vanished as if they had never existed. He began to worry, fearing that, in his eagerness, Redsnake had given himself away, but the anxiety proved groundless. When he trained the telescope on the top of the hill yet again, he saw the pickets being felled by shattering blows from tomahawks. Two scalps were soon waved triumphantly in the air. It was the signal for Skoyles to run back to his men. They mounted up at once. Caffrey rode beside his friend.

"They're still there, then," he said. "That's good news, Jamie."

"We don't know what state they're in yet."

Caffrey tapped his knapsack. "I've come well prepared."

Skoyles thought of Elizabeth Rainham. Physical wounds might be dressed, broken bones could be mended. But there were wounds to the mind that would never heal, deep, agonizing, and ever open, vile memories that could stalk a woman for the rest of her life. Skoyles hoped that Elizabeth had been spared such permanent injuries.

Night had been a prolonged torment for her. Elizabeth Rainham had been locked in the main bedroom of the house, the place where her Uncle David and Aunt Edith had spent almost ten happy years until her aunt had died of pneumonia. Lansdale's death had been more violent. Because he and his sons had refused to join the militia and fight against the British army, David Lansdale was hanged in his barn with Elizabeth's three cousins dangling beside him. On hearing the news of their execution, Elizabeth realized how barbaric her captors could be and she feared for her own life. When that was spared, she thought that she was being kept alive for their sport.

Several of the men had come to ogle her, flushed with drink and roused by her beauty. Their language had disgusted her and the lechery in their eyes had been terrifying, but she had not as yet been mauled. On the orders of their leader—a young lieutenant with the faint hint of a gentleman about him—the rebel soldiers had stayed their hands with great reluctance. It was only a matter of time, Elizabeth felt, before one of them would disobey the command and she would be unable to defend herself. There was no chance of escape. A guard was stationed outside the door and another in the courtyard. Even if she could have climbed through the window and dropped to the ground, she would have been quickly apprehended.

In any case, she did not wish to provoke them. The lieutenant had been kind enough to tell her that Harry Featherstone was still alive and being held with the other men, but that was all she knew. Confined to the bedroom, Elizabeth could do nothing but reflect on the seriousness of her predicament. She spent most of the night on her feet, afraid to lie on the bed in case she fell asleep and made herself even more vulnerable. On one wall was a portrait of her Uncle David. On another, the lovely face and warm smile of her Aunt Edith had been caught perfectly by the artist. Anything of real value had been stolen, but the room was still filled with touching mementos of its former occupants. Every time Elizabeth looked at one of them, she felt a knife through her heart.

The sound of heavy footsteps on the landing outside alerted her. A key was turned in the lock and the door swung open. Elizabeth backed away immediately. The man who entered was tall, rangy, and hirsute and had a livid scar across his face, as if he had been sliced open by a sword. He wore the blue uniform of the Continental Army and a sergeant's sash.

He was carrying a cup of water and a hunk of bread. He held them out to her with a lascivious grin that made his scar even more repulsive. Elizabeth fought to maintain her composure.

"I brought food and drink for you, ma'am," he said, eyes roving her body. "Just so as you don't think that we got no manners. Here—come and take it from me."

"Just put them down, please," she said, primly.

"As you wish, ma'am." He set the cup and the bread down on the little table under the window then he leered at her. "Don't I get a kiss for attending to your needs?"

"No," she replied crisply.

"No? Now that's real unfriendly of you, ma'am. I heard tell you English folk was so obliging." He used a foot to kick the door shut. "All I'm asking for is one little kiss."

"Go away!"

"Begging your pardon but there's something you don't seem to have noticed. I'm the man in charge," he said, patting his chest, "and you're the prisoner. I reckon that gives me certain rights, don't it?"

"If you don't leave me alone, I'll report you to the lieutenant."

He cackled merrily. "You'll need a mighty loud voice to do that, ma'am, seeing as how Lieutenant Muncie has just ridden over to the village two miles away. I'm in control here now. I make the decisions and you're one of them."

As he took a step forward, she reached out to grab an empty water jug that stood on the dressing table beside her. Elizabeth brandished it the air. The man cackled again.

"Hey, you got some spirit in you, ma'am," he said approvingly. "I like that. I think I'll make it *two* kisses now—one for the bread and one for the water."

"I won't touch either."

"You must have something, ma'am."

"No, thank you."

"Please yourself."

He shrugged his shoulders and turned away. Elizabeth dared to relax. She even put the water jug back inside its china basin. He was on her at once, swinging round to grab her by both wrists then pinning her against a wall so that he could take a first guzzling kiss that muffled her cry of disgust. When she struggled to get free, he flung her on the bed and looked down at her with a wild grin. Before he could move, however, he heard the crackle of flames and the frantic neighing of horses.

Leaving her where she lay, he rushed to the window and looked out. The stables were on fire and horses could be heard kicking madly against their stalls. Men were running out of the house to investigate. The sergeant rushed to the door and flung it open.

"Don't you go away, ma'am," he warned. "I'll be back."

He went out quickly and the guard locked the door behind him. Elizabeth was trembling with fear. The man's intentions were brutally clear. As soon as the lieutenant had left the farm, she had lost what little protection she had. A water jug would not keep the sergeant at bay. He could take his pleasure at will. The taste of his lips had made her stomach heave. When she got up from the bed, she sipped water from the cup to rinse her mouth, then spat it into the basin.

Voices were now raised in the courtyard, and she looked out to see frenzied horses being led out of the blazing stables. Smoke swirled everywhere. The sergeant stood in the middle of it all, waving his arms and barking orders. This was the man who would come to violate her, strong, uncompromising, and brutal. She could still smell the stink of his breath. Elizabeth could not believe her eyes when something hurtled through the air to strike the sergeant on the back of his skull and knock him to the ground, where he was trampled by a dozen flashing hooves. Other tomahawks seemed to come out of thin air to kill their targets. The next thing she heard was a series of gunshots from invisible men. The roar of the fire became deafening.

Elizabeth jumped back from the window, fearful that she might be hit by a stray musket ball and confused by the sheer pandemonium in the courtyard. If the stables were on fire, the inferno would eventually spread to the house and she would be burned alive. The thought sent another tremor through her. Dashing to the door, she tried to open it but it held fast. She began to scream for help. Footsteps thundered up the stairs and she heard the sound of a fierce struggle on the landing. Something then hit the floor outside with a resounding thud that made the boards shake under her feet.

The key was turned in the lock. Elizabeth backed away in panic, her head aching, her eyes misting over, her heart pounding like a drum. Outside the window, more gunfire was heard above the crackle of the fire. Horses were neighing, men were yelling. Elizabeth was certain that her own death was at hand. When the door opened, she put both hands to her face, afraid even to look. But the torture was at last over.

"Miss Rainham," said a familiar voice. "Are you hurt?"

Elizabeth lowered her hands, saw with amazement the figure of Captain Jamie Skoyles standing in the doorway, and, tears of relief streaming down her face, ran impulsively across the room to fling herself into his arms.

It took hours until the work was done. When the British prisoners were released, they saw the courtyard filled with dozens of redcoats, bringing pails of water from the river to put out the fire. Major Harry Featherstone immediately took command, but it was Jamie Skoyles who instructed the men in what they had to do, leaving his superior to comfort Elizabeth Rainham in the house and to issue a string of apologies for taking her to such a dangerous place. Of the rebel soldiers, only ten remained alive and they were put to work at once, digging graves for the men they had hanged in the barn, then burying the half-eaten remains of the British soldiers killed in the earlier ambush.

Two more redcoats were brought out of the shed where they had died overnight and given a decent burial. With muskets held on them, the rebels were forced to put heavy rocks on the graves so that the bodies could not be dug up again by ravenous wolves. Only when all the British casualties had been buried did Skoyles allow the American soldiers the chance to see to their own dead. It was a gesture that they had not extended to the enemy on the previous day.

Daniel Lukins was delighted to hear that his friend was still alive.

"We owe all this to Wolvie?" he said, smacking his hands together. "Whoever thought 'e'd turn out to be an 'ero—that long-legged fool who's always spoutin' poetry and suchlike at me? Good old Wolvie! I'm sorry that I stole 'is watch now."

"I'm not," said Skoyles. "If he hadn't fought with you, I'd never have known about a plot to assault me. Thank you, Lukins. Your warning was very timely."

"This makes us even, then, Captain."

"Even?"

"I saved you then and you saved me now."

Skoyles grinned. "I can't pretend that rescuing you was my main preoccupation when we set out from Skenesborough," he admitted, "but I'm pleased to see that you survived. Wolverton was worried that you might have been killed in the ambush."

"Not me, sir. I'm too small a target for the buggers."

"There may be something in that." He watched two men shoveling earth on to the last grave. "We're just about finished here now. I'd better go and call Major Featherstone."

"One moment, sir," said Lukins in a confidential whisper. "When they took the lady into the 'ouse, did they strip 'er naked and—"

"No," said Skoyles firmly. "Nothing untoward occurred, so I want no crude speculation among the men. I leave it to you to pass the word around. Is that clear?"

"Yes, Captain."

Skoyles walked back toward the house. His plan to create a diversion by setting fire to the stables had worked perfectly. The rescue had been a complete success, with minimal casualties on his side. No horses had been injured. They were rounded up to be taken back to camp. Tom Caffrey had been able to tend both the British wounded and those rebels injured in the attack. Sheer weight of numbers had made the outcome inevitable. Skoyles could take great satisfaction from it all, but the most memorable event for him was the embrace with Elizabeth Rainham. She had expressed more than simple gratitude for her rescue. During that fleeting moment in the bedroom, she had leapt over the boundaries of convention to reveal an affection that took them both unawares.

Sad to yield command to Major Featherstone, he was quick to see the advantage in doing so. It diverted Elizabeth Rainham. Featherstone had kept her in the house to hear what had happened to her and to give an account of his own imprisonment. Skoyles was glad that she had witnessed none of the gruesome events outside. Elizabeth had been spared the sight of the Indians taking their legitimate scalps, of her uncle and cousins being cut down from the rafters in the barn, and of the burial detail putting British dead beneath the ground.

Time alone with her in the house seemed to have a salutary effect on Harry Featherstone. When Skoyles went in to summon them, the major even stumbled through a subdued speech of thanks. But the gratitude shining in Elizabeth's eyes was the only reward that Skoyles wanted. A close friendship had been established.

"We're ready to leave now, Major," he said.

"What about this Lieutenant Muncie?" asked Featherstone. "According to Elizabeth, the fellow went off to the village earlier on."

"I sent a dozen men after him, sir, but he was no longer there. We must have frightened him off. He'll run back to the main army, wherever that may be."

"We'll find it," said Featherstone grimly. "Find it and destroy it."

"Yes, sir."

"You lead the way back to the camp, Skoyles."

"If you wish, sir."

"Miss Rainham and I will ride at the rear. I don't want her disturbed by the sight of those damned Mohawks flaunting their scalps."

"The Indians were crucial to the rescue plan, Major."

"I find that a matter of regret."

"Harry!" Elizabeth chided him. "They've earned our thanks."

"I'll make sure that I pass it on to them, Miss Rainham," said Skoyles. He lowered his voice. "The burial detail has finished its work now. Before we leave, I thought that you might care to pay your respects at the graves of your kinsfolk."

"Thank you, Captain." Tears threatened. "I'd like to do that."

"Take as much time as you wish, Miss Rainham."

"I will."

"I'll stay beside you," said Featherstone.

Skoyles gave each of them a nod, then left. Elizabeth bit her lip and tried not to cry, wondering if she could go through the ordeal of visiting the graves of her beloved relations. Later, there would be the additional trial of writing a letter to her parents, describing what had happened at Bitter Creek. War had taken on a frightening immediacy for her. Seeing her distress, Harry Featherstone reached out to enfold her gently in his arms. She was grateful for his support, but she took no real pleasure from the embrace. Over his shoulder, she was watching Jamie Skoyles walk away from the house.

Daniel Lukins was so pleased to be reunited with Marcus Wolverton again that he volunteered to cut the other man's hair without payment. Since he still retained something of the actor's vanity, Wolverton was ready to accept the offer. A man of unusual talents, the Cockney was a skilled barber who earned a regular income from his fellow soldiers. In view of the continual enmity between them, Wolverton had never let Lukins cut his hair before, and he had certainly never allowed the man near him with a razor, preferring instead to cultivate a mustache that he trimmed regularly. Since most soldiers were unshaven for days on end, the well-groomed Marcus Wolverton stood out from the common herd. In the past, Lukins had always mocked him for that.

With his customer perched on a stool outside their tent, the little barber snipped away with his scissors. He had a confession to make.

"Something strange 'appened back there in Bitter Creek," he said.

"Oh?"

"I missed you, Wolvie. I thought you was dead."

"I thought the same about you, Dan," the other revealed, "and it made me rather sad. I began to regret all the quarrels we'd had in the past. They seem so pointless now."

"They were," said the other. "Why did you start them?"

Wolverton stiffened. "You were the one who always did that!"

"Sit still or I'll cut your ear off by mistake."

"Then stop telling lies."

"Me? Tellin' lies? I'm the only truthful man in this 'ole regiment."

"That's the biggest lie of all, Dan Lukins." The barber laughed. "Now stop baiting me and get on with your job. I'm still waiting to hear what happened at Bitter Creek after I left."

"Then wait no more, Wolvie. I'll tell all."

Without any preamble, Lukins gave a long, colorful, rambling account of events at Bitter Creek, portraying himself as an unsung hero and insisting that it was he who had kept up the spirits of the prisoners when they were locked in the shed at the farm. So carried away did he become with his narrative that he even claimed to have assisted Jamie Skoyles in the rescue of Elizabeth Rainham.

"First time in my life I saved a woman's maiden'ead," he said with a snigger. "It was a peculiar feelin', Wolvie. In the past, I've always 'elped them to get rid of it. That lady owes me 'er thanks."

"You and Captain Skoyles."

"Well, yes, 'e did sort of assist me."

"He'd assist you with a boot up your backside if he heard you making ridiculous claims like that," said Wolverton. "I spoke to Sergeant Caffrey this morning. He told me that Miss Rainham was rescued from the house while you and the others were still bound hand and foot."

Lukins was indignant. "Who're you goin' to believe—'im or me?"

"You, Dan, of course," said the other, trying to mollify him, "as long as you have those scissors in your hand, anyway. The important thing is that you came back in one piece."

"I feels sorry for 'er. Miss Rain'am, that is."

"Why?"

"Marryin' someone like Major Featherstone. The man's a monster. Spent the night with 'im, I did. 'E treated us like dirt. I wouldn't want 'im as my 'usband, Wolvie, I know that. There!" he said, stepping back. "I've finished. Best 'aircut you ever 'ad. See for yourself."

He handed Wolverton a small mirror and the latter examined himself for some time, twisting his head to see it from all angles. Tom Caffrey strolled across to the two men.

"How's my patient this morning?" he asked.

"Wolvie's like a new man, sir," Lukins boasted.

"You've done an excellent job, Dan," said Wolverton, returning the mirror. "Are you sure that I can't pay you for the haircut?"

"I wouldn't take a penny from you."

Caffrey was impressed. "I'm glad to see that you two have settled your differences at last," he said. "It's one good thing to come out of that ambush."

"It is, Sergeant," said Wolverton. "I realized just how much I needed Dan—even if he does drive me to distraction sometimes."

"Me?" said Lukins, bending over him. "I'd never upset *you*, Wolvie. You're my best friend, I swears it. You keeps me sane in this mad'ouse they calls an army." He began to walk away. "Any time you wants a free 'aircut, you just give Dan Lukins a call."

"Take him up on the offer," Caffrey advised with a grin. "The only other free haircut you'd get here is from one of the Indians. How's that arm of yours today?"

"Still throbbing with pain, Sergeant."

"You were lucky that the musket ball didn't shatter a bone."

"I'm more relieved that Dan Lukins is still alive," said Wolverton. "More than half of us who went to Bitter Creek with the major were killed. Dan could so easily have been one of them. I felt such a thrill when I saw him again this morning, that I almost gave him this." He felt in his pocket for something then let out a cry of rage. "He's done it again!" he yelled. "The little devil has stolen my watch!"

Expelled from Skenesborough, the American rebels had been thorough. An army of axmen had worked tirelessly in the forest to make the overland route to Fort Edward completely impassable. Trees had been felled, branches arranged into forbidding lattice works, bridges destroyed, rocks used to block the tracks through the forest. The fort was only twenty-three miles away, but every foot of road would first have to be reclaimed. At one point, a two-mile causeway needed to be constructed across a swamp. British engineers and artificers labored in punitive conditions, supported by Canadian axmen. July rains pelted them and blazing sunshine toasted them. Fresh swarms of insects surged up out of the swamps to get into their noses, mouths, eyes, ears, and clothing. Those who toiled in the humid forest in their woolen uniforms were irresistible targets of blackflies, mosquitoes, deerflies, horse-flies, gnats, ants, ticks, and chiggers. Snakes proved particularly unfriendly.

Within a matter of days, surgeons were treating soldiers who had suc-cumbed to dysentery. The disease soon raged. Life in the camp was increas-ingly unpleasant. Suffocating heat was relieved only by violent storms. There was such a heavy fall of dew and mist each morning that it soaked the blankets on which the soldiers slept. Carving a way through the forest at the hottest time of year seemed to many to be an act of utter madness, a Herculean labor that would hold them up for weeks.

Yet the man who had set it in motion was bubbling with optimism. Gen-eral Burgoyne gave every appearance of enjoying his enforced stay at Skenes-borough. His accommodation was comfortable, his champagne and claret in good supply, and his mistress extremely compliant. Dining every day with his officers and gambling every night with the chosen few, he felt able to make the best of the situation. Summoned by the general one morning, Skoyles found him as cheerful as ever. They met in the room where the coffin of Colonel Skene's mother remained defiantly above ground.

"You were quite wrong to advocate Lake George," said Burgoyne.

"Was I, General?"

"I received a letter from General Phillips today. They're having an infernal time, trying to haul the gunboats, bateaux, and artillery over the portage from Ticonderoga. Soldiers and prisoners are working all hours."

"Our men fare no better in the forest," Skoyles argued. "If they go for-ward a mile a day, they feel it's an achievement. It's cost lives already, General, and not only because there are sharpshooters on the prowl. We had two more deaths from fever yesterday."

"Regrettable but unavoidable."

"Traveling by water would have been healthier."

"I'm a soldier, Captain, not a physician. My concern is to reach a destina-tion of my choice at whatever cost. It's a poor commander who turns nurse-maid to the lower ranks."

"Perhaps so," said Skoyles, "but we can ill afford to lose men."

Burgoyne nodded. "I agree with you there," he conceded. "We had to leave a garrison at Crown Point and another at Ticonderoga. When I wrote to Governor Carleton to send reinforcements, he replied that his orders did not give him the latitude to do so. Upon my conscience!" he exclaimed, stamping

146

a foot. "Had he let us pursue the rebels last summer, we'd have wiped out this so-called revolution by now. At the very moment when we could have struck hard, we were ordered to abandon the campaign and return to Canada."

Skoyles said nothing. Fond as he was of Burgoyne, he was not blind to the general's love of political intrigue. Skoyles was convinced that Burgoyne had used the failure of the British invasion the previous year as a means of discrediting Sir Guy Carleton in London. It was the main reason why Gentleman Johnny had replaced his former commander. Skoyles found Burgoyne a more likable and approachable man but he felt that Carleton had been badly treated by politicians who viewed the situation from a distance that was bound to distort it. Military honor—Skoyles had long ago discovered—was a matter of perception rather than actuality.

"I have some more work for you and my telescope," said Burgoyne.

"What are my orders, sir?"

"To make your way to Fort Anne, take note of its defenses, then move on to take a closer look at Fort Edward. If my reports are correct, General Schuyler is still there."

"Why do you need to send me?" Skoyles asked. "We already have scouting parties moving south."

"Yes," said Burgoyne, frowning. "Indians who wantonly disobey my instructions. They'd sooner loot a farm or take scalps from harmless civilians than gather intelligence. They're beginning to be more trouble than they're worth."

"I couldn't speak more highly of the men at Bitter Creek, sir."

"They seem to have been the exception to the rule. You did well there, Captain. And I've not forgotten the vital information you gave us about Mount Defiance. That's why I've selected you for this task."

"Do I travel alone?"

"That's up to you."

"If he's available, I'd like to take Redsnake. I trust him."

"Make what arrangements you will. Of course," he went on with a sly grin, "it does mean that we'll miss the pleasure of your company at the card table for a while but that might enable someone else to win."

"Much as I love cards," said Skoyles, "I prefer action in the field."

"Spoken like a true soldier!"

"When do I leave?"

"As soon as I can find my telescope," said Burgoyne. "Try to bring it back without any dents in it this time."

He searched among the piles of papers on the table until the instrument came to light. Burgoyne took a handkerchief from his sleeve to polish it slightly before he handed it over.

"Thank you, sir," said Skoyles. A thought nudged him. "Might I ask if there's any word of Miss Rainham? I've not seen her since we returned from Bitter Creek a few days ago. How is she, General?"

"Damnably grateful to you, Captain."

"The lady went through a terrible ordeal."

"That can be laid partly at my door," Burgoyne confessed. "I shouldn't have encouraged her to visit her uncle like that. Colonel Skene led me to believe that there was no risk involved. It seems that things have changed for the worse since he was last living in this area."

"You've spoken to Miss Rainham?"

"Yes, yes. She and Major Featherstone dined with me yesterday. Brave young lady. Held up well. You'd never have guessed that she'd endured such suffering. Not surprising to me, of course," he said. "Good breeding. Elizabeth is the daughter of Richard Rainham—an exemplary soldier. Resilience is a family trait."

Skoyles fished gently for information. "There's a rumor that we might have a wedding when we reach Albany," he said, artlessly. "Is that true, General?"

"You'll have to ask Harry Featherstone about that. It's his idea, and who can blame him? His bride-to-be has come all this way to be with him, and he's unable to do more than escort her to dinner. Harry's always been a red-blooded fellow," said Burgoyne, admiringly. "Understandable that he'd like to spend the night with his wife."

"But we're still in the middle of a campaign."

"By the time we reach Albany, it should effectively be over."

"Only if Brigadier St. Leger meets us there."

"Oh, I've no worries on that score," said the other blithely. "Barry St. Leger will do exactly what's expected of him. When he's reduced the forts in his path, he'll sail on down the Hudson River to join us at Albany with the forces we expect from New York City."

"Has General Howe dispatched an army yet, sir?"

"Probably."

"Have you had no confirmation of the fact?"

"I expect it every day, Captain. As you know, letters have difficulty getting through enemy territory. That's why more than one messenger is sent. General Howe will not let us down, I assure you," said Burgoyne with confidence. "Word will reach us at any moment."

The messenger had reached Albany before he was stopped by a patrol from the Continental Army. He tried to bluff his way past them in vain. The lieutenant in charge of the patrol ordered the man to dismount so that he could be searched. Fearing that he would be caught with vital intelligence on him, the messenger slipped something into his mouth. The lieutenant's suspicions were aroused. From the saddlebag of his horse, he took out a bottle that he kept for such occasions.

"Hold him tight and give him some of this," he said. "We'll get the truth out of one end of him or another."

Grabbed by two men, the prisoner was forced to drink the strong emetic. It soon had an effect. He began to retch violently and spewed the contents of his stomach on the ground. The men released him to search the vomit but the messenger moved quicker than they did. Retrieving the object that he had swallowed earlier, he popped it back in his mouth and tried to make a run for it. He was caught immediately.

"Give him a larger dose this time," the lieutenant ordered.

The man struggled hard and three soldiers had to hold him on the ground while a fourth poured the liquid down his throat. It was not long before the prisoner went into convulsions. He puked uncontrollably. The lieutenant seized the tiny silver bullet that had been regurgitated. When he had cleaned it off, he realized that it was hollow. Inside it, he found a piece of paper that contained the most startling news.

"General Howe is sailing to Philadelphia!" he announced. "He's not bringing his army to Albany, after all. Burgoyne is on his own."

They hanged the messenger by way of celebration.

CHAPTER TEN

Before setting off on his scouting trip, Captain Jamie Skoyles removed all trace of the British army. In place of his uniform, he wore the hunting shirt that had been so badly scuffed during his roll down Mount Hope, with some buckskin breeches and a round hat to replace the one lost at Ticonderoga. Though he took a musket, he left the bayonet behind, preferring instead to carry a hunting knife and a pistol. Burgoyne's telescope was in his pocket along with a map of the area. Using his local knowledge, Colonel Skene had advised him on the best route to take.

Skoyles was fortunate. Though the different tribes had dispatched men on foraging expeditions, several of the Mohawks were still at their camp. Redsnake was among them. He had a smattering of English and of French, so Skoyles was able to make himself understood by using a mixture of both languages. What the Indian could not do was to hold a conversation with him. That suited Skoyles. The last thing he wanted was a garrulous companion.

He put his trust in Redsnake because the Indian had shown his mettle at Bitter Creek, saving Private Marcus Wolverton from the ambush, then guiding the detachment sent out from Skenesborough. In the course of his second visit to the farm, Redsnake had acquired no fewer than five new scalps to add to his tally. The Indian seemed to have a respect for Skoyles that boded well. Unlike so many of his tribe, he would take orders. Had he allowed other Mohawks to go with him, Skoyles might have had more trouble controlling them.

Bay horses were taken because they blended more easily with the leafy surroundings. For the early part of the journey, they followed the road that had been hacked through the forest and on which a large and dispirited labor force was still working. Once they left it, they came up against the network of obstacles created by the American rebels. Skoyles hoped to pick his way past them one at a time, but Redsnake shook his head vigorously. He indicated with gestures that they should make a wide detour, adding miles to the journey but sparing them the frustration of trying to get horses over fallen trees or across swamps and streams that had been inconveniently deprived of their bridges.

Redsnake gave the impression of knowing exactly where he was going. He was a tall, thin, wiry man in his twenties with an inscrutable expression on his face. Apart from a breechcloth and couple of necklaces made up of animals' teeth, he wore only feathers and war paint. His eyes were sharp, his movements lithe, his instincts sound. He was armed with a tomahawk and a hunting knife. Skoyles had seen how proficient he was with both weapons.

Their speed varied. They were limited to a trot in the thicker parts of the forest but managed a steady canter at other times. Remaining alert for danger, Skoyles nevertheless let his mind dwell on Elizabeth Rainham. While she had preserved her virtue at Bitter Creek, she had lost her innocence about the nature of warfare; it had been a devastating experience for her. Skoyles wondered if it would make her think again about marrying a soldier and having to cope with the fears and anxieties of an army wife. At all events, he hoped that Elizabeth would not be persuaded to wed Harry Featherstone in Albany. It would seal her fate irretrievably. Since their momentary embrace at the farm, Skoyles did not simply envy the major. He desired Elizabeth for himself. And the more he thought about her, the more intense his desire became.

Bitter Creek had been an all too appropriate name for the farm. It had brought Elizabeth nothing but bitterness. She had ridden there with the anticipatory delight of seeing her uncle and cousins again after so many years. Instead, she discovered that the entire family had been hanged and the house looted. Only the timely arrival of redcoats from Skenesborough saved her from being raped. Skoyles regretted that the place held such disturbing memories for her. When he had first set eyes on Bitter Creek, it had struck him as exactly the sort of farm he had always wanted. To live in such a property with a wife and family beside him was his idea of perfection.

"Tired?" asked Redsnake, interrupting his reverie.

"No," said Skoyles.

"We rest?"

"Keep riding. There's no need to stop."

Their route was by no means wooded all the way. Steep cliffs and craggy mountains slowed them down, though they were rewarded with fine views when they clambered to a summit. Skoyles soon brought the telescope into play. Fascinated by the instrument, Redsnake insisted on being given it each time, mouth agape as he moved it from eye to eye. When it was returned to Skoyles's pocket, the Indian always watched covetously.

After looping eastward, they swung back toward Fort Anne, picking up a serpentine track that took them into dense forest. Redsnake was the first to notice the faint stink wafting in their direction. He called a halt and held his nose. Dismounting swiftly, they tethered their horses and went forward on foot. Skoyles soon picked up the stench as well and guessed its origin. During an earlier skirmish with a party of Mohawks, the rebels had suffered many casualties near a breastwork a mile from the fort. The garrison was too frightened of the Indians to venture out to bury their dead. Corpses lay strewn haphazardly on the battlefield, scalped, mutilated, or preyed upon by wild animals, all of them giving off the unmistakable reek of decay.

As they skirted the battlefield, Skoyles and his companion had to cover their mouths and noses with the palm of a hand. They pressed on until Fort Anne came into sight, keeping low to avoid being spotted by any sentries on the ramparts. Their stealth was unnecessary. When he trained the telescope on the fort, Skoyles saw that they were no sentries on duty at all. The entire garrison was streaming out of the gates. Smoke began to rise. Abandoning the fort, the rebels were set on destroying it.

Redsnake was impatient, nudging Skoyles to remind him to pass over the telescope. The Indian was forced to wait. Peering through the instrument, Skoyles had just seen someone he recognized, coming out of the gates on a horse. It was Ezekiel Proudfoot, looking fit and well. Skoyles smiled, pleased that the man was still alive, even if in the enemy ranks. Unfortunately, his former friend was the last person he was allowed to see. Skoyles suddenly felt a sharp blow on the back of his head, and he lapsed into unconsciousness.

"Do you know where Captain Skoyles is?" asked Elizabeth Rainham.

"On his way to Fort Anne."

She was dismayed. "Fort Anne? Is he involved in an attack?"

"No, Miss Rainham," said Tom Caffrey jocularly. "Jamie Skoyles is a brave man but even he wouldn't consider an attack when there are only two of them. He's on a scouting expedition."

"Oh, I see."

"Is there any message I can give him?"

It had taken Elizabeth a few days to recover from the events at Bitter Creek and to realize just how much she owed to Jamie Skoyles. Since her return to Skenesborough, she had been monopolized by Harry Featherstone and therefore unable to make contact with Skoyles. She felt guilty that she had not been able to express her gratitude properly and, with Nan Wyatt beside her, had come in search of him. Caffrey had met the two women outside Skoyles's tent.

"You might give him this," said Elizabeth, handing over a letter. "I was going to leave it in the captain's tent."

"I'll make sure that he gets it."

"When do you expect him back, Sergeant?"

"Impossible to say."

"I'll hope to catch him another time."

"Jamie will be delighted to hear that, Miss Rainham," said Caffrey, beaming. "May I ask how you're feeling now?"

"Much better, thank you."

"What happened at Bitter Creek was very upsetting for you."

"It taught me an important lesson," said Elizabeth seriously. "It was very naïve of me to treat a military campaign as if it were a pleasant excursion. I know better now."

"Stay in the camp where it's safe, ma'am," cautioned Nan.

"Oh, I will."

"Leave the soldiering to trained soldiers. I'd never have dared to ride off the way that you did." She turned to Caffrey. "I daresay that Polly takes the same view as me."

"She does," he agreed. "Polly knows how treacherous our enemies can be. She wouldn't venture outside the camp."

Elizabeth felt a twinge of remorse at the mention of Polly Bragg. She had been told to ensure that Nan Wyatt spurned the other woman in future but she had deliberately refrained from doing so. For one thing, she did not like being given orders, even if they came from Harry Featherstone. But the main reason she had disobeyed him was that the friendship between Nan and Polly was indirectly valuable to her. While the latter was primed to pick up any gossip about Elizabeth, her maid always brought back snippets of information about Jamie Skoyles. And Elizabeth had started to take an obsessive interest in him.

"Thank you, Sergeant Caffrey," she said. "We'll not detain you."

"No," Nan added. "I know that you and the other surgeons are always busy. Polly tells me that you're on duty twenty-four hours a day."

"It feels much longer than that somehow," he said.

"You must have so many thankful patients."

"They thank me best by staying alive."

"Do you ever get time to sleep?" asked Elizabeth.

"Sleep?" He laughed drily. "That's not part of my army rations, I'm afraid. I wish it was."

"You knew Captain Skoyles when he was in the ranks, I believe?"

"That's correct, Miss Rainham," he said cheerily. "He began as a private, just like the rest of us. Except that Jamie Skoyles was never quite like the rest of us. I could see from the start that he was destined for higher things."

"Why?"

"He's a natural leader. It was only a question of time before he was promoted. Gentleman Johnny has great faith in him," he stressed. "That's why Jamie was chosen to go to Fort Anne. There's nobody quite like him. Jamie Skoyles is the sort of man who never lets you down."

The first thing that Skoyles did when he regained consciousness was to put a worried hand to his head. He was relieved to find that his hat was still on and that he had not been scalped. In fact, the hat had prevented any wound being opened, but the back of his head was nevertheless throbbing violently. Skoyles knew at once why he had been struck by Redsnake's tomahawk. The Indian had stolen the telescope that he prized so highly. Skoyles guessed that the two horses would have disappeared by now as well. Redsnake had betrayed him, one more Indian who would desert the army and make off with his booty.

Skoyles took it as a compliment that he had not been killed when at his mercy. Nor had he been left defenseless. Redsnake had taken his hunting knife but left him with his musket, pistol, powder, and ammunition. They were small consolation to Skoyles. He had lost his horse, his guide, and his telescope. In doing so, he had lost the means to go on, to track the rebels all the way to Fort Edward. He would never catch up with the departing army on foot. All that he could do was to try to find his way back to Skenesborough.

When he got to the place where the horses had been tethered, he had confirmation that Redsnake had taken both of them. Skoyles began to retrace his steps, looking for some of the landmarks he had noticed on the journey there. Childhood experience came to his aid. During the years he spent in Cumberland, he had loved to explore the fells, often traveling several miles from home. Skoyles frequently got lost. With a combination of instinct and tenacity, however, he had always contrived to find his way safely back somehow. That early training had stood him in good stead on many occasions. It would not let him down now.

Skoyles did not linger. Breaking into a trot, he maintained it for a couple of miles, following the hoofprints whenever they were visible. He had no hope of overhauling Redsnake. The Indian would be hopelessly out of his reach. Skoyles loped on. It was the unremitting ache at the back of his head that made him eventually stop. He paused beside a stream, drinking some water and washing his face to refresh himself.

Setting off again, he reviewed the situation. Skoyles was not looking forward to his return. The report he would have to deliver to General Burgoyne would be embarrassing. Gentleman Johnny would be outraged at the loss of his beloved telescope. It was one of his many expensive accessories, and it also had sentimental value for him. All that Skoyles had learned on his trip was that Fort Anne had been vacated at speed by a nervous enemy. The intelligence would not atone for the loss of two horses, an Indian scout, and a telescope. He feared that he would lose Burgoyne's confidence and be ridiculed by Harry Featherstone. Worst of all, news of his failure on the mission would be immediately passed on by the gloating major to Elizabeth Rainham. That thought made his head pound even more.

It all helped to make him feel annoyed with himself for placing his trust in Redsnake. The temptation to steal the telescope and the horses had been too much for the Indian. Skoyles lengthened his stride, pushing himself harder by way of a punishment. His head still hurt but he lived with the pain. He had covered a few miles when he heard what sounded like a muffled shot. It put

155

him on his guard at once. After checking that his musket was still loaded, he moved on slowly, much more circumspect now.

The noise seemed to have come from his right. The neighing of horses and the startled cry of birds had followed the shot before dying away. His ears could pick up no other sound. Bent double, Skoyles crept on through the undergrowth. The trees then began to thin out and he caught sight of two horses about thirty yards away, tied to some bushes. Though he could not be certain from that distance, Skoyles thought that he recognized the animals as the ones that he and Redsnake had ridden. When he got closer, there was no doubt in his mind. They were the same horses. He had caught up with the Indian, after all.

Skoyles was puzzled. Whoever had fired the shot, it could not have been Redsnake, because he had no gun. Yet there was no sign of anyone else or of another horse. Edging forward, he caught sight of something that was protruding from behind a bush. It was a pair of bare feet and he knew instantly that they belonged to the Mohawk. Someone, apparently, had shot him. Skoyles wanted to make sure that he was dead. But he got no closer to the fallen man.

"That's far enough, mister," said a stern voice directly behind him. "Unless you want to join that Indian, throw down your musket."

"Who are you?" asked Skoyles.

"I won't ask twice."

There was enough menace and authority in the voice to convince Skoyles that he had to obey. Dropping his weapon to the ground, he put up both hands and turned slowly round to face a stocky individual of middle height who was holding a hunting rifle on him. The man was in his early thirties and there was an air of prosperity about him. He was well dressed and wore a broad-brimmed hat that he touched politely.

"My name is Isaac Harman," he said. "Who might you be?"

"Jamie Skoyles."

"And what is Jamie Skoyles doing in this godforsaken place?"

"I might ask the same of you, Mr. Harman."

"Not while I'm holding this rifle."

"Why didn't you shoot me in the back?"

"Because I wanted to find out who you were. Besides, I like to give a man an even chance. Take that Mohawk, for instance. I shot him right between the eyes."

156

"How do you know he's a Mohawk?"

"I've come across most of the Indian tribes hereabouts."

"Does that mean you live nearby?"

"I ask the questions, Mr. Skoyles," said the other, taking a few steps toward him. "Now, what are you doing here?"

"Looking for him," replied Skoyles, jerking his thumb over his shoulder. "His name is Redsnake. He knocked me unconscious and stole my horse."

"You're lying. If he had the chance, he'd have scalped you."

"Search him. He took my telescope as well."

The man patted his pocket. "I have it here, Mr. Skoyles," he said, watching his prisoner carefully. "Such a strange object to find on a dead Indian. I reckon it's about time you told me exactly who you are."

"A hunter."

"Not a very good one, by the look of it. There's no game on either of the horses."

"I was just starting out," said Skoyles.

"Do you shoot or trap?"

"Both."

"Why do you need to carry such a valuable telescope?"

"It was given to me by a friend."

Isaac Harman did not believe him. Since the other man had the weapon, Skoyles had to humor him while waiting for the opportunity to strike. Inside his belt under the hunting shirt was the loaded pistol. It would only take a second to bring it out. Harman came within reach of him and studied him with interest.

"You're no hunter, Mr. Skoyles," he decided. "Leastways, you're not here to hunt game. I get the feeling you were after human quarry. Am I right, sir?" Skoyles shook his head. "How come you know the Indian's name?"

"I thought he was a friend of mine."

"Then you know little about the Mohawks. Their name comes from the Algonquian word meaning 'man-eater.' Yes, that fellow you called a friend was a cannibal. His tribe has been known to roast their enemies alive and carve themselves a tasty portion as they do so." He gave a wry smile. "You're lucky. It's not just a scalp you lose if you cross a Mohawk."

"Why did you shoot him?"

"He came at me with his tomahawk."

157

"What were you doing here in the first place?"

"Ah-ah," Harman reminded him. "I ask the questions, remember?"

"Could I at least have my telescope back?"

"I've no proof that it actually belongs to you, Mr Skoyles."

"How else would I know that Redsnake had taken it?"

"He might have stolen it from its rightful owner."

"That's me," Skoyles insisted. "Look, the name of the maker is inscribed on it. I can tell you what it is."

"Very well," the other conceded. "We'll put that to the test."

It was the mistake for which Skoyles had been waiting. Harman tucked the butt of the rifle under one arm and kept his finger on the trigger. He then used his other hand to take the telescope from his pocket. At the very moment when Harman glanced down at the instrument, Skoyles made his move, diving forward to grab the barrel of the rifle and knocking the other man off his feet. The rifle went off, discharging its ball harmlessly into the air. Before Harman could recover, he found a pistol pressed hard against his temple.

"My name is Captain Jamie Skoyles of the 24th Foot," said Skoyles. "Consider yourself a prisoner of the British army."

Isaac Harman began to laugh uncontrollably.

Major Harry Featherstone arrived early at the house that evening so that he could have a private word with Burgoyne before they settled down at the card table with the others. The general was sympathetic.

"I can see your dilemma, Harry," he said. "Why wait at least a year to marry Elizabeth in a cathedral when our chaplain can perform the office in Albany? I'm sure that we could find a presentable church."

"That's what I told Elizabeth."

"Why is she against the notion?"

"Because it wouldn't meet with her parents' approval."

"Undeniably," said Burgoyne. "Richard Rainham is a stickler for the proprieties. He'll want to see his daughter married in Canterbury with the cream of the county in attendance. However, there are times in one's life when one has to flout parental wishes. I certainly did," he remembered with a chuckle. "Charlotte's father thought me such a highly unsuitable husband that he forbade his daughter to have anything to do with me. An elopement was the only course open to us."

"That's not the situation here," said Featherstone. "Elizabeth's parents are more than ready to accept me into the family."

"On their terms."

"Yes, General."

"Then perhaps you should effect a compromise."

"In what way?"

"Marry the lady in Albany and have a service of blessing in Canterbury Cathedral when you get back. In a sense, you'll then have two weddings, with all objections answered."

"Elizabeth may not see it that way."

"Tell her you love her so much that you want to marry her twice."

"Once is all that I crave, General," said Featherstone.

Burgoyne heard the edge of desperation in his voice. Featherstone was in a very awkward position. During the invasion from Canada the previous year, he had done exactly what many single officers did and acquired a series of mistresses with whom to while away the long summer nights. Burgoyne did not blame him for that, nor did he think it reprehensible behavior for a man engaged to be married. It was an accepted feature of army life. The presence of Elizabeth Rainham ruled out the option of a mistress, and Featherstone was finding that romantic love was a poor substitute for the delights of the flesh. Close to the woman he wanted, he was unable even to touch her. It was aggravating. He and Elizabeth could only consummate their love as husband and wife.

"By the time we reach Albany," Burgoyne observed, "Elizabeth will be twenty-one. That gives her certain rights of decision."

"She refuses to exercise them, General."

"Why?"

"I wish that I knew," Featherstone confided. "When I first raised the idea of marriage, Elizabeth was almost as excited as I was. Then we had that debacle at Bitter Creek. Since then, I fear, she's become a different person. She'll not even discuss the possibility."

"Give her time, Harry," Burgoyne advised. "What she saw at Bitter Creek was enough to disconcert anyone. Elizabeth is bound to brood on the death of her uncle and cousins. Give her time. She'll come round."

There was a tap and the door and it opened to admit two visitors. Expecting the other card players, Burgoyne was surprised to see Jamie Skoyles entering with a stranger.

"Excuse the interruption, General," said Skoyles, "but this will brook no delay. Allow me to introduce Lieutenant Isaac Harman. He's brought word from General Howe in New York."

"At last!" cried Burgoyne, shaking Harman's hand. "You're most welcome, Lieutenant. We were beginning to think that Sir William had forgotten us. You're the first messenger to get through."

"The others must have been intercepted, General," said Harman, removing his hat. "I thought at one point that my own embassy would fail, but Captain Skoyles turned out to be friend rather than foe. I've never felt so relieved in all my born days." He pointed to Skoyles. "You have a remarkable man here. The captain disarmed me when I was holding a rifle on him."

"That's the kind of thing Skoyles is inclined to do," said Burgoyne with a grin. "Isn't it, Harry?"

"Yes, sir," muttered Featherstone.

"You have the dispatch, Lieutenant?"

"Yes," replied Harman, taking it from inside his coat to hand it over, "but you won't be able to read it easily, I'm afraid. It's in code, General."

"In that case, I'll have to decipher it. Excuse us, gentlemen," he said, opening the door to the adjoining room. "Lieutenant Harman and I will be back in a short while."

Jamie Skoyles was left alone with Harry Featherstone. There was an uneasy silence that lasted for well over a minute. Skoyles tried to break it with a polite inquiry.

"May I ask how Miss Rainham is?" he said.

"Miss Rainham is well," replied the other stiffly.

"Has she recovered from the horrors witnessed at Bitter Creek?"

"She will do so in time. Not that it concerns you, of course. What happens to Miss Rainham is something that you'll never know. I've spiked your guns, Captain."

"My guns?"

"Yes," said Featherstone with a sneer. "From now on, you'll not be able to pump her maid for information. I've stopped the woman from speaking to Sergeant Caffrey's whore."

Skoyles bristled. "Polly Bragg is no whore, Major."

"She is in my eyes."

"When it comes to whores," said Skoyles pointedly, "I bow to your superior knowledge of the breed. But I'll not have you insulting Mrs. Bragg by attaching that name to her. She deserves respect."

"Not from me. She's been operating as your spy."

"That's not true."

"You told her to befriend Nan Wyatt."

"I did nothing of the kind, Major," Skoyles retorted, "and I resent the suggestion that I did. Polly Bragg takes no orders from me."

"Sergeant Caffrey does and he can instruct his whore."

"Stop calling her that!"

Featherstone was defiant. "I'll call that trull whatever I wish."

"Not in my hearing," Skoyles warned.

He squared up to the Major with his eyes blazing. Featherstone glared back at him but he did not take up the challenge. The tension between them was close to breaking point when Burgoyne came back into the room with Harman. The general concealed his disappointment well. His voice was almost cheerful.

"At least we know where we stand now," he announced. "It seems that General Howe has elected to sail for Philadelphia instead of coming to meet us at Albany." He snapped his fingers. "No matter for that. We can manage without him, and we still have Brigadier St. Leger to reinforce us. All is well, gentleman," he said, airily. "It has turned out to our advantage. We have just been granted an opportunity to steal all of the glory for ourselves."

The number of people in the field hospital increased every day. Private Marcus Wolverton was confined there until he was sufficiently well to return to his duties. The wound in his arm was still heavily bandaged and giving him continuous twinges. His thigh would also take time to heal. To take his mind off the discomfort, and to stave off boredom, he played cards that evening with Private Andrew McKillop, a chubby Scotsman who remained resolutely cheerful even though he had had a leg amputated as a result of the action at Bitter Creek. McKillop was propped up on a mattress outside his tent, seemingly oblivious to the pain he must be suffering. Wolverton could not understand how the man kept his spirits up.

161

"In your position," he admitted, "I'd be cursing high heaven."

"What's the point, Wolvie?" asked McKillop, shuffling the cards. "I'm not stupid enough to think that God will listen to anything I have to say. He washed his hands of me years ago."

"God has time for even the worst sinners."

"Including the one-legged variety?"

"He has a special place in His heart for them, Andy."

McKillop laughed. "I know you're trying to reassure me," he said, dealing the cards, "but there's no need. I'm not resentful. I may've lost a limb but I still have the rest of my body. I also have an occupation I enjoy, friends I love, and a commander I admire. What more do I need?"

"Life will be somewhat different from now on."

"I know that, Wolvie. I won't be able to march in battle with you, maybe, but I can still stay in the regiment. Sergeant Caffrey says there are lots of things I can do, especially when I'm fitted with my wooden leg. I can't wait for that to happen."

"You're an example to us all, Andy."

"Someone has to be or you'd have nobody to look up to."

"What about me?" said Daniel Lukins, coming over to them. "I tries to set 'im a good example. I does my very best to keep 'im on the straight and narrow. Wolvie looks upon me as 'is moral guardian."

Wolverton picked up his cards. "I look upon you as nothing but a common thief, Dan Lukins," he said, arranging the cards in order. "You've stolen my watch three times already."

"A man has to keep his hand in," said McKillop.

"Yes," Lukins added. "Besides, it weren't your watch in the first place, Wolvie. You filched it off that rebel officer at 'Ubbardton."

Wolverton sniffed. "Finders, keepers."

"That's what I said when I found it in your pocket."

"Go away, Dan. You're standing in my light."

"I just came to see if you've 'eard the rumor?"

"What rumor?" asked McKillop.

"Charlie Westbourne 'as finally lost 'is virginity."

"Never! Who was the unlucky woman?"

"There were five of 'em, Andy," said Lukins, cackling. "Four to 'old 'im down and one to make a man of 'im."

"Don't believe a word of it!" Wolverton warned. "Dan is lying again."

"No, I ain't. There *is* a rumor, and it did come from the Lieutenant, but the bit about the five women was wrong—there were only four." He dodged the punch that Wolverton flung at him. "No need to 'it me."

"There's *always* a need to hit you, Dan. You should be struck hard on the hour every day until you learn to tell the truth."

"This is the truth—I swear it!"

"How is Lieutenant Westbourne involved?" said McKillop.

"Because 'e was the one I over'eard, talking to another officer. They 'ad these worried looks on their faces, so I thought it was important to listen." He moved in closer and adopted a more conspiratorial tone. "The rumor is there ain't no reinforcements comin' from New York."

"But they were supposed to meet us at Albany," said Wolverton.

"General 'Owe is goin' to attack Philadelphia instead."

"That will take him further south—away from us."

"It's only a rumor, mind," said Lukins, "but I got an 'orrible feelin' that it may turn out to be true. I'm scared stiff."

"You're always scared, Dan."

"Well, I'm not," McKillop affirmed, exposing a row of tobacco-stained teeth as he grinned broadly. "We've got nothing to be frightened about. The British army is the finest in the world. We beat the French, we beat the Spanish, and we'll give these bloody Americans a damned good hiding as well."

"We could do it more easily with General Howe's army to support us," said Wolverton, "but that may not be possible. I hope that these wounds of mine heal up soon. It sounds as if I'll be needed."

McKillop sat up. "And me—I can still hold a musket!"

"You can't 'op around a battlefield on one leg, Andy," said Lukins.

"Try stopping me. I joined this army to fight."

"Well, I didn't, and I say it again—this rumor scares the pants off me. I think we should go back to Canada where it's safe."

"See it as a chance to make a name for yourself, Dan," Wolverton urged, hiding his own disquiet. "We're going to find a lot of action ahead of us. Who knows? If you kill an officer, as I did, you might be able to take a watch off him—then you won't have to keep stealing mine."

Lieutenant Isaac Harman was staying overnight in the camp before making the return journey on the following day. Jamie Skoyles invited the man into his tent so that they could talk at leisure. Harman was a New York loyalist who had enlisted in the British army the previous year. Skoyles admired his courage in volunteering to act as a messenger.

"I had no idea that you'd come as far south as Skenesborough," said Harman. "When I set out from New York, we'd not even heard the news that Ticonderoga had fallen."

"Why did it take you so long to get here?"

"Because I didn't hurry, Captain. Three of us were sent at the same time. Two were express riders, finding fresh horses as they went along and trying to outrun any pursuit. Their problem was that they looked exactly what they were."

"Messengers, riding hell for leather."

"Precisely, my friend, whereas I was posing as a man intent on buying land in New England. The disguise worked until I came up against you in the forest."

"I took you for a rebel," Skoyles confessed.

"So did lots of people, fortunately," said Harman. "That's why I haunted the taverns wherever I stayed. I could pick up information from the enemy that way. It was in a tavern in Albany that I heard that General Schuyler was going to send fifteen hundred soldiers to Fort Edward."

"That intelligence helped to spare my blushes, Lieutenant. I was due to press on to Fort Edward for the purposes of reconnaissance. Since you knew so much about the place, you saved me the trouble."

"Glad to be of assistance."

"You even caught Redsnake for me."

"That was unintentional. He tried to ambush me."

"It enabled me to get the horses and the telescope back."

"Did you tell General Burgoyne how the instrument went astray?"

"No," said Skoyles honestly. "He has enough on his mind at the moment. I didn't want to add to his worries."

"Gentleman Johnny doesn't seem to *have* any worries. When he deciphered that dispatch, he didn't turn a hair. It was almost as if he were glad that General Howe would not be coming."

"I can't say that *I'm* glad, Lieutenant. It will considerably diminish the impact we can make. Our aim was to isolate the rebels in the north."

"You may still do that, Captain."

"Not unless we win a pitched battle against them."

"It may not come to that," said Harman, sagely. "The rebels are in disarray. The loss of Fort Ticonderoga was a massive blow to them. They were still dazed by it when I got to Albany."

"We may have put the Continental Army to flight," said Skoyles, "but there are still the militias to call upon. They'll boost the numbers at General Schuyler's disposal."

"That's not the impression that I got, Captain."

"Oh?"

"I saw members of the New England militia on my way here. They looked like a rabble. Most of them of them had no uniform to speak of, and there was little sense of organization."

"They'll be organized enough on a battlefield," Skoyles argued. "It's dangerous to have no respect for an enemy. A war is not always won by the army with the smartest uniforms."

The discussion continued until Harman began to tire visibly. After shaking him warmly by the hand, Skoyles told him where he could sleep for the night and sent him off, grateful to have made his acquaintance. Alone in his tent, Skoyles felt a sudden need for company, and the face of Maria Quinn came into his mind. He regretted the way that he had abandoned her so swiftly during her earlier visit, and he wanted to make amends. Skoyles was tense, tired, and jaded. Maria Quinn would be the ideal antidote. He left the tent in order to find her, only to be met by the solid figure of Sergeant Tom Caffrey.

"Just the man I need," said Caffrey.

"Hello, Tom."

"Were you going somewhere?"

"Only to take a walk and get some fresh air," Skoyles lied, not wishing to take his friend into his confidence about Maria Quinn.

"I thought you'd still be out with Redsnake."

"I returned a lot sooner than I expected."

"Miss Rainham will be pleased to hear that."

"Miss Rainham?"

Caffrey handed him the letter. "She left this for you."

"When?" said Skoyles, pleased at the news. "And *why?*"

"Read it and find out."

Skoyles went into his tent with his Caffrey. Opening the letter, he studied it by the light of the candle. It consisted of only three sentences but he read them several times, searching for a message between the lines. His face was glowing.

Caffrey came over to him. "Well, what does she say?"

"Enough."

Elizabeth Rainham was about to retire early for the night. She would have appreciated company, but Major Featherstone had chosen to play cards instead. Elizabeth hoped that his decision did not foreshadow their marriage. To have a husband who preferred a game of whist to an evening with his wife was not an enticing prospect. On the other hand, she told herself, Featherstone was accepting an invitation from General Burgoyne that he could hardly refuse. It was a mark of favor in which she could take some pleasure. It never occurred to her that the reason why he was included in so many card games was that Major Harry Featherstone was a compulsive gambler.

She was on the point of undressing when she heard voices outside her tent. Nan Wyatt was instantly recognizable, but Elizabeth did not know the other woman's voice. After a while, Nan asked if she could come in to speak to her mistress, and she was admitted at once. Elizabeth could see that she was perplexed.

"Who was that?" she wondered.

"Polly Bragg, ma'am."

"What on earth is she doing here?"

"She brought a message for you," said Nan softly.

"From whom?"

"Captain Skoyles. He wishes to see you."

"*Now?*" said Elizabeth, taken aback.

"If at all possible."

"*Here?* No, it's out of the question. I couldn't possibly allow that, Nan. It would be most improper."

"The captain fully understands that, ma'am. He suggests that you meet somewhere else. If you agree, Mrs. Bragg will take us there."

"Did he say *why* he wants to see me?"

"He gave no reason, it seems," said Nan, "but I fancy that it may have something to do with that letter you wrote to him."

"I'd almost forgotten that."

"Had you, ma'am?"

There was a twinkle in the maid's eye that signaled her disbelief. Nan Wyatt was discreet. She was also very perceptive and had sensed the strong feelings that Elizabeth harbored for Jamie Skoyles. It was not her place to discourage them. Elizabeth was hesitant. The request had taken her completely by surprise and she was not at all sure how she should respond. Wanting to see him again, she knew that the situation was fraught with difficulties. If she agreed to a meeting, she would be giving herself away; if she declined to go, she risked offending a man for whom she had a growing fondness. Yet if she did see him—and if it came to the knowledge of Harry Featherstone—there would be terrible repercussions.

"What are you going to do, ma'am?" Nan prompted her.

"I don't know."

"Shall I tell Mrs. Bragg that you need more time to think it over?"

"No, no," said Elizabeth quickly. "Don't send her away."

"It's getting dark now. Nobody would see us."

"That's not the point, Nan. What I have to judge is whether or not it's appropriate behavior for me."

"Only you can decide that, ma'am."

"It's rather late. I was about to go to bed."

"Captain Skoyles has only asked for a few minutes of your time," said Nan reasonably. "But I can see that it's not convenient, so I'll tell Mrs. Bragg to convey that message to the captain."

"Wait," said Elizabeth, putting out a hand to stop her. "Perhaps I can spare a few minutes, after all. It's the very least that I owe him."

As he waited for her response, Jamie Skoyles felt very nervous, uncertain whether Elizabeth Rainham would come or, if she did, what he would say to her. He began to worry that he had read more into her letter than was really there. Short, formal, written in a neat hand, it simply expressed her sincere thanks for the way he had rescued her at Bitter Creek. Skoyles hoped that it said something else as well. He had borrowed Tom Caffrey's tent because it was closer to the encampment where Elizabeth was staying and could be construed as neutral ground. Had he invited her to his own tent, he was sure that she would have refused to come.

The sound of female voices told him that his agonizing wait was over. Polly Bragg held back the flap so that Elizabeth Rainham and Nan Wyatt could go into the tent. Skoyles had lit every candle available and they threw a lurid glow onto the canvas.

"Thank you for coming, Miss Rainham," he said.

"I'm not able to stay long."

"Of course."

She glanced around. "This looks and smells like the medical tent."

"Sergeant Caffrey loaned it to me. In fact, that's one of the things that I wished to make clear. You must be aware by now of the sergeant is very close to Mrs. Bragg and that she befriended your maid."

"It was the other way round," said Nan. "I befriended her."

"Perhaps you had better leave us alone, Nan," Elizabeth suggested.

"Are you sure?"

"Yes."

"Oh, I see. Very well, ma'am."

After glancing from one to the other, Nan backed out of the tent.

"I think I know what you were going to tell me, Captain," said Elizabeth, "but no explanation is needed. I never believed for a moment that you had set Mrs. Bragg to spy on me."

"Major Featherstone thinks differently. He accused me to my face."

"He spoke very unkindly of Mrs. Bragg. I've only just met her for the first time, but I found her extremely pleasant."

"Polly is a wonderful woman. She's nursed dozens of wounded men back to health. Sergeant Caffrey says that her help is invaluable. On the other hand," he admitted, "I can't pretend that her friendship with your maid was entirely innocent."

"That's neither here nor there," she said. "All that concerns me is that you did not deliberately employ her for your own purposes."

"Perhaps not, Miss Rainham, but I was ready to hear everything that she learned about you. It was more than idle curiosity."

"I was interested to hear any gossip about you, Captain."

"Major Featherstone will provide you with plenty of that, surely?"

"I preferred an account that had less prejudice in it."

Elizabeth gave a first smile and he responded to it with a grin. They were standing yards apart in the flickering light. Skoyles had never seen her look so lovely. There was an air of sadness about her that had not been there before, but it only served to enhance her beauty. Adversity had turned her into a mature woman.

"I'm sorry for what happened at Bitter Creek," he said.

"So am I, Captain. I've still not been able to find the courage to write to my parents about it. Mother will be heartbroken. Uncle David was her only brother." She hunched her shoulders. "Somehow, I've been unable even to lift a pen."

"Yet you wrote to me."

"Only because I felt that I'd been neglectful. I didn't thank you nearly enough for what you did at the farm. It's the second time that you've rescued Major Featherstone, and as for me . . ." Her voice faded to a whisper and she gave a wan smile. "Well, we both know what would have happened. Thanks to you, I was spared."

"Nothing gave me more relief than that, Miss Rainham."

He stepped in close to her and fought off the impulse to take her in his arms again. Skoyles could see the confusion in her eyes, a mixture of hope, interest, uneasiness, and cold dread. She bit her lip. It was as if she wanted to make some sort of declaration but was held back by fear of the consequences. No such fear hampered him. When he smiled down at her, it was with a warmth and frankness that revealed his true feelings. On the point of reaching out to him, she withdrew her hand at the last moment. Her discomfort was patent.

"I should not have come here, Captain," she said.

"Why? Are you afraid of me?"

"Not at all. I'm afraid of myself—afraid and a trifle ashamed."

"You've done nothing shameful, Miss Rainham."

"I feel that I might."

"Why did you write that letter to me?"

"To show my gratitude."

"But you were going to express your thanks in person," Skoyles noted. "According to Sergeant Caffrey, you came looking for me in my tent. Why bring a letter if you intended to speak to me?"

There was an uncomfortable pause. He could see her wrestling with her conscience. Acutely aware that she was betrothed to another man, she was nevertheless drawn to Skoyles in a way that she could not control. It was unnerving. Though she retained her outward poise, a battle was raging inside her. Instinct was fighting against precept, temptation against the firm commitment she had already made. Her upbringing had prepared her to cope with almost any situation but the one in which she now found herself. She was a realist. Opportunities to see Skoyles were few and far between. She knew that the chance of a moment alone with him might never come again. Whatever it cost her in terms of embarrassment, Elizabeth had to speak out now.

"I wrote that letter for one simple reason," she said, candidly. "I wanted you to know how I felt about you."

Turning on her heel, she rushed out of the tent. Skoyles went after her, but she did not look back. With Nan beside her, she hurried across the grass and was soon lost in the darkness. He stood outside the tent, bemused by her declaration, wondering if he had heard her aright. Skoyles took her letter from his pocket to sniff the scented stationery. It made his spirits soar. Elizabeth Rainham was genuinely interested in him. He could offer her none of the wealth and aristocratic status that came with a marriage to Harry Featherstone, yet she had broken through all the restraints and conventions that bound her in order to reveal her affection for Jamie Skoyles. He was thrilled.

Maria Quinn spent the night alone, after all.

CHAPTER ELEVEN

Lieutenant General Sir John Burgoyne understood the importance of visibility. Other commanders might have been content to spend the long wait in the relative comfort of Colonel Skene's house, dividing their time between leisurely dinners, endless card games, and nights of abandon with a voluptuous mistress. While he took abundant pleasure in all of these things, Burgoyne did not neglect his duties. He held regular meetings with his senior officers, inspected the troops from time to time, and made sure that he was seen in public by as many of his soldiers as possible. It was one of the reasons he was so popular. There was nothing remote and aloof about Gentleman Johnny. He was a familiar sight who could revive the most jaded spirits.

Burgoyne did not ignore the sweating fatigue parties who worked so hard to build a road through the forest. He rode out occasionally to see what progress they had made and to offer his encouragement. When the men were well into their second week of drudgery, they were visited yet again by their commander, in company, this time, with Captain Jamie Skoyles, who wished that the day were not quite so hot and humid. Burgoyne was pleased by what he saw.

"Excellent, excellent!" he called out to the axmen who were trying to remove yet another huge tree from their path. "Well done, men!"

"Wearing woolen uniforms is like working in a furnace," said Skoyles, dabbing at his brow with a handkerchief. "These men are heroes."

"Their reward is the knowledge that they're opening up a pathway to the enemy. We'll hound the rebels until they run out of hiding places."

"We'll have lost many men in the process, sir."

"I accept that."

"It's not just those who were killed by sharpshooters or bitten by poisonous snakes. Dozens have gone down with fever, hundreds have succumbed to dysentery."

"Fault of the climate. Unhealthy place to be."

"Colonel Skene thinks that this is Elysium, sir."

"Ha!" snorted Burgoyne, beating away a mosquito that had attempted to crawl under his wig. "Living in this wilderness and keeping your mother's coffin on a table is not my idea of Elysium. But, then, I suppose," he added with a wicked grin, "if I'd been born somewhere as heathenish as Scotland, I might believe that it was."

They swung their horses round and kicked them into a trot. Burgoyne gave a friendly wave to everyone they passed, and Skoyles saw the way that it always cheered the soldiers up. The captain waited until they were clear of swampland before he spoke.

"Have you no qualms about taking the forest route, sir?"

"None whatsoever."

"It's slowed us down completely."

"The calm before the storm, Captain."

"Even when they've finished cutting a way through, it will be not be a proper road. I was talking to one of officers in charge of the work," said Skoyles. "He told me that there are quagmires that will suck our wagons down into them if they carry full loads."

Burgoyne was unworried. "Then we simply unload them, drive the wagons on through, and replace their cargo when they're on firmer ground again. No problem is insurmountable."

"What about the lack of an army from New York?"

"That was part of my original strategy, I grant you, but I've no power to coerce General Howe into accepting it. If he prefers to chase the rebels out of Philadelphia, so be it. I wish him well. In any case," he continued, "it's not certain that no help at all will come from New York. Sir William is leaving General Clinton there. It may well be that he has orders to meet us at Albany."

"Was there any suggestion of that in General Howe's dispatch?"

"No," Burgoyne admitted, "but, then, it was sent some time ago, before news of our triumph at Ticonderoga reached the ears of our commander in chief. On receipt of that intelligence, Sir William may well have amended his plans."

"And if he has not?" asked Skoyles, hiding his concern.

"Then we have more than enough men for the task ahead. All that they require is firm leadership from their officers." Burgoyne turned to him. "Do you hear that, Captain? Confidence is our watchword."

"Yes, General."

"When you take your men into battle, you must not be troubled by even a ghost of a doubt. Confidence inspires—doubt only weakens."

"I learned that in my first skirmish, sir," said Skoyles. "A hesitant officer is a liability. Conviction is everything."

"Quite. Fortune favors us. We will press on to a famous victory. If we can take Ticonderoga, nothing can stand in our way."

"Word of its capture must have reached Congress by now. How do you think they will react, sir?"

Burgoyne laughed. "They are probably still wetting their breeches."

"Who will be blamed for the retreat?"

"General Schuyler, of course."

"General St. Clair was the fort's commander."

"His superior will have to take responsibility," said Burgoyne, "and rightly so. Both men will be thoroughly vilified. Lieutenant Harman, the messenger you escorted into camp, heard the angry talk in the taverns of Albany. People there are saying that St. Clair and Schuyler must have accepted bribes from us to surrender Fort Ticonderoga without even firing a shot."

"That's not true at all."

"It has the *appearance* of truth, Captain, and that's what counts in the long run. It spreads dissension. Even as we speak, Congress is probably deciding whether or not to replace General Schuyler."

"Would that be to our advantage, sir?"

"I don't think that it matters either way. They have no commanders to match ours," said Burgoyne with measured contempt in his voice. "Let them send a wealthy Dutchman like Philip Schuyler, a mad American like Benedict Arnold, or a renegade Englishman like Horatio Gates against us—we'll still fight our way to Albany.

"Will we, General?"

"We simply have to, man."

"Why?"

"Because of the wedding to be held there," said the other jovially. "Harry

Featherstone wants to marry his beautiful bride and—as a close friend of the family—I intend to be in Albany to give her away."

Skoyles felt as if he had just been hit hard in the stomach.

"I fail to see what objection you can raise," he said peevishly. "Ten days ago, you thought it a wonderful idea."

"Circumstances have changed, Harry."

"No, they haven't. We still love each other, don't we?"

"That's not the point."

"It's the reason we decided to get married in the first place."

"I know," said Elizabeth, "and it's the reason I endured that ghastly voyage in order to be with you. Everything was going well until we made that ill-fated visit to Uncle David's farm."

He released a sigh. "I've told you how much I regret that."

"You were not to blame."

"I feel that I was," Featherstone confessed. "At a time when you most needed protection, I was unable to provide it."

They were in Elizabeth Rainham's tent. Major Featherstone had come to escort her to dinner with General Burgoyne. He took advantage of a private moment together to try to persuade her that they should hold their wedding in Albany. Elizabeth's reluctance was beginning to irritate him. His manner became more forceful.

"The service of holy matrimony enjoins you to love, honor, and obey your husband," he reminded her. "Don't you think a little obedience is in order here?"

"You're not my husband yet, Harry."

"But you've pledged yourself to me."

"Not in front of a priest and congregation."

"Why are you being so difficult?"

"I don't mean to be," said Elizabeth with an appeasing smile. "I simply don't wish to be rushed into anything."

"Who is rushing you? We've known each other for years."

"I agree—and, during all that time, you've never been out of my thoughts. But that doesn't mean we have to get married in America."

"Why not, Elizabeth? Everyone approves of the notion."

"Everyone?" she said, bridling. "You've discussed this with other people? Harry, how could you?"

"I mentioned it to General Burgoyne, that's all."

"That's not all. If *he* knows, then Mrs. Mallard knows as well. And I daresay they've passed on the news to others. In all honesty," she said, her cheeks coloring with indignation, "this has upset me more than I can tell you. It was supposed to be our secret. Instead of that, it will be the talk of the camp."

"Elizabeth!"

"Who else did you confide in?"

"Nobody."

"Be honest with me, Harry," she pressed, "I can see in your face that you're not telling the truth. Who else knows about this?"

"One or two friends," he said with a dismissive gesture. "No more than that, I promise you." She turned away in disgust. "It was the natural thing to do, Elizabeth. I wanted to share my joy. You can hardly reproach me for that."

"No firm decision had been made."

"I thought that it had."

"Then you were too presumptuous," she said, swinging round to face him again. "All that I agreed to do was to think it over."

"You said, in so many words, that it was a tempting offer."

"It was—when the subject was first broached. Then I began to realize the arguments against it. Think how hurt my parents would be that they were not consulted. Think how cheated all our friends and relations in England will be that they were not here for the occasion." She shook her head. "No, Harry. Getting married in Albany would be a lovely gesture to make, but it's quite impracticable."

"I dispute that."

"We're in the middle of a campaign."

"That's what gave me the idea," he explained, spreading his arms. "What better way to celebrate a famous victory than by getting married?"

"You're assuming that victory can be taken for granted."

"I'd bet my fortune on it!"

"The rebels won't give up without a fight."

"I hope they don't. We'll be ready for them with cold steel and red hot musket balls." The prospect excited him. "It will be my finest hour as a soldier, Elizabeth. We'll crush those dregs of humanity under our feet."

"Supposing you get injured?"

"When I know that you're waiting for me?"

"You can't control what happens in battle. Look at Hubbardton."

"That was a mere skirmish," he said scornfully, "and I was never in real danger from the enemy—only from that imbecile Higgs. I'm an officer. I know how to conduct myself in action. All I need to spur me on is the promise of marrying you afterward."

"When we get back to England," she said.

"The wait will be interminable. I love you, Elizabeth," he declared, taking her in his arms. "I want you *now*. When I look at the others who are traveling with their wives, I feel insanely jealous and disadvantaged. We're three thousand miles away from home—we *need* each other."

"That's why I came, Harry."

"Then take the final step and marry me in Albany."

"I'm sorry, but I just can't do that. It would be wrong."

"Nothing feels more right to me."

Elizabeth broke away from him. His ardor was deeply troubling to her. She was not merely opposed to the notion of a wedding on foreign soil, she was having doubts about her choice of Harry Featherstone as a husband. It was vexing. For the most part, Elizabeth had loved him from a distance while he was abroad with the army. Now that they were close, she was getting to know him better and discovering aspects of his character that she found distinctly unappealing.

Featherstone was hurt by her change of attitude. Accustomed to her submission, he was now meeting with rejection. It stung him into a confrontation.

"Something has happened, hasn't it?" he demanded.

"Yes, Harry—the events at Bitter Creek."

"There's something apart from that. I've noticed it particularly over the past week. You're pulling away from me. It's almost as if you've lost interest in Harry Featherstone."

"Don't be silly!"

"Why else are you refusing to marry me?"

"Because I'd prefer to wait until we return to Canterbury."

"No," he probed, "there's another reason. I can feel it. You've become withdrawn, even distracted at times. You give the impression that your mind is on something else." He seized her wrist. "Or on *someone* else."

"Let go of me, Harry."

"Am I right? Is that what lies behind all this?"

"You're hurting me," she cried.

"I want an answer, Elizabeth."

"Well, this is not the way to get one." She shook herself free and rubbed her wrist. "Is that how you intend to treat a wife?" she asked with controlled vehemence. "By using your strength to bully her?"

"I apologize," he said, seeing that he had gone too far. "I apologize unreservedly. I wouldn't harm you for the world, you must know that."

"Not anymore."

"Elizabeth!"

"Take me to dinner, Harry."

"We must settle this first."

"It has been settled. I refuse to discuss the matter any further."

"That's unfair. I have a right to put my side of the argument."

"You just did that," she said, still massaging her wrist. "Now, please take me to dinner before I lose my temper completely."

Captain Jamie Skoyles had been invited to his commander's table as well, but he visited the field hospital first to show a friendly interest in some of the patients. Knowing that Elizabeth Rainham would be present at dinner, he had taken pains with his appearance. He wore his dress uniform and had had his boots polished until they shone. Most of the facial wounds he had picked up at Fort Ticonderoga had healed. Skoyles was now a portrait of military elegance. Marcus Wolverton nodded in approval.

"I wore a uniform like that once, sir," he recalled, "when I played the part of a villainous Captain Downey."

"Did you?" said Skoyles. "Was that at Drury Lane?"

"No, sir—Foote's Theatre." He laughed and nudged Private Andrew McKillop, who sat beside him outside the tent. "Now, there's an odd coincidence, Andy. Have you ever heard tell of Mr. Samuel Foote?"

"Not me, Wolvie," replied the Scotsman. "Who was he?"

"An actor and a playwright," said Skoyles.

"Quite right, Captain," Wolverton agreed. "His comedies were so rich and biting that we called him the English Aristophanes. The reason I mention him, Andy, is that he lost a leg—just like you."

"Poor man!" said McKillop.

"In his case, it was a little more embarrassing."

"What do you mean, Wolvie?"

"Well, you lost your limb in action," said Wolverton, "and there's honor in that. Mr. Foote lost his during some horseplay involving a duke. Just think of it—a Foote being deprived of its leg. Because of his name, he had to endure so much mockery. The Lord moves in mysterious ways and some of them are downright blooming cruel."

"What happened to the fellow?" said Skoyles.

"By way of compensation, he received the patent for a theater and built it in the Haymarket. Do you see the coincidence, Andy? He was a man after your own heart. Losing a leg didn't quell his spirit."

"It restored mine," boasted McKillop.

"Good for you!" Skoyles complimented him. "I wish that all of our wounded men had the same vigor. And you won't be the only soldier with a wooden leg, McKillop. We had a quartermaster in my last regiment who was fitted with a leg that he'd carved into the shape of woman."

"What name did she answer to, sir?"

"Christabel."

The men appreciated his visit. Skoyles had a sincere interest in them and was not simply there to win a specious popularity. Unlike many officers, Skoyles was totally at ease with the rank and file, understanding their needs and knowing their tribulations at first hand. Wounded men often felt forgotten and resentful. Skoyles made sure that those in his regiment did not suffer from neglect. He looked at the one-legged Scotsman.

"What made you join the army, McKillop?" he said.

"Nairn Blaine, sir."

"Who?"

"He owned the Running Stag," the other explained, "a tavern in my village. I was always getting into fights there and causing damage to his property. Mr. Blaine gave me a choice. I could either join the army and fight for my country—or he'd have me locked up."

"We've good reason to be thankful to this Mr. Blaine then. You've been a credit to us. By the way," said Skoyles, looking round. "Where's Private Lukins today? As a rule, he's never far away from you, Wolverton. What's happened to him?"

"He's deserted, sir," said Wolverton.

"Are you serious?"

"Dan Lukins has certainly *talked* about it. He's lost his nerve. Ever since we heard that there's no army joining us from New York, he's been very jumpy. Dan thinks we'll be hopelessly outnumbered."

"That's not the case at all," said Skoyles.

"No," McKillop added. "Besides, one of us is worth ten of them."

"The rumor gave Dan a real fright," said Wolverton. "I don't believe he's run away, but I fancy that he's gone to ground somewhere."

Skoyles was puzzled. "How did Lukins get wind of the rumor?"

"He overheard Lieutenant Westbourne talking about it."

"The blazes, he did! That means he'll probably have passed the news on to anyone prepared to listen."

"Dan Lukins will have told half the army by now."

"Idiot!"

"Is it true, sir?" asked McKillop. "Have *you* heard the rumor?"

"Yes," replied Skoyles tactfully. "I brought the messenger from General Howe into camp. At this point in time, the situation in New York is unclear. We must remain optimistic. What we don't need, however, is someone like Private Lukins, running around in a panic and spreading unnecessary fear among the other men." He took a deep breath. "I'll make sure that he understands that."

Daniel Lukins bided his time. With his knapsack packed and his redcoat turned inside out so that it would be less conspicuous, he hid in the trees until the pickets were relieved by their replacements. The soldiers began to chat with each other. While they were distracted, Lukins made his move, coming out of cover and scuttling through the undergrowth. The little deserter soon vanished into the forest. One more name could be crossed off the roll.

The food was exceptional, the wine plentiful, and the atmosphere wholly agreeable, yet Elizabeth Rainham did not enjoy dinner at the house that afternoon. It was not only the presence of Lucinda Mallard that disconcerted her, nor even the way that the other guests seemed to accept her. What really irked her was that she was identified solely as Major Featherstone's future wife and treated accordingly. Though she had coveted the position in the past, she now found it annoyingly restrictive. Elizabeth's unease was compounded by the fact that Featherstone, seated opposite her, was still seething after their earlier quarrel and drinking heavily to subdue his pulsing anger.

There was an additional source of discomfort for her. Elizabeth was at the other end of the table from Jamie Skoyles, too far away to catch anything but a few words of what he was saying. It was the first time for over a week that she had been in the same room as Harry Featherstone and Skoyles, and it caused her profound gloom. Trapped beside one man and forced to behave in the way expected of her, she was longing to be with the other. Her emotions were in turmoil. Whatever she told Featherstone, she knew that her friendship with Jamie Skoyles was the cardinal reason why she had determined not to get married in haste. It would put her hopelessly beyond the reach of the one person who had aroused real passion in her.

Included among the dinner guests were General Riedesel and his wife, with Major and Lady Acland, two couples who seemed to be the paradigms of happy marriage. Their palpable contentment only made Elizabeth feel more discontented. She admired them without wanting to emulate them, convinced, in any case, that life with Harry Featherstone would never be give her the deep satisfaction that she saw in the faces of the two married women. Elizabeth wanted something else now.

General Burgoyne abruptly shifted attention to her.

"Have you named the day yet, Elizabeth?" he inquired roguishly.

"I'm sure that I don't know what you mean, General," she said.

"Come, come now. There's no call for secrecy here. We all know that you're going to marry Major Featherstone, splendid fellow that he is. The only question to be decided is whether you do it sooner or later."

Elizabeth was firm. "Later," she said.

"I thought that Albany was mentioned as a likely venue."

"It was, General," Featherstone agreed over the murmur of interest that the announcement had ignited. "And it has not been ruled out, I assure you. My own view is that it would be the perfect time and place for the ceremony. Elizabeth and I are still discussing the possibilities."

She was about to contradict him when they heard distant gunfire. The women were startled, but the men paid no heed to the noise. Burgoyne sipped some claret before offering an explanation.

"A firing squad," he said, calmly. "I'll have no thieves in the ranks. When we have limited provisions, we have to watch them carefully. If a man disobeys my orders and steals food, he must expect no quarter. Don't let it spoil the meal for you, ladies," he urged, indicating the dishes on the table. "Eat as much of this wondrous repast as you wish." He switched his gaze back to Elizabeth. "Were you on the point of saying something, my dear?"

"I think that Miss Rainham made her feelings clear," said Skoyles, sensing that she was in need of rescue. "It's a matter that she and the major are entitled to discuss in private without anyone else prying into their affairs. What I wanted to ask you, General," he continued, turning to Burgoyne, "was whether any news had come from Brigadier St. Leger?"

"Not yet, Captain."

"By my reckoning, he should have reached Oswego by now."

"I'm sure that he has. The brigadier has probably left Lake Ontario behind and is now transporting his craft over the portage to the Mohawk River. Ladies and gentlemen," he said, raising his glass. "I give you a toast to a gallant officer—Brigadier Barry St. Leger!"

"Brigadier St. Leger!" they echoed.

Burgoyne was exhilarated. "It does my heart good to have such fine men at my command," he announced. "All things proceed to a happy conclusion. In a day or so, we'll be able to march to Fort Edward. In a week or so, we may have word of the brigadier's success. Our men are primed for action, their spirits are high, their mind on victory. And there's another unexpected bonus to report," he said, gratefully. "The Indians are at long last starting to behave themselves."

Everyone who met Jane McCrea remarked on her hair. Long, red, silken, and luxuriant, it almost touched the ground when it was unfurled. Jane was a tall, well-formed, attractive woman in her early twenties, who lived with her elder brother in the area near Fort Edward. While her brother became a colonel in the New York militia, she remained a staunch Tory and refused to move to the safety of Albany with him. Instead, Jane stayed at the cabin of the elderly Mrs.

McNeil, a talkative widow of formidable size. Both of them had good reason to welcome the approaching British army. Jane McCrea was engaged to David Jones, a young officer who was part of the American Volunteer Corps that traveled with the invading force. Mrs. McNeil was the cousin of no less a person than Brigadier General Simon Fraser.

The two women were eating a meal at the cabin when a wild-eyed Negro came banging on their door. They recognized him as one of the slaves from a nearby farm. Exhausted from running so far, he barely had the breath to get out his warning.

"The Indians have killed and scalped everyone at our farm," he cried, gesticulating madly. "Leave now while you still have a chance."

The slave did not wait to see what their response would be. Forcing himself into a run once more, he headed for the cover of the nearest trees. The women were thrown into a panic, not knowing whether to flee or stay. Mrs. McNeil kept a musket in the cabin, but it would not ward off an attack by marauding Indians. She started to close the shutters on the windows. Jane was agitated, having heard gruesome tales of what Indians did to their victims. Both hands went instinctively to her hair.

Mrs. McNeil was at the rear window when she saw them coming. All that she and her guest could do was to hide. Grabbing the food off the table, she told Jane to open the trapdoor to the cellar. If the women hid down there, the Indians might think that the cabin was unoccupied. Jane heaved on the trapdoor and stood aside for the old woman to go first. Vital seconds were lost as Mrs. McNeil tried her best to maneuver her substantial bulk through the entrance to the cellar. She had to force her ample bosom past the rough timber.

Before Jane could follow her, the door burst open and two Ottawa Indians burst in, tomahawk in one hand and knife in the other. Vivid war paint was smeared over their faces. Fresh scalps hung from their belts. Blood had dripped onto their naked thighs.

When they saw the women, they let out a whoop of triumph.

By the time the news reached him, General Burgoyne had brought his army to the blackened ruins of Fort Anne. He was in his tent when Simon Fraser reported the outrage to him.

"Miss McCrea was *killed?*" said Burgoyne in alarm.

"Killed, scalped, mutilated, then covered in leaves and rolled naked into a hollow."

"What about your cousin? Was Mrs. McNeil murdered as well?"

"No," said Fraser. "Since they had no horse for her, they stripped her naked and made her follow on foot. My cousin was in a dreadful condition when she reached our advance camp. Unfortunately, she's a rather heavily built lady, and none of the women with us had clothing large enough to fit her. For the sake of modesty, I had to lend her my greatcoat."

"I'll need to speak to your cousin, Simon."

"I suggest that you wait for her to calm down first, sir."

"Why?"

"She has a tongue that could strip the bark off trees when she's been provoked, and she's still in a ferocious mood. In any case," Fraser went on, "my cousin didn't actually witness Jane McCrea's murder. She had lagged far behind by then."

"How did the atrocity first come to light?"

"The young lady's hair was uncommonly long and beautiful, it seems. Her scalp was seen dangling from the belt of an Indian by David Jones, the loyalist officer Miss McCrea was engaged to marry. They had to restrain him from attacking the Indian on the spot."

"I can well imagine his feelings," said Burgoyne. "These are grim tidings. I've no doubt that our enemy will make full use of them."

"The killer must be punished immediately."

"He will be, Simon. Order the Ottawa tribe to assemble."

"I've already done so, sir. I spoke to their leader."

"That slippery Frenchman, La Corne St. Luc."

"He claims to have some measure of control over them."

"Not enough, patently. Well," Burgoyne decided, "it's time we taught them something about British justice. We can't allow innocent civilians to be butchered in this way." He shook his head in disgust. "This is truly appalling, Simon. I'd rather put my commission in the fire than have the government suppose that I condone such unheard-of barbarities. How misled I've been! I thought that the Indians would be our secret weapon—but they're turning out to be a nightmare."

Along with other officers, Captain Jamie Skoyles and Lieutenant Charles Westbourne were included in the party to visit the Ottawa camp. That was not unusual. Whenever he spoke to the Indians, the British commander felt it important to put on a show, arriving on horseback with a large delegation and behaving with due ceremony. The Indians were recent arrivals, having made the long journey from Canada to catch up with the army at Skenesborough. Stone-faced and watchful, they stood around in small groups as Burgoyne led his men into the camp.

"Is it true what people say about them?" asked Westbourne, riding beside Skoyles. "Are these the most vicious of the Indians?"

"None of the tribes is famed for civilized behavior, Lieutenant."

"Major Featherstone reckons that these are the worst."

"They've never been friends of ours," said Skoyles. "That much I know for a fact. Twenty years ago, when they fought against us on the side of the French, they were responsible for the terrible massacre at Fort William Henry. They slaughtered our wounded, violated and killed the women, then turned on the children without mercy. The man who led them that day is still their leader."

"Chevalier La Corne St. Luc. What sort of man is he?"

"Judge for yourself, Lieutenant. Here he comes."

The commander of the Ottawas was a tall, thin, swarthy Frenchman in his sixties with long gray hair and a face that had been stamped by time with a complex series of scars and wrinkles. Wearing a colorful robe and a feathered headdress, he nevertheless stood out from the braves around him by virtue of his color, manner, and bearing. La Corne St. Luc gave General Burgoyne a cautious welcome in his heavy accent.

"We know why you have come," he said, arms folded.

"Then let's not waste any words on it," the general declared. "A hideous crime was committed. Deliver up the malefactor, and we'll take the fellow straight off to hang him."

"I'm not able to do that, General."

"Why not?"

"Because the man is innocent of the murder."

"You *dare* to say that," Burgoyne retorted, "when he has the audacity to flaunt the young lady's scalp? Who on earth is this fiend?"

"His name is Wyandot Panther."

"Hand him over at once for execution."

"You would be punishing the wrong man, General," said the other coolly. "Wyandot swears that the lady was shot by rebels near Fort Edward. She died of her wounds."

"That's an arrant lie and he'll hang for it."

"No, General. Look around you." He indicated the whole of the camp with a dramatic sweep of his arm. "What you see are loyal friends. We journeyed for weeks to reach you, and we are ready to fight for the British. But if you try to hang one of my men," he threatened, "the rest of them will desert you on the spot and ravage the countryside all the way back to Canada."

Burgoyne was adamant. "I'd rather lose every Indian in this army than connive at their enormities."

The other man smiled. "You are too soft-hearted, General."

"I'm a soldier in the British army and I abide by its rules."

"They mean nothing at all to the Ottawas. You have your way of fighting a war. We have ours. Together we can conquer the enemy."

"Not if you let your men loose on defenseless women."

"They will restrain themselves in future. You have my word."

"What I want is the surrender of Wyandot Panther."

"Take him and you lose the entire tribe."

Burgoyne began to waver. Watching it all from nearby, Skoyles was dismayed at the way that they were being balked. The murder of Jane McCrea was an act of brutality that simply could not go unpunished. If clemency were shown, it would be seen by everyone as clear evidence of the general's inability to stop the excesses of the Indians. Even someone betrothed to a loyalist officer was not safe from the savages who traveled with the British army. Skoyles had protested against the use of Indians from the start. They were incorrigible. When he had made the mistake of trusting one of them—Redsnake—he had been betrayed. As he saw Burgoyne dismounting from his horse, Skoyles fumed in silence.

"What's happening, Captain?" asked Westbourne.

"They're going into the chief's teepee to discuss terms."

"No terms are required, surely? General Burgoyne has given his order. All they have to do is to hand over the killer and we can leave."

"Their commander has suggested a compromise."

"Compromise?"

"We spare the life of the Indian and, in return, the chief gives us another litany of promises that he has no intention of keeping." He gazed around the blank faces of the watching Ottawas. "The general is being tricked," he decided. "No matter what concessions you make to these people, they're going to desert us sooner or later."

"Do you think so?"

"It's inevitable."

"That would rob us of so much fighting power—and we've had enough desertions as it is."

"Prepare yourself for more, Lieutenant."

"Why?"

"Because we're moving closer to a battle all the time," said Skoyles. "That's when our soldiers' loyalty is really put to the test—under fire."

"How can anyone desert a man like General Burgoyne?" said Westbourne in bewilderment. "He is an inspiration to us all."

Skoyles chose his words with care. "He's a fine soldier and the most decent commander I've ever served under. The general has earned the immense popularity that he enjoys. However," he went on, "I doubt very much if the terms he is about to accept from the Indians will inspire anyone. We came to arrest a murderer and we'll leave empty-handed."

"Not if strict promises are extracted from La Corne St. Luc."

"Such promises are worthless."

"But they might bind the Ottawas to us."

"I wish that were true, Lieutenant," said Skoyles wearily, "but I fear that I have to stand by my prediction."

"What's that?"

"This whole tribe will desert us within a week."

"They've all gone?" said Marcus Wolverton in amazement. "The Ottawas have run out on us?"

"Every last one of them," Tom Caffrey told him. "And the worst of it is, they plundered our stores before they went."

"Thieving devils!"

"Good riddance, I say!" Andrew McKillop observed. "The longer we kept them, the worse it would have got. They kill anything that moves."

"I feel sorry for the people they meet on the way back home," said Caffrey with a sigh. "The Ottawas are so ruthless."

"That's why we employed them, isn't it?" noted Wolverton. "So that they could be ruthless to our enemies. They were hired to frighten."

"They just took their money and left."

On the very day after General Burgoyne's visit to their camp, the whole tribe had flitted away. The terms he had extracted from the Indians had no power to secure their loyalty. Reactions in the camp were mixed. Many thought that the army would be better off without the Indians, but even more were worried by the sudden depletion of their forces. As a fighting unit, they had been markedly weakened.

Tom Caffrey was making his rounds at the field hospital. A sudden downpour was keeping all his patients under cover. Wolverton and McKillop were sharing a tent with two other injured men.

"How does that feel now?" said Caffrey as he finished changing the dressing on the stump of McKillop's right leg. "Still painful?"

"I hardly notice it, Sergeant."

"At least, you survived. One of the farmers that the Ottawas killed nearby had the soles of his feet sliced off."

Wolverton shuddered. "Before or after he died?"

"Before," said Caffrey. "They like to watch a victim suffer. When they went, the Indians left a whole trail of heinous crimes behind them."

"We heard tell of a minister they cut down in his own church," said McKillop. "Then they raped his wife and daughter before hacking them to pieces. Have they no respect for human life at all?"

"None at all, Andy," said Wolverton.

"Civilians were not to be harmed. The general made that clear."

Caffrey pursed his lips. "Jane McCrea is the person I have most sympathy for," he said. "I hate to think what she had to endure before that savage put her out of her misery. We'll get the blame for it, mark my words. Every rebel newspaper in New England will print the story on its front pages—a lovely young woman was butchered by someone in the pay of the British army." He put the rest of the bandages away in his knapsack. "No word from Private Lukins, I take it?"

"None," said Wolverton sadly. "Dan has left us as well."

"Maybe he joined the Ottawas," McKillop suggested.

"No, Andy. Even Dan would never stoop that low."

"Is it true that he took your watch with him?" asked Caffrey.

"Yes, Sergeant. I'm not sure which hurts me most—losing Dan Lukins or losing that watch. It was the fourth time he stole it. Or, to be truthful," he said with a tired smile, "it was the fourth time that I *let* him steal it."

"Why did you do that?"

"It was a sort of game we played."

"He looked up to you, Wolvie," said McKillop, puffing on his pipe. "Yes, I know that you two were always at daggers drawn, but Dan really admired you for being so educated."

Wolverton grimaced. "What use is education to a private soldier?"

"A lot of use," Caffrey argued.

"It's a handicap, Sergeant, a real burden. It makes me stand out from the others and that gets me laughed at. Education was no help to me at Hubbard-ton," he said wryly. "When an enemy soldier is pointing a weapon at you, it's no good giving him a soliloquy out of *Hamlet*. All that he understands is a musket ball through the heart."

"I like to listen to you quoting Shakespeare," said McKillop with a grin. "You have the voice for it, doesn't he, Sergeant?"

"I agree," said Caffrey, trying to cheer the man up. "Perhaps you can go back to the stage one day, Wolverton. With luck, you might even get the chance of appearing in one of General Burgoyne's plays."

"That's exactly what I'm doing at the moment," said Wolverton bitterly. "I have a minor role in John Burgoyne's tragedy about the war against the American rebels. So do you, Andy," he told McKillop. "In the cast list, they have us down as Wounded Soldiers. We're not allowed any speeches, of course. Those are reserved for the officers. We just sit on the side of the stage and bleed convincingly."

"Stop it, Wolvie!" McKillop protested. "You give me the shivers."

"There's no call for you to be so cynical," said Caffrey. "Until your wounds heal up, you can enjoy a rest. Make the most of it, Wolverton."

"That's what *I'm* doing," said the Scotsman. "I love it."

"There you are—Private McKillop has the right attitude."

"Even if I don't have the right leg!"

Caffrey shared a laugh with him but Wolverton saw no cause for amusement. He reached for the battered copy of Shakespeare's sonnets that he always kept with him and began to read them to himself, losing himself in the intricate verse of another age. They were soon interrupted. The flap of the tent was held back and a head popped in.

"We found another man in the forest, Sergeant," said the newcomer, "but I'm afraid this one is way beyond your help."

"Do you know who he is?" asked Caffrey.

"Someone from the 24th Foot, though his jacket was turned inside out for some reason. He was dead when we found him."

Wolverton was on his feet. "Where is he?"

"Outside on the stretcher."

"Let me see."

The man's head withdrew and Wolverton limped quickly out of the tent. Caffrey followed him. Reaching for his crutch, McKillop hauled himself to his feet so that he could hobble after them. They stood in a circle around the forlorn figure on the stretcher outside. The rain was still falling but it could not wash away the dried blood on the face of Private Daniel Lukins. His bid for freedom had been summarily halted by three separate musket balls. One had pierced his skull, leaving a scarlet star on his forehead at the point of entry. A second had gone through his cheek and shattered the bone. Only the third one had met with some resistance.

Shaken by the violent death of his friend, Wolverton slipped a hand into the sodden jacket of the little man on the stretcher. When he took out the watch that Lukins had repeatedly stolen from him, he saw that a musket ball had shattered the glass and lodged in the works. The watch had stopped ticking.

"Well," he said, his voice hoarse with pity, "at least we know the exact time when he died."

Skill with a sword was an important part of an officer's training. The slash of a blade could kill a man instantly if the blow was powerful and well directed. It could even stop a horse. Jamie Skoyles had saved himself with his sword more times than he dared to count. With constant practice, he had learned to use its sharp edge to slice open an enemy and its fearful point to stab a man to death. When he did not kill, he had inflicted wounds that completely disabled an adversary. With a sword in his hand, he felt able to take on anyone.

Skoyles was far too strong, quick, and nimble for Lieutenant Charles

Westbourne. When the rain eased off, the two of them found a quiet corner of the camp where they could fight a mock duel, but Westbourne spent the whole time on the defense. Sparks flew as their swords clashed and the noise drew a few curious spectators. They were not surprised to see how easily Skoyles confounded his less experienced opponent. After ten minutes, Westbourne was gasping for breath.

"Enough, enough!" he cried, backing away.

"Would you like to try your luck with a spontoon instead?"

"No, Captain. You'd only put me to shame again. Whatever weapon we choose, I'll end up as the loser."

"Not if I fight with a handicap," Skoyles volunteered, taking the sword in his left hand. "Come at me again, Lieutenant."

"But I'd have an unfair advantage."

"Would you?"

"Undoubtedly."

"Prove it."

Westbourne took his stance and the fight resumed. It was Skoyles who was on the defensive now, parrying every thrust from his opponent and using his feet cleverly to get out of difficulties. Having gained the upper hand at last, Westbourne grew bolder and tried to use some more enterprising strokes. Skoyles was equal to everything that the other man could offer, bringing the bout to an abrupt end with an unexpected thrust and a sudden flick of his wrist. Westbourne's sword spun out of his hand and landed on the grass. The spectators clapped.

"How on earth did you do that?" asked Westbourne balefully.

"With plenty of practice."

"But you'd never have the sword in your left hand in battle."

"Oh, yes, I would," said Skoyles. "It happened when we invaded from Canada last summer. A musket ball hit me in the right shoulder during a skirmish near Crown Point. I was unable to defend myself with the sword in that hand. If I'd not been able to use the left hand, I'd not be alive now." He saw Sergeant Caffrey approaching. "Tom will confirm it. He was there at the time. It was his probe that removed the musket ball."

"Yours was one of many I took out that day," said Caffrey, reaching the swordsmen. "Excuse me for disturbing you, gentlemen. I wonder if I might have a private word with you, Captain?"

"Of course."

Skoyles took him aside. Westbourne, meanwhile, reclaimed his sword from the ground and drifted away with the other officers, still dazed at the way he had been so easily disarmed. Skoyles saw the sadness in his friend's eyes.

"What's amiss, Tom?"

"Dan Lukins is dead. They brought him in on a stretcher."

"Shot as a deserter?"

"No, Jamie," said Caffrey. "It looks as if he was brought down by enemy sharpshooters. It was a more honorable way to die, I suppose. Wolverton is inconsolable. He can only use one arm but he insisted on helping to bury Lukins. They'd known each other for years."

"Dan Lukins was a good soldier," Skoyles observed. "He might have had a wandering hand and a wicked tongue but he'd fight like a demon when he needed to. I'm sorry to hear that he's dead and even sorrier that he deserted."

"So am I. If hardened soldiers like Lukins are starting to walk out on us, we're in serious trouble."

"Where is he buried, Tom? I'd like to show my respects."

"Follow me."

"He did me a big favor," said Skoyles, falling in beside the sergeant as he moved away. "I'll never forget that. Lukins overheard the plot by Harry Featherstone to have me soundly beaten. If I hadn't been warned, those two Canadians might have done some real damage. Lukins saved my skin."

Caffrey licked his lips. "That's the other thing I need to mention to you, Jamie," he said, looking embarrassed. "It concerns that little brawl we had with those two men."

"What about it?"

"Well, I have a confession to make."

"Go on."

"I'm afraid that Polly spoke out of turn," said Caffrey. "She forgot my warning that nobody else was to hear a word of it. Polly was speaking to Miss Rainham's maid and it slipped out."

"Bugger it!" exclaimed Skoyles, coming to a halt. "I told you at the time that I didn't want a single person to know about it—not even Polly. The incident was over and done with, Tom. It was best forgotten."

"Polly promised to keep it a secret."

"Then why didn't she?"

"Heaven knows! She's so upset that she feels like biting her tongue out. She and Nan Wyatt were talking about Major Featherstone earlier today and—before Polly knew what she was saying—out it came."

"That's all we bloody well need!" Skoyles marched off again.

"Mind you," said Caffrey, catching up, "Polly tried to make amends for her mistake. When she realized what she'd said, she begged Nan not to say anything about it to Miss Rainham."

Skoyles was bitter. "What chance is there of that happening?" he asked. "The woman is bound to inform her mistress. In other words, the one person in the world I wanted to keep from hearing about that business is now aware of it. Elizabeth Rainham knows."

"What do you think she'll do, Jamie?"

"I'm not sure," Skoyles admitted, clenching his teeth, "but there'll be consequences. And they won't be very pleasant for any of us."

"At least, she'll see that bastard of a major for what he is."

"Think how much suffering that will bring her."

"She needs to be rescued from him, Jamie."

"This is not the way to do it. Harry Featherstone will go wild if she challenges him, and Miss Rainham will bear the brunt of it. She shouldn't have been told a thing."

"That was my fault," admitted Caffrey, "but I'm not entirely sorry. The fact is that he did pay two Canadians to beat you senseless, and he deserves to be exposed for it."

"He was, Tom. We left those two axmen in his tent."

"It needs to be made public so that he can be shamed."

"I disagree," said Skoyles. "These things happen in the army, as you well know. The best way to settle scores of this kind is in private. No good can be served by telling other people about them."

"What will happen now?"

"I have a nasty feeling that all hell will break loose."

"It may be that Nan *won't* tell her mistress about it."

"Yes," said Skoyles with heavy sarcasm, "and it may be that the rebels will surrender without a fight, hand over their arms, and turn into peaceable colonial citizens. Then we can all sail back to England as conquering heroes." He turned to his companion. "Of course, she'll tell her," he insisted. "What maid could keep a secret like that to herself? By now, Miss Rainham will know the ugly truth."

"That could work to your advantage, Jamie."

"How?"

"Be honest," said Caffrey, nudging him, "you *want* her, don't you?"

"That's immaterial."

"I don't think so. What better way to prize her apart from the major than by showing him in his true colors? You save his life at Hubbardton and how does he thank you—by hiring two men to kick seven barrels of shit out of you! That will get her sympathy."

"I don't need her sympathy."

"We both know what you need, Jamie, and this may be the way to get it. Miss Rainham will turn to you now. Grab her while you can."

"Not on these terms."

"Then you must be mad," said Caffrey in tones of disbelief. "Ever since you met the woman, you've been panting for her. In your position, I'd take her on any terms at all."

"It's not as simple as that, Tom."

"It always has been in the past. You want her like a house on fire and she's obviously sweet on you, especially after the way you rescued her at Bitter Creek. What's holding you back?"

"You wouldn't understand."

"This is not like the Jamie Skoyles I know," said Caffrey censoriously. "If it was any other woman, you'd have loved her and left her by now. And what better way to get your revenge on the major? Reach out and *take* her."

Skoyles felt uneasy. There was an uncomfortable truth in his friend's comments and it silenced him. He could not even explain to himself what made Elizabeth Rainham so different from all the other women, and why he deliberately pulled back from any real pursuit of her. With someone like Maria Quinn, it had all been so easy and natural. Once mutual affection had been established, they dispensed with any further social niceties and hopped into the nearest bed. It was a warm, pleasurable, satisfying relationship that involved no serious commitment on either side. They were playing by accepted rules. Neither he nor Maria had even bothered to look beyond the current campaign. Both were simply enjoying an intimacy while it lasted.

Elizabeth Rainham was, in many ways, even more desirable than Maria, but she brought complications in her wake. Not only was she betrothed to someone who had emerged as a dangerous enemy of Skoyles, she was also a friend of General Burgoyne. Two men in senior positions stood between Elizabeth and Skoyles. Even that would not have deterred him if he felt that he could offer her something more than he was giving to Maria Quinn, but he was not sure that he could. Maria was a mature woman with an uncomplicated liking for carnal pleasure. Elizabeth Rainham was a virginal young lady who would need more than the prospect of illicit passion to lure her into bed.

They had been walking at a steady pace. Skoyles was too preoccupied to notice that they had now reached the edge of the camp where the dead had been buried. Caffrey had to poke him in the ribs to stop him. Skoyles blinked and looked at the uneven rows of graves, marked only by rough crosses fashioned out of thick twigs. Most of the soldiers there had perished from disease, but there were some who had died of wounds picked up in earlier skirmishes. Skoyles was dismayed to see how many deaths there had been.

It was not difficult to identify the grave of Daniel Lukins because someone was keeping vigil beside it. Having helped to bury him, Marcus Wolverton was standing over the last resting place of the Cockney and mouthing words that went unheard. Skoyles moved across to him.

"I'm sorry we've lost him," he said gently.

"He knew the risk he was running, sir. Desertion is a crime."

"The worst crime of all for a soldier. I'd have shot him myself if I'd seen him sneaking away from us. But that doesn't mean I can't mourn him," said Skoyles. "Lukins served under me for five years. You get to know a man pretty well in that time."

"That's what I thought," said Wolverton. "I'd have wagered anything that Dan would never run away from the British army—and yet he did. I still can't understand why."

"No hint of it beforehand?"

"Not really, Captain. When he got back from Bitter Creek, he was his old self. He was even boasting that he saved Major Featherstone's lady from being raped." Skoyles was jolted by the mention of Elizabeth. "Dan was the same lying little reprobate he'd always been. On the other hand, he was very worried that we're to get no help at all from General Howe—but, then, so are the rest of us."

"Lukins shouldn't have listened to rumors."

"That's what distresses me, sir," said Wolverton, unable to keep a sob out of his voice. "Because he was scared of what he overheard, he let me down badly. I take it personally, you see. Dan didn't just desert the army—he ran out on me."

"Your lips were moving when I came up," noted Skoyles. "What were you saying?"

"I was quoting the last speech from one of Shakespeare's plays. They were words spoken about Coriolanus to the effect that, although he'd done terrible things in his life, he still deserved a noble memory. I suppose that's what I feel about Dan Lukins."

"That he should have a noble memory?"

"A memory of some kind, anyway."

"Why did you choose that play?"

Wolverton turned to him. "Coriolanus was a deserter, sir."

CHAPTER TWELVE

He knew that it was a mistake. After another session at the card table with his senior officers, Jamie Skoyles had strolled back toward his tent in a strange mood. Though he had won a fair amount of money, it had given him no sense of satisfaction, even though much of it had come from the pocket of Harry Featherstone. Nor had Skoyles enjoyed the cut and thrust of military conversation. Instead of relaxing as usual into his privileged situation at the table, he had been heartily relieved when the last game had been played.

Wanting simply to get some much-needed sleep, he was puzzled to see a flicker of light through the canvas of his tent. Someone had lit a candle. Skoyles was extremely careful never to leave a naked flame unguarded, so he realized that he must have a visitor. When he put his head into the tent, he saw that Maria Quinn was waiting for him.

"I told you that I could be patient," she said with an inviting smile.

"How long have you been here?"

"Long enough."

"Did anyone see you come?" he said with slight alarm.

"No, no, Jamie," she replied, getting up to pull him into the tent. "I waited until it was dark, then slipped in like a thief in the night." She put her hands on his arm. "Don't I get a welcome?"

"Of course."

Skoyles kissed her on the lips and felt the familiar surge of desire. At the same time, he was telling himself that it would be a mistake to let her stay, to make love to her again, to allow her to come between him and his growing obsession with Elizabeth Rainham. He wanted to break away, to put her off her with plausible excuses, then escort her back to her own part of the camp. Yet, once she was in his arms, he could not let Maria Quinn go. She was irresistible. Skoyles was slightly disturbed that she acted on her own initiative and came unbidden. It was a dangerous precedent, and he would insist that it never happened again. Meanwhile, he was going to take what was on offer and be grateful for it.

"Where've you been?" she asked, undoing the buttons on his coat.

"Playing cards."

Maria pouted. "You'd prefer to do that than be with me?"

"I had no choice," Skoyles explained. "General Burgoyne invited me and I couldn't possibly turn him down."

"What about me, Jamie? Can you turn me down?"

"Not tonight."

"Not any night, I hope," she said, removing his coat and laying it aside. "Were you surprised to see me?"

"I was, Maria."

"Surprised but pleased."

"Yes."

"Show me *how* pleased you are."

When she flung her arms around him, Skoyles shook off the nagging sense of guilt and responded with ardor. He knew that it was wrong, but he could not help himself. A romance with Elizabeth Rainham was only the vaguest possibility, whereas Maria Quinn was right there for him. No pursuit was involved. No courtship, no strategy, no waiting. She had come to him with an enchanting readiness. Pulling her to him, Skoyles began to unhook the back of her dress.

It was only in the morning that he realized how big a mistake it had been.

The journey from Fort Anne to Fort Edward had been slow, laborious, and depressing. Since the road turned away from Wood Creek, the British army could no longer use bateaux for carrying supplies and were forced to transfer them to the wagons. Hastily built and badly overloaded, the two-wheeled carts churned up the soft mud into a rutted morass that soiled the boots of the infantry, spattered their uniforms, and hampered their movement. When the dilapidated Fort Edward finally came into view, the spirits of the tired marchers lifted noticeably. Putting the despised wilderness behind them, they emerged into the sunlight and camped on the east bank of the Hudson River. The army could at last enjoy some leisure while they waited for the heavy guns to arrive by water from Fort Ticonderoga.

Lieutenant Charles Westbourne shared the general optimism.

"I feel as if we've reached civilization again," he said. "We can see farmhouses, fields of grain, berries ripening on the bushes. It's a far cry from the exigencies of Skenesborough."

"A definite improvement," Skoyles agreed.

"More to the point, General Schuyler abandoned the fort because he knew that he couldn't hold it. The enemy is retreating before us."

"That's not entirely true, Lieutenant. The garrison from Fort Edward may have pulled back to Saratoga, but we still have enemy forces to the east. If they can work their way around to our rear, they could cut off our own means of withdrawal."

"That's unthinkable, Captain. You heard the general's decree."

"Yes—we never retreat."

"There'd never be a reason even to consider it," said Westbourne breezily. "I have it on good authority that the general is so convinced that victory is within our grasp, he has written to Lord Germain for permission to return to England before winter."

"I sincerely hope that his confidence is justified."

"Do I hear a note of doubt in your voice?"

"You do," Skoyles admitted. "One of my main concerns is that we've stretched our supply line to the point where it will snap. Provisions are low and, before he abandoned the fort, General Schuyler turned much of the surrounding countryside into a desert. An army needs to eat, Lieutenant. Wholesome rations are vital."

"We simply forage farther afield."

"That course of action has already been forced upon us."

The two officers were talking outside Skoyles's tent. Their attention was diverted for a moment by the arrival of a handful of men from local farms, who walked into camp with a jaunty air. One of them carried a musket, another wore a rusty sword, a third had a sickle. Westbourne pointed them out to his companion.

"Even you must be heartened by the number of new recruits," he said.

"In the week or so that we've been here, almost four hundred loyalists have joined us."

"Unfortunately, less than half of them are armed, and those that are lack any training and discipline. As for the rest," Skoyles went on, critically, "they're not reliable. Few are here because of an overwhelming urge to serve King George. Some merely want to earn money, others to protect their district, and others again to work off some petty feelings of revenge against their enemies. They are forever wrangling about who is to be an officer or in what corps they would deign to serve. These are not *soldiers,* Lieutenant."

"They'll have their use."

"Only if they bring in cattle, clear roads, and guide troops on the march. Beyond that, they'll be a hindrance."

"At least, they'll not disgrace us like the Indians."

"That's true."

"What the Ottawas did to Miss McCrea was unforgivable."

"That particular outrage will return to haunt us," said Skoyles, "even though precise details of what happened are still unknown. It's already deprived us of David Jones, the loyalist officer betrothed to Jane McCrea. He and several friends went back to Canada in disgust."

"I think that even General Burgoyne is sick of the Indians now."

"He is, Lieutenant. At the card table last night, he said that their only preeminence consisted in their ferocity. I'm bound to agree."

"Reports of Jane McCrea's death have already appeared in some newspapers, it seems. How on earth can word travel so fast?"

"The enemy always has spies in our camp."

"We should root them out, Captain."

"That's easier said than done," Skoyles told him. "We just saw those raw recruits arriving in camp to swear their allegiance to the British cause. It may be that one of them is in the pay of the Continental Army. How are we to know? War has a nasty habit of blurring the line between friends and enemies. One can trust nobody."

"Like that friend of yours we captured at Hubbardton."

"True. Ezekiel Proudfoot is a case in point."

"What happened to him?"

Skoyles was reflective. "I don't know, Lieutenant," he said, "but I've a feeling that Ezekiel will surface before too long. He wants desperately to be involved in this conflict somehow. I suspect that it's only a matter of time before our paths cross again."

Sunday found Ezekiel Proudfoot in the village church. When the order had been given to abandon Fort Edward, he had not fled south with General Schuyler but elected instead to go east so that he could visit friends who lived near Manchester. Proudfoot joined the family at prayer that morning, glad to be back among people he knew rather than in a crumbling fortress with its demoralized garrison. He had now been forced to leave three forts in a row and did not wish to repeat the experience. After so much time spent among dejected soldiers of the Continental Army, he had been refreshed by a week on a farm among old friends.

But even in a quiet little church, the war could still intrude. The preacher was barely halfway through his sermon when the door suddenly opened and an officer from the local militia marched down the aisle. Recognizing the man, the preacher broke off in midsentence.

"Are you the bearer of any news, Colonel?" he asked.

"Yes," replied the newcomer, turning to face the congregation and raising his voice. "General Burgoyne, with his army, is on the march to Albany. General Stark has offered to take command of the New Hampshire men." There was an immediate buzz of interest. "If we all turn out, we can cut off Burgoyne's march."

"When do you want us, Colonel?" asked a voice from the back.

"Now, my friend."

The speaker rose to his feet. "Then what are we waiting for?"

Every man there stood up. The preacher quickly gave them permission to leave, and they rushed out in answer to the call to arms. Sensing that he might witness some action again, Ezekiel Proudfoot was among them. If John Stark was in command, there was no danger of a fort—or anything else, for that matter—being surrendered. Stark would not give the enemy the time of day without a fight and a mouthful of abuse to accompany it. The volunteers streamed away excitedly from the church, turned, in the space of seconds, from devout worshippers into willing soldiers. Nobody moved with more alacrity than Ezekiel Proudfoot.

It was a scene more typical of an English village green than of an army camped beside the Hudson River. In the blazing sunshine of an August afternoon, an impromptu game of cricket was being played between two regiments. A pitch had been paced out, wickets set up, and two cricket bats hewn out of wood. Strips of leather had been twisted into a ball. Though it appeared to the watching Germans to be a strange, confusing, rather pointless game, it had both a grace and a sophisticated violence that recommended it to the Englishmen involved. Their commitment was unambiguous, their pleasure self-evident.

Part of the fielding side, Jamie Skoyles had distinguished himself as a bowler, securing four wickets with the speed and cunning of his underarm deliveries, then patrolling the outer edge of the field and taking three excellent catches. He was so absorbed in the game that he did not notice that Elizabeth Rainham was among the spectators, seated with Lady Harriet Acland and Friederika von Riedesel and using a parasol to ward off the sun. Impressed by Skoyles's performance, she had applauded him with a willingness that went beyond mere approval.

When the batting side had been dismissed, it was time for the 24th Foot to take their turn at the crease. As the self-appointed captain of the side, Major Harry Featherstone insisted on being one of the opening batsmen and chose Charles Westbourne as his partner. It was no casual decision. While the lieutenant was a competent player, he had nothing like Featherstone's power or range of strokes. The major would be able to outshine him with ease, determined, as he was, to show Elizabeth what a gifted player he was.

When the innings began, Skoyles watched from the margin of the field, noting how Featherstone made sure that he always faced the bowling by scoring in even numbers, then taking a single run at the end of each over. Westbourne had no chance at all to bat. Given his propensity to hit the ball a great distance, the major pushed the score along at a respectable speed. Skoyles admired his skills. Always ready to learn from a superior batsman, he took particular interest in his footwork and timing.

"I must congratulate you, Captain," said a voice beside him.

"Miss Rainham!" he said, turning in surprise to see her. "I had no idea that you were here."

"I've always liked watching cricket. You were on good form today."

"Thank you. I'd hate to let the regiment down."

"There's no fear of that."

She moved in slightly closer. Skoyles could see little of her face under the parasol, but her proximity nevertheless excited him. It was an unexpected treat for him to be alone with her in the middle of a large crowd, able to enjoy a private conversation in a very public place. After an exchange of pleasantries, Elizabeth turned to the subject that had brought her across to him.

"I need to ask you a question," she began, "and I hope for an honest reply."

"You'll get nothing less from me, Miss Rainham."

"I am sure." She needed a moment to compose herself. "Something came to my attention over a week ago and I refused to believe it at first. To be frank, I dismissed it as silly tittle-tattle. However, as time went by, I came to wonder whether there might not be a grain of truth in the accusation. Do you know what I'm talking about, Captain?"

"I think so."

"Then answer me this—and you'll know how embarrassing it is for me even to raise this topic: Did Major Featherstone employ two men to assault you at Skenesborough?"

It was a question that he had feared and one that he tried to obviate by ensuring that no mention of the incident ever leaked out. Now that it had, his instinct was to protect her from knowing the worst about the man to whom she was betrothed.

"I can't say, Miss Rainham," he replied evasively. "It's true that two men did try to attack me one night, but I had forewarning of it and was able to take countermeasures. What I could not tell you for certain is who set the two men on to me."

"Who gave you the warning?"

"Private Lukins."

"Is he the man who is supposed to have heard the plot being hatched?" Skoyles nodded. "I may need to speak to him."

"That's impossible, I'm afraid. Dan Lukins was shot dead." He saw the parasol waver in her hand. "There's absolutely no suggestion of the major being implicated," he assured her. "Private Lukins was a deserter. He was killed by enemy sharpshooters."

"Why did he run away?"

"We'll never know."

"Do you believe that what he overheard was true?"

"Unhappily—yes."

"So it *was* the work of Major Featherstone?"

"I've no proof of that, Miss Rainham."

"*Somebody* was behind the plot."

"Undeniably."

"Then why are you so hesitant? I asked for an honest answer."

"Two men were hired by someone to ambush me," he told her, "and I'm forced to accept the possibility—the possibility only—that the man who engaged them was indeed Major Featherstone."

She was profoundly agitated. "Why did you not tell me?"

"I did not wish you to know."

"But you might have been seriously hurt."

"Even then I would not have confided in you."

"But this is important to me, Captain," she argued. "The major is engaged to marry me. If he is capable of such despicable behavior as this, I need to know about it. Why conceal it from me?"

"Because it's a matter between Major Featherstone and myself."

"That's not an adequate explanation," she said, looking up as a ripple of applause signaled another fine scoring shot from Featherstone. "You saved his life at Hubbardton—is *that* how the Major repaid you? I shall take this up with him immediately."

"I wouldn't advise that, Miss Rainham."

"Why not?"

"Because it will only bring you a lot of upset."

"That's irrelevant."

"I tried to spare you any pain by keeping the incident to myself."

"Well, I'm glad that I found out about it now. My maid picked it up from Mrs. Bragg and felt it her duty to pass the news on to me. It seemed too farfetched to believe at first—so completely out of character—but now I can see that it's the truth."

"Forget it," he counseled.

"How can I?"

"Because it will only cause rancor between you and the major."

"That won't hold me back, I promise you. I'm shocked that he could even consider doing such a thing. Brother officers should respect each other, not indulge in this kind of subterfuge." She looked up at him. "Did you not think of reporting the incident to General Burgoyne?"

"No," said Skoyles quickly, "and if you're unwise enough to do so, I'll deny that it ever took place. Disagreements between officers occur all the time. It's something that we have to take in our stride."

"Well, I'll not take it in *my* stride."

"You must."

"No, Captain. There are some things I could never overlook and this is one of them. I keep thinking of what might have happened if you had not been forewarned. You could have sustained serious injury."

"I didn't."

Her voice softened. "I *care* about you."

"And I care about *you,* Miss Rainham."

The edge of a cricket field was an odd place for such a declaration to be made by both of them, and it robbed them of any further words. They simply looked at each other and traded unspoken thoughts. They moved a step closer. When Skoyles remembered his night with Maria Quinn, he felt a stab of guilt and wished that her visit had never taken place, but he was not going to let recrimination rob him of a special moment. His arm rubbed against hers. His smile touched off her own. The silent conversation was cut short by a burst of applause, and Skoyles turned his head to see a ball hurtling toward them out of the air. Harry Featherstone had put all his strength into the shot, hitting the ball high into the sky before starting to run. Skoyles caught the ball as it was about to land on Elizabeth's parasol. He tossed it to one of the fielders chasing madly after it. In the middle of the pitch, one of the batsmen halted abruptly.

"Run!" yelled the spectators. "Run, Major, run!"

But he was deaf to their entreaties. Harry Featherstone had caught sight of Elizabeth and Jamie Skoyles. Stopping midway between the two wickets, he glared at them in disapproval, forgetting that he was playing cricket and throwing Westbourne into a state of confusion. The other batsman was about to be voluntarily run out. Even from that distance, Elizabeth could see the fury in the major's eyes.

"Excuse me, Captain," she said. "I'd better go."

Brigadier General John Stark was a spare, sinewy man in his late forties with piercing blue eyes and a large nose. Difficult, touchy, cantankerous, and fiercely independent, he was not inclined to suffer fools gladly, even if they were members of Congress. The roughness of his tongue was legendary. Renowned as an Indian fighter, he had also served with distinction both at Bunker Hill and at Trenton, believing, erroneously, that his gallantry would be rewarded by promotion. When it was denied him, he retired to his farm on the Merrimac River, deeply offended that junior officers had been promoted over his head by scheming politicians who had their own favorites.

Fearing the imminent approach of the British army, the General Court of New Hampshire swiftly voted to make John Stark a brigadier general. He accepted the belated honor. Taking over the independent command, he achieved startling results. In less than a week, twenty-five separate companies had signed up to follow him. The New Hampshire Militia soon had fifteen hundred men at its disposal, responding to the enormous popularity of Stark himself and to the threat of General Burgoyne to the west. In the entire state, more than one in every ten males had offered to bear arms.

Ezekiel Proudfoot volunteered to fight in his individual way.

"It's good," said Stark, poring over the sketch. "You're a fine artist, Ezekiel. This picture of yours really comes alive."

"It's meant as a warning to others," Proudfoot explained. "Jane McCrea was one of their own, engaged to a loyalist officer. If *she* could be treated in that barbaric way, what hope would our womenfolk have?"

"Indians are a danger to us all. That's why I killed so many of the pesky varmints when I marched with Rogers's Rangers in the French and Indian war. They'll cut a man's eyeballs out just for the fun of it, and God help any woman who falls into their murderous hands." He gave the sketch to Proudfoot. "This drawing of yours makes that crystal clear."

"The man responsible was an Ottawa. They've since deserted."

"It makes no difference, Ezekiel. Other tribes still travel with the British. Each is as bad as the other—Indians are Indians."

"That was my feeling."

"Until I was appointed," said Stark, pausing to light his clay pipe, "all that stood between New Hampshire and Burgoyne was Seth Warner and the remnants of the battle at Hubbardton—about one hundred fifty men." He puffed hard until the tobacco was alight. "That was a sad day for us."

"I know, sir—I was there."

"Ebenezer Francis was one of our best commanders."

"He was brave to the last."

"It takes more than bravery to win against the British."

They were in a camp that had been set up in Vermont to the southeast of Fort Edward. Having raised his army, Stark had to equip it, and he set about locating weapons, ammunition, bullet molds, cannon, tents, camp kettles, wagons, ropes, and all the other necessities of warfare. Uniforms were a luxury that could not be afforded. Rum had been high on his list of priorities.

"I had to tell that to the Committee of Safety," he said. "No army can survive for long without a supply of rum. They seem to think that patriotism is a strong enough drink." He chewed on the stem of his pipe. "Politicians! They know nothing at all about fighting."

Proudfoot had been given a cordial welcome by John Stark. Though the grizzled soldier knew of the engraver only by reputation, he appreciated the value of an artist who could record deeds of American valor. Stark intended, with his men, to provide some stirring military action that Proudfoot could commemorate in a print.

"How did they treat you as a prisoner, Ezekiel?" he asked.

"Very well, sir, but, then, I had special privileges."

"Privileges?"

"I knew one of their officers," said Ezekiel. "Captain Jamie Skoyles, a decent man and a good soldier to boot. We were close friends at one time—in one sense, we always will be. It was he who spoke up for me and arranged to have me taken to Skenesborough instead of being sent off with all the other prisoners."

"What did you learn at the camp?"

"That they were still cock-a-hoop at the capture of Ticonderoga."

"We should have properly garrisoned it," Stark protested. "We've known since the start of the year that the British would invade from Canada as soon as milder weather set in. Schuyler should have tightened its defenses when he had the chance."

"There was a chronic shortage of men and supplies at the fort. General St.

Clair felt that he could not hold out—especially when the British got cannon on the summit of Mount Defiance. To my eternal disgust, we fled."

Stark was forthright. "That idiot, Arthur St. Clair, should be dismissed," he said bluntly, "and so should General Schuyler. Both of them abandon defensive positions too easily. When Schuyler surrendered Crown Point last year, I gave him a piece of my mind. They should have resisted the British until they ran out of ammunition." He laughed harshly. "At least, it taught Schuyler to keep out of my way. Instead of coming here himself, he sent General Lincoln, that fat fool from Massachusetts, in his stead."

"Why?"

"To give me a message."

"Not a very welcome one, by the sound of it."

"No," Stark retorted. "Schuyler wanted to take charge of my men. The gall of it! I go to all the trouble of raising a militia and what does our esteemed general do? He sends word that we must march to Stillwater. He got short shrift from me, Ezekiel."

"What did you say?"

"I told General Lincoln, in plain terms, that I considered myself adequate to command my own men. I'm not at Schuyler's beck and call."

"He *is* in command of the Northern Department."

"Not for much longer, I hope. Besides, I'm not answerable to him or to Congress. Neither of them appointed me. If Schuyler thinks that I'm being insubordinate," said Stark, sucking on his pipe, "I don't care a fiddler's fart. *I* make decisions affecting my men. This army is *mine*."

It had cost Harry Featherstone his wicket. Distracted by the sight of Elizabeth Rainham and Jamie Skoyles, he had lost interest in the game and just stood in the middle of the pitch. When the ball was thrown in to the wicket keeper, the major was still stranded halfway down the pitch. Charles Westbourne remained in the safety of the crease but his partner was dismissed. Though the crowd gave Featherstone generous applause, they were mystified at the way he had surrendered his wicket.

Since he was the next man in, Skoyles had to take the bat from the major as the latter stalked off the field. It was thrust angrily into his hand. Featherstone growled something that Skoyles chose not to hear. A true competitor, the captain's mind was now solely on the cricket. He wanted to win. After a few words with Westbourne, he took up his stance at the other end and faced his first ball, sweeping it expertly away off his legs and collecting three runs. It meant that the lieutenant now had the opportunity to bat at last. Westbourne seized it, literally, with both hands, scoring two runs off his first shot.

The game was short-lived. With both men in aggressive mood, the bowlers were hit all over the ground, and the fielders were kept racing to and fro. Runs came thick and fast. The opposition team had only made a modest score, and it was left to Westbourne to pass it by striking a ball for four winning runs. As they came off the pitch, he and Skoyles were cheered to the echo. Fellow members of their regiment were overjoyed. The victory had been comprehensive.

Skoyles did not join in the celebrations. Now that the game was over, he could think only of Elizabeth Rainham. With the major standing beside her, she was seated with the other ladies, denying Featherstone the chance to speak to her properly. When she saw Skoyles, she got up and beckoned him over, ignoring the spluttering protests from the other man. At her suggestion, all three of them strolled away until they found a place by the river where they could speak in private.

"Elizabeth," Featherstone demanded, "what *is* going on?"

"I'll tell you in a moment."

"And why did you drag Skoyles along? We don't need him at all."

"We do, Harry," she said. "The captain is involved here."

"In what way?"

"He was an innocent victim."

"I think that I had better leave you," said Skoyles, not wishing to be part of the argument. "I'm not sure that I belong here, Miss Rainham."

"You don't," snapped Featherstone.

"Yes, he does," Elizabeth insisted, lowering her parasol so that she could confront the major. "Is it true that you hired two Canadians to attack Captain Skoyles in Skenesborough?"

"No, of course not!"

"There was a witness, Harry. Someone overheard you."

"Then he's a confounded liar."

"Two men did try to ambush the captain but, providentially, he'd been warned that they'd be there and suffered no injury. According to Private Lukins, *you* were the person behind the attack."

"Lukins!" snarled Featherstone. "That scheming little rogue!"

"Don't speak ill of the dead, Major," Skoyles interjected.

"I'll say what I like about that vermin. Telling tales about me, is he? If the wretch were not already dead, I'd wring his filthy neck for him."

Elizabeth persisted. "The fact remains that an ambush was set," she reminded him, "and it must have been at someone's behest. Tell me true, Harry: Did you or did you not speak to one of the Canadian axmen behind some wagons?"

"I refuse to answer that," said Featherstone, blustering.

"Private Lukins was nearby at the time."

"Then he mistook someone else for me."

"You're a very recognizable figure, Harry. It was you, wasn't it?"

"I'll not be interrogated like this!"

"Miss Rainham," said Skoyles, "I did warn you that nothing would be served by pursuing the matter."

Featherstone was dumbfounded. "You discussed this with *him* behind my back?" he cried. "How could you, Elizabeth?"

"Because I wanted to find out the truth."

"And you'd take his word over mine?"

"It was not Captain Skoyles who named you."

"You must excuse me," said Skoyles, moving away.

Elizabeth tried to stop him, but to no avail. Skoyles knew that he was in the way. Consumed with anger, Featherstone stared after him before rounding on Elizabeth.

"I'm ashamed of you," he said.

"Why?"

"For listening to a false allegation like that from Skoyles."

"But he didn't make it," she explained. "Captain Skoyles didn't even want to talk about the incident. As far as he was concerned, it was best left in the past. I could not take it so lightly. The evidence points so clearly to you, Harry."

"What evidence? The gossip of a nobody?"

"You ordered that beating, didn't you?"

"No, Elizabeth."

"Didn't you?" she repeated. "I'd rather know the worst."

"Do you really think me capable of such a thing?"

"Yes, Harry. It pains me to say it—but I do."

Her gaze was steady, her manner positive. Featherstone could see that she would not easily be fobbed off. Since a witness had overheard him, he had been unmasked.

"Who told you about this?" he asked.

"Answer my question first. Did you issue the instructions?"

"Elizabeth—"

"Yes or no?"

He gnashed his teeth. "It was no more than Skoyles deserved," he mumbled at length. "The fellow is insufferable."

Elizabeth said nothing. She was seeing him in an entirely new light now, and it was very unflattering. Featherstone tried to strike back.

"Who told you?" he inquired.

"Nan Wyatt. She heard it from Polly Bragg."

"Polly Bragg? But I told you that your maid was to have nothing to do with that jabbering whore. You *disobeyed* me, Elizabeth."

"I did what I thought fit."

"Sending your maid out to pick up all the scandal of the camp."

"No, Harry," she countered. "Allowing Nan to develop the one real friendship that she's made since we came here. I've met Mrs. Bragg and take her to be an agreeable woman. I certainly see no reason why she and Nan have to be kept apart."

"Let me be the judge of that," he insisted.

"Why?"

"Because I'm going to be your husband. I make the decisions."

"Like the one to have Captain Skoyles attacked?" she said, arching an eyebrow. "Some of your decisions are open to question, Harry. I'm bound to tell you that I think the less of you for having made them."

"Let me explain."

"No explanation is necessary. When I asked for the truth, you lied to me disgracefully. And now you're trying to justify what I consider to be a deplorable action."

"You're getting things out of proportion," he said, trying to mollify her with a sickly smile. "There was no malice behind that assault on Skoyles. It was meant as a joke, that's all, some harmless fun to relieve the boredom."

"You look upon physical violence as harmless fun?"

"They would not really have hurt him, I made that clear. They were simply hired to give Skoyles a fright."

"You're lying to me again, Harry," she said coldly. "A moment ago, you said that the captain was insufferable and that he deserved a beating. This was no joke. You behaved dishonorably, and you've forfeited a great deal of my respect as a result."

"Wait!" he said, restraining her by the arm as she tried to leave. "There's no need to take this so seriously. You must understand."

"I fear that I already do so." He released her arm. "I suggest that we keep apart for a while. In the circumstances, I think it the only sensible way to proceed—don't you?"

General Burgoyne read the second message from his commander in chief in private. It was unequivocal.

My intention is to Pennsylvania where I expect to meet Washington but if he goes to the northward contrary to my expectations and you can keep him at bay, be assured that I shall soon be after him to relieve you.

Burgoyne was so shaken that he poured himself a glass of brandy and downed it in one gulp before he read on. There was no comfort in the rest of General Howe's letter.

After you arrive at Albany, the movements of the enemy will guide yours; but my wishes are that the enemy be drove out of this province before any operations take place in Connecticut. Sir Henry Clinton remains in command here and will act as circumstances may direct. Putnam is in the High-lands with about 4,000 men. Success be ever with you.

All hope of assistance had gone. Howe had not simply taken his army to Philadelphia, he raised the specter of General Washington, the American commander in chief, turning his attention to events in the Northern Department. If that was the case, Burgoyne would be in even deeper trouble. Howe's promise to come to his aid in that event was worthless. By the time he reached Albany, there might be no British army left to help.

The letter had arrived in strips wound tightly around a quill pen. Thrusting the pieces of paper into his pocket, Burgoyne decided to keep the contents of the missive to himself. A sociable man who liked to confide in his senior officers, he felt that this was an occasion to protect them from bad news. He stepped out of his tent to find Captain Jamie Skoyles standing there.

"Colonel Baum is awaiting your orders, General," said Skoyles.

"He shall have them at once."

Mounting his horse, he rode to the spot where the German was ready to parade his men. Skoyles rode with him. What they saw was a mixed force that comprised 175 dismounted dragoons, 200 Brunswick grenadiers and light troops, a squad of Hesse-Hanau artillerymen with two three-pound cannon, 300 loyalists and Canadians, and a small number of Indians. A detachment of 50 British marksmen from the 34th Foot was due to join them from the vicinity of Stillwater. Including the musicians, there were, in all, some 800 men. A group of German women was also to accompany the expedition, as was the irrepressible Colonel Philip Skene.

Lieutenant Colonel Friedrich Baum was, in some ways, an unlikely choice as the leader of the disparate force, recommended though he might have been by General Riedesel. Now fifty, Baum was a capable, diligent soldier who had seen action in the Seven Years War. While he had been given command of a dragoon regiment in 1776, he had never led more than fifty men into battle. His most glaring defect was that he spoke no English. Putting him in charge of such an important undertaking was a risky exercise.

Skoyles owed his presence there to his knowledge of German, a language that he had mastered by dint of courting the young women of Prussia when he was posted there. He doubted very much if some of the honeyed phrases he had perfected in the bedchamber would be of any use in the forthcoming conversation. Burgoyne inspected the troops, then told Skoyles what Colonel Baum's orders were. They were duly translated. The German was astounded to hear them. Having been instructed to make a round trip across the Green Mountains to Rockingham and back to Albany—a daunting trek of two hundred miles—he was now being sent to Bennington, a mere thirty miles to the southeast.

Skoyles translated the colonel's baffled response for Burgoyne.

"He asks why you countermanded his earlier orders, General."

"Because I am led to believe that there are horses, supplies, and a large number of potential recruits near Bennington. Colonel Skene has urged me to send troops to the town because there is an enemy magazine there that is only lightly guarded. If we can seize those weapons and ammunition, it will be greatly to our advantage."

Through his interpreter, Baum accepted the explanation without complaint, but he was clearly disturbed by the last-minute change of plan. He said something in German to his companion, Major Maiborn. With his band playing, he then marched his men out of the camp in a southerly direction toward Fort Miller. Skoyles felt obliged to comment.

"I understood that this was to be a secret expedition, sir," he said. "The sound of those drums rule out any chance of secrecy."

"The colonel would not leave without his musicians."

"It's not my place to criticize, General, but the road to Bennington runs through dense forest. It's a haven for enemy sharpshooters. Don't you think that a much larger force should have been sent?"

"Not according to Philip Skene."

"With respect," said Skoyles, "the colonel's advice has not always been entirely sound. May I remind you what happened at Bitter Creek?"

"This is a different matter, Captain."

"More rain is likely, and that will slow them down badly. It will take them at least two days to march to Bennington."

"So?"

"Enemy scouts will be aware of their movements and report them to General Schuyler at Stillwater. Are you not afraid that he'll send speedy reinforcements to Bennington?"

"No, Captain," said Burgoyne with undue sharpness. "To begin with, I do not believe that General Schuyler is still in command. My guess is that he will have been replaced by Benedict Arnold."

"He is just as likely to dispatch men there."

"Stop speaking out of ignorance."

"I beg your pardon, sir."

"What you do not realize is that word has come from Brigadier St. Leger, who is besieging Fort Stanwix. The rebels will not wish that to fall. Arnold or Schuyler or whoever is in charge will want to send all available men there." His stare was challenging. "Do you have any more ill-informed observations to make?"

213

"Only this, General," said Skoyles doggedly. "When the colonel rode off just now, I overheard a remark he made to Major Maiborn. There was a note of alarm in it. The rough translation is this: How can they be expected to forage *and* mount an attack on Bennington?"

"Because I wish to kill two birds with one stone."

"Supposing that they meet heavy resistance?"

"The rebels have insufficient numbers."

"That situation could change."

"My intelligence indicates otherwise."

"How reliable is it?"

"Don't be so impertinent, man!"

"But if they *were* to encounter problems at Bennington—"

"Who is in command of this damned army, Captain Skoyles?" said Burgoyne, irritably, silencing him with a gesture of his hand. "When I require your counsel, I shall ask for it."

"Yes, General. My sincere apologies."

"In future, please refrain from making any comments that pertain to military decisions taken by your superiors."

"I will, sir."

"Good day to you, sir!"

Pulling his horse's head round with a tug of the reins, Burgoyne rode off at a brisk trot. Skoyles was smarting from the rebuff. A genial commander who had always solicited advice before was now haughty and irascible. Having taken the pains to work out a detailed plan for Colonel Baum and his men, Burgoyne had canceled it without warning and sent them off on a totally different expedition, one for which they were neither prepared nor equipped. As he nudged his own horse forward, Skoyles wondered what had happened to make the general behave in a way that was so untypical of him. It was troubling.

The unquestioning confidence that Skoyles had once had in his commander was eroded even more.

General Stark was not a man for delay. As soon as he caught wind of the approaching enemy force, he rushed his militia to Bennington in order to defend the magazine there, and sent out patrols to hinder Colonel Baum and his men. Reports came in every day. One of them made him burst out laughing. Ezekiel Proudfoot was curious.

"What's the joke, General?" he asked.

"It's one that was played on these flat-faced Germans who are bearing down on us. It seems that Philip Skene is with them."

"Yes, I heard a lot about Colonel Skene when I was held prisoner."

"*Colonel* Skene now, is it?" said Stark with amusement. "He was only a major in the militia when he lived at Skenesborough. Whatever his rank, he's no judge of character. When some of our men joined them, claiming to be loyalists, Skene urged that they be accepted and gave them slips of white paper to wear in their hat so that the Indians would know they were on the British side."

"Except that they weren't," Proudfoot conjectured.

"No, Ezekiel. When the Germans next came under attack, the so-called loyalists gathered at their rear so that they could shoot some of the officers in the back." Stark slapped his thigh. "They not only killed a number of men, they frightened off some of the Indians."

"That still leaves a sizable force, General."

"We have double their number."

"But they are practiced mercenaries," Proudfoot reminded him. "You've not had time to train your men, let alone supply them with proper weaponry and uniforms."

"Yes," Stark conceded, "that's true, but it will not stop me from giving battle. Look at the faces all around you, Ezekiel. These men came to fight, none more so than John Stark."

Proudfoot could see what he meant. As he gazed around the camp, he could sense a confidence he had not felt at Hubbardton. The militiamen wore a bewildering variety of dress—loose coats of every possible color, homespun shirts and vests, garments that fastened below the knee, buckskin breeches, or long linen trousers. Calfskin shoes, ornamented with buckles, were the favored footwear, and Proudfoot noticed that nearly everyone wore a broad-brimmed hat with a round crown. Each man carried a powder horn, a bullet bag, and a flask of rum.

"No two of them seem to have the same gun," Proudfoot said.

"As long as it works," said Stark, "I don't care what weapon they carry.

The Germans will face British, French, Spanish, and American muskets. There're even a few Kentucky rifles."

"But no bayonets."

"A handful."

"That's where the enemy does have the advantage."

"Only if they get close enough to use them," said Stark. "The same goes for their dragoons. They're used to fighting on horseback with sabers. It's a fearsome way to die. We need to keep those swords at bay."

"How many horses have they collected along the way?"

"Not nearly enough to put those dragoons back in the saddle. The Indians captured some horses at Cambridge, but when Colonel Baum refused to pay for them, they killed the animals outright."

"The dragoons must have been livid at that."

"Fit to bust with fury, Ezekiel. Cavalrymen hate to walk, especially if they have to carry those heavy sabers."

"They may well find horses between Cambridge and here."

"Let them," said Stark, gazing around his weird assortment of men. "I have no fears. The enemy may *look* much more like an army—but our militia will fight like one."

Jamie Skoyles had neither seen nor heard of Elizabeth Rainham for days, but he was able to gauge how things stood between her and Harry Featherstone by studying the latter's behavior. The major was brusque and detached, spurning any company and refusing every invitation to an evening of cards. When the occasion presented itself, he took out his anger on the lower ranks. A rift had clearly been opened between him and Elizabeth. Judging by the way Featherstone glowered at him whenever they met, Skoyles could see that he was being blamed. He hoped for an opportunity to speak alone to Elizabeth but it was denied him. Returning from a patrol with Brigadier Fraser, he learned that he would not even remain in camp.

General Burgoyne sent for him. Skoyles was relieved to find that his commander had recovered his characteristic buoyancy. He detected a faint smell of alcohol on his breath when Burgoyne spoke.

"I've an assignment for you, Skoyles," said the general.

"Indeed, sir?"

"Since you expressed some worries about Bennington, I've decided to send you there." He handed a letter to Skoyles. "Deliver these orders to Colonel Breymann and translate anything that he does not fully understand. Colonel Baum has asked for reinforcements. You are to accompany them to Bennington."

"Does that mean Colonel Baum is in difficulties?" asked Skoyles.

"Not at all," replied Burgoyne airily. "He is holding a position near the town where some fifteen hundred or so rebel militia have gathered."

"That's almost twice as many as the colonel has at his command."

"Do not presume to teach me arithmetic, sir. I can count. The real difference between the two forces is one of character, not number. Our men are battle-tried professionals; theirs are ignorant farmboys who scarcely know which end of the musket the ball comes out of."

"You're being unfair to them, sir," said Skoyles. "Some of those men have to shoot game in order to eat. They know how to hit a target."

"So do we—especially with our artillery. I've ordered Breymann to take two six-pound cannon with him. The rebels have nothing to compete with those."

"May I ask a question, General?"

"Of course."

"Why send a German corps instead of a British one?"

"Question of pride, man," said Burgoyne with a touch of arrogance. "I wouldn't send my own troops on a secondary action like this when I have Brunswickers here. It's exactly the kind of mundane exercise for which they're well fitted."

"Must it be Colonel Breymann who is dispatched?" said Skoyles. "It's common knowledge in the German camp that he and Colonel Baum are anything but friends."

"All the more reason they should fight beside each other. That's the way to forge a bond. There's no room for petty differences in combat." He snapped his fingers. "Give my compliments to Colonel Breymann and deliver my orders."

"Yes, General."

"One moment," said Burgoyne as the other man turned to go. "I know that you had doubts about this whole expedition, but it seems to have been a signal success. Baum has not only found enough horses to mount his dragoons, he is sending hundreds of oxen back to camp. I hope you'll have the grace to admit that you were wrong."

217

"I do so without hesitation."

"When you reach Baum, give him my congratulations."

"I will, sir."

"That is all."

Skoyles paused. "May I ask who is in command of the rebels?"

"Does it matter?" asked Burgoyne complacently.

"I think so, General."

"Well, I don't. We have the measure of their best commanders. Whoever is in charge at Bennington, he and his men will be swept contemptuously from the field and you, Captain Skoyles—be grateful to me for this—will be there to witness their humiliation."

Ezekiel Proudfoot had never seen such carnage. Wherever he looked, men were lying dead or suffering from horrific wounds that condemned them to a slow and agonizing end. The crackle of gunfire was constant, underscored by the booming of cannon and the neighing of injured horses. Smoke hung over parts of the battlefield like a pall. Though he carried a sketchbook, he found it difficult to know on which piece of action to concentrate, and he resorted to drawing whatever caught his eye at any particular time, abandoning one place to rush to another in search of a new subject. At Hubbardton, he had remained stationary on the ridge. Bennington, he soon discovered, was a very different battle.

Colonel Baum had made a strategic error, unwisely dispersing his forces among several locations. His dragoons commanded the position on a stone-covered hill behind a log breastwork, and 150 loyalists were sent across a river to build a breastwork there. The rest of his army was scattered piecemeal, taking what cover they could find. General John Stark was quick to exploit the folly of the enemy commander. Troops from the New Hampshire militia circled to the right of the dragoon redoubt while a force of Vermonters worked its way around to the left to take on Baum's rear guard. With Stark at its head, the main American assault hit the redoubt itself, lapping around the base of the hill and enveloping the Germans.

The loyalists, Canadians, and Indians soon lost their nerve. After holding their positions for a short while, they took to their heels and fled the scene, several of them cut down by rebel bullets as they did so. All the action now shifted to the hill, and Proudfoot got as close to it as he dared. Outnumbered and outmaneuvered, the Germans did not give in. In spite of their heavy casualties, they held their position for two hours until their ammunition ran out, a fact signaled with dramatic suddenness by the explosion of their reserve wagon.

Leaping up, Colonel Baum drew his sword and ordered his men to cut their way out with their cavalry sabers. Within a minute of issuing the order, he was dropped to the ground by a musket ball. The loss of their leader deprived the Brunswickers of the urge to fight on. Raising their arms, they walked forward in an attitude of surrender. Proudfoot saw them coming down the hill under armed guard. Now that the fighting had at last stopped, he had a subject for his next engraving.

Captain Jamie Skoyles had heard the faint sounds of battle in the distance and he encouraged Colonel Heinrich Breymann to make more speed. It was a request that he had made at every stage of the journey. The march from Fort Edward had been painfully slow. With nearly six hundred men and two cannon mounted on carts, Breymann had, for the most part, managed no more than half a mile an hour. Continuous rain pelted them, mud clutched at their feet, and they had great difficulty hauling their carts uphill. Crossing a river ate up even more precious time as the men had to wade through the water in single file. When the ammunition carts overturned, there were more delays.

What maddened Skoyles most of all was the German addiction to marching in formation. Every so often, they would pause to dress ranks as if appearance were more important than making progress toward the beleaguered force of Brunswickers. There was a worrying lack of urgency about the whole expedition. When Skoyles tried to complain, he was firmly admonished by Breymann, a curt individual with a well-earned reputation for bullying.

One of the other officers confided to Skoyles that, in his orders, Burgoyne had said that he was sending the reinforcements out "in consequence of good news received from Baum." How the awkward situation in which Colonel Baum found himself could be construed as good news, Skoyles did not know, but at least he was able to understand why Breymann was so unhurried. In conveying no sense of crisis, Burgoyne had unwittingly slowed the relief column down. With reluctance, Skoyles was forced to entertain serious doubts about his commander's judgment yet again.

They were miles from Bennington when the shooting was first heard and—to Skoyles's relief—they did quicken their step a little. The sounds of conflict grew steadily in volume as they got closer, and they were all struck by the intensity of the fighting. Gunfire was unceasing. The cries of dying men and the anguished neighing of horses soon reached their ears. Then they heard a massive explosion, far louder than that from a single cannon. Shortly after that, the noises gradually faded away, to be followed by an eerie silence.

Riding with a battalion of light infantry and grenadiers, Skoyles had to quell the impulse to kick his horse into a gallop. Desperate as he was to get to Bennington, he realized that one man could make no difference on a battlefield. Only the arrival of a sizable force would have any impact. Breymann did not disguise their approach. He ordered the band to strike up so that everyone would know that they were coming. To the captured Brunswickers, the music had a decidedly hollow ring to it. Reinforcements had come too late.

The battlefield was a sorry sight. Scattered across the hill were the uniformed bodies of dozens of German soldiers. More corpses lay in the other positions that had been taken up. Hundreds of prisoners were being marched away through a taunting crowd. General John Stark had inflicted something close to a massacre. While his rustic rifleman had beaten a professional army with their daring, accuracy, and mobility, those same men had now lost all discipline. With so many dead soldiers on the ground, the temptation for plunder was too great to resist. Weapons were being seized, jackets stripped from their owners, money, watches, rings, and anything else of value snatched by the scavengers.

Skoyles looked on with disgust. Desperately sorry for the loss of so many Brunswickers, he blamed Breymann for not arriving in time to save them and rebuked himself for his failure to make the colonel move at a faster pace. But his real fury was reserved for Burgoyne, who had treated the call for reinforcements as a polite request rather than an urgent summons. In telling Breymann that he was responding to good news from Baum, he had effectively condemned a large number of people to death. For an instant, Jamie Skoyles felt ashamed to be wearing a red coat.

Battle was joined again in a number of places. Many of the militiamen were too busy drinking their rum to take much interest, but Stark quickly assembled the rest, and he was strongly supported by Colonel Seth Warner and the Green Mountain Boys. Skoyles was with the grenadiers who took up a position near the river and opened fire. They were too far away from the enemy for their volley to have any effect, but they reloaded smartly and fired again. Their main problem was one that they shared with Baum's men. Rebel soldiers did not stand still to return fire. Shooting from behind a tree, they would race to another hiding place in order to reload. And because their rifles had a longer range, they could pick off the grenadiers at will.

Having no men under his direct command, Skoyles could do little more than ride up and down the line to offer encouragement. When his horse was shot from beneath him, he rolled on the ground until he collided with a grenadier whose whole face had been shot away. Grabbing the man's musket, powder horn, and ammunition bag, Skoyles took his place among the others and shot at the first target that presented itself. The odds were heavily against the Germans, but they refused to give ground. Skoyles was proud to fight beside them.

The battle raged on into the evening and shadows began to fall. German resistance was fierce, but Skoyles knew that the outcome was never in any doubt. The enemy had more men, more ammunition, and a better knowledge of the terrain. In John Stark, they had a far better leader than Colonel Heinrich Breymann, who lagged at the rear trying to bring his artillery into action, a feat that was made impossible when the horses pulling the cannon were shot. When Skoyles exhausted his supply of musket balls, he took some from a wounded grenadier, continued firing, and had the satisfaction of bringing down more attackers.

The end, however, was in sight. Weary, embattled, and running out of ammunition, the reinforcements could hold out no longer in the fading light. Breymann finally accepted defeat and decided to parley. He gave the order to the band, and they beat out the appropriate drum call. But the untrained Americans did not recognize the signal and continued to fire regardless. They could not be stopped. It was a clear demonstration that each side was fighting a different battle. While the Brunswickers adhered to the rules of engagement, the rebels improvised wildly. The drum call was meaningless to amateur soldiers. All that Colonel Breymann could do was to order a retreat. Abandoning their cannon, their carts, their dead, and their wounded, the Germans fled ignominiously from the field.

Skoyles fired a last deadly shot before joining them.

CHAPTER THIRTEEN

I t was not until the following afternoon that the routed army limped back into camp at Fort Edward. Fatigued, downcast, and soaked to the skin by the rain, the Germans were a pitiful sight. Many carried injuries and wore bloodstained bandaging around heads, arms, or legs; all of them were nursing their wounded pride. Of the dragoons who had fought with Colonel Baum, a mere nine had survived, the rest were killed or captured. In all, some nine hundred men had been lost at Bennington, nearly all of them regular soldiers. Those who watched the bedraggled men trudge back into camp realized, with a jolt, that almost a sixth of Burgoyne's army had disappeared.

Colonel Breymann reported first to General Riedesel. It was left to Captain Jamie Skoyles to give an initial account of the disaster to General Burgoyne and Brigadier Simon Fraser. He met them at the house where his commander had set up his headquarters. Though he tried to be as objective as possible, there was a degree of implied criticism in Skoyles's report. Burgoyne was quick to allocate blame.

"Colonel Breymann was clearly at fault," he said. "His army was too slow and ponderous. He was leading a force of tortoises."

"We knew that before he left," Fraser pointed out. "That was why I opposed the notion of sending the Germans. British soldiers would have got to Bennington in half the time."

"That may be true, sir," said Skoyles, "but the importance of speed was never impressed upon Colonel Breymann. He believed that Colonel Baum was in no danger and therefore took his time. In that sense, he was only following orders."

"Baum must be censured here," Burgoyne decided, eager to shake off any responsibility for issuing the wrong orders. "His dispatches were full of optimism. They did not call for immediate reinforcements."

"Too small a force was sent in the first place," Fraser argued.

"It's easy to say that in hindsight, Simon."

"According to all the evidence we have, the rebels were able to put almost two thousand soldiers in the field. Colonel Baum had no chance."

"He should have managed. His folly lay in advancing too close."

"Colonel Baum and his men fought with outstanding bravery," said Skoyles, keen to give them their due. "I've spoken to the handful of dragoons who managed to escape. They all praise their commander. The causes of their defeat were a shortage of ammunition and the superior number of the enemy. When it comes to false optimism," he went on, "the person we should single out here is Colonel Skene."

"I couldn't agree more," said Fraser.

"It was on his flawed advice that the Germans were sent to Bennington in the first place. Colonel Skene gave the impression that they would be sure to find an endless supply of horses, cattle, and new recruits—not to mention a magazine with only a light guard on it. Instead of bringing in more loyalists," said Skoyles with emphasis, "this misbegotten expedition has lost the ones that we already had."

"I could not foresee that, Captain," said Burgoyne. "Skene told me that Tory sympathies ran high in this part of New England."

"Rebel sentiments dominate, General. That's obvious from the speed with which the militia was raised and from the vigor with which they fought. It was one of the most distressing things we witnessed," Skoyles recalled. "When we reached the battlefield, we saw loyalist prisoners being dragged off, tied to a horse in pairs, and jeered at by their captors."

"They'll get no mercy when they're returned to their localities," said Fraser sadly. "Each and every one of them will be hanged."

"Nothing is served by dwelling on that," said Burgoyne testily. "The reality is that no army can get through a campaign without sustaining losses of some kind. We are still in good shape and of good heart. Albany is within striking distance."

"Do we have news of Brigadier St. Leger?" asked Skoyles.

"He is besieging Fort Stanwix."

"And you expect the fort to surrender?"

"Of course."

"We should take nothing for granted, General," Fraser suggested.

"The last dispatch was more than encouraging."

"I'm pleased to hear that," said Skoyles."

"And there's more good news for us," Burgoyne continued, seeking to divert attention from the tragic events at Bennington. "Congress has finally had the sense to replace General Schuyler."

"With whom, sir—Benedict Arnold?"

"No, Captain—with General Gates." He allowed himself a smile. "His mother was housekeeper to a duke's mistress, so you might say that he has aristocratic affiliations. He certainly has no blue blood of his own. He and I once served as lieutenants together in the Duke of Bolton's regiment. An honest fellow, if rather loudmouthed, but somewhat dull and limited when it comes to military affairs."

"He might have more support in New England than General Schuyler was able to garner," said Fraser worriedly. "This appointment may not be such good news, after all."

"You don't know the fellow as well as I do," said Burgoyne. "He's a disappointed man, a jaded soldier who sold his commission in the British army, then came to America and swallowed the deadly poison known as republican ideals. It has warped his judgment. Rely on me," he went on confidently, "we have no reason to fear a commander like Granny Gates."

Horatio Gates was so pleased to hear of the victory at Bennington that he went out of his way to visit Brigadier General John Stark, congratulating him on his success and assuring him that he had protested against the way that Stark was overlooked for promotion.

"There'll be red faces in Congress after this," said Gates, "and I daresay that General Schuyler will be embarrassed as well. They did not appreciate you, John. They realize what fools they were now."

"All that I wanted was my own command, General."

"And how well you deployed your men! It was exemplary soldiering and just the kind of success that we needed. You proved two things at Bennington. First, that the British are not invincible."

"Nor their hired German mercenaries," said Stark.

"Second—and this is more significant—that, if properly led, a militia can defeat regular soldiers in a pitched battle."

"It was the hottest fight I've ever been involved in," Stark confessed with a grin. "It was like a continual clap of thunder. There were moments when I felt we'd descended into the nether regions."

"What were your casualties?"

"Very light—around forty killed or wounded."

"Set against huge losses on the other side."

"Don't forget their weapons, General," said Stark. "We captured a horde of brass cannon, muskets, bayonets, sabers, and pistols. Horses, too, of course. There's also plenty of shot that can be used again. Our heavy guns were reduced to firing stones at the enemy."

"That must change, John," Gates confided. "Our men need proper equipment, better food and greater discipline. They also deserve some uniforms in which they can take pride. I'll procure some. Our uniforms may not be as flashy as those worn by Gentleman Johnny and his redcoats, but they'll signal that he's up against a real army."

Gates was a solid man of fifty with thinning hair, a pale, round face, and easy deportment. Stark admired him, and not only because the new commander of the Northern Department had ridden several miles to meet him. Gates had been popular in New England ever since he had championed their claim to the New Hampshire Grants in opposition to those of New York State, whose advocate had been none less than Philip Schuyler, the man he had replaced. Gates's appointment was bound to stimulate recruitment, coming, as it did, in harness with the cheering news about Bennington.

The two men were in Stark's tent in the militia camp. Waiting quietly in a corner was Ezekiel Proudfoot. Gates noticed a couple of sketches that were lying on a stool. He picked one up.

"I didn't know you were an artist, John," he said.

Stark laughed. "These hands were made for fighting," he said, extending his palms, "not for drawing pictures. No, that's the work of Ezekiel Proudfoot here," he said, beckoning the artist over. "He was with us at Bennington and made dozens of similar drawings. Ezekiel gave me those as souvenirs."

"I've seen and admired your work before, Mr. Proudfoot," said Gates, shaking his hand. "It's a potent weapon for us."

"Thank you, sir," said Proudfoot. "I did sketches of Ticonderoga and the battle at Hubbardton as well, but they were confiscated by the British. This is one of my best, I think," he went on, indicating the last piece of paper. "It's my idea of what Jane McCrea must have suffered."

Gates took the sketch to study it. The scene was full of drama and menace. Against a dark background of trees, a beautiful young woman was kneeling on the ground, her arms outstretched in an appeal for mercy. Two seminaked Indians were holding her. One was about to strike her with his tomahawk, while the other, also armed with a tomahawk, had a firm grasp on her long hair. There was a deliberate contrast between the darkened bodies of the men and the pallor of Jane McCrea's face, arms, and exposed neck.

"Can I keep this?" asked Gates, struck by the drawing.

"If you wish, General."

"Good. I hope that you'll be staying around. I don't think it will be long before we can offer you some more action."

"I'm glad to hear that," said Proudfoot. "When I was held prisoner, the British took all my engraving tools. I'll need to go back home to Albany to get some more. But I won't miss any action, have no fear. I'm drawn to a battle like a bear to honey. I've a nose for it, General."

"So have I," said Stark.

"How long have we got, General?"

"Weeks yet, I'd say, Mr. Proudfoot," replied Gates. "Burgoyne has to build up his supplies before he moves on, and he gained neither horses nor forage at Bennington. His men have to build a bridge across the Hudson," he pointed out, "and that will take time. Once he crosses to the western bank of the river, of course, he'll have severed his supply line to Canada."

"That will put him in a very awkward position," noted Stark. "He'll be unable to retreat and unable to go forward without a fight."

"We have to be ready for that fight, John."

"How many men do you have?"

"Over seven thousand, at a guess—mainly Continentals, but with New York and Connecticut militia in support. Best of all, we have Daniel Morgan's Rifle Corps from Virginia."

Proudfoot was delighted. "Dan Morgan!" he exclaimed. "His name alone will loosen the bowels of the British army."

"He suffers from rheumatism, but that won't keep him away from a battle. He has a score to settle with the British," said Gates. "He was once give five hundred lashes for striking one of their officers. A lesser man would have perished from such a flogging."

"Not Dan Morgan—he's an American phenomenon." Stark's joy was tempered by caution. "What's the enemy strength?"

"Since Bennington, they can't have more than five thousand able men."

"I heard tell that they had reinforcements coming down the Mohawk River," said Proudfoot. "Is that true, General?"

"Not any more," said Gates with a chuckle. "Nicholas Herkimer repulsed them at Oriskany and the siege of Fort Stanwix was lifted by Arnold."

Stark clapped his hands together and laughed. "By God, these are wonderful tidings! It means that the British army has been given a bloody nose three times in a row—Bennington, Oriskany, and Fort Stanwix. Wait a moment!" he said, scratching his head. "Wasn't it renamed Fort Schuyler last year?"

"Not by me."

Proudfoot grinned. "How did the general take the fact that he's been relieved of his command?"

"I don't know," said Gates with a shrug. "He's still sulking in his tent. Forget about Schuyler," he added. "He'll play no part in future deliberations. I want my best commanders around me—men like Daniel Morgan and John Stark. We need to raise more men and to train them properly for the battle ahead. If we do that," he concluded, "we'll be able to take all of the swagger out of Gentleman Johnny Burgoyne."

It was evening by the time Jamie Skoyles visited the medical tent and Tom Caffrey had to work by candlelight. During the battle at Bennington, Skoyles had picked up another lurid array of bruises on his body. His jacket had been pierced three times by musket balls, one of them grazing his side and leaving a long streak of dried blood as a memento. With his friend stripped to the waist, Caffrey cleaned up the wound before bandaging it.

"Why didn't you come to me sooner, Jamie?" he asked.

"I had to report to the general first, Tom. After that, I felt duty bound to speak to General Riedesel to explain what happened. My version of events differed somewhat from that of Colonel Breymann."

"Yes—yours is the honest one."

"The colonel was sent on a mission with insufficient intelligence. The blame for that must lie with General Burgoyne."

"Did you tell him that?"

"Not in so many words."

"I wish that someone would," said Caffrey. "The gossip is that we lost nine hundred men at Bennington and that the Indians have deserted. The further we go in this campaign, the fewer men we have. Doesn't that worry the general?"

"It doesn't seem to, Tom," said Skoyles, reaching for his shirt. "He dismissed the whole episode with a smile as little more than the loss of a foraging party. That wasn't how the rest of us saw it."

"What was Old Red Hazel's view?"

"General Riedesel was justifiably angry. He warned the general of the dangers along the road to Bennington and recommended a force of at least three thousand men. His advice was ignored."

"Yet again."

"Whereas Colonel Skene's—unfortunately—was not."

"I sometimes begin to wonder whose side that man is on."

"His own, Tom." Skoyles put on his shirt. "His decisions are always sponsored by self-interest, and that means to our disadvantage."

The tent flap opened and Polly Bragg put her head in.

"Excuse me, Captain," she said, "but there's someone to see you."

"Now? It's hardly convenient. Can't he wait?"

"It's Miss Rainham."

Skoyles was startled. "*Here*—on her own?"

"I can see that Polly and I are in the way," said Caffrey, winking at his friend and moving away. "My quarters are all yours."

He went swiftly out of the tent and left Skoyles wondering if he should do up his shirt or put on his coat over it. Before he could make up his mind, however, Elizabeth stepped into the tent. She saw the bandaging around his body.

"I heard that you were wounded," she said in consternation. "Is it serious, Captain Skoyles?"

"Not at all," he replied, turning his back on her to do up his shirt. "If you'll pardon me, I'll make myself more presentable."

"What happened? I'm told that you went to Bennington."

"I went and I was shot at. Luckily, I was only grazed."

"Thank goodness for that!"

"Tom Caffrey has looked after me. I feel like a new man." He tucked his shirt inside his breeches then turned to face her. "I must say that it's very kind of you to take such an interest in my health."

"I'm interested in everything about you, Captain," she said before she could stop the words coming out. She lowered her head demurely. "Nan Wyatt, my maid, was talking to Mrs. Bragg, who happened to mention that you'd been injured in battle. I just wished to reassure myself that the injuries were not bad."

Skoyles understood at once. Knowing that he would be in the medical tent for a while, Polly Bragg had alerted Nan Wyatt, who, in turn, had confided in her mistress. The meeting with Elizabeth had been engineered by his friends, and that made Skoyles self-conscious. He shifted his feet. It was ironic. A man who was completely at ease with someone like Maria Quinn felt curiously nervous in the presence of another woman.

"It's a pleasure to see you again, Miss Rainham," he said.

She looked up at him again. "Thank you."

"I'm sorry that I had to leave so suddenly after the cricket match, but I had a strong feeling that only two people were needed in that particular conversation."

"You were right, Captain."

"Far be it from me to come between man and wife," he went on, fishing for a response. He saw her wince. "I trust that any differences have been reconciled by now."

"I've not seen the major since that day," she admitted.

"Indeed?"

"His behavior toward you was unwarrantable."

"Major Featherstone is my superior. That's warrant enough for any behavior in the army. I make no complaint, Miss Rainham."

"But you should. Why are you being so noble?"

"I'm simply doing what I always do," he explained, "and that is to tolerate the antics of a superior officer. I've done it for many years now, so I'm well used to the process. That's the way the army works." He searched her eyes. "When do you expect to speak to the major?"

"I don't know."

"He must surely miss you."

"Perhaps."

"Any man would miss someone like you, Miss Rainham."

"Do *you* miss me?"

"It's not my place to say," he replied, biting back the words that he wanted to utter. "You're betrothed to someone else."

"And if I were not?"

"You must know how I feel about you."

"Yes," she said gently, "I do, and I thank you for your friendship and understanding. It's my own feelings that I'm more worried about."

"Your own?"

She gave a nod. "I fear that they may be improper."

"Nothing you do could be improper, Miss Rainham."

He could see her trembling as she fought against an upsurge of emotion. She seemed to be on the point of tears. Skoyles moved in close, wanting to offer his arms but somehow unable to do so. It was Elizabeth who acted on impulse. She hurled herself at him with the abandon she had shown at Bitter Creek, but this time she did not break away. The embrace went on for several minutes, his hands caressing her body, her head nestling into his shoulder, her tears of joy dampening his shirt. When she finally drew her head back, there was a mingled pleasure and apprehension in her eyes.

"I should not be here," she murmured.

Skoyles stroked her cheek. "Do you intend to leave?"

"Not yet."

And she accepted a first, lingering kiss on the lips.

"The nerve of it, Harry!" exclaimed Burgoyne. "The sheer audacity of it."

"What does General Gates's letter say?" asked Featherstone.

"It's not a letter, it's a string of insults. On my instructions, under a flag of truce, Doctor Wood carried my missive to Gates, protesting at the treatment of wounded prisoners at Bennington and complaining, in the strongest language, at the way that the loyalists were refused quarter in the battle when they offered to surrender."

"What was his reply?"

"Listen to it. Gates is indignant.

"*That the famous Lieutenant General Burgoyne, in whom the fine gentleman is united with the soldier and the scholar, should hire the savages of Amer-*

ica to scalp Europeans and the descendants of Europeans, nay, more that he should pay a price for every scalp so barbarously taken, is more than will be believed in England, until authenticated fact shall in every gazette convince mankind of the truth of this horrid tale."

"Ha! So ends this sermon from the Reverend Horatio Gates!"

"No apology for the way his rabble behaved at Bennington?"

"Not a whisper."

"From what I hear, it is *they* who acted like savages."

"Gates will hear no condemnation of his militia," said Burgoyne, snatching up a sheet of paper from the table. "Not content with daring to criticize me, he had the impudence to send me this."

"What is it, General?"

"A piece of vile provocation."

He handed the paper over. They were in the room that Burgoyne had commandeered as his office. The table was littered with maps and papers. An empty glass stood beside a decanter of brandy.

"It's a sketch of Miss Jane McCrea," he said, "purporting to show what happened to her. Unless I'm mistaken, it's the work of an artist whom we took prisoner—one Ezekiel Proudfoot. When he was captured, I saw several of his sketches. I recognize his style."

"I remember the damn fellow well," said Featherstone, looking at the drawing. "He was a friend of Captain Skoyles and, by rights, he should have gone to Ticonderoga with the other prisoners. He escaped from Skenesborough."

"And is free to use his talents against us." The general took the sketch back. "This is not what happened at all. When David Jones reclaimed the lady's hair from that Ottawa Indian, there was no blood or skin on it. Jane McCrea hadn't been scalped at all. It may well be that Wyandot Panther was telling the truth. She was shot by rebel soldiers here at Fort Edward, not slaughtered and raped by an Indian."

"Tell that to General Gates, sir."

"He'd pay no heed," said Burgoyne, holding up the sketch. "*This* is the version he wants to promote. We're at the mercy of artistic falsehood here, Harry. If something like this reaches a wider audience in the form of prints, it will do us a lot of harm."

Featherstone was bitter. "And all because Skoyles insisted on bringing his friend to Skenesborough," he said. "If Proudfoot had gone to Ticonderoga, he'd still be there—out of harm's way."

"They say the pen is mightier than the sword. I have a horrible presentiment that the engraving may turn out to be mightier than both, especially when it's been produced by someone like Ezekiel Proudfoot."

"I blame Skoyles."

"He was not responsible for the man's escape."

"I begin to wonder."

"Take care, Harry," Burgoyne warned. "That's a serious accusation to make against another officer. I'd absolve Skoyles of any complicity. He's shown his mettle time and again during this campaign, both as a scout and as a soldier. You should know that—he saved your life."

"Yes, sir," said Featherstone, trying to suppress his open hostility toward Skoyles, "but that was in the past. We must look to the future."

"Naturally."

"The auguries are not good, General."

"On the contrary," Burgoyne retorted, "they are excellent. Our army has rested, we've been joined by another group of Mohawks, and we still have loyalists coming in from time to time."

"Granted, sir. But against that you must set the substantial losses we suffered at Bennington, the fact that other Indian tribes deserted us, and—this latest blow—the retreat of Brigadier St. Leger and his men."

"That was a reversal, I admit, but I allowed for it in my contingency plan. We still have an army capable of beating anything that Gates and his preposterous soldiers can throw against us." He adopted a pose. "I'm a gambling man, Harry, as you know. When we cross the Hudson River, I'll be taking the biggest gamble of my life. But I feel in my bones that it's the right thing to do."

"So do I, sir," said Featherstone, emboldened by his commander's overweening confidence. "If we can force the devils to fight a pitched battle on our terms, we are bound to win."

"Think what that will do for us when we get back to England."

"We'll be feted as heroes for the rest of our lives."

"I look for an earldom out of this."

"You deserve a dukedom, General."

"Thank you."

233

"Your judgment at every turn has been exemplary," the other flattered him. "The plan you conceived for the invasion of America was a brilliant piece of strategy."

"Our journey to Albany will be celebrated for two things. We will finally bring these skulking revolutionaries to book. That's one thing."

"And the other?"

"You shouldn't need to ask me that, Harry," Burgoyne teased, reaching for the brandy decanter. "Albany will always have a place in your heart. It's where you and the divine Elizabeth will be married."

"Yes," said the major uncertainly.

"Well, try to look a little more pleased about it, man."

Featherstone could not quite manufacture a smile.

Jamie Skoyles and Elizabeth Rainham met whenever they could. In such a large camp, with so many pairs of eyes on them, it was very difficult for them to achieve any privacy, and most of their encounters were, of necessity, in public. Nan Wyatt was a ready accomplice, able to voice her disapproval of Major Harry Featherstone at last without incurring her mistress's anger. The maid's presence as a chaperone made apparently accidental meetings possible. At times, Skoyles would simply be talking to Tom Caffrey when—by prior arrangement—Elizabeth walked past with Nan and exchanged a few casual words with him. It was a contact of sorts.

The call of duty limited Skoyles's freedom. When he was not leading a scouting expedition, he was helping to supervise the construction of the bridge of rafts across the Hudson River. Until that was completed, the army was forced to cool its heels at Fort Edward. No matter how busy he was, Skoyles always found a moment for an occasional visit to the field hospital to check on his men. After weeks of convalescence, Private Marcus Wolverton was fit for duty. Skoyles found him with Private Andrew McKillop, sitting outside a tent and regaling his friend with some passages from Shakespeare's plays.

"Well done!" said Skoyles, arriving in time to hear a speech from *Macbeth*. "You've lost none of your talent, Wolverton."

"I was accustomed to larger audiences than a one-legged man, sir."

"Larger, maybe," said McKillop, "but not more attentive. I've just had a wee slice of Scottish history. Those words are music to my ear. I feel very privileged. General Burgoyne has musicians to play to him every evening—I've got Wolvie."

Wolverton smiled wistfully. "Dan Lukins used to say that I quoted Shakespeare as if I had six large plums in my mouth."

"And a dozen up your arse," McKillop remembered.

"Exactly the kind of remark I'd expect from Lukins," said Skoyles with amusement. "For all that, he admired you, Wolverton."

"I know, sir," said the other, "but he had a strange way of showing it." He pulled a face. "That's the trouble with this army. As soon as you grow to like someone, they either desert or get killed. In Dan's case, he did both—the little fool!"

"You've other friends to take his place," McKillop put in, "and I'm not going to run away or get shot. You've got me for life, Wolvie."

"How long will that be?" Wolverton turned gloomily to Skoyles. "It's only a question of time before I'm in the firing line again, isn't it, sir?"

"We'll fight another battle sooner or later," Skoyles agreed.

"Where?"

"If only we knew. The enemy is waiting for us to cross the Hudson first. They won't let us get to Albany without a tussle."

"Do we know where they are now, Captain?" asked McKillop.

"A few miles from Stillwater, building up their defenses."

"When do we cross the river?"

"At the end of the week—with luck."

"That means we'll have been here almost a month."

"A month of waiting, watching, playing cards, and getting rained on every other day," said Wolverton. "Why ever did I join the army?"

"In the hope of meeting me," said McKillop, grinning at him.

"That makes it all worthwhile, Andy!"

"Ignore the sarcasm in his voice, McKillop," said Skoyles. "He really means it. You're what every actor craves—a captive audience."

He spent a few more minutes with them before taking his leave, waving to other patients he knew as he did so. Skoyles was close to Tom Caffrey's tent when Harry Featherstone came into view. The major bore down on him.

"Found you at last," he said. "The general wishes to see you."

"Yes, sir."

"*Now*," rasped Featherstone, sensing his hesitation.

"I just wanted a word with Sergeant Caffrey first."

"General Burgoyne is more important than an assistant surgeon."

"I appreciate that, Major. I'll go at once."

Before Skoyles could move, however, Caffrey came around the angle of the tent with Polly Bragg and Elizabeth Rainham. A rendezvous between Skoyles and Elizabeth had been arranged with their friends acting as a convenient cover. When she saw Skoyles waiting there, Elizabeth gave a radiant smile that congealed on her face as she caught sight of Featherstone. The major was surprised and hurt.

"Elizabeth!" he exclaimed.

At any other time, Skoyles would have considered it an honor to be singled out for the assignment. It appealed to his sense of daring and would enable him to render a great service to his army. What made him reluctant was his blossoming friendship with Elizabeth Rainham. To leave camp for any length of time meant separation from her, and that was a source of pain. However General Burgoyne's orders could not be disobeyed. Skoyles was told to penetrate the enemy camp, take full inventory of its defenses, then escape as soon as the opportunity arose.

Slipping out of camp at night, Skoyles intended to complete his work as swiftly as he could. He wore his hunting shirt, buckskin breeches, and round hat. With his hunting knife in its sheath, he also carried the Kentucky rifle and ammunition that he had taken from the militiaman who had shot one of the Indian scouts and died a grisly death as a result. The weapon was slow to load and lacked a bayonet, but it was more accurate than the Brown Bess muskets of the British army, and its longer range gave it more potency. Skoyles had practiced with it regularly until he was proficient with the rifle. In his pocket, once again, was Burgoyne's telescope.

Knowing that there would be enemy scouts in the vicinity, he moved warily. He used one of the bateaux to ferry himself and his horse to the western bank of the Hudson. His route took him slightly inland now as he followed the southerly course of the river. After ten miles, Skoyles was within reach of the rebel camp and could see their fires in the distance. Aware of the importance of conserving his energy, he dismounted, tethered his horse so that it could graze in a hollow, and snatched a few hours' sleep while he could.

Up at the crack of dawn, he rode forward half a mile until he came to a stand of trees. Skoyles climbed up the tallest of them and, with the aid of the telescope, took a long look at the encampment. General Gates and his army occupied a position on Bemis Heights, the plateau that rose above the river and commanded the route to Albany. Strong fortifications dominated road and river, turning both northward and westward to form three sides of a box. The camp was protected at the front by a ravine, and in front of that was closely wooded ground, intersected by tiny creeks and wagon tracks.

Skoyles had seen enough. It was time to join the rebel army.

"What's your name?" asked the sergeant.

"Daniel Lukins," lied Skoyles.

"Where are you from?"

"Hubbardton."

"Why do you want to join us?"

"To kill the British," said Skoyles, spitting on the ground. "I lost a brother and several friends in a skirmish against them near my home. Their Indians plundered our farm."

"It's taken you a long time to enlist."

"I had my brother's wife to comfort and a farm to rebuild, but I never forgot what they did to us at Hubbardton. When I was free to move again," said Skoyles, "I pretended to be a Tory and joined the British at Fort Edward. Take me to General Gates and I'll furnish him with good intelligence."

The man looked at him with suspicion. He was a sergeant in the Continental Army, a short, stubby individual in his forties with a tufted beard and deep-set eyes. Ready to welcome any new soldiers, he wanted first to make sure that they were genuine recruits.

"You know our terms of service, Daniel Lukins?" he said.

"Yes, Sergeant."

"This is the Continental Army. If you sign on, we own you for two years. We're not like the militia—you can't run off after two months."

"That suits me, sir," said Skoyles determinedly. "Just put me where I can stain those redcoats with blood."

The man appraised him. "You have the look of a soldier about you," he decided. "I think you've seen service before."

"I have. It was the British army that brought me to America, my brother and me together. We were mere lads when we marched with General Wolfe. We took to the country," Skoyles explained, "and stayed on after we left the army. I wanted to be a farmer—until what happened at Hubbardton."

"What rank did you reach?"

"Sergeant."

"Describe your uniform."

"My coat was lapelled to the waist with blue facing, our regimental color. The buttonholes of the coat were of white braid, those on the waistcoat were plain. Because I was a battalion sergeant, I had a halberd but no pouches."

"Sash?"

"Crimson worsted with a blue stripe. It was worn round the waist."

"I remember it well," said the other. "When I was in the British army, I served in the 16th Foot. Our facings were yellow." He offered his hand and Skoyles shook it. "You're welcome, Dan Lukins," he said, "if you're prepared to join us as a corporal. The pay is just over seven dollars a month."

"I didn't come here for the money, Sergeant. I've got fire in my belly. I'm here in order to fight."

"Then you will. Come and meet General Gates."

Skoyles followed him through the camp, relieved that his disguise had been convincing and his answers persuasive. He did not think that Daniel Lukins would mind his name being appropriated. Posthumously, the Cockney was doing the British army a favor. Skoyles missed nothing. As they walked between the rows of tents, he looked everywhere and made a mental note of what he saw. The rebel camp was larger than the one at Fort Edward and—although it was less organized—there was a prevailing mood of optimism.

When they reached the commander's tent, Skoyles was told to wait outside while the sergeant went on in. Horatio Gates was sufficiently interested in what he heard to come out into the daylight. He weighed the newcomer up before speaking.

"So you wish to be a corporal in the Continental army, do you?"

"I just want to fight against the British, General."

"Do you believe in the notion of an American republic?"

"I believe in anything that will drive those redcoats off our soil," said Skoyles. "King George has grown fat off us for too long."

"Sergeant Rymer tells me that you were recently at Fort Edward," said Gates, still uncertain about him. "What did you learn?"

"As much as I could, General."

"Tell me."

Skoyles divulged all the facts and figures that he had rehearsed with General Burgoyne before leaving the camp, speaking freely but making sure to give nothing of crucial importance away. Gates was impressed. The intelligence accorded with what enemy spies had already gleaned but it was more up-to-date.

"When does Gentleman Johnny expect to cross the river?"

"At the end of the week," said Skoyles, "when the bridge is ready."

"And the morale of his men?"

"Very low, General. They have not recovered from the reverse at Bennington. It preys on their mind."

"So it should."

"The army is also weakened by disease. Dysentery has been a scourge, and camp fever is rife."

As he had been instructed, Skoyles went on to paint a picture of a shattered army with despondent officers, trying to lull Gates into a fatal overconfidence. The general liked everything that he heard.

"Take him away, Sergeant Rymer," he said, finally. "We've a good man here. I wish that everyone who joined us had the same attitude." He regarded Skoyles. "Carry on, Corporal Lukins."

"Yes, General," said Skoyles.

"We'll put your intelligence to good use."

Gates went back into his tent and the sergeant led Skoyles away to go through the formalities of joining the Continental Army.

"You've sound fortifications," observed Skoyles, looking at the many earthworks and breastworks that had been constructed. "Who built all these, Sergeant?"

"If I could pronounce his name, I'd tell you. A Polish engineer, and a genius at his trade. He helped to design the Delaware forts protecting Philadelphia, and earned a commission as colonel. He's one of our best weapons, as you can see."

Skoyles knew that he was talking about Tadeusz Kosciuszko, a gifted man who had been drawn to the rebel cause by its republican ideals. During his time in America, the Pole had acquired a reputation that made even General Phillips speak of him with envy. Skoyles could understand now why Bemis Heights was so well defended by the trunks of trees, logs, boulders, and rails. A barn had been turned into a makeshift fort, complete with a powerful battery. Other batteries guarded the extremities of the camp. Kosciuszko's fortifications bespoke a sense of impregnability.

Safe within his disguise, Skoyles also felt impregnable. He had even taken in the rebel commander. Having been at the camp for less than half an hour, he already had a good idea of its strengths and weaknesses. Skoyles was still congratulating himself on his success when he recognized the man walking toward them.

It was Ezekiel Proudfoot.

The frustration was overwhelming. Unable to stand it any longer, Harry Featherstone went to her tent and demanded some time alone with her. Elizabeth Rainham was cautious.

"I'd prefer it if Nan stayed," she said, "if you don't mind."

"I do mind. She's done enough damage already."

Nan was stung. "I beg your pardon, Major."

"Get out."

"That's for Miss Rainham to say, sir."

"Get out, woman!" Featherstone ordered.

Nan looked to her mistress who, after a pause, gave a nod. The maid went quickly out of the tent but remained within earshot. Elizabeth found the strength to face her visitor calmly.

"How long is this going to go on?" he asked her. "It's weeks since you've spoken to me properly. We're engaged to be married, Elizabeth, so I'll not be treated like a leper."

"I find the situation easier to bear when we're apart, Harry."

"And what about *me?*"

"You managed perfectly well without me last year," she pointed out. "Your letters were full of complaints about the weather, but you also talked of the many occasions when you wined, dined, and played cards."

"That's all that I *could* do," he said, omitting any mention of the fact that, in her absence, he had enjoyed other female company. "When you were far away, I could cope; when you are right under my nose—and I'm forbidden to see you—then I'm in agony."

"I'm sorry to hear that."

"Then why continue like this? I'm heartily fed up with making excuses to General Burgoyne when you refuse his invitations to dinner, and I'm sick of lying to my fellow officers about you."

"Then tell them the truth: We have drifted apart."

"*You* may have done so, Elizabeth. I most certainly have not."

It was strange. As she looked at him now, she could see all the things about the major that had made her fall in love with him. Featherstone was an elegant man with the aristocratic air of a true officer. There was also something faintly unnerving about him, a quality that made her simultaneously frightened and reassured. It was that hint of danger in his character that had appealed to her most, yet it was now the thing that repelled her.

"You never told me what you were doing yesterday," he said.

"Yes, I did. I was visiting the hospital."

"We have surgeons to look after the wounded."

"And nurses," she said. "Kind women like Mrs. Bragg who give up their time to tend the sick and injured. Men are grateful for the sight of a female face."

"I *know*—I'm one of them."

"Harry!"

"Have you any idea how painful this is for me?"

"The pain will gradually fade in time."

"The opposite has happened in my case," he said, "and I'll stand no more of it. I'll not be made the laughingstock of the whole camp."

"That wasn't my intention."

"Then talk to me, be with me, dine with me. People are starting to pass derogatory comments, Elizabeth. They think that a rift has opened between us."

"You were the one responsible for that, Harry."

"Can't we consign it all to the past and start anew?"

"I think not."

"We can, if we both try." His voice took on a pleading note. "Have you forgotten all the promises you made to me when we were in Canterbury? You swore that you'd do anything to be with me."

"That was before I saw you for what you really are."

"I'm still the same man, Elizabeth," he insisted, taking her by the shoulders. "The man that your sister chose until she was cruelly taken from us. Don't you remember what Cora said to you?"

She bit her lip. "Only too well."

" 'Love him in my stead, Elizabeth.' That's what she told you."

"Yes, it's true—and I found it easy to do so."

"What's changed?"

"I don't know."

"Have I lost *all* of your respect?"

"No," she said, "I still admire you as a soldier who's prepared to risk his life in defense of King and Country. Beyond that . . ." She ran her tongue over her dry lips. "Beyond that, Harry, my feelings are unclear. When my sister died—and when she wanted me to enjoy the happiness that she had hoped to share with you—I was only too ready to love you. But I was young and inexperienced. I was caught up in an infatuation."

"And now?"

"Things have altered. I simply can't feel the same about you any more. That may sound cruel, but you deserve honesty." She straightened her back. "You brought it on yourself, Harry."

He glared at her. "It's *him,* isn't it?" he decided. "That's what really came between us—Captain Skoyles. Until he came on the scene, you were only interested in me. Then you met him."

"It's not as straightforward as that."

"Oh, I think it is, Elizabeth. If I'd engaged two men to assault any other officer, you'd not have turned a hair. Because the intended victim was Skoyles, you had a fit of righteous indignation."

"It was a dishonorable thing to do, Harry, and, whoever the victim was, I'd have protested strongly."

"I doubt that," he said. "Skoyles has been a thorn in my side from the start. After Hubbardton, he even dared to invite you into his tent."

"Only because I asked to thank him on your behalf."

"I owe the fellow no gratitude!"

"Well, I do. He rescued us both at Bitter Creek."

"Does that mean you have to throw me aside for him?"

"No, Harry."

"*He* was the reason you visited the hospital yesterday, wasn't he?" he accused. "You didn't go to see the wounded men at all. You went there to meet Captain Skoyles. Admit it—*admit it, Elizabeth!*"

He reinforced his demand by shaking her so vigorously that she let out an involuntary cry of pain. Nan Wyatt came into the tent immediately and stared in disbelief at what she saw. Featherstone released his hold and mouthed an apology before going swiftly out of the tent. Nan rushed to put a consoling arm around Elizabeth, who tried to stem her tears.

"He knows," she whispered. "The major knows."

"Why didn't you betray me, Ezekiel?" he asked. "You know why I'm here."

"Yes," said Proudfoot, "but I had a debt to repay. Thanks to you, I'm not languishing in Fort Ticonderoga with the other prisoners."

"There's a big difference. In helping you, I didn't put myself in any danger. You, on the other hand, could be charged with harboring an enemy soldier."

"I'll take that chance."

"Thank you."

"Besides, there's another reason why I didn't give you away."

"Is there?"

"I was pleased to see you."

They were seated together on a grassy knoll near the edge of the camp. Skoyles had signed the relevant papers, been given a regiment, and was now a putative member of the Continental Army. Across his knees was the corporal's blue uniform that he had been issued. Proudfoot glanced at it.

"You've been demoted, Jamie," he mocked. "You should have held out for a captaincy—not that you'd have enjoyed it for long."

"I was happy to be back in the ranks for a while."

"We've good soldiers, the equal of anything you can muster. And our militias are full of brave fighting men."

"I know," said Skoyles, feeling the side that had been grazed by a bullet. "One of those men wounded me slightly at Bennington."

"You were *there?*"

"Until we were chased from the field."

"I watched the whole battle, Jamie."

"That luxury was not afforded to me."

Skoyles had been stunned when he first encountered Proudfoot at the camp, and he was mightily relieved that his true identity had not been revealed. There were plenty of trees from which the rebels could hang him. Proudfoot had kept him alive.

"I was glad that you escaped, Ezekiel," he confessed.

"Why?"

"Because I hated to see you under armed guard, especially as you are no soldier. It was almost as if I *wanted* you to go free."

"Who's showing friendship toward the enemy now?"

"I led the search party for you. When we found that the redcoat in the woods, I realized that you'd got safely away and I was content."

"Even though you knew that I'd use all my skills against you?"

"Even then."

"We are two of a kind, Jamie," Proudfoot commented. "I wore a red uniform to escape from your army and you're putting on a blue one in order to join mine. Both of us are turncoats."

"Only by compulsion."

"Unless you could be persuaded to stay with us."

"On a corporal's pay?" said Skoyles with a grin. "It's not exactly an irresistible temptation. I know there's a bounty of twenty dollars and the promise of land, but the land is only in the gift of Congress if you happen to win this war."

"I believe that we will. Bennington was a turning point."

"Campaigns are full of turning points. I've fought in too many to be worried by a single reverse. You've gallant soldiers, I'm sure, but have you the commanders who can bring out the best in them?"

"Only time will tell." Proudfoot studied him quizzically. "What do you see yourself as, Jamie—British or American?"

"British."

"Yet you've always nurtured the idea of buying land and settling down here. What would that make you?"

"A British colonist."

"Only if this corner of the colonial empire survives. Supposing—for the sake of argument—that we break away from King George. Does that mean you'll accept defeat and go back to England?"

"No, Ezekiel," said Skoyles. "I've lived on my dream far too long to abandon it now. Win or lose, I'll be staying here."

"Then you'll become one of us."

"No, I'm British through and through."

"You will," Proudfoot argued. "So stop shilly-shallying. These men you see around you will be your fellow countrymen—and so will I. Why not become one of us sooner rather than later?"

"Stop trying to corrupt me."

"I'm simply appealing to your common sense."

Skoyles laughed. "If I had any of that, Ezekiel," he said, "I'd never have joined the army in the first place. It was an act of sheer madness that, somehow, I've never quite managed to regret."

"But you regret things you'd done in the name of that army."

"Very much so."

"Have you ever looked at it from the opposite angle?"

"In what way?"

"Well," said Proudfoot, "imagine, just for a moment, that England has been invaded and conquered by France. Instead of being at the head of a mighty empire, the country would be nothing more than a French colony, subject to the laws, dictates, and whims of a foreign power. Can you envisage that, Jamie?"

"Quite easily."

"In those circumstances, what would someone like you do?"

"Resist the enemy in every possible way."

"Just like us! Welcome to America!"

"That's false logic," said Skoyles earnestly. "In the sense that you mean, America does not exist. It comprises thirteen fractious colonies that squabble with each other all the time. They have to be reminded who founded and who funded them. You're merely one part of the biggest empire in the world, and I'm proud that I can help to maintain it."

"I don't see you as King George's lackey somehow."

"I'm a true subject, Ezekiel."

"Subject to all the dictates of that grotesque tyrant?"

"Stop trying to win me over to your side."

"I think that the tide of events will do that."

"Have you never heard of loyalty?"

"Loyalties can change. Look at our generals—many of them learned their trade in the service of the British army."

"Including your own General Gates."

"He marches to a different drum now, one that beats out the pure, clear sound of American republicanism."

"It has a discordant note to my ear," said the other skeptically. "Our commanders are kindred spirits. They're both crafty politicians with an eye on self-advancement. General Burgoyne got where he is by talking down Sir Guy Carleton in London. In exactly the same way, General Gates gained his command by undermining his predecessor. That's not American republicanism, Ezekiel—it's naked ambition."

"Ambition is only a means to an end."

"Then it can be used to justify any atrocity."

"I dispute that. However," he went on, "I can see that this is not the ideal moment for a philosophical discussion, or even for a conversation between friends. It's time to choose sides. You know the one that I'm on." He offered his hand. "Goodbye, Jamie."

Skoyles shook his hand. "Where are you going?"

"To take a long, slow walk around the perimeter of the camp. That should give you plenty of time to decide what to do. When I've had my stroll, you see," he warned, "I'll feel obliged to report to General Gates that I've just seen a British spy in the camp." He hauled himself up. "I wish that we didn't have to part this way."

"Blame it on American republicanism."

"I'd rather blame in on your pigheadedness, Jamie."

Skoyles rose to his feet. "I always looked upon my pigheadedness as a shining virtue," he said with a smile. "Perhaps the only one I've got." He slapped the other man's arm. "Goodbye, Ezekiel—and thank you."

"You'll be back one day."

"Oh, I will. But I'll have the British army with me next time."

On September 13, 1777, led by Brigadier General Simon Fraser and his advance guard, the British troops set off with colors flapping in the wind and bands playing to cross the Hudson River. On the following day, the Germans followed them. There was no turning back now. With an army of little more than five thousand men, General Burgoyne moved slowly south until they reached the village of Saratoga, where he took over General Schuyler's sumptuous mansion as his headquarters. He ordered his men to reap the harvest in the fields that Schuyler's wife had found too wet to burn when she fled from the house. Then he made arrangements for dinner.

The army was unsettled. Many of the officers were aggrieved that their commander had not consulted them about the move from Fort Edward, and there was perturbation among the rank and file as well. News of St. Leger's defeat had reached everyone by now, and it caused general anxiety. They felt isolated. Elizabeth Rainham was more concerned about the absence of Jamie Skoyles. Since the only way that she could find out about him was to speak to Burgoyne, she accepted his invitation to dinner, even though she knew that Lucinda Mallard would be present.

There was another advantage to her appearance as one of the guests. Harry Featherstone would view it as a gesture of kindness to him, and he would be appeased. It might even still his suspicions about her. In order to learn the whereabouts of Skoyles, she was prepared to endure the major's company beside her, and the inevitable comments that would be made about their forthcoming marriage. Elizabeth arrived early at the house, hoping to catch the general on his own. Burgoyne was giving instructions to the musicians whom he wanted to play during the meal.

"Ah!" he said, breaking off when he saw Elizabeth. "Someone is hungry, I see."

"It's always a delight to come to your table, General."

"Then why have you spurned us so many times?"

"I've not been at my best recently," said Elizabeth, inventing an excuse. "I felt tired and slightly feverish."

"Oh dear! Nothing serious, I hope."

"No, General. It seems to have gone away now." Other guests could be heard arriving at the front door, so she blurted out her question. "I've not seen Captain Skoyles in camp for a day or two. Where is he?"

"I sent him on an assignment, Elizabeth."

"May I know what it is?"

"It's highly secret, I fear. I can't discuss it."

"How long do you expect him to be away?"

247

"I'm not sure," he confessed. "Why do you ask?"

"No reason. Idle curiosity, that's all."

"There's nothing idle about you, Elizabeth," he said shrewdly. "Curious, maybe—and an inquisitive nature is a good thing—but never idle. As for Skoyles, he's acting on my orders."

"Where?"

"That's privileged information," he said. Six other guests came into the room, Simon Fraser and William Phillips among them. The general beamed. "Well, now," he declared, "everyone is remarkably punctual today—except Major Featherstone, that is. Where have you hidden him, Elizabeth?"

"Harry will be here soon."

"Then why don't we all have a glass of punch while we await him?"

He signaled to the man beside the punch bowl, and the waiter began to fill the glasses and hand them to the guests. Elizabeth was the first to receive hers. When she saw Mrs. Mallard enter, she took a long sip of the liquid to brace herself against what lay ahead. Featherstone was the last to appear, and he had clearly been drinking beforehand. Though his gait was steady, his cheeks were reddened and his eyes faintly glassy. He went into an elaborate pantomime, kissing the hand of every woman there with excessive courtesy and making a flattering remark to each one. Featherstone even treated Lucinda Mallard as if she were the social equal of everyone else in the dining room. The last person he approached was Elizabeth, and he kissed each of her hands in turn.

General Burgoyne raised his glass of punch in a toast.

"To King and Country!" he declared.

Everyone took up the toast and sipped their drink.

"We move on to certain victory, ladies and gentlemen. I have followed my instincts and opted for boldness," he told them with a merry chuckle. "I have crossed the Rubicon."

"Hail, Caesar!" cried Featherstone, lifting his glass to Burgoyne.

"Hail, Caesar," echoed the others.

They took their seats at the table and the first course was served. Food was strictly rationed for the common soldiers, but Burgoyne saw no reason to stint himself or his guests. His cooks had prepared a delicious meal, and there was claret to accompany it. The quartet played music by Haydn. The atmosphere was relaxed. It was a most civilized way to pass the early afternoon.

Elizabeth joined in the general chatter as a way of escaping a more private conversation with Featherstone beside her. His air of elation worried her, and it could not be put down solely to drink. She feared that he had misinterpreted her decision to be there as a sign that all was now well between them. It was not until the main course was served that she understood why he was in such a mood of celebration. Featherstone leaned across to her and whispered in her ear.

"Have you heard the rumor about your friend?" he taunted her.

"What friend?"

"Captain Skoyles."

"No, I haven't," she said, trying to keep the concern out of her voice. "Why—what's happened to him?"

"Nobody knows," he said with an obvious satisfaction. "He was sent on a mission by General Burgoyne with orders to return as soon as possible. He was expected back today, but we've seen neither hide nor hair of him. If he doesn't show up tomorrow, only one conclusion can be reached, Elizabeth."

"What's that?" she asked, cheeks burning.

"Skoyles must be presumed dead—and good riddance to him!"

CHAPTER FOURTEEN

Jamie Skoyles had been given a chance to escape from the rebel camp. The pull of an old friendship had saved him from immediate exposure as a spy, but Ezekiel Proudfoot could help him no further. It was only a matter of time before the alarm was raised and a search instituted. Skoyles knew that he must not get caught. Having deceived General Gates himself, he could expect no mercy. The rebel commander would take a particular relish in having him strung from a tree. Skoyles intended to disappoint him and put one of the sturdy oaks to better use.

When his presence in the camp was reported to Gates, it would be assumed that he had fled after being identified by Ezekiel Proudfoot. Patrols would be sent out to apprehend him. Skoyles reasoned that the safest place to be was where he already was. Stuffing his new uniform into the knapsack that had been provided for him, he had therefore sidled off toward a cluster of maples, oak, and white pine. The moment he was out of sight, he chose the largest of the trees and, slinging his rifle over his shoulder, shinnied up it as quickly as he could. He selected a bough near the top that was strong enough to bear his weight and completely sheltered by leaves. Skoyles settled down to wait in his temporary refuge.

Twenty minutes later, he heard the commotion. Orders were barked, patrols were formed, and horses cantered out of camp. The irate General Gates was taking no chances. In the unlikely event that the spy was still in the camp, he had ordered a systematic search. A detachment of men combed the whole area, starting at the frontal defenses and working their way slowly back in a long line. When they had reached the tree where Skoyles was hiding, he could hear them far below, discussing the gruesome punishments they would like to inflict on a British spy. Skoyles was grateful that he had evaded them for the time being.

He made his move in the dead of night. Climbing down from the tree, he stretched his aching limbs, then stripped off his clothes and changed into the uniform that he had been given. The other garments were put into his knapsack. To the naked eye, he now looked like any other soldier in the Continental Army and felt confident enough to stroll among the tents without fear of being challenged. His nocturnal walk was more than exercise. Skoyles had been taking a closer look at the camp so that he could estimate its strength and later describe its layout and fortifications.

When he had committed all the details to memory, he made his way to the edge of the camp. Since the search for him would be concentrated to the north, to prevent him from rejoining his army, he had chosen to strike due south, in the direction of Albany. First, he had to get past the pickets. Skoyles fell back on the device he had used at Bitter Creek and created a diversion. Having borrowed a kettle from beside one of the campfires, he filled it with a handful of stones. When he crept up behind the pickets, he chose his moment, then flung it hard in the direction of some bushes. It rattled noisily on impact and drew three sentries out of position. By the time they discovered that they had been fooled, Skoyles was clear of the camp and running at full speed.

When dawn came, he was once more up a tree, sleeping in a maple to avoid capture and to escape the attention of any hungry animals that sniffed their way through the virgin forest. There had been no pursuit. Skoyles decided that the pickets would report the incident during the night as a case of desertion, and that, unbeknown to them, had the ring of truth. Corporal Daniel Lukins had indeed deserted from the Continental Army. After drinking water from a creek, he washed himself, then explored the main road that led to Albany. Rain had softened the mud and the imprint of many horses could be seen. Heavy reinforcements had obviously gone to the camp from the rebel stronghold.

Sound carried a long way through the forest, so he did not use his rifle in case the noise attracted attention. To get food, he resorted to a trick he had learned as a boy in Cumberland, sitting patiently beside a rabbit hole until—after an hour or so—a pair of ears emerged from it. They were instantly seized and the animal killed outright. When skinned and gutted, the rabbit was soon being roasted over a fire. While he waited for his meal, Skoyles was able to reflect on the meeting with Ezekiel Proudfoot, pleased that the bond between them had somehow been strengthened even though they were nominally in opposition. Their friendship, it seemed, went beyond narrow political allegiances.

Proudfoot had been right about one thing. Skoyles was fighting an enemy who would one day be his neighbor. Win or lose, when the war was over, he planned to buy land and remain in America. Would he prefer to do that as a member of a Republic of the United States or as a colonial whose fate was in the hands of a distant monarch? When he tried to answer the question, Skoyles found that his sympathies were divided. After twenty years in a red coat, he felt strangely comfortable in the uniform of the Continental Army.

Restored by the meal, he lingered close to the road in hopes of seeing a lone horseman whom he could waylay and deprive of his mount. To that end, he kept his blue uniform on as a convenient disguise. When horses had finally appeared that afternoon, however, they came in a sizable number and Skoyles had to hide in the trees as they trotted past. He could see at a glance that it was a rifle corps made up of wiry men in fringed hunting shirts and round hats. Skoyles counted upward of four hundred of them. What disturbed him was the sight of the tall, weather-beaten man who rode at their head. Though he had never seen him before, Skoyles knew that it could only be the legendary Daniel Morgan.

It was news that had to be conveyed urgently to General Burgoyne along with details of the enemy camp. By now, Skoyles realized, the British army must have crossed the Hudson to the western bank and pushed as far south as it dared without provoking a major engagement. To reach them, Skoyles elected to make a wide detour to the west. After changing back into his hunting shirt and breeches, he carried the uniform in his knapsack, traveling on foot after dark and hoping that his sense of direction would guide him. Skoyles was out of luck. Losing his way, he had stumbled on a rebel patrol and was pursued through the woods for most of the night. He had to climb another tree to escape.

Daylight taught him that he was only half a mile from the Hudson River and still south of the rebel camp. A more troubling discovery was that batches of militia seemed to be heading for the camp at regular intervals. Enemy numbers were growing. More to the point, scouting patrols were getting larger and more frequent. Skoyles had decided to take a more direct route back to his camp, even though it meant waiting for dark once more. He spent the intervening period searching for the means that would carry him past the pickets at Bemis Heights. A stone-filled kettle would not suffice a second time.

The log he chose was over five feet in length, stout enough to support him, yet light enough for him to drag to the river. He had fashioned a paddle out of a branch he had cut from a tree and shaped with his knife. As night started to wrap him in a blanket of darkness, he launched his craft with his rifle strapped to the log by a series of fronds. Skoyles sat astride it and paddled. The Hudson River was cold but strangely comforting. He felt safe.

That feeling disappeared when he got close to the camp. Eyes would be trained on the river and on the road. Skoyles tried to offset danger by keeping to the middle of the water and lying full length on the log. In the gloom, he merged with his crude boat and looked like another piece of driftwood in the river. Once clear of Bemis Heights, Skoyles sat up and brought the paddle back into action again. After a couple of miles, he steered himself across to the bank and disembarked. His legs were soaked and his arms aching, but he had escaped detection.

Reclaiming his rifle, he headed northward in the direction he believed would lead to the British camp. An hour later, he was picking his way through a wood when he sensed peril ahead. Before he could react to it, bodies suddenly emerged from the undergrowth and he was confronted by a group of armed men, who poked their bayonets threateningly at him.

"Drop that gun!" a voice demanded. "You're our prisoner now."

Skoyles laughed. "The devil I am, Private Wolverton!" he said as he recognized the actor's distinctive tones. "I'm a captain in your regiment so you can stop prodding me with that bayonet of yours, or I'll shove it so far up your backside that your eyes will pop out."

The council of war was held at midnight in the dining room of the house. Generals Burgoyne, Phillips, Fraser, and Riedesel stood around the table in the quivering light of a dozen candles and studied the sketch that Jamie Skoyles was drawing. He had given them a highly attenuated version of his stay in the rebel camp and said nothing at all about his encounter with Ezekiel Proudfoot. Skoyles regarded that as private information that would, in any event, only cloud the issue. What the commanders sought was knowledge of the camp and the likely deployment of its soldiers.

William Phillips took special note of all the fortifications.

"That confounded Pole is a brilliant engineer," he conceded. "Even with our heaviest cannon, it will be difficult to batter down some of those breastworks. They're positioned in the ideal places."

"We'll find a way to circumvent them," said Burgoyne, then he translated his comment into French for the benefit of Riedesel. "How many men do they have, Skoyles?"

"I can't give you an accurate figure, sir," replied Skoyles, "because reinforcements were coming in all the time. Among them was a rifle corps led by Daniel Morgan."

"Morgan!"

They were all startled by the news. Even Riedesel was acquainted with the reputation of Daniel Morgan and his riflemen, who, though listed as belonging to a Virginia regiment, were drawn from several states. From the expressions on their faces, Skoyles could see that the rebel army was suddenly treated with slightly more respect.

"They have a minimum of seven thousand men," he explained, "made up of Continentals and militia. Before we discount the latter as rank amateurs, I'd advise you to recall what happened at Bennington."

"Tell us about General Gates," Fraser suggested.

"He looked every inch a soldier, sir," said Skoyles, "and he's working hard to improve his army. The militia still lacks proper uniforms and equipment, and the Continentals are little better off. They have uniforms, but several have worn out their shoes by marching, and I saw a few with bare feet. Notwithstanding that, there was a sense of discipline about the Continental Army."

"Imposing discipline was the one thing that Horatio Gates *could* do," Burgoyne conceded. "But he's only been in charge for a few weeks, so he'll not have had time to lick his army into shape. That's in our favor."

"So is our superior artillery," Phillips remarked.

"And the fact that we are *British*." Burgoyne remembered that Riedesel was at his elbow. He forced a smile. "And German, of course."

"The days ahead are critical," said Fraser. "We have to keep our men under a tight rein, General."

"We will, have no worries on that score." He looked at Skoyles. "There was a most regrettable incident earlier today, Captain. The enemy has not exactly been strewing rose petals in our path. They prefer to destroy bridges ahead of us to cause further delay. A party of them got within a mile of us this morning."

"That wouldn't have happened when we had all the Indians with us," said Skoyles. "They frightened scouting parties away."

"I still view their disappearance as a boon. Anyway," Burgoyne continued, "some of our men so far forget their orders that they went ahead and foraged in a potato field. They were caught by the enemy."

"Instead of simply capturing them," said Fraser, taking up the story, "they shot or wounded nearly all of them. No quarter was given."

"Disgraceful!" Burgoyne exclaimed. "Fourteen men, whom we can ill afford to lose, were killed. And all because they disobeyed. Well, it won't occur again," he resolved. "I've issued a general order to remind the rank and file that the life of a soldier is the property of the king. From now on, anyone caught advancing beyond our sentinels will be hanged. I'll not have scavengers in my army."

"If it were left to me," said Phillips, "I'd tie the buggers to the end of a cannon and fire the bloody thing myself! They deserve to have their balls cut off and strung out on a washing line."

It was Skoyles who translated for Riedesel this time, softening the artilleryman's outburst into polite German. Burgoyne unrolled a rough map of the area and marked their present position with a cross.

"We must move forward tomorrow," he announced. "Skoyles?"

"I think that we might camp near this spot, General," said the other, indicating a point on the map. "I noticed it when I made for the rebel camp. It's called Sword's Farm. We'd have the river at our back."

"So be it," Burgoyne decided. "What better place to unsheathe the sword of justice than at Sword's Farm? Thank you, Captain. Your advice has been invaluable." He jabbed a finger at the map. "The decision is made—Sword's Farm it is."

Elizabeth Rainham was fretful. Unable to stay in her tent, she wandered restlessly among the camp followers early that morning with Nan Wyatt at her elbow. Elizabeth seemed impervious to the mist and deaf to the sounds of hectic activity from the main camp. The thought that Jamie Skoyles might have been killed had lit a fire of anxiety inside her head, and she could not douse the flames. What intensified her apprehension was the fact that she still had no idea where Skoyles had gone or what his orders had been. Adding to her pain was the memory of the look on Harry Featherstone's face when he told her that Skoyles must be presumed dead. The major had been almost triumphant. Any affection that Elizabeth still felt for him had been removed forever.

"Try to put it out of your mind, ma'am," Nan advised her softly.

"I wish that I could."

"Worrying about the captain will not bring him back. We should return to our tent. It sounds to me as if we'll soon be on the move."

"On the move?" Elizabeth was confused. "Where are we going?

"I daresay that we'll soon be told."

"Perhaps I should try to speak to General Burgoyne again."

"No, ma'am," said Nan. "If the troops are pushing forward, he'll be far too busy to speak to you."

"But I *must* know what happened to Captain Skoyles."

"It will become clear in time."

"You think he's dead, don't you?" said Elizabeth, rounding on her. "You agree with Major Featherstone. He won't be coming back."

"All I know is that Captain Skoyles is missing," the other said soothingly, taking her arm. "He's been into enemy territory on his own before now and he's always survived. Have more faith in him, ma'am. He'd hate you to suffer in this way on his behalf. Be hopeful."

"How, Nan? I've given up all hope."

"Well, I haven't—and I have enough for both of us."

"If I lose Captain Skoyles," Elizabeth murmured to herself as she confronted the prospect, "then I lose everything."

Confirmation soon reached them that the army was pulling out. There was a flurry of activity all around them and a heady buzz of speculation about where they were going. Drums could be heard beating in the main camp. Elizabeth agreed reluctantly to go back to her tent, resigned to the fact that some terrible fate had befallen Skoyles. At the very moment when they had been drawn closely together, he had been snatched away. She was so convinced he had been taken from her that she did not at first believe Polly Bragg when the woman came rushing up to them through the crowd.

"Captain Skoyles is back, ma'am," said Polly breathlessly.

"Back?" asked Elizabeth. "Are you sure?"

"Quite sure."

"Is he alive?"

"Very much alive, according to Tom."

"There!" said Nan. "I told you that he'd not let you down, ma'am."

"Captain Skoyles is *here?*" said Elizabeth, slowly taking it in.

"Yes, ma'am," said Polly. "He wanted you to know that he's safe."

"Thank you, Mrs. Bragg. That's wonderful news."

Elizabeth let out a cry of joy, then collapsed into Nan's arms.

It was a bad day for a battle. After camping near Sword's Farm, the British army awoke on Friday, September 19, to be greeted by cold, rain, and low-lying fog so dense that it made any kind of reconnaissance quite impossible. General Burgoyne had to wait for hours until the sun began to disperse the fog. He was then able to dispatch his forces. The order of march consisted of three divisions. Captain Jamie Skoyles was part of the elite right wing that set off under the command of Brigadier Fraser. General Riedesel led the left wing along the river road, accompanied by Major General Philips. Burgoyne remained with the column that moved forward in the center.

Most of the field in front of them was heavily wooded but, on the right, there was an open area around a clutch of cabins known as Freeman's Farm. This was the target for Fraser and the right wing, a force that comprised grenadier and light infantry battalions, and the 24th Foot, with two German regiments under Colonel Breymann in support. The remaining Indians, Canadians, and loyalists were in front or on the flanks. The mood was positive. In spite of all their setbacks, the troops were inspired by the leadership of Burgoyne, whose popularity was as high as ever. There was no fear of a repetition of Bennington. A famous British commander was now in charge.

The terrain slowed them down and soon split up the columns in a way that made communication between them well nigh impossible. First to reach the Great Ravine, the right wing was forced to travel farther west to find a place where it could cross the stream. Skoyles estimated that they were now almost two miles from the center column. They followed a circuitous route along high ground so that they could cover the march of the main army, and drive in any enemy troops they encountered.

In a battle that began almost by accident, it was the main army that met the first resistance. Unknown to them, Daniel Morgan's riflemen had taken up their positions behind a rail fence, in a log cabin, and behind trees or high in their branches. When the skirmish line appeared, the backcountry marksmen fired with such devastating effect that the redcoats fell in droves. Roused by this initial success, Morgan's men pursued the fleeing soldiers hard without realizing that they were actually heading toward the main British force. When they came under concerted attack themselves, the riflemen scattered at once. Fearing that his beloved corps would be destroyed, Daniel Morgan ordered them to withdraw to the woods by using his high-pitched turkey call.

Burgoyne, meanwhile, moved his men on to Freeman's Farm, and battle really commenced. Fresh American units came up in support of the riflemen, pinning the British down. The contrast between the two armies was stark. While the redcoats stayed in traditional shoulder to shoulder formation and fired ear-splitting volleys time and again, the rebels preferred to fight from cover, retreating when charged, then pushing forward once again when they regained the initiative. Burgoyne was outraged that they aimed specifically at his officers, sending man after man with braid epaulets crashing to the ground. To a commander who had been reared on European rules of engagement, it was an abomination.

Burgoyne himself was everywhere, scorning danger as he rode up and down the lines of his infantry to exhort his men to greater efforts. Wherever the fighting was fiercest, he charged off to rally his troops, brandishing his sword. His voice was lost in the cacophony of musket fire, cannon fire, and the agonized cries of dying men. Wounded horses added to the uproar and confusion, threshing about on the ground or staggering a few paces before collapsing once again. So furious and unrelenting was the battle that it was difficult to determine with whom the advantage lay. Freeman's Farm was a scene of utter chaos.

General Gates took no direct part in it all, preferring to direct operations from his tent at Bemis Heights and keep the bulk of his men in reserve behind the fortifications. It was General Benedict Arnold who led the army on the battlefield and who acted as their talisman. Now in his midthirties, Arnold was a dark-haired, dark-skinned man of medium height with a restless energy and an iron determination. He looked upon Horatio Gates as an untried commander, a military theorist who had never smelled gunpowder before, and whose decisions were therefore questionable. When Gates heard of the enemy's approach, and refused to sanction an attack, it was Arnold who dispatched Daniel Morgan and his rifle corps with Brigadier Enoch Poor's men in support.

Ezekiel Proudfoot went with them, carrying his satchel but having no weapon apart from a walking stick he had cut himself. When the fighting started, he broke away from the rebel soldiers to climb a tree that would give him at least a partial view of the engagement. As at the battle of Bennington, so much was happening simultaneously that he did not know where to look or what to sketch first. The first soldier who was portrayed on his paper, however, was Benedict Arnold, leading his men from the front and showing a fearlessness that verged on lunacy. A veteran of many battles, Arnold was as ubiquitous as Burgoyne, spurring his horse to places where the battle was at its most ferocious and using his sword to slash at any of the enemy within reach.

Thousands of men were embroiled in a death grapple across a wide panorama. From high in the tree, Proudfoot could only pick out a very few individuals, but he was bound to wonder whether Jamie Skoyles was somewhere near Freeman's Farm. He was certain that his friend had escaped the rebel camp and had no feelings of guilt about helping him. Now, however, they were on opposite sides again. Proudfoot hoped that, when he came to sketch the carnage in the aftermath of battle, he would not find Skoyles among the countless dead who would litter the field. A cannon boomed in the distance, and the whole tree shook violently as it was hit. Proudfoot clung on tight. He was not going to be robbed of his privileged view of history.

Ordered to hold the ridge on the right, Simon Fraser's men saw little action but witnessed a great deal of it and were eager to be involved. Their chance eventually came when reinforcements streamed up from Bemis Heights on the left flank of the rebel combatants. Fraser sent a detachment under Major Harry Featherstone to head them off. When they intercepted the enemy and were put under pressure, Captain Jamie Skoyles was ordered to lead a second detachment of the 24th Foot. He responded with characteristic zeal, issuing his commands as he took his men down from the ridge.

Featherstone's detachment was grateful for the support, though the major wished that anyone but Skoyles had brought it. Recrimination was momentary. Both men were too immersed in the battle to think about their personal animosity. Making sure that they were clearly visible to the troops, they kept on the move on their horses, using their swords to convey signals and interrupting the volley firing with an occasional bayonet charge. Though they lost several men, the others maintained their discipline, stepping over the fallen as they pushed the rebels back.

Freeman's Farm was the major cauldron of the battle, sizzling away for hour upon hour until muscles became tired, ammunition began to run out, and the sheer scale of the casualties on his side began to alarm even Burgoyne. While his numbers were finite, the Americans were able to feed more and more men as required. One British regiment, the 62nd Foot, had lost over three-quarters of its men. Burgoyne sent an urgent summons to General Riedesel on the left flank. It was time to bring the Germans into play.

Hindered by having to rebuild bridges along the way, the Germans had been last to reach the line of battle and were unsure of what to do. When attacked, they had resisted stoutly, and Phillips had introduced his artillery, powerful weapons against an army that used no cannon at all. On receipt of the summons from Burgoyne, Riedesel swung right toward Freeman's Farm with five hundred men and some artillery pieces, arriving in time to find the British main army severely pressed. The Germans dressed ranks and joined in the battle, supported by cannon fire that raked the enemy flank with grapeshot.

It was a crucial intervention. Supported on both flanks, Burgoyne was able to hold out until fading light and complete exhaustion ended the hostilities for the day. It was a stalemate. The rebels withdrew to Bemis Heights, and the smoke of battle finally cleared. When a rough count was taken, it was found that the British and Germans had lost, in all, almost six hundred men, twice as many as the Americans. But since they held the field, Gentleman Johnny was determined to claim a famous victory. Lifting his sword into the darkening sky, his voice rang out like a clarion call.

"We've beaten them!" he cried joyously. "The day is ours!"

Night was filled with noise. The cannon might be silent, but their roar had been replaced by the howling of wolves and the groans of the wounded, who still lay on the battlefield. Sergeant Tom Caffrey was one of the many surgeons who went out to scour the area with stretcher bearers, looking for men they could save and those they had to bury. Of those who were still alive, the majority would be dead by morning from their wounds, but they were nevertheless carried back to the field hospital that had been set up. It was disheartening work.

"I thought that the day was ours," Caffrey observed cynically. "If that's the case, why do we have so many more dead bodies than the enemy?"

"A good question," said Skoyles.

"I've lost count of the number of officers who've been killed."

"That was deliberate, Tom. Anybody wearing epaulets became a prime target." He fingered his sleeve. "I've got a few more holes in my uniform as a result."

"You should have stayed in the ranks, Jamie."

"The Americans took their toll of those as well."

Skoyles had joined the search because he wanted to find some of his own men who had been shot in the woodland where they had fought. Like others who accompanied the medical teams, he carried a musket, conscious that rebels would be hunting their own casualties as well and taking the opportunity to relieve fallen redcoats of their weapons at the same time. Occasional shots were exchanged in the dark. The battle was still not over.

Caffrey examined another wounded man, gave him a few cheery words of comfort as he bandaged his wound, then helped him onto a stretcher to be borne away. He looked wistfully after him.

"Lieutenant Osborne will be dead within an hour," he said.

"Was there nothing you could do, Tom?"

"You saw his arm. It was virtually shot away. He's lost so much blood that the wonder of it is that he's still alive now. What gives a man the willpower to hold on like that?"

"I don't know," said Skoyles, "but I admire his courage."

"If only that were enough!"

They were in woodland now, moving warily among the trees in search of survivors from the 24th Foot. One corpse they found was eerily lifelike, seated on a log with his back against the trunk of an oak, looking for all the world as if he was simply resting. Caffrey identified six different bullet wounds in his chest. A second man was discovered with a yawning gap where his nose had been, a third with his intestines spilled out in front of him. A private, found alive, was examined by Caffrey and dispatched to the hospital. Skoyles was attracted by faint moans deeper in the wood.

"I think I know that voice," he said, quickening his steps. "It sounds like Charlie Westbourne."

"Then let's find him."

"Once we engaged the enemy, I lost sight of him."

They followed the pitiful lament and eventually tracked him down. Lieutenant Westbourne had been sensible. Shot in the thigh and unable to walk, he had dragged himself into the shelter of a bush and stemmed the bleeding by taking off his jacket so that he could use his shirt as a bandage. His sword had been employed to make a tourniquet, twisting the bandage tight around his limb. Westbourne was thrilled to see familiar faces conjured out of the gloom.

"Thank you, thank you," he said, effusively. "I prayed that somebody would come."

"You've done my work for me, sir," noted Caffrey, inspecting the wound. "All we need to do is to get you back and I'll take that bullet out of your leg. I wish that everyone had your instinct for survival."

"I was shot in the first charge. I felt as if I'd been amputated."

"With luck, we can save the leg."

"And a fine officer with it," added Skoyles.

"What was the outcome, Captain?" asked Westbourne. "All that I could do was to lie here and listen to the battle. It seemed to go on forever." He smiled hopefully. "Did we win?"

"According to General Burgoyne, we did."

"What's your assessment?"

"At best, an honorable draw," said Skoyles, "with this worrying addendum. We committed our whole army. General Gates kept a large part of his men back, yet the troops who fought still held their ground. That will encourage them."

"And they'll have other militias coming in all the time," said Caffrey. "As our numbers dwindle, theirs will swell. This is not what I'd describe as a resounding victory."

"But we held the field?" said Westbourne.

"Yes, Lieutenant—and all the corpses that cover it. Let's get you a stretcher," he went on. "I'm afraid you'll face something of an ordeal when we get back to the hospital."

"The bullet must come out, Sergeant. I can bear the pain."

"I'm not talking about your wound, sir. You're going to undergo an experience you've never had before, so brace yourself now."

"Why?"

"When I've finished with you," teased Caffrey, "I'm going to pass you on to one of the nurses. You'll be in the tender hands of a woman at last, Lieutenant. Can you endure *that* pain?"

After a long time apart from his brother, Ezekiel Proudfoot was overjoyed to see him again. Reuben had joined the rebel camp with one of the Massachusetts regiments in the Continental Army. Though the soldier was bigger and more powerful and had a darker complexion than Ezekiel, there was a strong family likeness between them. In the wake of the battle of Freeman's Farm, they found a moment to catch up on each other's news. Reuben was interested to see his brother's sketches of the battle and frustrated that he had not been directly involved in it.

"General Gates should have given us the chance to take them on," he said, handing the sketches back to Proudfoot. "By all accounts, we had the British on the defensive."

"No doubt about that, Reuben."

"Had we sent in more men, we could've destroyed them."

"That was Benedict Arnold's claim," said Proudfoot, "but I'm afraid that General Gates disagreed with him. In fact, he's accusing Arnold of insubordination because he dispatched troops without permission."

"The British army was coming at us. That's permission enough."

"You and Arnold are obviously of the same mind."

"We are," said the other. "I regard Arnold as a real hero. He should have been given command of the Northern Department. Time and again, he's proved himself in battle. When did General Gates ever take part in a serious engagement?"

"This morning, Reuben."

"What do you mean?"

"He had a violent quarrel with General Arnold, who is not a man to mind his language. Some of the insults they fired at each other could be clearly heard by all of us close to the tent. General Gates may not have earned a reputation on the battlefield," said Proudfoot, "but he'll not shirk a fight with his staff officers. He was bristling with anger."

"What did he say?"

"That he was taking Daniel Morgan's men under his own direct command, and that he might have no further use for Arnold."

Reuben was flabbergasted. "No further use for him?" he cried. "He's the best soldier we have. It's madness to get rid of him. Everyone who fought in the battle says that Arnold was a magnificent leader."

"He was." Proudfoot held up his sketch of Benedict Arnold. "That's why I tried to capture him on paper."

"Yes, it's a good likeness," said Reuben admiringly. "You've caught him in action, which is where he wants to be."

"Arnold will fight all day for our cause. He makes me proud to be an American. With a leader like that, we've someone to rival Burgoyne."

"Envy is at work here, Ezekiel. I think that Gates wants to rob a better man of his share of the glory."

"Too true. From what I hear, Arnold is barely mentioned in the account of the battle that Gates sent to Congress. It's almost as if he never took part in the engagement."

"That's plain dishonest."

"Everyone who was there knows that."

"Battles are won by generals who lead their men in the field, not by those who hide in their tents like Gates." Reuben bunched his fists. "We have the numbers. We have the advantage. Why doesn't our commander let Arnold take us out there to finish them off?"

"Because we're desperately short of ammunition."

"I'd fight with my bare hands, if need be."

"Not against those bayonets, Reuben. Even you wouldn't be that rash. No," said Proudfoot, "what happened at Freeman's Farm depleted our supply of ammunition badly. The quartermaster has sent an urgent message to General Schuyler in Albany, telling him of our plight."

"Schuyler!" snorted the other. "What use is he?"

"We need someone to help us out."

Reuben Proudfoot was impatient. Having joined the army in search of action, he hated to be deprived of it by what he saw as the perverse decisions of his commander. With the burly physique of a farmer, and the skill of a true marksman, he was a good soldier, spurred on by high ideals to do what he could to drive the British out of America. Uncertain motives had brought many young men into the army. Reuben was not one of them. He was a republican with a missionary ardor.

"Do you remember Jamie?" his brother asked.

"Who?"

"Jamie Skoyles. He stayed with us at the farm all those years ago."

"Yes, I remember him," said Reuben. "The last I heard, he was a sergeant in one of the British regiments."

"It's Captain Jamie Skoyles of the 24th Foot now."

"You mean, that he's *here,* fighting against us?"

"Yes, Reuben. When I was taken prisoner, he did me a favor."

"I hope he expects none from me in exchange."

"No, that debt has already been settled."

"I liked Jamie when he was with us, and I know that he became a close friend of yours, but that makes no difference to me," warned Reuben. "If he's a redcoat, he's an enemy that has to be destroyed. I'm sorry, Ezekiel. Don't expect me to show him any mercy."

"It's very unlikely that you'll meet on the battlefield."

"I hope that we do. All that I'll see is another target for my rifle. A captain, is he?" he said with a grim smile. "Then I'll take even greater pleasure in killing Jamie Skoyles."

The field hospital consisted of a row of tents and a deserted barn that had been taken over by the British surgeons. So many soldiers had been wounded in battle that there was not room under cover for all of them. Some were left out in the open, propped against trees or sleeping on a blanket on the ground. Jamie Skoyles made the rounds of his own men, pleased that there were relatively few of them since the 24th Foot was not heavily involved in the battle. With the bullet removed from his thigh, Lieutenant Charles Westbourne was among those who would recover. Days after the engagement, he lay on a bed of straw in a corner of the barn.

"How are you feeling now, Lieutenant?" asked Skoyles.

"Rather fraudulent, if truth be told."

"Fraudulent?"

"Yes," said Westbourne, looking around. "Compared to most people here, I got off lightly. Sergeant Caffrey had to carry out several amputations to keep people alive, and some have got wounds that will take months to heal. Last night," he added with a shiver, "the burial detail never stopped. Among others, they took away the man lying beside me. He'd been shot in the throat and died in great pain."

"Like so many others," Skoyles observed sadly. "Instant death is not a blessing that everyone enjoys on a battlefield. Still," he went on, trying to sound more positive, "I rejoice in your good fortune. Tom Caffrey tells me that you'll make a full recovery in time."

"I want to be ready for the next battle, Captain."

"There's no hope of that."

"Why? Is General Burgoyne intending to strike again soon?"

"Left to him, we'd have attacked on the day after the battle," said Skoyles, "but, luckily, his senior officers objected to such reckless action, and the news from General Clinton resolved the issue."

"What news is that?"

"Good tidings at last, Lieutenant. Reinforcements have finally arrived in New York City, enabling Clinton to lead a foray up the Hudson in our favor."

"Then we are saved!"

"Not necessarily," said Skoyles, introducing a note of caution. "They have a long way to come and will need to reduce some forts on the way, but the threat of an attack from Clinton will scare the enemy. That will definitely help us. The word from New York City also helps to take away the unpleasant taste of other news that's just come in."

"Oh?"

"It seems that the American militia attacked the portage between Lake Champlain and Lake George. Under the command of General Lincoln, they captured the men we left there, released the rebel prisoners being held, and burned all our sloops and bateaux."

Westbourne was shocked. "All our vessels?" he gasped.

"Our supply line to Canada went up in flames."

"Pray God that Sir Henry Clinton comes soon!"

"There's no way back for us." Skoyles saw that Polly Bragg was approaching them. "Ah, here's your nurse. I'll bid you farewell."

"No, no," said Westbourne, "don't leave me alone with her."

"She's only coming to change the dressing on your leg. I think it's high time that you overcame your fear of women, don't you? They've done splendid work for us here, in the worst possible conditions."

Skoyles greeted Polly Bragg and handed the patient over to her. Westbourne tried to detain him so that he would not be alone with a woman, but Skoyles was more interested in speaking to another of the nurses. Elizabeth Rainham was outside the barn, holding a canteen of water to the lips of a wounded man with bandaging around his eyes. She looked tired and harried. Her hair was tousled. Skoyles waved to her and she came across to him, taking care not to tread on any of the supine bodies on the ground. Skoyles noticed that the edge of her skirt was besmirched with mud. When she got close to him, he could see the perspiration on her brow.

"You should take a rest," he advised her.

"I'm needed here, Captain."

"You've been on duty for hours."

"I'll do anything I can to help," she said, "and so will Nan. It would be cruel and selfish of us to remain in our tent while there's so much suffering that could be allayed here. We've seen what Mrs. Bragg and the other women have been able to do for the casualties. Nan and I were anxious to lend them our support."

"It's much appreciated, Miss Rainham."

Talking to her in public imposed a formality on Skoyles that felt artificial now that they had become so close. He drew her aside into the shade of a tree so that they had a small measure of privacy. She gave him a weary smile of thanks.

"I'll wager that you never expected to be doing anything like this when you set sail from England," he said, desperate to touch her but afraid to do so. "I hope that it's not too much of a shock for you."

"I was terrified at first," she admitted. "I was given the impression that I'd spend the whole campaign involved in nothing more than pleasant social occasions." She displayed her reddened palms. "Instead of which, I end up with blood on my hands."

"Has it frightened you away from army life?"

"Not if I can be near you, Jamie."

"Thank you," he said, hearing the deep affection in her voice. "It would almost be worth getting wounded so that you could tend me."

"No, no!" she pleaded. "Don't say that."

"It was a joke, Elizabeth."

"The very thought of it upsets me," she said. "It's only by the grace of God that you were not killed or wounded at Bennington or in the battle here. Look at these poor men," she went on, glancing at the field hospital. "Some of them have hideous injuries. The man I was giving water to just now was blinded in the battle. Others have lost arms, legs, or part of their faces. Their lives will never be the same again."

"I know," he said with a sigh. "But, at least, they survived. In the week since the battle at Freeman's Farm, dozens of our casualties have died. They're soldiers who can never be replaced."

"Until the reinforcements arrive under General Clinton."

"It would be unwise to rely on them. The enemy will be aware of their movement up the Hudson Valley, and they'll not allow us to wait until help comes from New York. Instead of aiding us," he told her, "the news of Clinton's approach may provoke an attack from the rebels."

"More deaths, more wounds, more unspeakable horrors."

"The issue can only be settled on a battlefield, Elizabeth."

"Then give me your promise," she said, clutching his hand. "If and when you do take up arms again, promise me that we'll meet—however briefly—before you leave camp."

"I promise."

"Thank you, Jamie. I couldn't bear it if you went off to battle and got yourself—"

"Nobody is going to kill me, Elizabeth," he said, interrupting her. "I have too much to live for now."

"So do I," she said. A wounded man groaned in agony nearby. "I'll have to go now. Somebody needs me. Remember your promise."

Skoyles was unequivocal. "I shall."

While she went off to tend the wounded soldier, he picked his way in the opposite direction, stepping around dozens of bodies. Skoyles did not get very far. One of the other volunteer nurses was kneeling beside a man whose hand had been shot away. As Skoyles approached, Maria Quinn stood up to confront him. Her face was lined by fatigue and her apron stained with blood. There was a hurt look in her eyes. His guilt stirred at once. Skoyles had neglected her badly.

"I haven't seen you for over a week, Jamie," she complained.

"I know. I'm sorry about that, Maria."

"What happened?"

"I've been far too busy."

"Too busy to think of me?"

"Not at all," he said defensively, looking over his shoulder to make sure that Elizabeth was not watching them. "I thought about you a lot, but that's all I could do."

"Why?"

"We fought a hard battle, Maria—as you can see—and there'll be another one to fight very soon. I have to remain alert at all times."

"Is that what you told *her?*"

"Who?"

"The woman you were talking to a moment ago," she said, letting her jealousy show. "Did you tell her that you were on duty all the time?"

"I was simply asking after one of my men," he lied.

"That's not what it looked like to me."

"I just wanted to know how Lieutenant Westbourne was doing."

"Who is she, Jamie?"

"One of the nurses."

"I'm one of the nurses as well, but you didn't come looking for me, did you? What's going on, Captain Skoyles?" she demanded "Why haven't you been near me for a week?"

"I told you, Maria. I haven't had a free moment."

"You found a moment to talk to that woman."

"Forget her."

"Did those times we spent together mean *nothing?*"

"Of course," he said, trying to appease her. "They meant a lot."

"Then why have you been avoiding me?"

"I haven't."

"Let me come to you tonight," she whispered.

"No, that's not possible."

"But there may be another battle tomorrow. I must see you."

Skoyles was squirming with embarrassment, yet, at the same time, he could see what had attracted him to Maria Quinn. Hands on hips and flushed with anger, she was more appealing than ever. Skoyles was very tempted. Though he had just made an assignation with Elizabeth, he could not stop himself from giving another commitment.

"We'll meet again soon, Maria," he said.

"When?"

"In due course."

"*When?*" she repeated.

"Before the next battle."

"Do I have your word on that?" He hesitated. "Well, do I?"

"Yes."

Skoyles forced a smile, then walked quickly away, realizing that he had given the same promise to two women and knowing that he would have to hurt one of them very much. Maria Quinn had made great sacrifices in order to be with him on the campaign, and she deserved more than mere gratitude. The times they had spent together had been highly enjoyable. In seeing her before the battle, however, he would be betraying Elizabeth Rainham, and the very notion of that brought on an attack of prickly heat. Maria Quinn belonged in one part of his life and Elizabeth in another. Both wanted his attention, but it could not be shared. No compromise was possible.

The encounter with Maria had one salutary result. It forced him to examine his friendship with Elizabeth Rainham more carefully. Skoyles tried to be as objective as possible. Did he want her for herself, or was she simply a means to settle a score with Harry Featherstone? He would certainly take pleasure from enticing the major's lady away from him. That was undeniable. Featherstone was unworthy of her. He was a gambler, a heavy drinker, and an inveterate rake who had pursued other women while Elizabeth was still at home.

Yet those same charges could be leveled at Skoyles as well. Nobody relished a game of cards or a drinking bout as much as he did, and he had slept with Maria Quinn long after he first took an interest in Elizabeth. Skoyles was no saint. He had as many faults as the next man. Like most soldiers, he took his pleasures where he found them and moved on without a backward glance. Maria Quinn was only one of many women he had encountered over the years. While they were together, he had cared for them, but he had always cast them aside in the end and done so without remorse.

Guilt was a new sensation for Skoyles, and he was finding it a very disturbing one. He felt guilty about his deliberate avoidance of Maria and about the fact that she could still arouse his lust. Could he really love Elizabeth Rainham while he had such strong feelings for another woman? And did Maria Quinn mean so little to him that he could discard her so easily? Skoyles was deeply confused about what he really wanted and from whom he wanted it. His mind was in turmoil. When he got back to his tent, he was still not sure which of the two women he would visit on the eve of the next battle.

General Horatio Gates had a streak of vanity in his nature. Conscious of the fact that Benedict Arnold had featured in some of the sketches made by Ezekiel Proudfoot, he wanted to make sure that he, too, might one day appear in an engraving. As a consequence, Proudfoot was invited to his commander's tent to add a portrait of him to his collection. Gray-haired, ruddy-cheeked, and with his glasses perched on the end of his nose, the general looked as if he deserved his nickname of Granny Gates.

Seated at a table with his paper in front of him, Proudfoot got to work. He had drawn the merest outline of his subject when they were interrupted. Benedict Arnold came, unannounced, into the tent.

"How much longer are we going to wait?" the newcomer demanded. "We have an army of eleven thousand men out there, General, while the British have less than half that number. Why the delay?"

"I'm waiting until the time is ripe," said Gates irritably.

"And when will that be, I pray—when Sir Henry Clinton has fought his way here? Do you *want* the enemy to have reinforcements?"

"Of course not."

"Then why dither?"

"I am not dithering, General Arnold."

"No," said the other, scornfully, "you're standing here so that you can

271

have your portrait drawn. That's hardly the way to prepare for a battle ahead—unless you think that an image of General Gates in his tent will frighten away the British army."

"Sarcasm does not become you, General."

"Inactivity does not become an army. They are keen to *fight,* man."

"And they will, in due course."

"When will that be?"

"When I decide."

"Make that decision *now,*" Arnold urged. "We need a victory to restore confidence. General Howe defeated Washington at Brandywine over a fortnight ago, so the British have their tails up. Burgoyne will have heard that news by now and it will bolster him."

"We've had our successes as well—Bennington, for instance."

"Yes," retorted the other, "and what happened to those heroes from Stark's militia? They arrive here in camp, then, after a few days, they say that their term of service is up and ride out of here."

"I'd no power to keep them."

"You did, General. Had you attacked the enemy while we had Stark's men at our disposal, they would have helped us to send the British running for their lives."

"I was not ready to sanction an attack at that time."

"You are *never* ready, General. You dither like an old woman."

"I resent that remark."

"Strike while the iron is hot."

"The only thing that's hot at this moment is that mischievous tongue of yours. Curb it, sir."

"Because of your hesitation, we lost John Stark and his men."

"Only for a time," said Gates, enjoying the opportunity to surprise Arnold. "I received intelligence yesterday that Stark has captured Fort Edward and is on his way south with a thousand men."

"Were he to bring ten thousand, you'd still not lead them into battle."

Proudfoot was fascinated to see Benedict Arnold at close quarters. There was a suppressed power in his compact frame and a sparkle in his eye that set him apart from Gates. Arnold walked with a limp as a result of a wound he had received during the invasion of Canada. Proudfoot was in the presence of an undoubted military hero, and he was mystified that Gates accorded the man such scant respect.

"All that you know about is fighting," said Gates with disdain. "If you understood British politics a little more, you'd realize that our position may not be under threat at all."

"It will be if Sir Henry Clinton gets here."

"Clinton is in no hurry. He and Burgoyne are rivals. They've never been on friendly terms. Why should Clinton strain himself to help a man who has ambitions to succeed Howe as commander in chief?" He peered over his glasses. "Clinton wants that position for himself. He'll not be thwarted by Burgoyne."

"Then why is he coming up the Hudson Valley?"

"To make a gesture. Time is on our side, General."

"Not if we dawdle much longer," Arnold argued. "Do you wish to be squeezed between two British armies?"

"That will not happen, I assure you. Gentleman Johnny's army has been badly mauled, and I've sent out patrols every day to harass his pickets. Burgoyne is an inveterate gambler," he declared. "Despair may dictate that he risk all on one throw. He has far too much pride to retreat, and he can't afford to wait for Clinton. He will come to us."

"At a time of his choosing. Why let him take the initiative?"

"Because he'll play into our hands."

"One of the oldest rules of warfare is that attack is the best means of defense. We should follow that advice."

"No, General," said Gates, trying to impose his authority, "that would be rash in this instance. Besides, it's no concern of yours. You will take no part in any future battle."

"According to your reports," said Arnold bitterly, "I took no part in the engagement at Freeman's Farm. Congress will hear nothing of my feats that day. Benedict Arnold was invisible. It's only because of our artist here," he added, indicating Proudfoot, "that people will know the truth. I was *there*."

"You were, indeed, General," said Proudfoot.

"Your engravings are famed for their accuracy, Ezekiel, and I thank you for that. You are certainly drawing General Gates in his favored setting," he said with vehemence. "You will only ever catch me in the saddle, whereas he is always lurking behind the lines in his tent."

"Good day to you, sir!" Gates yelled.

But his visitor had already left in disgust. There was a long, embarrassed pause. Proudfoot did not know whether to leave or to continue with his drawing. Gates looked over at him.

"You say that you have a brother in the Continental Army?"

"Yes, sir. Reuben is with a Massachusetts regiment."

"Rank?"

"Sergeant."

"What's the feeling among his men?"

"They're getting impatient, General," said Proudfoot. "It's two weeks since the battle at Freeman's Farm, where they were kept in reserve. They lust for action. You've eager soldiers out there, sir."

"Too eager, in most cases."

"Yes, sir."

Gates turned away to ponder. Several minutes passed. He was so engrossed in thought that Proudfoot wondered whether the general had forgotten that he was there. At length, Gates resumed his earlier pose.

"Carry on," he said calmly. "I'm ready for you now. That pompous little fellow, Benedict Arnold, won't disturb us again."

The decision produced mixed reactions. When he first heard of it, Jamie Skoyles was in Brigadier Fraser's tent. The other man summoned to hear the news, in strictest confidence, was Major Harry Featherstone.

"We move out tomorrow," Fraser announced. "General Burgoyne will take fifteen hundred picked men and ten cannon to reconnoiter the enemy position. We've been chosen to accompany him."

"It's about time," asserted Featherstone.

"You approve of the plan?"

"Completely, sir."

"Jamie?"

"I have reservations, sir," Skoyles admitted. "What begins as a reconnaissance mission could very easily turn into a pitched battle, and we lack the numbers for that."

"It sounds to me as if you lack the spirit for it," said Featherstone.

"Not at all, sir. I'll obey my orders to the letter."

"So will I," said Fraser, "but I do so with misgivings. We're in no state for another major engagement. We lost too many men at Freeman's Farm, and desertions have mounted ever since."

"But we *won* that battle, sir," Featherstone reminded him.

"We gained more honor than victory, Harry."

"The rebels were driven from the field."

"They simply fell back to their fortifications to avoid unnecessary loss of life," said Skoyles. "Our men are jaded, Major. Autumn is here and they have nothing but summer clothing to keep out the nighttime chill. Rations have been cut to a third. This is hardly the way to prepare an army for battle."

"Would you simply let them wither on the vine?"

"No, sir. I'd consider an early withdrawal."

"Withdrawal?" said Featherstone with disgust. "That's sheer cowardice, Captain."

"It's common sense," said Fraser, "and it's what I advocated myself. Among others, I was backed by General Riedesel."

"The Germans are always the first to retreat."

"That's unjust, Harry."

"And ungrateful of you," Skoyles added. "The Germans saved us at Hubbardton and again at Freeman's Farm. They deserve more than a sneer from you, Major."

"The Brunswickers and the Hessians share the same faults," said Featherstone. "They're too slow, too methodical, and, as a rule, too late."

"Would you rather fight without them?"

"If they could be replaced by British soldiers."

"That's a luxury none of our commanders can hope for, Harry," said Fraser. "With an insufficient army, we are forced to hire foreign mercenaries. I'm happy to have them with us."

"So am I, sir," said Skoyles.

"Well, I'm not," said Featherstone. "I mean, they don't even have the decency to learn our language."

Skoyles smiled. "Have you had the decency to learn *theirs,* sir?"

"Of course not! It's a barbarous tongue."

"This is no time to quarrel about that, Harry," said Fraser briskly. "Now that I've acquainted you with the general's orders, keep them to yourselves. We must not alarm the men. As Jamie pointed out, there's always the danger that tomorrow's venture may lead to a battle."

"I hope and pray that it does!" Featherstone exclaimed.

"Then you must also hope and pray that you come through it unscathed. We know that the rebels have a huge advantage in numbers. We also know that they have a tribe of Iroquois on their side. That means that they'll be a much tougher proposition than they were last time."

"We have our artillery, sir," noted Skoyles, "with Major Phillips to deploy it. That could tilt the balance in our favor."

"Quite so, Jamie. But, whatever happens, there are bound to be losses. Tonight is the time to write letters to your families and loved ones," he suggested, "in case you are in no position to do so tomorrow." He looked at Featherstone. "Take leave of Miss Rainham while you may, Harry. There's no use pretending that we'll all come back alive."

A strange look came into the major's eye. He glanced at Skoyles.

"No, sir," he said quietly. "We must confront the truth. Some of us are doomed to perish on the battlefield."

Polly Bragg delivered the letter and Nan Wyatt passed it on to her mistress. Elizabeth Rainham read it with a mixture of concern and excitement, dismayed to learn that Skoyles was part of a force that would leave camp on the morrow, yet elated at the thought he would pay her a farewell visit that night. Unfortunately for her, he was not the only one. Conscious that he might be taking part in another fierce engagement, Harry Featherstone sought to use that fact to his advantage. He called on Elizabeth in her tent and tried to play on her sympathy.

"We're being deployed tomorrow," he told her.

"Another battle?" she said, pretending to be surprised.

"More than likely. This may be the last time we meet."

"Don't say that, Harry!"

"The possibility has to be faced. You saw how many casualties we had the last time we fought them. I may join their ranks tomorrow."

"I hope not."

"Do you mean that, Elizabeth?"

"Of course, I do."

"Then you still care enough about me?"

Elizabeth was in a quandary. Anxious to get rid of him before Skoyles came, she could not do that by telling him the truth. It would lead to a protracted argument and send Featherstone off in search of his rival. On the other hand, if she expressed an affection that she did not really feel, she would be misleading him.

"I asked you a question," he said.

"I know."

"Do you still care?"

"I care for anyone who's about to fight in a battle," she said.

"That's not what I want to hear, Elizabeth. Don't you realize what I'm telling you? The enemy has a huge advantage in numbers. If we do take them on, you may never see me again."

"I'll pray that that's not the case."

"I was hoping for more than prayer."

"You have my full sympathy, Harry."

"There are better ways of expressing sympathy," he said, reaching out to stroke her hair. "Let's put our differences behind us, shall we? I know that I've let you down in some ways and I'm profoundly sorry about that, but I feel that none of that matters now. Let's forget it."

"If you wish."

"Try to remember what brought us together in the first place. To me, you were never just a replacement for Cora. You were so much more than that. You were your own woman and I loved you for it." He took her by the shoulders. "Be mine again, Elizabeth. Just for tonight—be mine again."

"No, Harry."

"Even though I may be killed tomorrow? Please—let me stay. We may not have that wedding in Albany, or even in Canterbury Cathedral, but we can spend just one night as man and wife, can't we?" He pulled her close. "I *want* you, Elizabeth. I've earned you, surely."

"No," she said, breaking away. "You can't ask that of me."

"Isn't it why you came all this way from England?"

"I came to be with the man I love, Harry, not to be tricked into bed like this. It's wrong of you to ask," she chided. "I expected better of you."

He needed time to compose himself and to change his approach. Seeing that he blundered, Featherstone tried to make amends.

"I apologize," he said. "It was foolish of me to think that I could snatch a few hours of pleasure before I go off tomorrow. It was unfair to you, Elizabeth, and I hope that you'll forgive me."

"I will if you leave me alone, Harry."

"Just tell me that you still care—then I'll go."

He took her by the hand and looked deep into her eyes. Elizabeth felt threatened. She did not want to lie but it was the only way to get rid of him. She even conjured up a smile.

"Yes, Harry. I still care."

He kissed her hand, gave her a token bow, then left the tent. She felt so dizzy that she had to sit on the edge of the camp bed. It was a long time since she and Featherstone had been alone together and the rift between them had widened. After his conduct that night, it had widened even more. Elizabeth cared for him enough to hope that he would come through any battle unscathed but she feared having to face him again.

With a deliberate effort, she cleared her mind of Harry Featherstone and thought only of the person who had replaced him in her affections. While she waited for him to come, Elizabeth whiled away the time reflecting on the changes that he had wrought in her life. Having left England in order to be with one man, she could only envisage her future with someone else now. Captain Jamie Skoyles had none of the prospects or social advantages enjoyed by Harry Featherstone, but that did not matter. In every way, Skoyles was the better man—more honest, more honorable, more interesting, more reliable, and much more able to make her feel like a real woman. While Featherstone was more acceptable to her parents, she knew that she had made the right choice.

Long before he arrived, Elizabeth had reached her decision. Given the fact that Skoyles might be involved in hostilities on the following day, it was tempting Providence to make too many plans for a future together. He was hers, here and now. She had to seize her opportunity. It was a huge and dangerous step to take. Elizabeth would be flouting convention and doing something that she had been taught to regard as anathema. She would also be committing an act of betrayal against the man to whom she was betrothed and whom she had sworn to love forever.

Notwithstanding all that, she was still ready to follow her heart. In circumstances like the present ones, her upbringing counted for nothing. Rules of behavior during a war were instinctive rather than imposed. Elizabeth was ready to brave disapproval and surrender to her emotions. When Skoyles finally arrived, she ran to his arms.

"You got my letter?" he asked.

"Yes, Jamie. It upset me very much."

"Why?"

"Because you may be fighting another battle."

"Not until tomorrow, Elizabeth. In fact—"

"Don't say anything else," she said, putting a hand to his lips. "We may only have tonight. Let's not waste a moment of it."

She clung to him for a moment with an element of desperation. Then she stepped back, looked lovingly up at him, and began to unhook her dress. Jamie Skoyles smiled and stared in wonder at her. Elizabeth Rainham was his at last. She was no longer beyond his reach. He felt an upsurge of love that swept aside all other considerations.

Maria Quinn was not even a faint memory.

CHAPTER FIFTEEN

"Are you sure, Ezekiel?" he asked, grabbing his brother anxiously by the arm. "Is that what General Gates said?"

"Word for word. I was in his tent, Reuben."

"He's forbidden Benedict Arnold to join in any battle?"

"I'm afraid so," said Proudfoot.

"Then he's lost all my respect. What's wrong with Gates?" said Reuben, upset at the confirmation of his worst fears. "Has he never heard of Arnold's trek to Canada? How he built a navy to take on the British on Lake Champlain? Has he forgotten who raised the siege at Fort Stanwix?" He released Proudfoot's arm. "And don't remind me that it was renamed after General Schuyler," he went on, angrily, "because he's another useless commander who should be taken out and shot."

"You're being unfair to Schuyler. It was he who persuaded the Iroquois to join us. More importantly," Proudfoot continued, "the general responded to Gates's urgent call for more ammunition by sending out men to strip the lead from the windows of Albany, so that it could be melted down and poured into bullet molds. He deserves thanks."

"Perhaps," said the other grudgingly.

"You might even learn to use the name of Fort Schuyler."

"That's too much to ask of me, Ezekiel. I'll not forgive him or Granny Gates for letting General Arnold down. Don't they recognize genius when they see it?"

The brothers were strolling near the edge of the camp at Bemis Heights. It was the morning of October 7, 1777, and Reuben Proudfoot was even more irritated by what he assumed was the unwillingness of General Gates to meet the enemy in battle again. Ezekiel Proudfoot took a more rounded view of affairs. Having met both Gates and Benedict Arnold—and having committed both of their portraits to paper—he had his own opinions of the two men.

"Arnold's genius is plain for all to see," said Proudfoot. "The problem is that he's only too aware of it himself. It makes him arrogant."

"He's entitled to be arrogant."

"Not in the presence of his commander."

"You are surely not taking Gates's side here?" Reuben challenged him.

"I take no side at all. I'm simply saying that Benedict Arnold can sometimes be his own worst enemy."

"Horseshit!"

"He is, Reuben. He's wild and undisciplined."

"That's what makes him such a great leader."

"Even great leaders must learn to obey orders."

"What orders?" cried Reuben. "All we've done since we got here is to sit on our hands. Gates hasn't even allowed us to go out on patrol. How can we fight for liberty if we're penned up here on Bemis Heights?"

Proudfoot had no answer. He loved his brother but had never shared his pugnacity. Even as a boy, Reuben had enjoyed a fight for its own sake and he hated to be kept away from any action. Conquest of the British army did not just mean a military victory to him. It would herald a Republic of the United States of America, and Reuben was more than ready to lay down his life in that cause.

Drums began to beat in the distance. Reuben identified the sound.

"That's a call to arms from our advance guard!"

"Are you sure?"

"I should be, Ezekiel," he said, embracing his brother. "I've been waiting to hear it for weeks now. The British are coming. Granny Gates will have to let us fight now."

Serious doubts about the reconnaissance expedition had afflicted Jamie Skoyles beforehand. When the men set out late that morning, his doubts had hardened into fears. Skoyles was worried by the size of the force that General Burgoyne led out of the camp. If the sole aim was to reconnoiter enemy positions, a hundred men would suffice and draw far less attention to themselves. As it was, the fifteen hundred soldiers were supplemented by Canadians, Indians, and loyalists, taking the total to over two thousand, and making it impossible for them to move with any stealth. Apart from the creaking of the ammunition wagons and the sounds of the heavy guns being hauled over the crisp, dry leaves in the woodland, there was the steady beating of drums to alert the enemy.

Taking so many men away also weakened the defenses at the camp, and that also disturbed Skoyles, because it left the remaining soldiers vulnerable to enemy attack. Burgoyne's decision to move forward was a colossal gamble, but Skoyles—a seasoned gambler himself—felt that it was doomed from the start. On a personal level, the expedition robbed him of any chance to revel in his memories of a blessed night spent in the arms of Elizabeth Rainham. There was an added poignancy Elizabeth's twenty-first birthday fell on October 7, and he would not be there to help her celebrate it. Instead, he would be following the orders of a man whose judgment he—and many others— considered to be ruinously defective.

Gentleman Johnny was untroubled by any doubts. Leading an army of British and German professional soldiers, he felt capable of taking on any opposition. Yet the men who had cheered him before they departed from the camp were not fresh troops. They were tired, hungry, and exasperated. Regular attacks from rebel skirmishers at night meant that they were deprived of sleep, and their meager rations were barely enough to sustain them. They were no longer the well-drilled army that had left Canada on a wave of optimism, but a ragged collection of individuals who had difficulty in dressing their lines.

As at the battle of Freeman's Farm, the British army was divided into three elements. Brigadier Simon Fraser occupied the right with the 24th Foot, supported by the light infantry under the Earl of Balcarres. General Riedesel was situated in the center with some of Colonel Breymann's grenadiers and four artillery pieces. Major Acland and the British grenadiers marched on the left flank, with heavy artillery in support. The three columns advanced beyond the two British redoubts that had been constructed. When they emerged from woodland into a wheat field, they were spread out over a wide area.

Skoyles was astonished when Burgoyne gave the order for his men to display, form a line, then sit down in double ranks with their weapons between their legs. Foragers, meanwhile, proceeded to cut the wheat or standing straw. Skoyles was bemused. Was this the object of their advance? A foraging expedition did not need over two thousand men. Why send so many? Skoyles was apprehensive. With the majority of the soldiers in such an exposed position, they were—literally—sitting targets.

General Horatio Gates received the intelligence from James Wilkinson, his deputy adjutant general, a man who had once urged the evacuation of Fort Ticonderoga. Wilkinson had no thoughts of retreat now.

"They are foraging, General," he reported, "and endeavoring to reconnoiter your left. I think, sir, they offer you battle."

"What is the nature of the ground and what is your opinion?"

"Their front is open and their flanks rest on woods, under cover of which they may be attacked; their right is skirted by a lofty height. I would indulge them."

"Well, then, order Morgan to begin the game."

Gates had finally decided to attack.

Jamie Skoyles heard them coming before they appeared. Pouring down from Bemis Heights like a torrent, the rebel soldiers attacked the front and rear of the right wing. Within minutes, Skoyles and his men were fighting for their lives. Nor were they the only object of enemy ferocity. The whole British and German line was under assault by an army five or six times their number. Skoyles and the other officers deployed their men as best they could, but sheer weight of numbers drove them back into the woods. The British artillery was rendered less effective by the presence of stout trees that could shield the enemy, who had the advantage of fighting in a way that most suited them. Daniel Morgan's rifle corps and Henry Dearborn's light infantry were in their element. It was battle on their terms.

Volley firing from lines of British infantry could not hold back soldiers who emerged from cover to shoot, then darted behind a tree trunk to reload. Even the threat of a bayonet charge did not deter them. Both the Continental Army and the various militias had waited too long for battle to be cheated of victory. Skoyles was impressed with the courage and enthusiasm of their repeated charges. Whenever they were driven back, the rebels simply regrouped and came at the British again.

The noise was even more deafening than it had been at Freeman's Farm. Rebel soldiers howled for blood or screamed in pain as grapeshot raked them. The sound of artillery and musket fire was interspersed with the cries of dying men and wounded horses. Hooves thundered across the wheat field. Drums beat out their tattoos. Wheat and straw were forgotten now. Both sides were harvesting human blood.

As in earlier engagements, the rebels made a special effort to kill enemy officers. The letter of protest that Burgoyne had sent to Gates about this unacceptable conduct had been ignored. Americans were under no compulsion to abide by British rules of engagement. Victory was all to them. By killing or disabling officers, they weakened the whole structure of the opposing army and brought that victory nearer. Skoyles was made all too aware of rebel tactics. Shortly after his men were attacked, his hat was shot off and a bullet removed the heel of his boot.

His horse was the next to be hit, struck in the chest and rearing up so high that Skoyles was dislodged from the saddle. As he fell to the ground, he rolled swiftly away so that he was not crushed beneath the weight of the animal as it came crashing down after him. Skoyles got to his knees in time to defend himself against a rebel soldier who came racing through the trees at him. Intending to dash a British officer's brains out with the butt of his rifle, the man instead found his weapon deftly parried by a sword that flashed in Skoyles's hand to run him through with one clean thrust.

Bullets whistled all round him, but the greatest danger for Skoyles was directly behind him. It was only by chance that he glanced over his shoulder. Riding toward him, with murder in his eye, was Harry Featherstone, bristling with hatred and ready to exploit the confusion of battle. Skoyles had only a split second to take evasive action. Had he not dived out of the way, the slash of Featherstone's sword could have taken his head off. In fact, all that was detached was one of the epaulets on Skoyles's shoulder. Before he could get up to pursue Featherstone, the major had ridden off into the trees to continue the fight against the real enemy. Skoyles turned his own anger upon the rebels.

Ezekiel Proudfoot took to the trees once again. Since the only way he could get any view of the battle was from above it, he climbed the tallest oak he could find and surveyed the field. Everywhere he looked the British and German soldiers were under severe fire, pressed back by Continentals and militia, who seemed to be reinforced time and again. In some part of the battlefield, Reuben Proudfoot would be hurling himself into the fray, but because his brother did not recognize the colors of each regiment, he was quite unable to decide where Reuben might be.

Disorder reigned supreme. It was a scene of violent struggle, random cruelty, and, in some places, mounting panic. Smoke billowed from the heavy guns. Charges were made, repulsed, then made again with greater commitment. Examples of outstanding bravery and intense suffering were everywhere. Blood stained the wheat field red.

All that Proudfoot could do was to rely on his memory, consigning images, incidents, advances, retreats, and untold gory deaths to the back of his mind for later use. His hand was shaking far too much for him to draw any sketches. He had witnessed battles before, but Proudfoot knew that this one was markedly different. What he was looking at was nothing less than a fight for American liberty, a decisive engagement that could turn the whole war in their favor. Such a battle needed a leader around whom the rebels could gather. He soon appeared, galloping toward the Brunswickers with suicidal audacity. It was the man whom Proudfoot had last seen in his commander's tent.

Drunk on rum and consumed with rage at the attempt to deny him a role in the battle, Benedict Arnold spurred his horse on and urged his men to follow him. When a redcoat tried to bayonet him, the American hacked him to death with his sword, then beat off two more British bayonets before riding to another part of the field. Arnold was brave, impetuous, foolish, dauntless, indefatigable, and utterly heroic.

It was a memory that Ezekiel Proudfoot would never forget.

The British army had its own heroes, none more prominent than Simon Fraser. Under fierce attack, the 24th Foot nevertheless managed to retain a semblance of order and hold the right flank. That was not the case with the redcoats on the left flank, who had been pushed back by the force of the rebel onslaught, their officers slain, their artillerymen and their horses shot dead, and their guns captured. The Germans under Riedesel fared even worse in the center of the action. Though they fought with typical order and gallantry, they endured savage losses. Bullets that did not kill or wound them dented the shiny metallic fronts of their caps, adding a continuous series of pinging sounds to the general hullabaloo.

Simon Fraser could see the immense difficulties that the center faced. Rallying his men, he brought a detachment of them toward the harried Germans. Jamie Skoyles was among them, having acquired a stray horse whose rider had been killed. Sword held aloft, he followed the brigadier toward the part of the field that was bearing the brunt of enemy attack. Skoyles yelled orders to his men, but it was Simon Fraser who really inspired them. Riding back and forth in his brilliant uniform, he was a highly visible figure on his handsome gray mount.

While others were losing their nerve, Fraser was telling his men to form a second line and they were rushing to obey. He was leading by force of personality. Fraser did not go unnoticed by the enemy. Skoyles urged him to stay out of range of rebel sharpshooters but the brigadier spurned danger in order to encourage his men. Three shots were fired. The first hit the gray horse's crupper and the second went through his mane. Skoyles implored his commander to draw back. The third shot made the decision for him. Hit in the stomach, Fraser slumped forward in agony over the horse's neck.

Skoyles kicked his own animal into a canter at once, riding up to the wounded brigadier and supporting him with one arm as he carried him back behind British lines. No individual loss had such a lowering effect on others. The only man capable of organizing proper resistance against the rebels had been eliminated from the battle. General Burgoyne was utterly disheartened. Simon Fraser was his closest friend and confidant. When he saw the wounded Scot being taken from the field, he gave the order for retreat. With their tails between their legs, and leaving masses of dead or wounded redcoats on the battlefield behind them, the British army pulled back to their two redoubts. In just under an hour, Burgoyne's bold gamble had been revealed as an act of monumental folly.

With the help of an ensign, Skoyles took the stricken man from the field of battle as quickly as they could. When they reached his tent, they helped Fraser from his horse and carried him inside. Blood was still oozing from his wound. Skoyles was pleased that the first surgeon on hand was Tom Caffrey. Removing Fraser's jacket and undoing his shirt, Caffrey examined the wound. The marksman's bullet had passed through the victim's stomach and penetrated the backbone. All that the surgeon could do was to stem the bleeding and dress the wound.

"Tell me, Sergeant," said Fraser bravely, "to the best of your skill and judgment, if you think my wound is mortal."

Caffrey glanced sadly at Skoyles then took a deep breath.

"I am sorry to inform you, sir," he said softly, "that it is, and that you cannot possibly live four and twenty hours."

"So be it."

Suffering intense pain, and tormented by the knowledge that the British army was losing the battle, Simon Fraser nevertheless accepted his fate with extreme dignity.

Elizabeth Rainham was in despair. She could not believe that so much pain could come on the heels of so much pleasure. Her nocturnal joy with Jamie Skoyles had been followed by a day of high anxiety as she fretted over the safety of her lover. The sounds of battle had been all too audible, and she resigned herself to the fact that there would be heavy casualties. When she saw Simon Fraser being carried on a stretcher into the little house occupied by Friederika von Riedesel and her family, Elizabeth was distraught. If the commanding officer of the 24th Foot had been wounded, what of those who fought beside him?

"Hope for the best, ma'am," Nan Wyatt counseled her.

"Injured men are being brought back every minute."

"Then that proves Captain Skoyles must have escaped injury."

"Unless he is lying dead somewhere," Elizabeth said softly.

"You've vexed yourself about him before, ma'am, and in vain."

"But this is a pitched battle, Nan, and the Americans will try to kill as many of our officers as they can. Captain Skoyles is a marked man. Truly, I fear for his life." Her maid enfolded her in a maternal embrace. "Where can he *be?*"

After the shooting of Simon Fraser, a mood of melancholy descended on the British officer corps. As they pulled back to the redoubts, there were somber faces and slack shoulders. Not a glimmer of Gentleman Johnny's famous swagger remained. Jamie Skoyles responded in the opposite way. Heartbroken at the loss of his revered commander, he rode back to join the battle with an increased determination. Revenge was the only way to alleviate his grief, and he was eager to exact it. Fraser had been singled out for destruction. The brigadier had told Skoyles that he saw the man who shot him—a sharpshooter, perched in a tree, who aimed at him three times in a row. It was a deliberate assassination.

Skoyles got no farther than the Breymann Redoubt. Named after the colonel whose men constructed and held the fortification, it was a large breastwork, built of logs that had been laid horizontally between upright posts, and running to two hundred yards in length. It was equipped with several brass cannon and commanded a clearing across which any attack would have to come. By the time Skoyles reached it, the redoubt was already under fire from the Massachussets regiment led by Colonel John Brooks. The captain did not hesitate to join in the resistance.

Leaping from the saddle, he tethered his horse and rushed to the palisade. When a man close to him was shot in the mouth, he reeled backward and fell to the ground, a waterfall of blood gushing from between his shattered teeth. Skoyles relieved him of his musket, powder horn, and ammunition bag before taking up his position. Bullets thudded into the timber in front of him and sent splinters flying into the air. Poking his musket through a gap between the logs, Skoyles fired a first shot and downed an American infantryman.

Even a cursory glance told him that their situation was hopeless. They could not hold out indefinitely against such superior numbers. Colonel Breymann might roar at his men and threaten them with his sword, but they could not achieve the impossible. What they might do was to delay the enemy until retreating British soldiers could attack them from the rear, but even that would give them only a temporary respite. The rebels got closer and closer until they made a concerted effort to storm part of the redoubt. Skoyles had just reloaded his musket when he saw dozens of men trying to clamber over the breastwork.

He shot one of them, dislodged a second with a swing of his musket, then pulled out his sword to beat a third away. It was the fourth man who almost cost Skoyles his life. When his head appeared over the top of the palisade, the American's features were contorted with a mingled hatred and rage. Skoyles nevertheless recognized him at once. It was Reuben Proudfoot, the brother of Ezekiel, bearing a striking resemblance to the engraver. For a brief moment, the battle seemed to stand still as the two men eyed each other. Skoyles even smiled as fond memories flooded back.

"Jamie?" asked Reuben, blinking. "Is that you?"

"Yes."

"I'm sorry. I have to do this."

Skoyles felt the urge to offer his hand in an improbable gesture of friendship, but Reuben was bent on slaughter. Hauling himself up, he cocked a leg over the palisade then took aim at point-blank range. Skoyles had no time even to think. His sword flashed again, knocking the barrel of the musket aside even as it discharged its bullet. In another lightning movement, Skoyles turned the point of his sword on Reuben Proudfoot and thrust hard under his ribs until he pierced the heart. Only when he had withdrawn his weapon did Skoyles realize what he had done. He felt a stab of guilt. Reuben, meanwhile, had dropped his musket and now fell forward into the arms of the man who had killed him. Skoyles caught him, laid him gently on the ground, and had a moment's sad reflection before he rejoined the fray. Reuben Proudfoot vanished instantly from his mind. With a speed born of long practice, Skoyles went through the sequence of actions needed to reload his musket. He then peered through a gap in the logs.

The rebels had been driven back but they were massing for another attack. Cantering up and down in front of them, exhorting them on to victory, was a startling figure on a mettlesome horse. He wore the uniform of a major general and seemed to be heedless of danger. Skoyles knew him by sight, name, and reputation. It was Benedict Arnold, a soldier who brought his own brand of madness to the battlefield and who had the same uplifting effect on the rebels as Simon Fraser had had on the British. Nothing but total mastery of the field would satisfy Arnold. He wanted to obliterate the enemy.

Skoyles slid his musket through the gap and bided his time. When the demented rider came within range again, Skoyles pulled the trigger, but he had not aimed at Arnold. Instead, he brought down the horse. It collapsed and rolled over, pinioning its rider and breaking the leg that had been fractured before at Quebec. Seeing what had happened to their leader, the infantry stormed the redoubt again. Skoyles heard Arnold's voice rise above the din.

"Don't hurt the soldier who did this," he bellowed. "I hold no grudge. He was only doing his duty!"

It could not be said of those around Skoyles. Short of ammunition and seeing the futility of fighting on, many of the Germans began to forget their duty. They left the barricade and ran. Colonel Breymann went berserk, hurling abuse at his men and lashing out at them sword. The musket ball that killed him came from a German weapon. One of his docile grenadiers had been pushed too far by the tyrannical officer. It was the signal for a stampede. Freed from the attentions of their harsh and unpopular colonel, the rest of the men abandoned their post and fled. In order to avoid capture, Jamie Skoyles went with them.

The battle of Bemis Heights was, effectively, over.

General Horatio Gates understood the true meaning of the American victory. Led by him, soldiers, who, in many cases, had never even borne arms in battle before, had humbled the finest army in the world. It was a result that would echo loudly throughout the thirteen states and bring thousands more to the rebel cause. Though he had never stirred from his tent during the encounter, Gates felt able to take considerable credit for the success. His timing had been perfect. Coming into the commander's tent, Ezekiel Proudfoot was among the first to congratulate him.

"Well done, General!" he said, shaking his hand. "There'll be plaudits from Congress and from General Washington after this."

"The approval of Congress will be welcome, but I care nothing for Washington's opinion. He loses too many battles."

"You have just won a famous victory that even our commander in chief must acknowledge."

"I was determined to vanquish Gentleman Johnny."

"You rubbed his nose in the dirt. This has made your name, sir. You'll henceforth be known as the hero of Saratoga."

"We had thousands of heroes in the field today," said Gates with an attempt at modesty. "Each one deserves his share of the glory."

"One, in particular," noted Proudfoot. "General Arnold."

Gates bridled. "All that he deserves is a stern rebuke. He willfully disobeyed my orders yet again."

"But he led the troops magnificently, sir."

"He should not even have been there," said Gates, petulantly. "I stripped him of his command. When I heard that he'd joined the battle, I sent a man after him to recall him but Arnold outran the fellow."

"I can vouch for that, sir. I saw him clearly from my position in a tall tree. General Arnold rode hell for leather into the enemy lines as if intending to take on the whole army by himself. He set the most inspiring example to others."

"Insubordination is never inspiring, Ezekiel. What would happen if every soldier flouted my orders? There'd be anarchy on the battlefield." He sniffed loudly and pushed his glasses up his nose. "How is he now?"

"Still in great pain. They brought him back to camp on a litter."

"The man is lucky to be alive," said Gates, "and we must all be grateful for that. But he is still an arrant fool." He glanced at Proudfoot's sketchbook. "I hope that you did not waste your time on a drawing of Benedict Arnold. He's not worthy of it."

"I disagree," said Proudfoot stoutly. "I did sketch the general but, in truth, he deserves a portrait in oils."

Colonel James Wilkinson came briskly into the tent.

"Do we have any idea of casualties yet?" asked Gates.

"Yes, sir," replied Wilkinson. "Early reports suggest that the British lost almost nine hundred men, killed, wounded, or taken prisoner. We've only had thirty deaths listed so far, with less than a hundred wounded."

"And no prisoners?"

"None, General. They were in no state to take prisoners."

"Those figures are miraculous," said Gates. "We've not only beaten the redcoats, we've kept our army largely intact."

"And captured all of their artillery," Wilkinson observed. "We've drawn their teeth, sir. The British cannot bite back."

"How long will it be before they accept that?"

"General Burgoyne will not surrender easily," said Proudfoot.

"His pride will keep our demands at bay for a while," Gates decided, "but his position will grow weaker every day. We have him surrounded. His army has been reduced to a shambling remnant of the mighty force with which he set out from Canada, and he's lost some of his best officers. His men are on short rations. They've no spirit to take us on again. All we have to do is wait."

"Clinton is still coming up the Hudson Valley," Wilkinson noted.

"He'll not be here for a while yet—and Burgoyne knows it. We'll keep Gentleman Johnny bottled up here, and harass his pickets day and night with skirmishers." Gates's smile was cold and calculating. "We'll bring the great beast to his knees in time."

The tent flap was held back and a tentative head appeared.

"I've a message for you, General," said the newcomer. "Delivered under a flag of truce." The officer stepped into the tent to hand over the missive. "If there's to be a reply, sir, I can deliver it."

"Thank you." Gates opened the letter. "It's from General Burgoyne," he explained as he read it, "written on behalf of Lady Harriet Acland, requesting permission for her to be admitted to our camp so that she can nurse her husband. She's heard that he was badly wounded."

"True, sir," said Wilkinson. "Major Acland was shot in both legs."

"Then his wife must be allowed to be with him," Gates announced, sitting down to dash off a note authorizing the visit. "Deliver this to the lady and ensure that she's treated with the utmost respect." He handed the note to the messenger. "Let them see that we are magnanimous in victory." He waited until the man had left before speaking. "It may help to bring their surrender a little closer."

The British army had tasted victory so often in decisive battles that it did not quite know how to cope with a crushing defeat. Jamie Skoyles shared the general malaise. He and his fellow soldiers moved about in a daze. In the immediate aftermath of the battle, there were duties to be done and Skoyles met all his responsibilities. He first scoured the field in order to rescue wounded soldiers, then he helped to organize burial details for those who had perished in the fray. The numbers on the death roll were horrifyingly high.

When his work was finished, he reported to General Burgoyne so that he could take part in the collective recrimination of the officer corps. It was a grim experience. The commander in chief tried to wrest some glory from the day, but Skoyles preferred to accept the bitter truth. They had been hounded from the battlefield by a finer army, inspired by a superior vision. While the redcoats fought merely to subdue colonial ambition, the rebels set their sights on freedom. The motley army of Horatio Gates wanted a way of life that was not controlled from three thousand miles away in England.

Skoyles did not win any popularity when he pointed this out to his colleagues, most of whom were still searching for excuses to lessen the impact of their comprehensive defeat. He was shouted down more than once. Relieved when it was all over, Skoyles trudged back to his tent, wanting nothing more than the chance to clean himself up, reflect on what had happened, and give his weary body a rest. He needed to be alone for a while. Skoyles was shocked and sobered, therefore, when he discovered that a visitor was waiting in his tent.

Seeing the dried blood on his face, Maria Quinn ran to him.

"You've been wounded, Jamie!"

"It's nothing serious," he said. "I picked up a few scratches, that's all. Save your sympathy for those with real injuries."

"I watched them being brought into the field hospital on stretchers. They were in a terrible state. There was nothing at all that we could do for many of them."

"I know, Maria."

There was a long pause. Standing so close to her, Skoyles felt awkward and slightly ashamed. The last time she had come of her own volition to his tent, he had reached out gratefully for her. He could not do that now and she sensed his reluctance.

"You gave me your word, Jamie," she said, quietly. "You promised that I'd see you again before you went into battle."

"There was no time," he told her, prevaricating. "General Burgoyne made the decision on the spur of the moment, and we were called to arms. I didn't even have a chance to get a message to you, Maria."

"Yes, you did."

"What do you mean?"

"I'm not the only woman who followed this army because of a man," said Maria sharply. "There are dozens of us. When the word spread that there might be another battle next day, most of the women were sent for. I was one of the few left behind. That was the message that Captain Skoyles had for me. I was not wanted."

He hung his head. "I'm sorry about that."

"So was I, Jamie. You've always kept your promises before."

"I know," he admitted, feeling guiltier than ever, "but it just wasn't possible this time, Maria. There were too many things to do. An officer has responsibilities. There were preparations to make."

"Then why weren't you here to make them?"

"What?"

"I waited for hours," said Maria accusingly. "I came to this tent and waited half the night for the man who had asked me to leave Montreal so that I could be with him."

"That's not what I said," he corrected. "I didn't ask you to come, Maria. You were the one who suggested it. I told you that I could give no firm commitments. We'd be at the mercy of the fortunes of war."

"But you didn't try to stop me, did you?"

"No," he conceded, "I was glad that you came. I was touched."

"Then what happened?" she asked, adopting a softer tone and caressing his shoulder with her palm. "I thought that we wanted each other, Jamie. I'd have gone anywhere in the world to be with you—yet you couldn't spare me that one night. Why not?"

"Maria," he said, taking her by the wrist to stop her stroking him, "I didn't mean it to turn out this way. When I made that promise, I intended to keep it. You're very dear to me. But," he went on, steeling himself to tell her the truth, "someone else has come into my life and my feelings for you are not quite the same any more. However," he added, hastily, as he saw fury in her eyes, "I hope that we can still be friends."

"Friends!" she said, scornfully. "I didn't come all the way from Canada simply to be friends with you."

"It was bound to end some time."

"Yes, but not like this. What kind of a man are you? How could you pretend that I was your lover when your mind was on someone else? It's so cruel, Jamie. It's so hurtful."

"It was not deliberate."

"I thought you were mine."

"I was, Maria—for a time."

"But only until you found someone better."

"That's not what happened," he said earnestly. "I didn't go looking for anyone, I swear. I didn't need to when I had you. But I was carried away by the turn of events. It's the only way I can explain it."

"Oh, I think there was a much simpler explanation than that."

"No, Maria."

"You had your fill of me," she said bitterly, "then tossed me away without a second thought."

"It's not true."

"Don't tell me any more lies. I've heard more than enough already. I can see that I was mistaken in you, so—if you'll forgive me, Captain Skoyles—I won't offer you my friendship." She pushed past him and opened the flap of the tent. "You don't deserve it."

"Maria!"

He reached out to stop her, but she was gone. Skoyles was rightly chastened. It had been a painful encounter, but her censure was just. He had behaved badly to her. In choosing Elizabeth Rainham, he was trying to turn his back on a former existence that was symbolized by Maria Quinn. None of them would escape unhurt. Maria had been the first and most obvious victim. Skoyles had agonized for hours before rejecting her, and he was now smarting from her retaliation.

Elizabeth would also suffer. She had only given herself to him because she was ignorant of Maria's existence and of that element in his character that drove Skoyles to become involved with such women. When she learned the truth—and he was determined to be honest with her—it would cause her immense heartache. What he did not know was whether her love was strong enough to accommodate it. Skoyles flopped down onto his camp bed. Having lost on the battlefield, he felt as if he had just endured a more personal defeat.

News that Jamie Skoyles was alive and uninjured brought the most intense relief to Elizabeth Rainham. It was the best possible birthday present for her. Like everyone else in the camp, she was appalled to hear of the fate of the British army, and of the loss of almost a half of the men whom General Burgoyne had led out that morning. Elizabeth was also saddened to learn that some of the officers whom she had come to know during her time with the army—Major John Dyke Acland, Sir Francis Clerke, Captain John Money, Major Griffith Williams, and Captain Thomas Blomfield—had all been wounded and taken prisoner. Brigadier General Simon Fraser was on his deathbed, and that troubled her most of all. The grim tidings, however, were tempered by the news about Jamie Skoyles.

Elizabeth knew that he would come to her eventually. There would be lots of things for him to do first, but she was prepared to wait. Seated on the camp bed, and by the light of half a dozen candles, she read from a book of poems that she had carried with her from England. The familiar words brought her pleasure, but she could not savor their magic to the full. Her mind was too preoccupied.

It was almost midnight before she heard the scrunch of footsteps outside her tent. Putting her book aside, Elizabeth stood up excitedly and adjusted her hair. When the tall, uniformed figure came into the tent, she rushed forward to put her arms around him, withdrawing at once when she realized that it was Harry Featherstone.

"Expecting someone else, were you?" he said accusingly.

"No, no," she lied. "Of course not."

"Then why did you pull away from me?"

"You shouldn't be here, Harry. I want to go to bed."

"Is that why you have you all these candles blazing?"

Featherstone had obviously been drinking. To fend off the misery of defeat—and of his failure to kill Jamie Skoyles—he had reached for a bottle of brandy. It had dulled his grief but sharpened his desire. As he gazed at Elizabeth in her night attire, he was aroused even more. She looked so beautiful and enticing. His eye then fell on her left hand. He moved toward her.

"Where's the ring I gave you?" he demanded.

"I always take it off at night."

"You swore to me that it would never leave your finger. When we exchanged rings at our betrothal, you gave me your solemn word that you'd wear mine forever."

"I'm not able to keep that promise, Harry."

"You must."

"No," she returned, "and you know the reason why."

"I'll not be thwarted, Elizabeth. There's too much at stake. You were mine when you set sail from England, and you'll *stay* mine."

"That's not possible."

"Yes, it is," he insisted, fumbling in his pocket. "It's your birthday and I have a present for you—something to show my love."

"Keep it, Harry."

"But I bought it for you."

"Keep it," she repeated, putting a hand on his wrist to prevent him from taking anything from his pocket. "Whatever it is, I don't want it. Everything between us is over. I'll never wear your ring again."

"Don't say that!" he snarled. "You're still betrothed to me."

"Not anymore. After what I've learned about you, I couldn't bear to be married to you—not even for Cora's sake. It's all over, Harry. Our betrothal is at an end." Elizabeth could not disguise the truth from him. "There's someone else in my life now."

"So that's why you rejected me last night."

"Yes, Harry."

"I have a rival. Now I wonder who that is," he said with a sneer. "Could it be the gallant Captain Skoyles? Have you fallen for his rather grisly charms? If you have, you're certainly not the only one, Elizabeth," he warned her. "You'll just the latest in a long line of conquests."

"I'd like you to leave."

"Or maybe the conquest has already taken place? Is *that* what's happened, Elizabeth? You refuse to let *me* come anywhere near you," he said resentfully, "but you let Skoyles put his grubby hands all over you."

"I want you to leave."

"No!"

"Please, Harry."

"I'll leave when I choose," he told her, pushing her toward the bed. "There's something that I want from you first, Elizabeth—something I've waited far too long to enjoy. And since you're ready to give it away free," he said, contemptuously, "then I'll take my share."

"Get out of here!" she cried.

"Afterward."

"Harry!"

"If I can't have you as a wife," he said, grabbing her roughly by the shoulders, "then I'll have you as a woman."

She tried to scream but he clapped a hand over her mouth. Forcing her down on the bed, Featherstone got on top of her and stifled her protest by kissing her full on the lips. The taste of brandy made her wince in disgust. His hands clutched at her breasts, his knee parted her thighs. No matter how hard she struggled, Elizabeth could not dislodge him. He was determined to take her by force. When she felt his sweaty palms on her naked body, she went completely numb, too horrified at what was happening to offer even token resistance.

Featherstone gave a laugh of triumph and started to peel off his uniform. Before he had even removed his coat, however, he was seized from behind. Jamie Skoyles had rushed into the tent. Fury lent him extra power. When he saw what Featherstone was trying to do, he hauled him away from Elizabeth and flung the man to the ground. Sitting astride him, Skoyles hit him with an unrelenting series of punches that left him bruised, bleeding, and barely conscious. He then got both hands on the major's neck. If Elizabeth had not interceded, he would have strangled the man.

"Leave him, Jamie," she begged him. "That's enough, that's enough."

"He deserves to die for this," said Skoyles.

"Just get him out of here."

Taking the major by the throat, Skoyles pulled him upright. Blood was running from Featherstone's nose and from gashes above both eyes. Two of his teeth had been knocked out in the onslaught. Still badly dazed, he looked at Skoyles with a mixture of fear and hostility.

"If you come anywhere near Miss Rainham again," Skoyles warned, still holding him, "you'll answer to me. Is that clear?" The other man gave a grunt of defiance. Skoyles punched him hard in the stomach and made him double up with pain. "Is that clear, Major?"

Featherstone capitulated and gave a nod of assent. Opening the flap of the tent, Skoyles hurled him out into the darkness before turning to embrace Elizabeth. She was trembling from her ordeal and crying with gratitude. It was minutes before she was able to speak.

"It was terrifying," she confessed. "I'd never have believed that Harry could do such a thing. Whenever we met in England, he was always the perfect gentleman."

"The perfect gentleman tried to kill me on the battlefield."

"Never!"

"He did, Elizabeth. The major slashed at me with his sword when he thought I was off guard. He rode off before I could challenge him."

"That's dreadful!" she exclaimed. "You must report him."

"To whom? It would be my word against his, and who would believe the junior officer? No," he went on, "the only person who'd know that I was telling the truth is Simon Fraser and he'll be dead by morning—God rest his soul!"

She was aghast. "You mean, Harry will get away with it?"

"Oh, I think he had his punishment in here just now," said Skoyles, kissing her on the forehead. "He realizes that you belong to me, and that's the worst punishment of all for the major. It's the thing he fears most—public humiliation."

"I was so worried that you might not come back to me, Jamie."

"Nobody was going to stop me."

"What will happen to us?"

"I don't know," he admitted. "I can't believe that even General Burgoyne will be stupid enough to engage the enemy again. We suffered terrible losses in the field today. Our artillery is now in the hands of General Gates and his men. They could blow us to pieces."

"Will we have to surrender?"

"I see no other way out. When we had the chance to withdraw to safety, the General spurned it. As a result," he said, bitterly, "we lost half of our reconnaissance force and some of our best officers. I used to admire him in the past but not anymore. General Burgoyne has a lot to answer for, Elizabeth."

"He seemed so confident of victory."

"Sheer bravado. It cost hundreds of lives."

"Supposing he's forced to surrender," she said. "What then?"

Skoyles shrugged. "That's up to the rebels. My guess is that the soldiers will be taken prisoner and marched off somewhere so that we can take no further part in the war."

"What about the rest of us?"

"There'll be other arrangements."

Elizabeth was alarmed. "We'll be *separated?*"

"I'm afraid so," he said. "But you'll be treated kindly. General Gates is not a vindictive man. He, too, was an English gentleman once." He pulled her close and kissed her gently on the lips. "Whatever happens—wherever you go—I'll find you, Elizabeth."

"How?"

"I've no idea, to be honest. I just know that I will. As long as you stay in America, I'll track you down. This war won't go on forever."

"General Burgoyne thought that it would be over by Christmas."

"I never believed it would be that easy."

"He gambled everything on winning."

"There's a lot more fighting to come yet."

"And will you be involved in it, Jamie?"

"Of course," he said proudly. "I'm a soldier. Fighting is my profession. It's what I love. It's what I do best. I'm ready for the next battle, Elizabeth. I'm just relieved that I won't have to fight it under the command of General Burgoyne."

"And meanwhile?" she asked.

"Meanwhile," he said, mindful of his vow to be honest with her, "you need to know a little more about me, Elizabeth. We must talk."

Only the American officers were given the privilege of a single grave. The rank and file who had been killed in the battle were put into large pits that had been dug near Bemis Heights. Ezekiel Proudfoot watched as his brother's body was lowered into the mass grave. Even in death, there was a rebellious quality about him, a defiance that not even a redcoat officer's sword could cut out of his heart. Reuben lay between a man from a New Hampshire Regiment and another from the 11th Virginia Rifle Corps. They all belonged to the same regiment now.

When the chaplain had conducted the burial service, those present filed past the graves and tossed a handful of earth onto them. Proudfoot noticed that Lieutenant Colonel John Brooks, his brother's commander, was among them. He went over to him.

"Excuse me, Colonel," he said. "My name is Ezekiel Proudfoot. My brother, Reuben, was glad to serve under you, sir."

"Thank you, Mr. Proudfoot. Your brother did not let us down."

"Does anyone know how he was killed?"

"It was while we were trying to storm a redoubt."

"Was he killed by a redcoat?"

"No," said Brooks, "it was probably by a German grenadier."

Proudfoot was satisfied. Somehow the information made his brother's death easier to bear. Collecting a handful of earth, he dropped it over Reuben's upturned face, then walked sadly away.

"Unconditional surrender!" Burgoyne exploded, throwing the letter aside. "Horatio Gates must have taken leave of his senses. While I still have red blood in my veins, I'll surrender to nobody."

"Least of all to a vile toad like Gates," said William Phillips.

"It would go against the grain."

Jamie Skoyles gave a rough translation for the benefit of General Riedesel. The British army had withdrawn to Saratoga and the four men were in the house that had once belonged to General Schuyler. Burgoyne was far too impatient to speak in French to Riedesel and requested Skoyles's aid as an interpreter. The captain was glad to be present at such an important discussion. When the German commander made a comment, Skoyles translated it for the others.

"The general feels that the retreat was handled badly," he said. "He believes that we should have pushed on while he covered our rear."

"How could we push on when the men were falling asleep on their feet?" asked Burgoyne. "We all needed to rest."

"Yes," Phillips added. "The troops were so exhausted when we got here that they didn't even have the strength to cut wood and light fires. They just dropped to the ground in the pouring rain and lay there. I've never seen such a bedraggled army."

"If we'd struggled on," Skoyles resumed, "then we would have got clear of Saratoga before the rebels cut off our escape route. That's what worries General Riedesel."

"He is not in command of this army," said Burgoyne peremptorily. "Nor is he even my deputy. Remind him of that, Skoyles."

When he translated the words into German, Skoyles's tone was much more emollient. He received a nod of thanks from Riedesel. By rights, Skoyles knew, the man should have been second in command because it was a position that no artillery officer could hold. Distrusting the German, and wanting his friend to act as his deputy, Burgoyne had gotten round army rules by appointing William Phillips in second place as an emergency measure.

"What will Gates do next, General?" said Phillips.

"Make another crucial mistake, I expect," replied Burgoyne. "He's made two already. He should have chased us from the battlefield when he had the chance, and he should never have sent that absurd demand for unconditional surrender. The man is unfit to command."

"Nevertheless, he does hold all the cards."

"Only until Clinton gets here."

"We can hardly rely on that," said Phillips. "The last report put him at Fort Montgomery. That's well over a hundred miles away."

General Riedesel whispered something to Skoyles.

"What's he muttering now, Captain?" said Burgoyne tetchily.

Skoyles translated. "The general wishes to know if you've reached a decision, sir."

"Of course, I've reached a decision. I refuse the terms point-blank."

"And the alternative?"

"We play for time. Tell that to the general," Burgoyne advised him, "then you can take that lugubrious countenance of his out of here. No further discussion is needed."

When Skoyles had translated, he and Riedesel left. Once outside, the German offered his hand in thanks, then marched away. Tom Caffrey had been waiting for his friend to emerge from the meeting.

"Well?" he asked. "What happened, Jamie?"

"We stay here."

"Do they know how short we are of rations?"

"As long as Gentleman Johnny can dine in style, he has no worries about food. It was the thing that really upset General Riedesel and his wife," said Skoyles. "We were trounced by a better army and chased from the field. Yet when we reached here, our commander made merry with Mrs. Mallard and his intimates as if it were a celebration."

"We've precious little to celebrate."

"I know that, Tom."

"Eleven more lads died today, and there are others who'll not be with us for long. And all because Gentleman Johnny had visions of glory!" he said with rancor. "After what that man did, he ought to hang his head in shame."

"He'd rather drink his champagne and sport with his mistress."

"Everything depends on General Gates now," said Caffrey. "I hear that he let Lady Acland visit their camp to tend her husband's wounds. She's a brave woman, Jamie. Did you know that she was pregnant?"

"Yes, Tom. And she's such a delicate creature. This war has awakened bravery in the most unlikely people."

"I just wish that General Burgoyne was one of them."

"Credit where it's due," said Skoyles, leaping to his commander's defense. "He showed exceptional courage on the battlefield and exposed himself to all kinds of danger. Nobody who saw him during the conflict could ever doubt his bravery as a soldier."

"I'm talking about his bravery as a man," Caffrey explained. "He led our army into disaster. Along with the other surgeons, I'm still trying to cope with the appalling results of it all. Is Gentleman Johnny brave enough to admit that he made calamitous mistakes?"

"No, Tom. That would require a brand of honesty that he simply doesn't possess. When he's not hosting dinners or sharing a bed with Mrs. Mallard," said Skoyles, grimly, "he'll be rehearsing his excuses for losing a battle against an army of untrained amateurs."

Over a week after the battle, General Gates finally received the document for which he had been waiting. It was delivered to the rebel commander by Colonel James Wilkinson, who had acted as his intermediary during the armistice that had been declared. Gates was thrilled. He showed the document to Ezekiel Proudfoot with glee.

"We have him!" he said.

"By the scruff of his well-bred neck."

"Gentleman Johnny has signed at last."

"Only because you gave him an ultimatum, General."

"It was the one way to coerce him, Ezekiel. He's been wriggling for days, refusing one set of terms, criticizing another, and doing all he could to delay us. I put a gun to his head. My only concession was to call his submission a Convention."

"You could have enforced complete surrender, sir," said Wilkinson, who was not entirely happy with the terms of the Convention that had brought hostilities to an end. "When someone is surrounded by an army four times the size of his own, he has no right to barter."

"We have an agreement," said Gates, "and that's all that matters."

"Congress may choose to think otherwise."

"That's its prerogative, James."

"No defeated army has ever been offered such advantageous terms," Wilkinson observed. "Instead of offering to surrender, General Burgoyne has only signed a Convention."

"A surrender by another name," Proudfoot commented.

"He'll not see it that way. Nor will Congress. Gentleman Johnny will boast that it's a concession he wrung from us—along with a number of others, I may say."

"We are civilized men," Gates told him, sharply, "and we should behave with generosity. That's why I'm allowing the British army to march from their camp with full honors of war, and to ground their arms by the river."

"I know, sir, but you're also granting them free passage to England, on condition that they do not serve in America again."

"Exactly, James. It takes a sizable British force out of the war."

"They'll soon be replaced," said Proudfoot. "Would it not be more sensible to keep them here as prisoners of war, useful hostages in case they are needed?"

"That's my opinion as well," said Wilkinson.

"You've read the Convention," said Gates. "I'll abide by it."

"General Washington will complain."

"Washington *always* complains, and I don't see it as my function in life to appease him by unnecessarily harsh treatment of an enemy that has agreed to lay down its arms." He waved the document in the air. "It's immaterial whether this is headed Convention or Articles of Surrender. Even our commander in chief should be able to weigh its significance."

"Yes," said Proudfoot happily, "we beat the pants off the British."

"We did more than that, Ezekiel. We forced a redcoat general to recognize us for what we are—not rebels or riffraff or seditious colonials. We've earned respect at last," Gates insisted. "We've finally gained our true identity. Gentleman Johnny has signed a document that calls us what we are—*Americans.*"

When Jamie Skoyles caught sight of him, he could not at first believe that it was his old friend. Ezekiel Proudfoot was strolling through the British camp as if searching for someone. Seeing Skoyles, he trotted across to him and shook him warmly by the hand.

"What the devil are you doing here, Ezekiel?" asked Skoyles.

"Trading on a friendship," said Proudfoot. "When I was staying at Fort Ticonderoga, I got to know Colonel Wilkinson very well. He had business with General Burgoyne today, so I prevailed upon him to bring me along in the hope that I might see you."

"I couldn't be more pleased."

"Unless the circumstances were reversed, of course."

"That would be preferable," said Skoyles with a grin, "but, alas, we never stood a chance of winning that battle. The Americans are worthy victors. They beat us soundly."

"I revel in that, Jamie, though my joy is tinged with sadness."

"I can understand why. Your brother, Reuben, was killed."

Proudfoot was surprised. "How do you know that?"

"I was there at the time," said Skoyles. "We were trying to hold the Breymann redoubt from one of the Massachussets regiments that was being urged on by General Arnold."

"So I believe."

"When they stormed us, I saw your brother climbing over the fence. He was as close to me as you are, Ezekiel. In fact, for a moment, I thought that it *was* you."

"And did Reuben recognize you?"

"Yes," Skoyles replied, "he even said my name. Then he raised his rifle to kill me. I admired him for that. He didn't let friendship stand in the way of duty—but, then, neither could I. It was him or me, Ezekiel. Luckily, my sword was quicker than his trigger finger."

"It was *you*, then?" said Proudfoot. "You killed my brother?"

"I fear so."

"Dear God! I'd hoped that it hadn't been a redcoat—least of all you, Jamie." Tears came as he grappled with the news. "What a cruel thing war can be! It set a brother I love against a friend I revere." He stared at Skoyles. "It pains me to say this, but you deserve the truth. If I'd been able to choose which of you should die, it would have been you, Jamie. My brother was fighting for a superior cause. I'd sooner have one less redcoat than lose a patriot like Reuben."

"Your brother did say that he was sorry," Skoyles recalled, "but that didn't stop him from trying to put a musket ball between my eyes. I just wish that it hadn't been him, Ezekiel."

"At least I know what happened now," said Proudfoot soulfully. "That helps. And if I'm honest, Reuben was not long for this life. As soon as they put a rifle in his hands and gave him a license to shoot at redcoats, it was only a matter of time before he died. He was always too impulsive."

"So was Benedict Arnold."

"He was impulsive but magnificent. I'll show you."

Proudfoot opened the flap of the satchel that hung from his shoulder and took out a sheaf of drawings. He found a sketch of Arnold that he had drawn during the battle of Freeman's Farm. It showed the general in distinctive pose, riding in front of a brigade of rebels, sword held high and face suffused with passion. Skoyles was complimentary.

"That's exactly how he looked at the redoubt as well."

"He was carried from the field with a broken leg."

"Yes," said Skoyles. "I shot his horse from under him. I could have aimed at General Arnold, but I had too much respect to kill him. I don't think he holds it against me."

"And neither do I, Jamie. I don't blame you for Reuben's death or for General Arnold's injuries, though I regret both bitterly." Proudfoot put his sketches away again. "I've been given permission to be there when General Burgoyne goes through the formal surrender. General Gates wants a sketch of the ceremony that can be turned into an engraving."

"It will be a historic moment."

"I hope that I do it justice." His eyes filled with sadness. "Well, I suppose that I must accept we'll never see each other again, Jamie. You'll sail back to England with the others."

"No," said Skoyles. "I'm staying in America. This is my home now."

"But how *can* you stay?"

"I'll find a way somehow. There are years of fighting ahead yet, and I don't want to miss out on them. I intend to be on the winning side next time—and that means killing some more American brothers of yours." He took his friend by the shoulders. "Can I ask you a favor, Ezekiel?"

"Of course."

"I'd like you to draw a portrait for me."

Proudfoot grinned. "Captain Jamie Skoyles in dress uniform?"

"Oh, no," said Skoyles with a fond smile. "I'm not that vain. What I want is a portrait of a very special lady."

At ten o'clock on the morning of October 17, 1777, the British and German troops paraded. They marched out with their drums beating and their colors held high, enjoying the full honors of war. Though they tried to beat the "Grenadiers' March," the drummers could put no enthusiasm into their work, and the tune sounded flat. When the defeated army passed the American ranks, there was no jeering, no laughter, and no derisive comments. The victorious rebels simply stood and watched. Farmboys as young as fourteen and old men in unsightly wigs stared at the redcoats and their allies in wonder. The one discordant note came when an American band struck up the music of "Yankee Doodle" in mockery, but it soon faded away. A dignified silence returned.

The British soldiers led the way. They were followed by the Germans, many of whom had acquired pets they wished to keep—a bear, a deer, foxes, raccoons, rabbits. Human pets had also been added to the cavalcade in the course of its travels. Among the camp followers that straggled behind the soldiers were dozens of slatternly women who had been gathered up along the way to provide comfort and entertainment. In view of both armies, General Burgoyne drew his ivory-handled sword, bowed, and offered it to General Gates in a token of surrender. With equal courtesy, Gates bowed to the other man, then returned the sword. It was a gesture that brought tears to the eyes of Gentleman Johnny.

Jamie Skoyles was part of the Convention Army that set off on a two-hundred-mile march that would take them over the Green Mountains and through the Connecticut Valley until they could strike off toward Cambridge, Massachussetts. Ahead of him, Skoyles could see Major Harry Featherstone, who had had the sense to keep well clear of him, and who still bore the facial wounds from their last encounter. Behind him, Skoyles left Elizabeth Rainham, who was to be escorted to Albany in due course with General Burgoyne and others. There was no danger that Skoyles would ever forget what Elizabeth looked like. In his pocket, drawn with admiration and skill by Ezekiel Proudfoot, was a vivid portrait of her.

The road to Saratoga had been long, hard, and increasingly bitter. It had been a personal Damascus for Skoyles. Having set out from Canada as a British officer, he no longer felt as dedicated to his calling as he had been. It was not merely a case of disenchantment with General Burgoyne. It was the fact that Skoyles had been fighting against men whose ambitions he was coming to share. American rebels simply wanted to live in a free country where they could bring up their families in peace. They did not want to be ruled by a distant monarch who had never even set foot in the colonies. In Skoyles's opinion, their cause was just and, after the two battles at Saratoga, it had taken on a whole new resonance.

As the prisoners of war marched away, autumn sunshine broke through the lingering mist, giving the trees a stark brilliance and turning the Hudson River into a fast-flowing mirror that threw up shimmering images. Birds were singing. It was going to be a pleasant day.

Under his red coat, Captain Jamie Skoyles felt a persistent itch.